This book is dedicated to my wife Anna.

Without her support, I don't get to first base.
***
I also dedicate this book to the memory of six great cops/partners:

Anthony Falco Sr.   Joe Esposito   Remo Franceschini
      Joe Favor   Jim Carroll   Charlie Hart

THE CASE OF THE AMOROUS CADDY

ANTHONY CELANO

1

It Started with a

Putt

THE THIRTY-FIVE YEAR OLD DENNIS BUMPER was a cabdriver with a natural talent for playing golf. He was so capable that he went on to land a part-time job caddying at the Stanley Burrows Golf Club, an exclusive, private concern on Staten Island.

Being a privately owned club, Stanley Burrows came with a membership quota. Admittance to the club was by invitation or sponsorship. In addition to golf and other recreational activities the club offered, there was a full bar with spacious dining and entertaining areas. Since membership was costly, club members tended to be well off financially.

For Bumper, caddying wasn't work, it was fun. The compensation he received from the seasonal gig was a fine financial supplement to his regular job.

Bumper understood that his worth as a club caddy would be measured by his knowledge of the variations connected to each of the eighteen holes on the course. His ability to exceed this yardstick of competency made Bumper a frequently requested caddy among club members. Furthering his appeal was his ability to tactfully advise golfers when they were in doubt as to how to proceed with their next shot.

One club member who insisted on Bumper being her caddy was Judith Vanidestine, the wife of a plastic surgeon. Aside from the benefit of an improved game, Judith was thrilled over outshining the others in her regular foursome. Judith's cordial association with her caddy turned out to be trouble in the long run.

Problems began the July before Judith Vanidestine's December murder. Bumper's value on the golf course caused the doctor's wife to be exceedingly nice to him. Such attention to someone like Bumper, who never received a second look from females, was enough to turn the caddy's head. Bumper began looking forward to caddying for the married Judith. It soon became the only thing that mattered to him.

Their hours on the golf course led to Bumper developing feelings for the plastic surgeon's wife. Fueled by her attention, this interest eventually graduated to unhealthy proportions. Bumper came to liken caddying for Judith to being on a date with her.

Bumper perceived the slightest common courtesy extended by Judith to be evidence of a special connection. If Judith smiled when she spoke to Bumper, it was perceived as chemistry.

"I hope you're taking good care of Digger," the country club member said one day, as if the caddy's hamster was of importance to Judith.

"Digger's in good hands, Ms. Vanidestine," Bumper assured her. "Thank you for your concern."

"Is Digger much work, Dennis?"

"No, no trouble at all," he replied before advising, "Be careful on this hole; the greens are very fast."

"Digger is lucky to have you. I know I'd be lost without you, Dennis," voiced Judith, flashing a toothy smile. The caddy saw this exchange as a breakthrough moment. *She needs me,* he thought wistfully.

The club member's newfound accuracy in sinking golf balls so delighted her that she reacted by overwhelming the caddy with flowery accolades at every opportunity. This diet of flattery deepened Bumper's affection for Judith. By August he was hopelessly in love with the golf club member.

Once bitten by the love bug, the smitten loner was careful not to reveal his true feelings. Only Bumper's friend, fellow churchgoer Sammy Angelo, was taken into Bumper's confidence when it came to Judith Vanidestine.

Bumper and Sammy bonded because they were similar in several respects. Their strongest commonality rested in their religious inclination. Both were God-fearing men who never married. They also shared a history of being social outcasts in their younger days. There was one distinct difference between the friends. Sammy was a pacifist, whereas the caddy was capable of violence when the right buttons were pushed.

Bumper's volatility could be traced back to his youth. At an early age he was callously treated by cruel peers who targeted him for having an excessive curvature in his upper back. Cruel nicknames such as "Bump the Hump" and "Quasimodo" effected Bumper emotionally. His unwed mother, unequipped for dealing with her son's sulking, sent Bumper to the local parish priest for guidance.

After a series of privately held meetings, the well-intentioned clergyman suggested that Bumper take up weight training as a diversion from his troubles. The priest believed that muscles would build the youth's confidence and stem his victimization at the hands of bullies. This recommendation proved to have mixed results.

Once armed with brawn, it dawned on Bumper that having such a physical advantage gave him the whip hand. He wasted no time in seizing the opportunity to enact revenge. Bumper embarked on a campaign to settle scores with a portfolio of people who had found pleasure in tormenting him. One by one, Bumper trounced those who referred to him in derogatory terms. It wasn't long before his brutal mission earned Bumper the reputation as a local mental case not to be trifled with.

By the time Bumper reached adulthood, the days of people teasing him for his humpback were long over. Bumper never forgot the kindness afforded him by the parish priest. Their sessions together not only remedied Bumper's problem, they also influenced him spiritually. Bumper went on to embrace church teachings with the same enthusiasm he put into weightlifting. He attended Mass regularly, followed the commandments, and earnestly committed himself to living a righteous life.

It was at a church function that Bumper came to meet Sammy Angelo, a man several years his senior. Sammy was drawn to the church for similar reasons as Bumper. He, too, had been picked on as a youth due to a physical malady.

A smallish man with a neatly trimmed beard, Sammy was plagued by a condition that caused him to sweat excessively. Regardless of the temperature or lack of activity, Sammy's shirts were always wet. This noticeable affliction made Sammy a prime target for bullying while growing up. The difference between the two friends was that Sammy didn't seek revenge on everyone who ever called him "Soaky Sam." He simply stuck to the teachings in the good book and turned the other cheek. Sammy let go of his bad memories upon entering adulthood.

Sammy helped get Bumper into a reasonably priced apartment in his Sunset Park building after the death of Bumper's mother. It had been Sammy who had introduced Bumper to golf.

* * *

IT WAS A BEAUTIFUL MORNING WHEN Judith arrived at the golf club with her friends. Scheduled for an early tee off, the foursome was comprised of women in their late thirties to early forties. Each participant was poised, fit, and married to a successful man. Thanks to cosmetic surgery, all of the ladies appeared a little younger than they actually were.

However, only one in the foursome interested Bumper. Every drop of desire in him was set aside for Judith, the plastic surgeon's wife. As far as Bumper was concerned, the others in the foursome didn't even rate as spillage.

"What do you think, Dennis . . . a nine iron?" asked Judith.

"No, I think you may be better off with a nine hybrid," replied the caddy, handing Judith the appropriate club. He then advised her on how far to bring the club back.

"Thank you," she warmly said. "I'll try it."

As Judith got in position to hit the ball, the caddy struggled to keep his eyes off the golfer's shapely figure. He fought to control the lust within him that was triggered by Judith's toned body.

Judith was beside herself with joy after placing the white ball exactly where she intended it to go. "Yes!" the broadly smiling club member shouted. "Dennis, you're an absolute gem!"

The caddy's shy smile smacked of satisfaction. His thinking was not on Ms. Vanidestine's next shot but on the words she expressed. *She called me a gem,* thought the puffed-up caddy.

From that point on, Bumper couldn't keep his eyes off Judith. He followed her visually as closely as he did the golf balls that sailed across the course. He ardently cleaned her golf balls and clubs just to receive the reward of additional smiles of approval from Judith.

Each modicum of attention bestowed on the caddy was forever stored in Bumper's mind. Later, when alone, he was able to draw upon those reflections to satisfy the intense yearning he had for the wedded club member.

Concealing his passion for Judith had become exceedingly difficult for Bumper. While the caddy did his best to keep his romantic inclinations in the shadows, his interest was quite evident to anyone taking the time to look at him. The caddy's eyes followed the plastic surgeon's wife wherever she went. The juices of *amore* percolating within Bumper had no shut-off valve to quiet the tempest.

To meet his mounting desire for more of Judith, Bumper purchased the latest cell phone model, one capable of taking pictures. Armed with this newfangled device, the caddy began discreetly photographing the object of his affection while she was busy swatting golf balls. A number of shots captured Judith bending over. The naughty photos he took weren't to be shared. Not even his friend Sammy Angelo warranted a look at them.

On occasion, Bumper also caddied for Judith's husband. Those outings weren't fun for the caddy. Every time he looked at the plastic surgeon he felt further removed from Judith. The caddy considered the highly successful Doctor Vanidestine as a barrier in his quest for Judith's affection. Feeling inadequate in comparison to the prestigious physician, his dislike blossomed into full-blown hatred.

* * *

THE SIXTY-ONE-YEAR-OLD, gray-haired Doctor Gordon Vanidestine was well established because of his ability to correct facial imperfections. His professional success had much to do with his astute mind for business development.

As a young doctor with limited finances, he came upon an idea after having a conversation with a neighbor who owned a dress shop in the garment center. Vanidestine learned that the neighbor's attorney also represented, and was a ranking member of, the Performance Club, a Midtown Manhattan private club that catered to the show-business crowd. Upon learning this, Vanidestine mentally put together the beginnings of a business plan.

The plastic surgeon banked on his belief that an attractive appearance was of vital importance among those in the entertainment industry. He was convinced that by gaining access to the circle of prestigious club members, he'd be able to grow a business.

Once I tap into these celebrities and get a couple as patients, there is no telling how far I can go, thought the doctor.

The one obstacle that gave Vanidestine pause was the cost factor connected to being a member of the fraternity in question. After some consideration he decided that, whatever the cost, it would be a sound investment he'd be making in himself.

With some mild cajoling, Vanidestine's neighbor arranged for the plastic surgeon to meet with his labor attorney. In addition to the Performance Club, the lawyer represented a number of noted restaurants and assorted entities. Doctor Vanidestine, who tended to be a natty dresser, wore his best suit in an effort to impress Fred Klein, the attorney in question.

Klein, a handsome man who sported a thick head of hair and a neatly trimmed beard, welcomed Vanidestine by waving him into his office. Casually dressed, the attorney rose from his desk and extended his hand.

"Have a seat," said Klein after shaking his visitor's hand. "I'm Fred Klein."

"Thank you. I'm pleased to meet you, Mr. Klein."

"Call me Fred. So my client tells me you're a plastic surgeon; that's impressive."

As the two conversed, Klein learned of Vanidestine's history with the attorney's client. He then explained his own history with the doctor's neighbor. As Klein spoke, the plastic surgeon noticed a photograph of the lawyer with the late actress Jayne Mansfield. The doctor found this to be even more impressive than his being a topnotch attorney. Seeing Klein and the actress together in a picture convinced Vanidestine that he was on the right track. Access to celebrities like the talented Ms. Mansfield was just what the plastic surgeon was looking for.

"So why do you want to become a member of the Performance Club?" Klein eventually asked. Vanidestine, who was prepared for such a question, replied well enough to impress the labor lawyer. From Klein's perspective, the plastic surgeon was a solid candidate who was worth his sponsoring for club membership.

Klein, being a business development guru, was a visionary when it came to networking. Having an active hand in the formation of an entity composed of numerous networking groups, he saw in Vanidestine a path to explore the feasibility of forming a physician's networking group. Thinking how such a group would make a handsome addition to his portfolio, Klein pitched the business development idea as a win-win opportunity. The plastic surgeon jumped at the chance to potentially expand his chances at gaining new work. With the backing of Fred Klein, Doctor Vanidestine took a giant step toward his goal of enhancing his business. As things turned out, he was destined for great things.

After gaining membership to the Performance Club, the plastic surgeon calculated that the best way to gain the attention of club members would be by showcasing his talent. With this in mind, he offered to fix the oversized snout of the gregarious club manager for free. This proved to be a brilliant strategy in that the manager became a walking endorsement of the doctor's surgical skills. Over the years, Vanidestine's business blossomed with many famous people added to his patient list. His fees were not to be left in the dust. They skyrocketed accordingly.

Along with the plastic surgeon's success came lots of attention put forth by the opposite sex. This unsolicited recognition fostered the birth of an immense ego in the surgeon. Setting aside his glasses, Doctor Vanidestine now opted to wear contact lenses. As his hair thinned, he overcame the loss with a hairpiece. The surgeon raised a thin silver mustache after one paramour conveyed that a small brush would be an attractive addition. Now sporting the look of a thespian, he became even more in demand at the Manhattan-based club.

At the age of fifty, the plastic surgeon took up with an attractive fashion designer who impressed him with her youth, beauty, and warm personality. The doctor also liked the idea of going around with a hot woman who other men wished they were with.

Doctor Vanidestine subsequently married the fashion designer, who left her career to devote her time to being the wife of a prominent surgeon. Although quite satisfied with Judith, after years of marriage the union's sexual excitement dampened. This cooling off was mutual, with both parties agreeing to intimacy outside of their marriage.

Alma Horton, a model and actor who had a recurring role in a daytime television soap opera, was just the woman to accommodate Doctor Vanidestine's carnal wants. After surgically improving the twenty-seven- year-old Alma's nose, the surgeon found her most receptive to his overtures. His willingness to assume some of Alma's living expenses went far in advancing their relationship. To hide the added expenditures from his wife, the doctor fudged his business records in order to pay the recreational costs incurred.

Alma possessed the right attributes to anchor Doctor Vanidestine. She was bright, buxom, and beautiful, a combination that was enough for the doctor to overlook whatever demands she placed on him. Her cool sophistication made bedding her down seem like the greatest conquest imaginable. Put plainly, she possessed that rare magnetic power capable of training a man like a seal.

Alma complimented the plastic surgeon's business acumen, lauded his medical achievements, and flattered his ego with rave reviews as to his bedroom technique. After a while, Alma had him convinced that he was doing both Fred Klein and the Performance Club a favor.

* * *

BUMPER WAS DISAPPOINTED WHEN told he had been reassigned to caddy for Doctor Vanidestine's foursome. He was originally scheduled to caddy for the plastic surgeon's wife, Judith. Puzzled by the switch, he inquired as to why there was a change. Bumper learned that Judith Vanidestine had told her husband that Bumper was the club's finest caddy. The plastic surgeon, wanting to experience Bumper's ability firsthand, called for the change. While this irked Bumper, there was nothing to be done about it.

The doctor arrived at the country club accompanied by one of his guests, a man of physically large proportions.

"Oh, no!" thought the caddy as he watched the club member's guest slip on his golf shoes while in the parking lot. This was the

10

sort of behavior that the country club frowned upon. "I can't believe no one is saying anything," said Bumper under his breath as he watched the violator go uncorrected by his host. *This looks like the kind of jerk who'll ask to rub my back for good luck*, thought the caddy.

As the day progressed, Bumper began to find fault with everyone in the foursome. The big man was irritating in that he was a chatterbox who made excuses for every poorly placed ball. While this was not uncommon behavior among golfers, Bumper was unforgiving because the player was part of the plastic surgeon's foursome.

Another man in the foursome was a golf novice. Oblivious to golf etiquette, he was a distraction to the others trying to play the game in a timely fashion. Bumper repeatedly had to remind the man to wait his turn before hitting the ball and to pick up his ball in order to avoid holding things up.

Finally, there was the golfer the caddy nicknamed "Pencils," a shameless man when it came to keeping his score. Bumper viewed doctoring a scorecard to be an integrity breach. It was a form of cheating that the caddy considered reprehensible. Of all the foursome guests, he liked Pencils the least.

Halting play for refreshments midway through the game, Bumper overheard Doctor Vanidestine talking to those in his foursome. The caddy's mouth dropped as he overheard the plastic surgeon gleefully recount the details of a high-end golf outing he recently attended. The caddy cringed at hearing Judith's husband detail the antics that occurred at the booze-filled round of golf that came with a working girl assigned to each foursome. The caddy couldn't believe his ears as Judith Vanidestine's husband boasted of how he had his way, behind a tree, with a hooker.

Sex in the rough? Bumper thought. *Lap dances while riding in a golf cart? What kind of a golf club was this?*

Envisioning his precious Judith having relations with a husband he saw as lecherous was problematic for Bumper. His vexation was manifested in various ways on the back nine.

Out of spite, Bumper began sabotaging the plastic surgeon's golf game. Bumper intentionally misread the greens, gave faulty tips to Vanidestine when he was putting, and dropped the doctor's golf balls in precarious positions whenever possible. The caddy also recommended the wrong clubs to use.

Since the men in the foursome were playing for money, the anxiety caused by the plastic surgeon's lackluster performance gave rise to temper tantrums. A highlight for Bumper came when, after slicing a ball, an angry Doctor Vanidestine flung his driver. Bumper had to cover his mouth and look away to conceal his gloat.

"Don't just stand there!" barked the doctor while attempting a long, difficult putt on the fourteenth hole. Bumper was guilty of standing where his shadow fell across the putt line. "What the hell is wrong with you today?" shouted the frustrated plastic surgeon.

"Sorry," replied the caddy, adjusting his position.

On one hole Bumper began sneezing when the plastic surgeon was trying to concentrate on teeing off. The caddy's face-to-face contact with the doctor concluded at the completion of the final hole. Far from departing cordially, the doctor showed his displeasure by walking off in a huff.

The caddy cleaned their golf clubs once the members of the foursome headed to the locker room to shower and prepare for drinks. When no one was looking, Bumper urinated in the surgeon's golf bag. He then left it sitting alongside other unattended bags.

* * *

AFTER COMPLETING HER ROUND OF GOLF, Judith Vanidestine emerged from the locker room looking vibrant, fashionably dressed and, in the opinion of Bumper, drop-dead beautiful. The caddy monitored Judith's movements by creeping around the club taking sneak peeks at her. He zeroed in on Judith's crossed legs as she drank at the club bar with those she had golfed with. His pleasure was interrupted when her husband and his friends joined her group for drinks.

Seeing everyone enjoying themselves created a spark of jealousy within Bumper. *Judith can't possibly belong with that old man*, thought the caddy. *Without his money, he's nothing!*

The caddy headed home that day, frustrated. After wolfing down the couple of slices of pizza he picked up for the ride home, he decided to take his cab out on the road and make some money. While driving about Manhattan picking up fares, the part-time caddy remained in a foul mood as he rehashed unpleasant thoughts about Judith's husband.

##########

THE SUBSEQUENT STORM THAT followed Bumper's urinating in the golf bag led to an inconclusive investigation. While the plastic surgeon strongly suspected Bumper of committing the foul deed, his accusation lacked proof. The attorneys for the golf club, sensitive to the physical abnormality of the caddy, advised the club member that without concrete evidence that Bumper watered the golf bag, it was best to let the matter drop. Their position was not to take a chance with a New York legal system noted for generous settlements. The plastic surgeon had little choice but to concur.

The ugly side of Bumper surfaced the following day after hearing from a staff member at the club that Mr. and Mrs. Vanidestine had become embroiled in a physical altercation in the club parking lot the evening prior. While no one seemed to know exactly what caused the fracas, it was well established that the couple had been drinking. When Bumper began probing, he was informed that the plastic surgeon, in the heat of the moment, had shoved his spouse to the ground. Dennis became livid at hearing this. The scowl on his face made it clear just how perturbed he was.

"What was the fight over?" Bumper asked through teeth that met tightly.

"I don't really know," replied the staff member.

"Well, what was said?"

"All I heard was that her old man called her a 'bitch' and knocked her on her ass."

"What else was said?"

"That was all I got."

"And then what happened?"

"I don't know. I wasn't there . . . Hey, wait a minute—what's your big interest in this anyway?"

Not wanting to reveal his true feelings, Bumper backed off. "I have no interest in either one of them," he replied, quickly adding, "I was just curious because I caddy for both of them. What about the club . . . is it doing anything?" Bumper was worried that the battling husband and wife might have had their club memberships revoked.

"I don't think the club knows a thing about it. The whole mess was over pretty quick."

The thought of Judith being manhandled stuck with Bumper. *That parasite is gonna pay one day for pushing Judith around,* thought the infuriated caddy.

2

Differing Opinions

THE CAUSE OF THE CONFLICT BETWEEN JUDITH VANIDESTINE and her husband in the golf club parking lot had centered on Dennis Bumper. Empowered by alcohol, Judith vehemently challenged the plastic surgeon's assertion that Bumper urinated in his golf bag. The frustrated doctor, who was equally fortified, lashed out physically in his response to his wife's refusal to agree with him. Their discussion carried over to the following morning, at which time they more mildly resumed their quarrel.

"You have no proof that poor Dennis did anything," pointed out Judith.

Judith's defense of the caddy had much to do with her appreciation of Bumper's golf tutelage. Since Dennis began working as her caddy, Judith's game had improved steadily. Her enhanced performance earned her many accolades from those she regularly golfed with.

"I got all the proof I need to convince me," said the plastic surgeon.

"I just can't see how you can jump to such a conclusion."

"C'mon, Judith. You pity the poor bastard because of his humpback."

"His back has nothing to do with anything. He's a great caddy, and I'm continuing to use him regardless of what you think!"

"What? After I told you how awful he was with my foursome, you're still going to use him?"

"You pick your caddy, I'll pick mine," replied Judith snippily, before walking off.

* * *

BESIDES JUDITH BEING MARRIED TO Doctor Vanidestine, the plastic surgeon represented the sort of competition that Bumper knew he couldn't compete with. Lacking the impressive social position and affluence of the plastic surgeon discouraged the caddy from making his feelings known to Judith.

As far as Bumper could see, the only way to gain any traction with Judith was by disrupting the Vanidestine marriage. If Judith was in a place where she pondered divorce, he believed that she'd be vulnerable. Once in this mindset, Bumper felt he'd have an unobstructed path to win Judith's heart as she rebounded.

When in the company of his best friend, Sammy Angelo, Bumper found himself with an outlet to vent his feelings. When the caddy began trashing the plastic surgeon, it caused Sammy to worry about his dear friend.

"Dennis, this isn't normal," Sammy said bluntly. "You're talking crazy about this guy. It ain't healthy, feeling the way you do."

"I know, Sammy," acknowledged the caddy. "I'm just pissed off that Judith is married to a guy like that.
He's just plain no good. I can feel it in my bones. I don't know exactly what he's up to, but I know he has
to be up to something."

"Maybe he is and maybe he isn't, but whatever he's doing, his bride is apparently happy with him," pointed out Sammy.

"Judith's too wonderful a person to think negatively about anyone. She needs to be made aware of what that bum husband of hers is all about."

"Make sense, Dennis," pleaded Sammy. "This woman can figure things out by herself. This is none of your affair," he emphasized. "It's not your place to interfere in the relationship of a married couple."

"All I know is that I'm not forgetting for a minute what Jesus said, Sammy."

"And what was that, Dennis?"

"*Ye shall know the truth, and the truth shall make you free.*"

"That's from John 8:32," noted Sammy, who was himself well versed on things biblical.

"Correct, and Judith's gotta learn the truth about who she's married to!"

"What are you planning to do?"

"I haven't exactly decided yet, Sammy. I'm sort of stuck at a crossroad."

"Dennis, hold up a second. Before you go and do something foolish, why don't we sit down and talk to Father Billy? He helped me through my problems when I was down, and I'm sure he can provide you with sound advice."

"You know I have a lot of respect for Father Billy. But for right now, I'm gonna have to think things out on my own, Sammy."

"Well, how about we do this . . . before you actually do anything, will you at least think about talking to Father Billy? Will you promise me that?"

"I don't like making promises that I might not be able to keep."

"You can't think it over?" asked the concerned friend. "That's all I'm asking . . ."

"Okay. That I could do. Father Billy is regular."

The following day, when Bumper checked his mail, he found several religious pamphlets referencing how no one should covet his neighbor's wife. He knew the mailman must have been Sammy Angelo.

* * *

DENNIS BUMPER SHARED HIS ABODE with Digger, a Campbell's dwarf hamster. Bumper chose the name Digger for the hamster once he caught on that his pet's favorite pastime was to tunnel and explore.

17

While Digger might not have been able to communicate verbally, he did have value as good company for Bumper. The hamster represented a captive audience that Bumper could talk to without receiving feedback he didn't want to hear. The pet was also a responsibility that made him feel needed.

Both Bumper and Sammy Angelo were avid followers of their faith. Sammy, in particular, poured financial support into the struggling Sunset Park Church he attended regularly. The two friends resided in adjacent units on the fifth floor of their apartment house.

Prior to his nervous breakdown, the slightly built Sammy had been a workaholic who made a fine living. An established cartoonist for two nationally syndicated comic strips, his work was also regularly seen in a number of periodicals and magazines.

A victim of his own success, Sammy's financial gain came with a great deal of stress. Deadlines, demanding workloads, and dealing with difficult people eventually got the better of him. It took the intervention of Father Billy, a newly assigned Sunset Park parish priest at the time, to help see him through his health crisis.

Sammy found the plain-talking priest someone he could relate to. He felt the guidance he received from Father Billy to be practical. Sammy found himself more in sync with Father Billy than with any other priest he knew, and that included the senior priest at the church where he worshipped. Their conversation at the time of Sammy's issues was brief and to the point:

"Is it necessary for you to continue working?" asked Father Billy one afternoon when the two were chatting in the rectory library.

"I suppose I don't have to work, Father," replied Sammy.

"Then why work?"

"Well, my life has always centered on my work, Father."

"Do you have any family dependent on you?"

"No, Father. I never married."

"Are your parents alive?"

"No, they passed. I've been alone for quite a while."

"What about brothers and sisters?"

"I was an only child. My only family members are in Italy."

Upon hearing that, Father Billy seemed to perk up. "That being the case, you have no one to worry about other than yourself."

"I suppose so."

"Why, I bet that you must have a nice nest egg tucked away. Am I right?"

"Yes, Father. Fortunately, I'm solvent. I've always been a saver."

"Excellent," said Father Billy, who was clearly uplifted after hearing this. "Living modestly is a virtue, Sammy."

"Well, to be honest with you, Father, I was never the partying type. It was always all work for me. That was basically my problem. I just reached a point where I'm burnt out."

"Why not channel your efforts to a far greater cause?"

"I don't follow you, Father . . ."

"The Lord works in mysterious ways to help us, Sammy. You can be one of His ways. After all, one doesn't need to hog the entire loaf."

Sammy was now beginning to get Father Billy's drift. "I do what I can to support the church, Father."

"I know you do, Sammy. You're a generous man. But we must remember that it's far better to give than receive."

"Now that I'm not working anymore, do you think I should devote more of my time to the Lord?"

"Yes, Sammy. I think giving time is an excellent idea. But since you have no family to support, I suspect that donations to the needy would be a greater way to show your commitment to God."

"I don't mind contributing a little more to worthy causes, Father."

"Why, that's wonderful, Sammy. I'm so pleased that you realize that money should be used to help others. Never forget that the good work we do here on earth will bring us the greatest of rewards in the beyond. As long as we have our health, we have everything we need while here."

"Tell me, Father, who can I help?"

"Well, I know of a distressed family in dire need of five thousand dollars to offset a tragic house fire. They lack . . ."

"There is no need to explain to me, Father. Who should I write the check to?"

"Rather than writing a check, it's best to give me the cash, Sammy. I think it would be prudent for you to keep your generosity anonymous," advised Father Billy. "By filtering your assistance through me, you won't be pestered by those hitting you up for money all the time."

Sammy thought about this for a minute. "You know something Father, you're right. I don't need people coming around. Five thousand, right?"

Sammy Angelo's willingness to part with his money so easily gave Father Billy pause. *Maybe I underestimated how much he has tucked away*, thought Father Billy. Feeling it was too late to ask for more, he confirmed the amount.

"That's right, five thousand."

"You want it all in cash, Father?"

"Yes, Sammy. We want to avoid any embarrassment to the family accepting the money," explained the priest. "People do have their pride, you know. We must be respectful of that."

"Of course, Father."

"And remember, Sammy, I am here for you. You can call on me anytime."

"I know that, Father. I think I'll stop in the church to light a candle before I head home."

* * *

AFTER SUNDAY MASS, Bumper and Sammy ordered Chinese takeout. Sitting in front of the television in Sammy's apartment, the two friends enjoyed their food. During the commercials, Bumper began discussing Judith Vanidestine, who had become his favorite topic of conversation. As the caddy spoke of his deep feelings for the married woman, it was clear to Sammy that his friend's love had intensified.

20

"What on earth are you thinking, Dennis?" asked Sammy. "You can't continue to waste your life pining for this woman."

"I just can't help myself," said Bumper. "Since I'm Judith's regular caddy, I'm always around her."

"Thou shall not covet thy neighbor's wife," reminded Sammy. "Remember the commandments."

"I know it's wrong, but that's where my heart is."

"Can't you caddy for someone else?"

"I could, but I don't want to. She's in my system, Sammy. What more can I say? All I ever do is think about Judith."

"This isn't good, Dennis," warned Sammy, "not good at all. Think about your job at the golf club."

"That's another thing," acknowledged Bumper.

"Did you tell anyone else about this infatuation you have?"

"C'mon, Sammy, do you think I'm crazy? No one but you knows how I feel."

"That's one good thing. Tell me, has this married woman been encouraging you?"

"Yes and no."

The vagueness of Bumper's response caused Sammy Angelo to see innocence in his friend. Taking into account Bumper's physical deformity, he tried to be gentle in conveying his wisdom.

"It may help you to remember what William Shakespeare said, Dennis."

"What was that?"

"The devil hath power to assume a pleasing shape."

Bumper chuckled at hearing this. "Judith Vanidestine is no devil, Sammy," he assured his friend. "If anything, she's an angel."

"Has the angel come on to you?"

"Well, sort of."

"Can you be a little more specific?"

"For one thing, she always smiles at me when I caddy for her."

"And . . ."

"You don't understand, Sammy. Let me try and explain it better to you. When she looks into my eyes, I can see her eyes sparkle."

This statement caused Sammy Angelo to take a deep breath. He found it difficult to imagine anyone having sparkling eyes over Dennis Bumper. "I see," he finally said. "Are you sure it's her eyes that are sparkling and not yours?" Bumper ignored the question.

"And do you want to know what else, Sammy?"

"What?"

"I've never caught her once staring at my back."

"But face facts, Dennis . . . she has a husband."

"Don't you think I know that? I have to be very careful regarding her husband. If the plastic surgeon ever got wise, he'd get me fired from the golf club for sure."

"Well, isn't that a good enough reason to stay away from this woman?"

"I can't help myself when it comes to Judith. Besides, she depends on me to caddy for her."

"Oh, that does pose a problem. The husband and wife—they golf together?"

"No. Mostly she plays with her friends, and the doctor plays with his. That causes me to wonder how close they actually are."

"Be careful, Dennis," said Sammy as he shook his head disapprovingly. "When a man is caught sleeping with a married woman, they both die."

"The Bible says that?"

"That's straight out of Deuteronomy. You're playing with fire."

"The blood Jesus shed on the cross covers all sin," countered Bumper, "and that includes infidelity."

Sammy rolled his eyes. "The sins we commit can be forgiven only when we have a repentant heart. Do you have a repentant heart, Dennis?"

"Me? I'm not the one. Her husband is the one who needs to have a repentant heart."

"What do you mean?"

"Let's skip it," said the caddy, digging into his tray of pork fried rice.

At the conclusion of the movie they were watching, Bumper confessed to Sammy that he had urinated in the plastic surgeon's golf bag. Sammy was stunned, finding his friend committing such an act hard to believe.

"Go on. Who ya kidding," commented Sammy. "You didn't do any such thing."

"Honest, Sammy, I unloaded a river full."

"Dennis, you better keep this to yourself, or people are gonna think something is wrong with you."

"They couldn't ever prove it was me. Anyone could have taken a leak in his bag. It was left out for hours unattended."

"Aren't there cameras?"

"Not a one."

When Bumper communicated the story of Doctor Vanidestine's golf outing with the working girls, Sammy was further appalled. "Why, these people must all be crazy," he said.

"I'm telling you, Sammy, Judith's husband is wicked,"

"This is something out of Sodom and Gomorrah," said Sammy, referring to the notoriously sinful cities in the biblical book of Genesis.

"The good doctor could use a good dose of sulfur and fire," replied Bumper. Between the two churchgoers, there was no loss of biblical knowledge.

"Are you doing anything on Saturday for dinner?" asked Sammy.

"I was planning on driving the cab that night. What's doing?"

"I'm meeting Father Billy. Why don't you come and join us?"

"Where are you going?"

"We're going to the Little Spain Restaurant on 4th Avenue."

"If you're paying, I might go," replied the caddy, adding, "I know Father Billy ain't springing for it."

"It'll be my treat, Dennis."

3

Bumper Turns Shamus

BUMPER'S BEING A CABDRIVER was a job that suited him. He liked the work because it minimized his having to answer to a boss. He likened the responsibility of safely transporting passengers to captaining a vessel or piloting an airplane. At times, his occupation was an ego-boosting experience. Nothing proved this more than when Bumper assisted in the delivery of a baby in the back seat of his cab. His photo appeared on page three of the *Daily News* for that.

Prowling the streets of Manhattan in search of people in need of a ride had an ambiguity to it. In one sense it was therapeutic for Bumper. Aside from earning money, the hunt for fares provided a respite that helped take his mind off Judith Vanidestine. However, Bumper's work concentration was shattered anytime he saw something that reminded him of the married woman. A facial similarity, shape, or walk would be enough to renew his pining for Judith.

The disheartenment connected to the situation caused Bumper to grow bitter at times. Upon entering this foul sphere, Bumper began thinking of ways to undermine the Vanidestine marriage. The caddy proved to be quite creative in this undertaking.

Assuming that an irritated man would inevitably vent his anger at home, Bumper concocted ways of harassing Doctor Vanidestine. He believed once enough turmoil was created in the Vanidestine household, divorce would follow.

The time Bumper spent caddying for the plastic surgeon netted him lots of insights into the physician. The caddy remembered overhearing the doctor talk about his membership in the Performance Club, a private concern in Manhattan that catered to those in the entertainment world. Bumper thought that this venue would be an ideal place to commence his campaign to publicly humiliate the plastic surgeon.

The caddy advanced his nefarious agenda by telephoning Doctor Vanidestine at the Performance Club. Using an assortment of ruses, Bumper was able to get the surgeon to the club telephone on multiple occasions. Each time the doctor picked up the line, he was greeted by the vulgar sound of human flatulence as produced from a Whoopee cushion. When Bumper heard the plastic surgeon slam down the phone in anger, he had sufficient indication that he was getting to his target.

Doctor Vanidestine put things in check by no longer accepting phone calls at the club. He also stopped answering his cell phone if he didn't recognize the number of the caller. Those policies successfully put an end to the telephonic persecution.

Bumper soon came up with other ways to annoy the plastic surgeon. He gift wrapped a shoebox that he mailed to Vanidestine in care of the Performance Club. The Upper East Side return address on the package lent an air of legitimacy to the delivery. No one expected the haunting surprise contained within the box.

The plastic surgeon was glad to receive what he believed to be a gift from a satisfied patient. At the urging of his fellow club members, the doctor agreed to open the package. All on hand gasped upon seeing what was contained in the shoebox. The sight of a king size dildo resting atop a bed of lettuce smothered in live worms was a sight that jarred all in attendance. For the plastic surgeon, this was the final straw. Doctor Vanidestine dialed 911.

Vanidestine explained to the responding officers the history of how he was being victimized. After listening to the doctor's account, the officers prepared a complaint report. Once the report was completed, the guardians of the law explained to the complainant that the matter would be referred to the precinct detectives.

As it turned out, the detectives were unable to unearth any fingerprints of value from the package delivered at the club. Their interview of the plastic surgeon provided no information that enabled the investigators to further their investigation. Frustrated that his complaint had become a closed case, Doctor Vanidestine had little choice other than to let things go at that.

With the plastic surgeon no longer accepting packages, Bumper began to randomly pass by the Performance Club whenever he was driving his cab. Luck was on Bumper's side one evening when he happened to spot Doctor Vanidestine stepping out of a taxicab. Bumper abruptly pulled his own cab over so that he could observe the plastic surgeon. Bumper bit on his lip in anticipation as the doctor held the vehicle door open for his fellow passenger to exit the cab.

Doctor Vanidestine, who was dressed in a navy-blue suit, reached into the vehicle to take hold of what appeared to be a woman's hand. At first Bumper assumed the woman was Judith Vanidestine. It wasn't. Instead of the plastic surgeon's wife, a younger, equally beautiful woman emerged from the back of the taxi. Bumper was exhilarated by what he was witnessing, believing that he had just stumbled upon proof of the plastic surgeon's unfaithfulness.

Look at this! Bumper thought as he eyeballed the leggy, unidentified woman in the short skirt. He watched as the pair walked into the Performance Club together. This was an indescribably delicious moment for the caddy.

Bumper abandoned all thought of picking up fares at this point. He parked and waited patiently for the plastic surgeon and his female companion to exit the club. Ever vigilant, Bumper caught sight of the smiling couple ninety minutes later when they stepped out into the street. Seeing the doctor place his arm around the shoulder of the young woman made it clear as to what their relationship was.

"That's it. Get nice and cozy!" Bumper said under his breath as he observed the woman reciprocate by putting her arm around the doctor's waist. The public display of affection Bumper was witnessing made him wish he had a camera with him powerful enough to capture the moment on film. Bumper activated the cab windshield wiper washer to clear away the window dirt. He wanted his view to be unobstructed.

"Just look at this shamelessness!" Bumper proclaimed to himself with sincere outrage. "Why, she's young enough to be his daughter!"

When the plastic surgeon and his lady friend began strolling down the block, the cabdriver emerged from his vehicle. After feeding the parking meter, he proceeded to follow the pair on foot while cautiously allowing for some distance to accumulate.

They must be walking off their food, thought Bumper as he trailed behind his prey.

Doctor Vanidestine and the woman switched to holding hands once entering Central Park. They lazily walked as any two lovers would. Once deeper within the confines of the park, the plastic surgeon and his companion engaged in the touchy-feely behavior usually expected among the young. This public display of affection came complete with goofy smiles and extended kisses. When Doctor Vanidestine took a handful of the rear end of his romantic interest, the recipient of the squeezing displayed no apparent aversion to the intrusive overture.

Have they no shame! thought Bumper, who had concealed himself behind a large tree. *They're nothing more than heathens!*

When finished with their frolicking, Doctor Vanidestine and the woman casually made their way to an East Side piano bar. The couple entered the establishment unaware they were being tailed. Bumper positioned himself on the sidewalk where he

27

was able to peer into the front glass of the nightspot. Bumper's vantage point permitted him to see the couple order drinks at the bar.

Observing the plastic surgeon's girlfriend in the light impressed the wide-eyed Bumper, who marveled at her beauty. The frequent smiling and continued displays of physical affection he witnessed caused Bumper to become envious. He only wished that he was engaging in such billing and cooing with Judith, the plastic surgeon's wife.

Sure, have a good time, thought Bumper as he watched Vanidestine and his lady friend sing along with others who were standing around the piano player. *These two are getting frisky while poor Judith is probably sitting home alone wondering where this stinker of a husband is.* The thought of such unfairness began to gnaw at Bumper.

The plastic surgeon began to hit his musical stride when the piano player began playing a tune very familiar to him. The 1906 ditty, "Love Me and the World Is Mine," was an old song that Vanidestine's grandmother used to sing to him.

As the plastic surgeon sang along enthusiastically, he shifted his body and took a deep breath in preparation to cut loose with the most prominent part of the song. As he put forth vocally, the words suddenly ceased flowing mid-lyric. Vanidestine's open-mouthed pause came after he spotted Bumper standing on the sidewalk on the other side of the saloon glass. At that exact moment it dawned on the doctor who was responsible for the harassment he was being subjected to.

"You!" blurted out the surgeon, looking at the glass facing the street. Realizing that he was identified, Bumper disappeared from view in a flash. The caddy's hasty disappearance left no doubt in the plastic surgeon's mind as to who his tormentor was.

"What's wrong?" his friend asked, seeing the look of malaise on her lover's face. "What are you looking at?"

"Nothing's wrong," replied the surgeon stiffly. "C'mon. We're leaving."

Bumper had taken refuge in the Chinese Restaurant on the opposite side of the street. He concealed himself inside the eatery while maintaining a clear view of the piano bar. When Bumper observed Doctor Vanidestine and his companion leave the bar, he resumed his surveillance.

The trail ultimately ended at an apartment building on East 54th Street. The couple nodded their greeting to the doorman as they walked past him. There was little doubt that the plastic surgeon would likely be tucked in for the rest of the night.

Bumper, pretending to be an autograph seeker, asked the doorman if the woman with the older gentleman was someone famous. He was surprised at how quickly the doorman advised him of the woman's identity, a model and actress of some notoriety. The building employee identified her companion as her boyfriend. Satisfied at learning the identity of the plastic surgeon's paramour, Bumper returned to his cab and went back to picking up fares.

Bumper, having established that Judith Vanidestine's husband was involved in an extramarital affair, now had the evidence he wanted. What remained was the caddy having the nerve to communicate his discovery to Judith.

4

Calling Off the
Dogs

DOCTOR VANIDESTINE BEGAN WAVING away the smoke that was tickling his nose. Although he disliked his mistress smoking, especially while in bed, he held his tongue. The last thing he wanted to do was alienate the other woman. As it turned out, the physician didn't have to say a word. The expression on his face conveyed a distinct displeasure.

Noting the doctor's displeased look, the girlfriend assumed it was due to her smoking. To avoid exasperating matters, she put out her cigarette prematurely. Before rubbing her butt out in the astray she inhaled a long, final drag. She was careful to release the smoke in a direction that was least intrusive to the plastic surgeon resting beside her.

The naked woman then crossed one leg over her raised knee and began to teasingly wiggle her toes. Her intent was to make the doctor forget all about her smoking in bed. This was a ploy she had used successfully in the past. This time the strategy failed her. The doctor exhibited no reaction to the temptation that presented itself. Failing to rise to the occasion, the plastic surgeon remained on his back, glumly staring at the ceiling.

"I'm sorry, Gordon. I know you hate my smoking," she said, believing that her nicotine habit was the cause of her lover's coolness. "I really have been trying to smoke less."

"I'm not annoyed at your smoking," said the plastic surgeon. "I know you've been cutting down."

"What is it then?"

"I'm upset over what happened at the piano bar."

"You never did tell me what that was all about."

Doctor Vanidestine opened up to his mistress how he was being targeted for harassment at the Performance Club. After the nastiness was explained, the mistress grew concerned. The thought of a delivery of worms repulsed her.

"Only a sick person would do such a thing, Gordon," she said. "Anyone capable of doing something like that must be mentally disturbed."

"Of course, this is definitely the work of a demented mind," agreed Vanidestine.

"What on earth would warrant someone doing such a horrible thing?"

"That's what so baffling to me. I have absolutely no idea."

"Do you suspect anyone?"

"Now I do. That's what I find so upsetting."

"I don't understand . . ."

The plastic surgeon went on to elucidate how he saw the caddy from his golf club spying on him through the glass at the piano bar.

"Are you definitely sure it was the caddy?"

"It was him," stated the physician adamantly, adding curtly, "I should know my own caddy."

"Have you ever reported any of this to the police?"

"Yes, of course. The detectives said nothing could be done without proof. I really don't think they exerted themselves."

"Maybe the lawyer at the club could help you with the police."

"Who do you mean—Fred Klein?"

"Yes, you always said that he knows everyone."

"He does, but I feel awkward going to him."

"Why should you feel awkward?"

"He was the one who sponsored my entry into the Performance Club."

"That's even more of a reason you should go to him. With all the surgeries you performed on members of that club over the years, they should thank you."

"Perhaps you're right," said the plastic surgeon, thinking that his woman had made a good point. "I'll reach out to him."

* * *

WHEN THE PHONE RANG, the semiretired Fred Klein was at his Florida getaway having an amicable lunch with some friends. Checking the number on his cell phone, he saw it was Doctor Vanidestine calling. He wasn't surprised. Having heard from club members about the worm episode, Klein anticipated the possibility of hearing from the plastic surgeon.

"Excuse me, gentlemen. I have to take this call," announced Klein, leaving the table. When he reached a private area, he answered the phone. "Hello," said the attorney.

"Hello, Fred. It's Gordon Vanidestine. I have a little problem and was wondering if you could help me out by putting me in contact with the right people."

"If I can," said Klein. "What's the problem?"

After receiving all the details of the harassment, the lawyer rolled his eyes. Klein hated hearing of such difficulties. Feeling personally tainted for having sponsored Vanidestine's membership to the club years prior, the sensitive attorney shared in the plastic surgeon's embarrassment.

"I heard through the grapevine that you've been having issues," said Klein. "I didn't realize the magnitude of the matter."

"Yes, it's been pretty bad . . ."

Klein didn't have it in him to abandon the plastic surgeon. He felt an obligation to do what he could to help. "Maybe I can grease the wheels of justice, Gordon. I'll make some calls."

"Thanks, Fred."

"Sit tight. I'll get back to you."

The attorney telephoned the New York City police commissioner on his cell phone. "It's Fred Klein, Commissioner."

"Hello, Fred. How are you doing?"

"I'm fine, thanks. I was wondering if you could help a friend of mine. You don't mind my asking, do you?"

The top law enforcement officer wasn't in the habit of going out of his way for just anyone. His response was lukewarm. "What problem does your friend have, Fred?"

"Gordon Vanidestine is a fellow member of the Performance Club. He's recognized as one of the top plastic surgeons in New York City, Commissioner," advised Klein, using the plastic surgeon's status to his advantage. "He is being harassed and receiving little satisfaction from the police. I was hoping you could do something to alleviate his problem."

The commissioner warmed up considerably after learning that Vanidestine was a prominent plastic surgeon. "Why, of course, Fred. I'll do all that I can. You know that."

Klein rated high in the top cop's book because the attorney often introduced him to people and places where he, even as police commissioner, would not normally have access.

"Thanks, Commissioner. I owe you one," said the attorney.

The following day, thanks to the magic of Fred Klein, Doctor Vanidestine met with the police commissioner at the Performance Club for dinner. The police commissioner couldn't have been more accommodating. The top lawman's receptiveness had everything to do with his vanity.

Bothered by the large bags under his eyes, the commissioner saw the plastic surgeon in terms of an opportunity to receive corrective surgery in order to enhance his appearance. By the commissioner's way of thinking, his doing a favor warranted the expectation of receiving one in return. In this particular case the commissioner expected to be the recipient of a free surgical procedure.

At the conclusion of their discussion, the commissioner believed they had reached an understanding. The commissioner would have his chief of detectives address the plastic surgeon's

33

harassment problem, while the plastic surgeon would surgically remove the commissioner's bothersome under-eye bags.

* * *

DOCTOR VANIDESTINE WALKED TOWARD One Police Plaza slowly. He advanced cautiously, as would anyone approaching someplace unfamiliar. Having experienced limited interactions with the police, the plastic surgeon was in awe of the well-protected structure. He noted how access to the building was exceedingly controlled. Also surprising was the extensive compliment of gun-toting officers protecting both the police headquarters building interior and perimeter.

After making his way through the security point, the plastic surgeon affixed the security pass he was issued to his outermost garment. As instructed, he proceeded to an elevator bank that would take him where he needed to go. When the doctor arrived at the upper floor office of the chief of detectives, he was received by the chief's gopher, Detective Silverlake.

"Doctor Vanidestine?" asked the veteran detective. After confirming the visitor's identity, Silverlake added, "We've been expecting you."

Judging by his appearance, Silverlake could see that the doctor was a man of means. The quality of the clothes Vanidestine wore attested to that. The detective was in the dark as to the nature of the visitor's business with the chief. All Silverlake knew was that the doctor's presence was the result of a call that came down from the police commissioner's office. The detective had been around long enough to know that this meant a contract was in play to take good care of the doctor.

"I'll let the chief know you're here, Doc," said Silverlake.

"Thank you."

When the plastic surgeon entered the chief's sizable office, he was impressed. The chief's desk, a vintage piece of furniture, was massive. It sat in the center of the room with a long wooden table pressed against its center, forming a T-shape. Several chairs were positioned on each side of the table. The chief liked this arrangement because it left little question as to who was in charge.

"Have a seat, Doctor," said the chief, who rose from his desk to offer his hand. "It's nice to meet you."

"My pleasure," replied the plastic surgeon cordially. "You have a very nice office, Chief," complimented Vanidestine as he assumed a seat at the long table.

"It suits me. Do you see this desk?" the chief asked, proudly pointing to his work station.

"It's very nice. Is it an antique?"

"This was Police Commissioner Richard Enright's desk. It goes back to before the early 1920s."

The plastic surgeon nodded approvingly, as if impressed. He had never even heard of Enright. The .38 caliber revolver that hung from the chief's belt is what really caught the doctor's attention, as did the tiny green shamrocks that decorated the small leather ammo pouch that hung from the chief's belt.

"Do you prefer coffee or tea, Doctor?" Vanidestine shook his head in the negative. "Perhaps you prefer a bottle of water?"

"No, I'm fine, really."

"Okay, we're good," said the chief, dismissing Silverlake, who had been standing by in the office.

"So how do you know the police commissioner, Doctor?"

"We met through a mutual friend."

"I see. The commissioner is a good person to know. So tell me, what seems to be the problem?"

After hearing some of the details concerning the plastic surgeon's issue, the chief summoned Sergeant Al Markie to his office.

"Sarge, say hello to Doctor Vanidestine," said the chief. "I want you to take good care of him. See what can be done to put an end to his troubles."

"No problem, Chief," said Markie. "What's the situation?"

"The doctor will explain it all to you. Take him to your office and get to work on it." The chief then turned to address the plastic surgeon. "Don't worry, Doc, you're in good hands."

35

"Thank you, Chief," said Vanidestine, rising from his seat to follow Markie.

Once in Markie's office, the sergeant and Detective Oliver Von Hess interviewed Doctor Vanidestine. The plastic surgeon went on to articulate how he was being harassed.

"And you suspect this caddy is responsible," said Markie. "Do you have anything, other than what you've already told us, to support your suspicion?"

"That's the problem. I have no actual hard evidence," replied the plastic surgeon. "But really, isn't the caddy showing up at the piano bar proof enough that he had to be behind the harassment?"

"I'm afraid we're going to need more than what we have, Doctor."

"What's the caddy's name again?" asked Von Hess, injecting himself into the questioning.

"Dennis Bumper."

"Can you describe him please?"

"He has a humpback and. . ."

"The caddy has a humpback?"

After providing the investigators with a description of Dennis Bumper, Von Hess asked about the box the worms came in. "Was the box addressed in print or script?"

"Print, I believe," Vanidestine replied.

"Do you know where the box is now?"

"I have no idea."

"Do you know if the detective you dealt with dusted for fingerprints or saved the box?"

"I know they definitely dusted. I'm not sure about saving the box."

"Let me ask you something," injected Markie. "What possible motive could this caddy have to target you?"

"It's a mystery to me, Sergeant."

"Do you think he may be on drugs?" asked Detective Von Hess.

"I've seen no indication of that. But who knows?"

"Did you have words with the caddy, perhaps?"

"Not really . . . well, I did get short with him once."

"What over?"

"He was doing a horrendous job caddying for me, and I tend to believe his poor performance was intentional."

"We're not golfers," said Markie. "In what way was he doing a horrendous job?"

"He made a multitude of errors."

"Could you be more specific?"

"He gave bad advice when I was putting. He couldn't find my balls, every poor drive I hit he said ended
up in the woods . . . just little things like that."

"I see. Well, if it is this caddy, there has to be more of a reason behind all this," commented Markie. "Did you ever have any money dealings with him?"

"No, I never did."

"And you said there are no drugs involved?"

"Not that I'm aware of."

"Did he ever turn on you?"

"I don't understand the question, Sergeant."

"The sergeant's asking you if the caddy ever gave you an argument," clarified Von Hess. "Was he ever combative with you?"

"No, never, not even once. He'd lose his job if he ever tried anything like that."

"Are you sure you never inadvertently slighted him in some way?"

"If I did, it was totally unintentional. You know, the funny part of all this is that my wife gets on well with him."

"Where does your wife fit into this equation?"

"Dennis Bumper is basically her regular caddy."

"Do you get along well with your wife, Doctor Vanidestine?" queried Von Hess, now sensing a direction.

"Of course I do. Why do you ask?"

"Just asking," replied the detective, not revealing his line of thinking.

"Well, how about we do this, Doctor," said Markie. "We'll start by doing a background check on this caddy. Let's see where that takes us. In the meantime, take our business card. Be sure to let either of us know if anything new develops."

"How long before I'll hear from you, Sergeant?"

"Give us a couple of days."

The subsequent results of the background check netted no relevant information pertaining to the caddy. After ascertaining that there was no evidence preserved in the worm caper, the investigators had nothing go on, other than Bumper looking through a saloon window.

Markie and Von Hess could only think of one thing to do. When they later conveyed to Doctor Vanidestine their intent to have a talk with Dennis Bumper, the plastic surgeon discouraged them from doing so. Vanidestine was worried that approaching Bumper without proof would exacerbate things and, thus, intensify the harassment.

"Are you sure you want to call off the dogs?" asked Markie.

"Yes, I'm sure," replied the plastic surgeon.

Markie's efforts to sway the doctor were met without success. This being the case, all involved agreed to wait until the harasser slipped up and did something that might provide the proof they needed.

Sergeant Markie explained this decision to the chief of detectives, who reacted by shrugging his shoulders. "This guy just doesn't know how to help himself," observed the chief. "I'll post the commissioner."

The chief picked up the telephone to contact the police commissioner. After apprising his superior of where things stood, he was surprised at the commissioner's sudden lack of interest. The commissioner didn't share that the reason for his cooling was connected to his having to pay for the surgery that would correct his under-eye bag condition. The commissioner concluded their conversation with only a terse comment.

"Screw the sawbones," said the commissioner tartly. "Let the son of a bitch fix his own problems."

* * *

DENNIS BUMPER AND SAMMY ANGELO were leisurely walking along Shore Road. The friends were in the habit of doing this on pleasant summer evenings when Bumper wasn't driving his cab. During their walk, Bumper shared what he learned about Doctor Vanidestine. After digesting the details of Vanidestine's infidelity, Sammy weighed in.

"Dennis, all of this has nothing to do with you," announced Sammy. "I hope you realize that."

"Somebody has to wise up Judith, Sammy. He's making a fool of her."

"Dennis, we've been through this before," said the loyal friend, his frustration obvious. "They are a married couple. Their business is theirs, not yours."

"How can you expect me to ignore what her husband's doing?"

"Dennis, please listen to reason," pleaded Sammy. "You can't be taking sides in a problem between a husband and wife. Nobody knows what goes on in their house but them."

"I have all I need to know," declared Bumper emphatically. He was getting annoyed at his friend's failure to go along with him. "Judith is pure, and her husband is a cheating slime ball, and that's it in a nutshell!"

"Don't get mad, Dennis. I'm on your side. You know that," assured Sammy, realizing he had ruffled his friend's feathers.

"And aside from being a cheat, don't forget that he gets physical with Judith."

"She complained to you about that?"

"No, she never told me directly."

"Then how do you know that it's a problem?"

"The bastard knocked Judith to the ground in the club parking lot."

"Do you know what the argument was over?"

"What difference does that make, Sammy? I know all I need to know. He had no business getting physical."

"I can't dispute that with you, Dennis, but . . ."

"But nothing," barked Bumper. "Can't you hear me, Sammy? The cheating son of a bitch has a girlfriend tucked away in the city, and he's pushing Judith around. She needs me, not a husband like him."

"What God has joined together, let no one separate," said Sammy, citing Mark in the good book.

"Yeah, well, we're gonna have to see about that, Sammy."

"Now look, Dennis, how about we go see Father Billy and talk to him about all this? He'll guide you through this. Trust me."

"Not now, Sammy," said Bumper, abruptly ending the conversation.

5

The First Murder

MONTHS PASSED WITH BUMPER continuing to carry a torch for Judith Vanidestine. It was a crisp morning in December when the plastic surgeon's wife returned to her Todt Hill home on Staten Island. Judith Vanidestine was tanned, happy, and fulfilled. Her Florida golf holiday with her financial advisor exceeded expectations. Martin had been the paragon of attentiveness, both on and off the golf course. Her lover was the perfect supplement to her husband.

Like all her clothes, the stylish burgundy track suit Judith wore beneath her coat was of the highest quality. From afar she could be taken for a younger woman. The few traces of gray that ran through her long, dark hair were the only indicators that she was years beyond forty.

Judith placed her coat and travel bag on top of the sofa. She stood the powder blue golf bag that housed her clubs next to the living room fireplace. Thirsty, she then went to the kitchen to fetch herself a tall glass of water. Once her dryness was quenched, Judith proceeded to unpack. While doing this she telephoned her husband to let the doctor know she had arrived home safely.

During their chat the plastic surgeon informed his wife that he would be spending the next few days in Manhattan. He explained that he had several surgeries to perform, adding that he also had an evening event that required his attendance. The childless couple had long agreed to afford each other all the latitude necessary to maintain their relationship. Their conversation was truncated due to Judith being called away to answer the ringing doorbell.

Now who could that be? she wondered, after hanging up the phone. When she went to the front door she was surprised to see Dennis Bumper, a caddy at the Staten Island golf club she and her husband belonged to. She hadn't seen Bumper since the golf season had ended.

"Dennis, what are you doing here?" Judith asked, looking over his shoulder at the Yellow Cab parked in front of the house. "Is that taxi waiting for you?"

"It's my cab."

"Where is the driver?"

"I'm the driver," answered the caddy. "I'm a cabdriver. That's my regular job."

"You own your own cab?"

"No, I just rent it from the owner. We have an arrangement."

"Really?" asked Judith, expressing interest. Part of Judith's appeal was the ability to feign interest in things she couldn't care less about.

"I pay the owner a flat weekly rate. In return, he lets me hang on to the cab so I can use it whenever I want. Since he's retired, it works out good for both of us."

"I see. It's sort of like a pension for him."

"Sort of, I suppose."

"So what brings you here, Dennis?"

"Well, since you've always been so nice to me, I feel obligated to tell you something that I think you should be aware of," advised the visitor. The somberness of Bumper's tone suggested that something serious was afoot.

"Well, come in the house. It's freezing out here."

"Thank you, Ma'am."

"It must be very important for you to come to my home, Dennis, so please tell me, what is it?"

The caddy couldn't have appeared more solemn. "I probably should have told you months ago, Ma'am."

Her curiosity stimulated, Judith had the caddy take a seat in the living room. "Now what is it that you have to tell me?"

"I don't know how to tell you this without hurting you," began Bumper. His troubled look made it evident that what he had to say had been weighing heavily on his mind.

"Hurting me?" she asked with surprise. "What on earth are you talking about?"

"Well, errr, um," stammered the caddy.

Despite her husband's opinion of the caddy, Judith always exhibited great understanding when it came to Bumper. Sympathizing with his affliction, she could only imagine how awful it was to go around with a humpback.

Judith was totally unaware that Bumper harbored a deep love for her. His affection was a case of pining from afar. As a result of his amorous feelings, Bumper placed Judith on a pedestal. To Bumper, Judith Vanidestine was nothing short of perfection, both physically and morally. To the religious Bumper, the latter was the more significant of the two qualities.

The hump on the caddy's back did not warrant him an endless amount of Judith's time. "Come on now, Dennis. I'm very busy right now, so tell me what you came here to tell me."

"Your husband is cheating on you," finally blurted the caddy.

"What?" asked the plastic surgeon's wife, who was taken aback by what she heard.

"Doctor Vanidestine has a girlfriend on the side." Judith's stunned expression was misread by the caddy. His belief was that he just shattered the world of the woman he was enamored with. "I know this is hurtful to you, Ms. Vanidestine. But don't ever feel that you're alone. I'm here for you."

Judith looked at Bumper as if he had two heads. After letting out a deep sigh of frustration, she responded.

"Look, Dennis," she began, "I appreciate your concern, but you don't understand how things are." Judith's voice was flat and emotionless as she expressed herself. "My husband and I love each other deeply. We keep no secrets from each other. He and

I are on the same page, if you get my drift." Her drift totally escaped Bumper.

"I understand that you're a loyal person, Ms. Vanidestine," commented Bumper. "But you're too good for the likes of a . . . a philandering swine like him."

The caddy's words ignited a fire within Ms. Vanidestine that wasn't going to go out easily. She turned on Bumper with a vengeance.

"HOW DARE YOU!" she thundered with outrage. "Where do you get off coming to my house and talking to me this way?"

"Well . . ."

"First of all, my private life is none of your damn business!" shouted the outraged wife. "Secondly, any arrangement that I have with my husband is our affair!"

"I didn't mean to upset you . . ." said Bumper meekly.

"From here on out you better mind your own damn business. Now get the hell out of my house!"

Reeling from the lambasting he received, Bumper took a step back. "I just thought you should know."

"What makes you think I don't know? Do you think I'm stupid?" The questions caused Bumper to back off. "For your information, my husband and I have an arrangement," she barked. "He sees who he cares to, and I see who I want." The revelation caused Bumper's jaw to drop in disbelief.

"You mean . . ."

"Oh, shut up!" snapped Judith, cutting off the caddy midsentence. "If my husband were here, it would be just too bad for you. Why, if Martin was here there is no telling what could have happened."

"Martin?"

"Yes, Martin! The man I just came back from Florida with!"

Bumper, not wanting to hear more, cupped his ears with his hands. Judith stepped up her attack.

"Don't you want to know about Martin?" she asked with a sneer. "He's the wealth manager my husband and I use . . . and I screw his brains in every chance I get!" she crudely declared.

The caddy recoiled, staggering as if struck. Bumper's face turned grotesque as he beheld the woman he now considered to be tarnished. Bumper somehow mustered the courage to confess his feelings. "I loved you. Don't you understand?" said the caddy with a sad tenderness. "I would've married you."

Ms. Vanidestine cupped her hand over her eyes in disbelief. "You pathetic, twisted man," she said in a low voice. "Do you honestly think that I would ever stoop to taking you seriously?"

Judith's words were stinging enough to bring out Bumper's dark side.

"You disgust me," he announced.

"I disgust you? Why, you pathetic moral bastard . . . have you looked at yourself lately?"

"Have you no shame?"

"GET OUT OF MY HOUSE!" ordered Judith explosively.

"YOU SICKEN ME! Bumper roared back, his own temper now taking charge. The back and forth only further inflamed things.

"Listen, Quasimodo, I've had just about enough of you. You get the hell out of my house right now, or I'm calling the police." Judith's referring to Dennis as Victor Hugo's deformed character in the novel *The Hunchback of Notre Dame* cut deep.

"DON'T YOU EVER CALL ME THAT!" Bumper hollered, now truly triggered.

Ms. Vanidestine reacted by doubling down. "You heard me— get out QUASIMODO!"

"I TOLD YOU NOT TO CALL ME THAT!" warned Bumper.

"QUASIMODO! QUASIMODO! QUASIMODO!" taunted Ms. Vanidestine spitefully, equaling the caddy's volume. "Where are you going?" she asked as she saw Bumper scoot to the golf bag by the fireplace.

The caddy's steps were short and quick. Removing one of the irons from the bag, Bumper turned on Judith, swinging the club wildly at her. Judith raised her hands to deflect the rain of incoming blows. Her attempt to ward off Bumper's attack was futile.

The fierce blow that struck home dropped Ms. Vanidestine to the ground. Bumper stood over his victim and administered several more tee-off style swings that connected with Judith's head. When exhausted, the caddy ceased his onslaught, leaving his victim bloodied and lifeless.

Bumper threw down the golf club next to the dead woman's body. Although spent, he still possessed an intense curiosity that required satisfaction. He couldn't resist the urge to go through the homicide victim's pocket book. Bumper's interest was not in stealing Judith's money but, rather, to gain greater knowledge of her. The gum she chewed, the breath mints she favored, her lipstick, and so on were all important to him. Then, to his surprise, he found something of great interest in Judith's address book. Contained within the pages were the details of Judith's family and friends. Among these listings was Martin, Judith's lover. Oddly, there was no telephone number with the listing:

Martin Tamor, Wealth Manager
Tamor, Bacon & LaRoy
1285 Avenue of the Americas, 35th Floor, NYC
New York, New York 10019

Bumper threw the address book to the floor. He then fled the house to his taxi. Not thinking of consequences, he drove home to his Brooklyn apartment. Once there, Bumper retreated to his bedroom. Then he showered and climbed into bed. He pulled the blanket over his head for an added sense of privacy.

Once settled comfortably, Bumper began to wonder what caused Judith to become such a terrible person. Seeking a place to lay blame, he fleshed out possible causation factors. He came to the conclusion that Judith's fall from grace stemmed from the negative influences of her husband and wealth advisor lover.

Those two bastards are responsible for the ruination of Judith, reasoned Bumper. This position morphed into an indisputable fact in the mind of the caddy.

Finding peace beneath the covers, Bumper began to mentally relive his nasty exchange with the plastic surgeon's wife. *Both me and Judith are victims of sinister forces,*" thought Bumper. *Judith was corrupted by her husband and that guy Martin. They're the ones responsible for ruining both our lives!*

Bumper knew it was only a matter of time before he'd be caught for the Staten Island murder he had committed. Accepting this outcome, he intended to eventually turn himself in. It was at that point that he intended to call on the services of Father Billy. However, before doing that, there were two more murders to commit.

* * *

THE HIGHEST NATURAL POINT in New York City is Todt Hill. It's considered the most exclusive area on Staten Island. The Vanidestine home was a spacious, five-bedroom affair with wood-burning fireplaces. Tucked in the triangular space beneath the staircase leading to the second floor was a large fish tank. Assorted colorful fish could be seen aimlessly swimming about.

The mail carrier servicing the neighborhood usually delivered mail by late afternoon. The postal worker was a chipper man who loved the holiday season. Although an atheist, the veteran mailman wore a pin on the lapel of his coat that reflected a cross within a Christmas tree. The month of December was the time that he made it a point to ring doorbells and wish people a happy holiday as he handed them their mail. It was his way of reminding people that a Christmas gratuity would be appreciated.

The mailman waited patiently for someone to come to the door of the Vanidestine home. The plastic surgeon and his wife were generally good for a fifty-dollar donation. Since the front door was slightly ajar, he found it unusual when no one came to the door. Before moving on to the next house the letter carrier poked his head inside and called out, "Is anyone home?" When no one responded, he wondered why. When a second shout drew no response, he ventured a couple of steps deeper into the house, thinking the residents might have gone away and forgotten to lock their front door. He also considered the possibility that something was amiss.

Thinking it better to be safe than sorry, the mailman decided to investigate. *Somebody might be sick*, he thought, and he prepared to use that as justification for going inside if questioned.

"Is anyone home?" repeated the mailman as he entered the main room of the house.

The letter carrier let out a chilling shriek when he saw the battered body of Judith Vanidestine lying on the living room floor. He regained his composure only after fleeing the house. After taking a moment to gather himself, he turned around and reentered the house. Standing over the downed woman, it was clear to him that she was dead.

The mailman immediately dialed 911 to report his discovery to the authorities. Heeding the instructions of the police dispatcher, he awaited the arrival of the authorities. Overwhelmed by the sight of the grisly discovery, the mail carrier stepped outside into the cold air. While waiting for the police to respond, he noticed a neighbor leaving her home. Since misery likes company, the letter carrier couldn't resist the temptation of recruiting someone to join him in his wait. By the time the responding radio car arrived, the officers were met by the mail carrier and half a dozen neighbors who had been apprised of what had happened.

The officers designated the house a crime scene. They requested that the dispatcher notify the patrol sergeant that he was needed at the scene. The sergeant, upon his arrival, had the police officers cordon off the room in which Judith Vanidestine rested. He then posted an officer at the front door to restrict access of the unauthorized. Once the crime scene was preserved, the sergeant requested the presence of the precinct detectives.

The subsequent investigation was led by Detective Lieutenant Jake Nightshade, a veteran detective squad commander with many years of experience. Nightshade was accompanied by Detective Jessica Winters, a newly promoted investigator.

The precinct sleuths ascertained from the mailman that the interior lights of the house were on when the body was discovered. They further gathered that the front door had been left open. An inspection of the premises determined that the windows were locked, and there was no evidence of a forced entry. This meant that the killer was either let in or pushed his way into the house. This conclusion was supported by the fact that there was no indication of a robbery having transpired. The house wasn't ransacked, and the victim's purse contained hundreds of dollars.

The detectives noted that the coffee pot and other small appliances were turned off. They then closely examined the area surrounding the body of the homicide victim. They observed nothing to suggest that a struggle occurred. The furniture appeared undisturbed. A cursory look at the body revealed no defense wounds on the victim's hands. There was also no indication that the body had been dragged along the floor or moved. The bloodied golf club was found not far from the corpse, making it obvious that the iron was the murder weapon.

The forensic team that responded to the crime scene lifted fingerprints of value off the bloodied murder weapon, a Callaway six-iron. The clubs in the golf bag that stood beside the living room fireplace were also dusted for fingerprints, as were various areas of the house.

Since robbery was ruled out, the precinct detectives knew they needed to look elsewhere for a motive. They conducted a series of interviews of neighbors to verify the victim's identity and gain insights into the deceased. Their inquiry produced a sunny account of a married woman with no marital discord apparent. The postal carrier who discovered the homicide victim also recollected Mr. and Mrs. Vanidestine as being a pleasant twosome.

Detective Winters unearthed one lead in relation to the canvass she conducted. Two neighbors indicated that they had seen a yellow taxicab parked in front of the Vanidestine residence. They claimed to have never seen the driver.

The task of notifying Doctor Vanidestine of his wife's death fell on the shoulders of Detective Winters, a newly minted detective with limited experience. Being shorthanded, the squad commander had little choice other than to assign Winters to the case. Winters held a Master of Social Work degree. The sixty-two-year-old Lieutenant Nightshade felt that his detective required close watching because of her advanced degree.

"You run with this one, Jessica," advised the squad commander. "First thing you do is get a hold of the husband. He needs to be notified. After that, we start digging."

"No problem, Loo."

6

Patience Is a Virtue

THE FACT THAT MR. AND MRS. VANIDESTINE lived an unconventional lifestyle wasn't something they broadcast. While the couple had no shame over their behavior, they did try their best to keep their open marriage a secret. The couple feared that exposure of their lifestyle would run the risk of damaging the plastic surgeon professionally. Another concern of the childless couple was the fact that Mrs. Vanidestine had traditional elderly parents residing on Staten Island. Facing their scorn was unthinkable. This was information unknown to the detectives investigating the golf club homicide.

Detective Jessica Winters placed a call to Doctor Vanidestine's office. Unable to connect with the plastic surgeon, she left a message with his staff advising them that the physician was to contact her on a matter of grave importance.

Recognizing that something serious must have occurred, the office staff desperately tried to contact the doctor. Their efforts were unsuccessful. This lack of responsiveness wasn't surprising because the plastic surgeon was at a point in his life where he could afford to do what he pleased. Plainly put, he had already made his money.

"Did you notify the husband, Jessica?" Lieutenant Nightshade asked back at the precinct squad room.

"I left a message at his office," replied Winters. "This is kind of weird, considering he's a physician."

"What do you mean?"

"He hasn't gotten back to me. Apparently his staff couldn't get hold of him."

"It may not be as weird as it seems, kiddo . . . if he was the one who whacked his wife."

"According to everyone I've spoken to, they're supposed to be a loving couple."

"You never know what goes on behind closed doors, Jessica. The craziest shit can set people off."

"This was an exceedingly violent murder, Loo," noted the detective. "It smacks of rage." The comment made by Detective Winters impressed the squad commander.

"Good observation," complimented Nightshade. "The victim must have surely done something to piss somebody off. Maybe the husband caught her screwing around."

"That's possible, boss. At least we got the prints that were lifted off the murder weapon to work with."

"Yeah, that's something. Be sure to run those prints through every available system. I want them compared to anyone who has been fingerprinted—especially cabdrivers. Don't forget about that Yellow Cab being seen parked outside the house."

As a result of the fingerprint research, Detective Winters learned that one of the prints lifted from the murder weapon belonged to a cabdriver named Dennis Bumper. A check of Bumper's driving history with the Department of Motor Vehicles revealed that Bumper once received a moving violation while operating a taxicab.

Detective Winters identified the cab owner. At Nightshade's direction, Detective Winters set out to interview the owner of the medallion, a retired man who cooperated fully. He advised that he rented his cab to just one driver on a regular basis. He described Dennis Bumper as a God-fearing man plagued with a humpback. When queried as to where the taxicab in question was at the time of the Judith Vanidestine homicide, the detective was told that Bumper had it.

Questions about Bumper's temperament produced no indication of his being unstable. Bumper was described as a trustworthy person who always behaved like a gentleman.

"Are you sure he showed no signs of being prone to violence or having a temper?" asked Detective Winters.

"Oh, no, not Dennis," replied the cab owner. "I'd never entrust my cab to him if he was anything like that."

As Detective Winters continued her questioning, she came to find out that Bumper also worked as a caddy at a golf club. Upon hearing this, the detective brightened, believing she had made great headway.

Detective Winters promptly returned to her Staten Island squad to confer with Lieutenant Nightshade. After apprising her squad commander of what she learned, she indicated that she wanted to pick up Bumper.

"Let's think about this a second before you go running off half-cocked," said Nightshade.

"What's to think about, Loo?" asked Detective Winters quizzically. "We got the guy's prints on the murder weapon . . . what else do we need?"

"Jessica, in a homicide investigation you can't jump from A to Z. You gotta connect all the dots."

"So what do you want me to do?"

"For a start, find out what golf club this guy Bumper caddies at. Then see if the victim is a member of the club or is known to play golf there."

"I'll get right on it, Loo."

"Remember, always get the facts before you act," lectured Nightshade.

"Will do, Loo," replied the young detective, who was of the school that believes "He who hesitates is lost."

"There is one other thing, Jessica."

"What's that?"

"Even if we put the caddy and the victim at the golf club together, it wouldn't be out of the ordinary for the caddy's prints to show up on the murder weapon," pointed out the lieutenant.

"So where does that leave us, Loo?" asked the disappointed Winters.

"It would be helpful to establish some kind of motive, Jessica." Nightshade could see that Winters now assumed a very serious look about her. "Relax. Don't be in a rush," he said. "It takes catching a few of these homicides to get your A-game going. We all had to learn a little something along the way."

Detective Winters nodded her understanding. She had just stepped out of the squad commander's office when Nightshade's telephone began ringing. Seconds later Nightshade called out into the squad room.

"Saddle up. We got confirmation of three homicide victims over at the Barrett Houses. Let the games begin!"

"What about the Judith Vanidestine homicide, Loo?" asked Winters.

"Worry about that one later, Jessica. We got a new priority now. This triple is sure to make a big splash. Leave the Vanidestine case folder on my desk," instructed Nightshade. "We'll get to it when we can."

Lieutenant Nightshade wasted no time getting the office of the chief of detectives on the telephone. After notifying the chief of the triple, he mentioned that he was operating shorthanded.

"I know all about it," said the chief. "I don't need you to remind me of the lack of bodies. Every squad in the city is operating light."

"Sorry, Chief."

The relationship between the men had always been a warm one. The two had worked together years ago when both were young police officers working in Bedford Stuyvesant's high-crime 79th Precinct. The chief understood his old friend's dilemma but committed to no relief in terms of adding detectives to his squad.

"I know you understand that I got nobody to assign to your squad permanently," advised the chief.

"I'm not looking for support, Chief. I got everything covered. I just called to let you know that we got three dead in an apartment . . . all stabbed."

54

"Okay, Jake."

"Oh, and we also caught an interesting single homicide too, Chief."

"What's that one about?"

"The head of some woman was used as a golf ball in her house. She was bludgeoned."

"Any press interest?"

"Nah, we didn't even a get a call from the *Staten Island Advance* on it yet, Chief. This triple we got going out here is the one that's gonna dominate the news. "

"So you got it all covered, Jake?" asked the chief, not bothering to ask the name of the homicide victim.

"C'mon, Chief, we go back a long way. Three or four, what's the difference? I got it covered."

"I know you do, Jake. Just remember to keep me posted on your progress with the triple."

The triple homicide investigation ended a day after it began. The perpetrator had unexpectedly surrendered to the precinct and confessed to murdering his wife, her sister, and his mother-in-law. The reason he gave for killing them was bizarre. He claimed the victims had eaten the roast beef he had planned to eat.

Once the triple was put to rest, Detective Winters was free to concentrate on the Judith Vanidestine murder. The investigator immediately resumed her efforts to contact the dead woman's plastic surgeon husband.

* * *

DOCTOR VANIDESTINE WAS A WELL-ESTABLISHED professional. His reputation as an excellent plastic surgeon afforded him the independence to keep his patients waiting. He thought nothing of taking time off and rescheduling office appointments if he was tired or had something better to do.

The plastic surgeon often slept over at the illicit love nest he shared with his mistress. Being with the other woman always seemed to be a priority with him.

As was often the case, Doctor Vanidestine rose long after his girlfriend went to work. He cleaned up and put on fresh clothes that he kept at the apartment. By early afternoon he was at the Performance Club, where he was a member. At the club, he had the resident barber shave him and cut his hair.

The plastic surgeon then went to the card room where he played cards with several club members. When not playing cards, the doctor often could be found engaged in a game of nine-ball with cronies in the club pool room. Both activities were played for affordable stakes, so the games always remained friendly.

When the doctor's lover arrived at the club after work to join Vanidestine, they made themselves comfortable in the Barrymore Room where they enjoyed a cocktail. Afterward, they moved to the main dining room for dinner. When their hunger was satisfied, the couple proceeded to their apartment to watch a movie on television and later share intimate moments.

The plastic surgeon had been sleeping soundly when awakened by his young mistress, who tended to be noisy when getting ready for work. It took a few minutes for the plastic surgeon to get over his grogginess. Once composed, the doctor took a moment to check his phone messages.

It wasn't unusual for the plastic surgeon to receive lots of messages. What he found uncommon were the notices instructing him to contact a Staten Island detective forthwith. When Vanidestine spoke to Detective Winters, he was told that he needed to go to the police station that covered his residence. Winters provided no clarifying information. The detective only said that it was imperative that the plastic surgeon see her as soon as possible.

"Do I need a lawyer?" asked the doctor.

"No, that's not necessary," answered Winters. "You aren't in any trouble. I'll explain everything when you get here."

Before leaving for Staten Island the plastic surgeon telephoned his home. Getting no answer, he dialed his wife's cell phone.

When that was unsuccessful, the doctor took on a distressed look.

"Something bad must have happened," announced Vanidestine.

"What's wrong?" asked the mistress who had just emerged from the shower.

"I don't know. A detective just told me that I have to go to the police station on Staten Island right away. I have a bad feeling about this."

Seeing that Doctor Vanidestine was frazzled, his girlfriend offered to accompany him to the Staten Island precinct. The plastic surgeon declined her offer, citing that it would be inappropriate for her to show up at his side if there was, indeed, a problem.

"I don't have to go inside the police station with you. I can wait in the car. At least I'll be close by if you need anything."

"I'll be all right. Go to work. I'll call you later."

When the plastic surgeon arrived at the precinct, he was anything but all right. Clearly ill at ease, he stood before the precinct desk sergeant and asked for Detective Jessica Winters. When notified, Detective Winters went downstairs to the main lobby to meet the doctor. With Vanidestine in tow, the detective reported to the office of Lieutenant Jake Nightshade.

The plastic surgeon broke down when he was apprised of the circumstances surrounding his wife's death. The stone-faced lieutenant studied the distraught physician, who openly wept. Nightshade was specifically looking to see if tears were flowing down the doctor's cheeks. They were.

Unconvinced that the husband's emotional display was genuine, the squad commander continued to entertain the possibility that the plastic surgeon murdered his wife.

"Go and get Doctor Vanidestine some water, Jessica," ordered the lieutenant.

When the plastic surgeon regained his composure, Detective Winters commenced her questioning as to Vanidestine's whereabouts at the estimated time of Judith's homicide. Initially, the plastic surgeon didn't realize that he was being looked at as a suspect. Due to the inquiry that followed, it eventually dawned on him that his innocence was in question. The doctor, taking umbrage at this, reacted aggressively.

"I can't believe that you think I had something to do with killing Judith!" shouted Vanidestine. "Instead of me, why aren't you out trying to find the real person responsible!"

"You're not being accused of anything, Doc," said Lieutenant Nightshade. "We're only trying to eliminate you as a suspect." This explanation made things somewhat palatable for the plastic surgeon.

When the questioning concluded, Nightshade took a moment to speak privately with his detective.

"Well?" asked the lieutenant.

"I don't know, Loo. What do you think?"

"I'd say he's telling the truth, Jessica," replied Nightshade.

"How can you be so sure?"

"Someone wrongly accused reacts in an outraged manner, just as Vanidestine did. A guilty person usually doesn't get so emphatic. They just get a nervous look about them and are less passionate when claiming their innocence."

Once the issue of guilt and innocence was settled, all parties began to work cohesively toward a common goal. The plastic surgeon was able to provide just one piece of interesting information. The detectives listened closely as Vanidestine explained in detail how he believed he was being harassed by Dennis Bumper, the caddy at his golf club.

When asked how Judith Vanidestine got on with Bumper, the doctor had to admit that his wife got on well with the caddy. The information conveyed gave the investigators a possible direction to go in.

"Did you report this harassment to the police?" asked Lieutenant Nightshade.

"Yes, but the detectives did nothing."

"They did nothing?"

"Pretty much nothing. I even had two detectives from headquarters look into it. They also got nowhere."

"Who were the detectives from headquarters?"

"Sergeant Markie and Detective Von Hess worked on it."

Nightshade and his detective exchanged glances with neither commenting.

7

Tamor Gets the Hammer

FRESH FROM MURDERING JUDITH VANIDESTINE, Dennis Bumper remained unhinged. He had become fixated on killing both Judith Vanidestine's plastic surgeon husband and her lover, Martin Tamor. The unbalanced caddy felt an obligation to purge the duo from the earth for having corrupted Judith morally.

Having lived a pious life, Bumper had unwavering faith in the justness of his maker. He believed that ramifications such as eternal damnation wouldn't apply to him once he confessed his sins in a confessional to a priest.

The only difficulty Bumper could foresee was showing sincere remorse for his vile acts. It was something the caddy knew he'd have to work on. However, for now, Bumper had no time to worry about forgiveness. His immediate concentration was on hunting down Judith's husband and lover before being apprehended. Once his murderous mission was fulfilled, he had every intention of giving himself up to the law. Bumper decided on dispatching Martin Tamor first. Since Bumper had never met the financial advisor, he was curious as to what Judith's lover was like.

* * *

MARTIN TAMOR LIVED A LIFE that only a man of privilege could lead. A Manhattan resident, he was accustomed to dinner in the best restaurants with one of his many attractive female clients or a business associate.

The six-foot tall, forty-seven-year-old wealth advisor was a well conditioned bachelor who favored custom-made suits, monogrammed shirts, bold ties, and cufflinks. A deeply tanned, clean-shaven man, he had very few wrinkles. The salt and pepper hairpiece he wore added to his fine appearance.

Complementing his impressive facade was a smooth oratorical ability that transmitted confidence, friendliness, and professional competence. The combination of those qualities made Tamor particularly attractive to those of the opposite sex.

The acquisition of money and women were Tamor's only passions. In Judith Vanidestine he found someone who he believed qualified for his attention. Since Judith was in an open marriage, she came without threat of domestic turmoil causing embarrassment for Tamor. The wealth of the married couple was such that Tamor also made out well managing their money.

The Avenue of the Americas private office of the wealth advisor contained a number of framed photographs taken at the many golf outings he attended. In two golf foursome photos Judith Vanidestine could be seen smiling broadly as she stood next to Tamor.

On display in the office bookcase were the golf trophies Tamor had won over the years. There were also a number of professional awards visible. On his desk rested a framed photograph of a smiling Tamor with a girlfriend he had a long term relationship with. To those entering his workspace, all seemed nice and proper.

Tamor had photos of a different nature hidden inside his locked desk drawer. Those photos, which he personally took, were not for public consumption. They were naughty images that depicted his sexual conquests in various stages of nudity. Some of the photographs depicted the naked body of Judith Vanidestine, captured by Tamor during their trysts.

Tamor liked to gaze at his private collection of photographs from time to time. They represented something to be proud of, similar to the way the wealth manager felt about his golf trophies. Reliving intimate moments gave him great pleasure whenever there was a lull in his business.

* * *

BEFORE LEAVING HIS APARTMENT, Dennis Bumper removed an antique cobbler's hammer out of a drawer he used for housing work tools. The hammer was a family heirloom that had belonged to his shoemaker grandfather. After juggling the hammer in his hand, he was satisfied as to its sufficiency in terms of weight. He then placed the tool into his waistband. After zipping his coat, Bumper embarked on his mission.

When he arrived in Manhattan, Bumper parked his cab at a meter located not far from the business offices of Tamor, Bacon & LaRoy, a wealth advisory firm.

Not having the access pass necessary to gain entry onto the upper floors, Bumper was forced to bide his time. The right moment presented itself when the security officer assigned to the building elevator bank got distracted by someone asking a question. The caddy, managing to slip past the officer unnoticed, got onto a waiting elevator.

Upon arriving on the thirty-fifth floor, Bumper saw to his right two large glass doors. Seated at a desk behind the doors was a young woman serving as the firm's receptionist. The caddy briskly walked up to the desk as if he belonged.

"May I help you, sir?" asked the receptionist, taken aback by the visitor's physical appearance. She tried hard not to stare at Bumper's humpback.

"I'm here to see Martin Tamor," replied Bumper.

"Do you have an appointment?"

"Yes."

"May I have your name please?"

"Dennis Bumper," replied the caddy, not bothering to give an alias.

"I'm sorry, Mr. Bumper, but I don't seem to have you down in the appointment book."

Not having Bumper on her list of expected visitors, the receptionist telephoned Tamor to verify that the visitor was expected. When informed that he had no appointment with the wealth manager, Bumper instructed the receptionist to tell Tamor that he was there at the behest of Judith Vanidestine.

Curious as to what was going on, the wealth manager telephoned Judith. When no one answered her phone, he decided to let the visitor into his private office. When Bumper entered the room, he immediately closed the door behind him.

"Well, tell me . . . what's this all about?" asked Tamor, who was a bit spooked by the caddy's imperfect physical appearance.

Before answering, Bumper gazed at his surroundings. Tamor's window office faced Radio City Music Hall. To someone like Bumper, the view was impressive. He had entered a realm totally beyond his reach. Even Tamor's manner of dress was something unique to the caddy. The entire picture translated into something that embittered Bumper more than he already was. *A real big shot*, thought the caddy.

When Bumper began moving closer toward him, the wealth manager grew alarmed. Feeling threatened, he instinctively began to rise from his seat. He never made it. Bumper, quick as a cat, removed the hammer from his waistband. Seeing the raised hammer caused Tamor to pause, which was a grave mistake. The flat end of the tool struck the top of the wealth manager's forehead with great impact. Blood flowed liberally enough to conceal the round impression left by the blow.

The wealth advisor fell back into his chair and remained motionless. Seeing that his victim was still breathing, Bumper landed a second vicious blow. This one left no doubt as to the outcome. The dull thud of the hammer hitting its mark wasn't a pretty sound, even to Bumper.

Before leaving the private office, Bumper let the bloody hammer fall to the floor. He then wrote on a piece of paper, "IN CONFERENCE – DO NOT DISTURB," and taped it to the front of the office door upon exiting. On his way out he informed the receptionist that Mr. Tamor asked him to tell her that he didn't want to be disturbed.

Once back in his cab, Bumper got to thinking of the murderous path he was on. This, in no way, deterred him from planning to kill again.

* * *

WHEN THE MIDTOWN SQUAD DETECTIVE arrived at the offices of Tamor, Bacon & LaRoy he found a uniformed police officer standing guard in front of the closed door to the homicide victim's private office. The officer was there to preserve the crime scene.

The detective, who was working alone, entered the office cautiously. Careful to avoid contaminating the crime scene, he first visually inspected the office from afar. From what he could determine, there were no signs of a robbery. He did note the bloody hammer on the floor.

Moving closer to the body the detective was able to see that the victim's trouser pockets appeared to be undisturbed. A fancy watch was visible on the victim's wrist, and an emerald ring was visible on his pinkie finger. The detective established that there were no apparent defense wounds on the hands of the victim. This suggested that Tamor didn't endeavor to defend himself.

The responding detective called for the covering detective supervisor to respond to the scene. He then called for the crime scene unit to come and collect evidence. While waiting, the detective began to interview the office staff.

Since the victim's secretary had been on a break, the only witness of value was the receptionist. She informed the investigator that a man identifying himself as Dennis Bumper arrived at the office falsely claiming to have an appointment with the victim. The receptionist conveyed that it was only after the visitor mentioned the name of Judith Vanidestine that the crime victim agreed to meet with him.

The receptionist provided a detailed description of the visitor to the crime victim's office. She noted that the visitor would be distinguishable due to his having what appeared to be a humpback. Encouraged by this information, arrangements were made by the precinct detective for the receptionist to view photos. If that failed in terms of an identification being made, the precinct detective intended for the department artist to prepare a sketch of the wanted man. Once completed, the sketch would then be circulated to all precincts in an effort to identify and, subsequently, apprehend the suspect.

When the crime scene unit arrived they lifted fingerprints off the bloody hammer and note taped to the office door. When they completed their work, the covering detective supervisor authorized a search of the office. The supervisor watched as the precinct detective went through the victim's desk. When the investigator came upon the scrapbook containing nude photos of at least a dozen women, he handed it over to the supervisor.

"It looks like he was a busy boy," commented the supervisor as he went through the scrapbook. "I wonder if one of these gals is that Vanidestine woman."

"This might be her, boss," said the detective, holding up the picture frame containing the photograph of Tamor's girlfriend that he had removed from the victim's desktop.

"You'll have to identify this woman, whoever she is, and see what she has to say."

Since Tamor was now believed to be something of a womanizer, the detective and the covering supervisor began speculating as to a possible motive. One theory kicked around was that the murder might have stemmed from an extortion having gone bad. Another was that the homicide victim might have met his end at the hand of a disgruntled husband or boyfriend. Also voiced was the possibility of an angry client retaliating after receiving costly financial advice.

The detective planned to conduct an inquiry into the names Dennis Bumper and Judith Vanidestine. He hoped that the lifted fingerprints would lead to an identification of the killer.

8

A Pain in the Neck

BUMPER FELT THAT THE STATEN ISLAND residence of Doctor Vanidestine would be a risky place to ambush the plastic surgeon. Thinking that the doctor would eventually meet up with his mistress, he decided to concentrate on the apartment of the other woman.

In preparation for his attack, the caddy went to the closet where he stored keepsakes of his late father, a World War II army veteran. The souvenirs were kept in a cardboard box that rested atop an upper shelf in the closet.

Looking at the items contained in the box brought back memories of his factory worker dad. Bumper examined the medals his father had been awarded for his service to his country with pride. Since his father was never willing to discuss what he did to earn the war recognitions, Bumper always thirsted for information as to that part of his father's life. Bumper reflected on when he gained his first insights.

As a little boy, while waiting his turn for a haircut, he listened to his father converse with the barber. Bumper was intrigued by the stories of war being exchanged. His tales of the big brouhaha on the other side of the pond were fascinating to a boy who could never be accepted into the military due to a physical condition.

The hand grenade that his father took home as a reminder of the war he had fought in was another thing Bumper found fascinating. He stared at what his father used to refer to as a "pineapple" with wariness. It was the one thing in the box of treasures that he avoided handling.

It was the bayonet that Bumper zeroed in on. Believing it to be the weapon best suited for his purposes, he took it in hand. The caddy wondered how many men, if any, his father may have stabbed to death while engaged in hand-to-hand combat. Whatever the body count, Bumper's intent was to add one more to the list of unlucky warriors.

Having chosen a killing instrument, Bumper fished out a dish rag from beneath the kitchen sink. After encasing the blade in the rag, he stuffed the bayonet into his waistband. He then donned his winter coat and went to his cab with the sole purpose of hunting down Doctor Vanidestine.

* * *

BUMPER PARKED HIS TAXICAB on the street in close proximity to the residence of the plastic surgeon's mistress. He sat in the cab with the off-duty sign visible, indicating to the public that he wasn't available for fares. He watched with some bitterness as the doorman let people in and out of Alma's posh building. Down deep he felt that a husband poaching inamorata didn't deserve such fine digs.

When he grew tired of sitting in the cab, Bumper decided to get proactive. He approached the building doorman in an effort to gain information. With money loosening the doorman's tongue, Bumper learned that the plastic surgeon had spent the night with Alma Horton in her apartment. He further gathered that Vanidestine had not been seen leaving the building yet. The information gathered made waiting easier for Bumper.

Once back in his cab, Bumper maintained an eye on the building entrance. While waiting for the plastic surgeon to come out into the street, he passed time by watching the steady flow of people walking by on the sidewalk. Everyone seemed to be focused on where they were going, seemingly oblivious to what was happening around them.

When the plastic surgeon finally exited the building, Bumper jumped up in his seat. Vanidestine being alone made things perfect. The physician seemed to have aged since the last time Bumper had seen him. His walk lacked its usual confidence. Instead, he shuffled as would a burdened man with troubling things on his mind.

Bumper gripped his bayonet tightly and alighted from his taxi. Advancing quickly, he struck from the rear. The sneak attack saw Bumper's bayonet penetrate the back of the plastic surgeon's neck. The force of the overhand thrust dropped Vanidestine to one knee. The doctor instinctively winced as his shoulders rose toward his ears in answer to the pain.

The plastic surgeon placed a hand where the bayonet penetrated his flesh. He turned to face the source of his assault, only to be greeted by the point of the bayonet. This time Vanidestine's throat was punctured. The blow proved to be the final cut. It was a killing wound that severed the victim's jugular vein. The last thing Vanidestine saw was the crazed face of Bumper, the bayonet-wielding caddy.

Ignoring the screams emanating from the people on the street, Bumper rushed to his cab. In doing so he let the bayonet fall to the sidewalk. One person on the street had the presence of mind to try and memorize the license plate number of the taxicab Dennis escaped in. Someone called 911, and another thought to press a scarf against the surgeon's throat wound in an effort to stop the bleeding. Most of the spectators stood by, quietly staring at the downed plastic surgeon. They were aware nothing else could be done. The doctor was far beyond help.

When the police officers responded to the location of the homicide, there were several curious citizens who remained on hand to watch how things unfolded. The officers called for an ambulance and notified their superiors. Once the responding detectives established that Doctor Vanidestine was, in fact, dead, the crime scene unit was called in for evidence gathering.

The inquiry conducted at the scene proved worthwhile. A good description of the plastic surgeon's killer was obtained. The hump on Bumper's back was certain to make a future identification a lot easier. One witness furnished the investigators with a partial license plate of the yellow taxicab the perpetrator had fled in. Another identified the bayonet that was left behind on the sidewalk as the murder weapon. As in the case of the wealth manager's murder, fingerprints of value were lifted off the recovered murder weapon.

In police parlance, the homicide was a "ground ball." It wasn't going to be long before the perpetrator with the humpback was identified and picked up. Such an outcome didn't escape Bumper, who assumed that the law would soon get around to tracking him down. However, Bumper wasn't ready to be taken into custody. Having completed his homicidal trilogy, there was still one more thing Bumper needed to do prior to surrendering himself to the law.

* * *

BUMPER DROVE HOME to Brooklyn carefully. The holiday music coming from the car radio was uplifting. It enabled the caddy to see a bright side to his killings. He could move on now that the slayings were behind him.

After securing a parking space for his cab a couple of blocks from his home, Bumper walked briskly to his building. Instead of going directly to his own apartment, he went to see his best friend, Sammy Angelo, who lived in the same building. Sammy was in the process of preparing a liverwurst and Swiss cheese sandwich for himself when Bumper arrived.

"Just a minute!" shouted Sammy to the closed door. "I'm coming!"

Before the door was fully opened, Bumper rushed past his friend and entered the apartment.

"Hi, Dennis," greeted Sammy cheerily. "I was just making a sandwich. Do you want one?"

With everything going on, Bumper hadn't thought about food. Now that he did, he realized he hadn't eaten in a long time.

"I suppose I could eat something," answered Bumper.

"Sit down. I got liverwurst and Swiss cheese. You want mayo or mustard on yours?"

"Mayo, please," replied Bumper.

Bumper took a seat at the kitchen table. Sammy detected that something wasn't right with his friend.

"Are you okay, Dennis?" asked Sammy. "You look all worn out."

"I've done some bad things, Sammy . . . real bad."

Sammy stopped what he was doing to look at his friend more closely. "What are you talking about?"

"I'm not proud of the things I did, but they needed doing," answered Bumper, remaining vague.

Bumper was looking down at the tabletop as he spoke. It was if he were a naughty boy confessing to poor behavior.

The concerned friend now looked at Bumper more carefully. He wondered what was going on. Sammy couldn't help but notice the blood on his friend's clothes.

"Is that blood you got on you, Dennis?"

"Yeah, Sammy it is. Things got a little messy."

"What the hell happened? Did you have a problem with somebody you picked up in the cab?"

"No, it was nothing like that. I'll explain everything once we start eating. I'm starting to feel a little faint."

Sammy quickly made the sandwiches and put them on plates. He then poured two glasses of Coke. When finished, he took a seat at the kitchen table across from his guest.

"So what the hell is going on with you, Dennis?"

"I'm in big trouble, Sammy," began the caddy. "I'm . . . I'm a murderer."

"You're a what?" asked Sammy, who was about to bite into his sandwich.

"I killed Judith Vanidestine," confessed Bumper.

The stunned Sammy put down his sandwich. "Are you serious?"

"No joking. I killed Judith. She's the one from the golf club that's married to the plastic surgeon."

Sammy realized that his friend was being truthful. "Dennis, I know who she is. We spoke of her often enough. It must have been some kind of accident . . . right?"

"It was no accident, Sammy. I just lost it . . . I got mad and killed her."

"But you were nuts about her . . . "

"Judith was brainwashed, Sammy. They did a job on her; they changed her. They poisoned her against me."

The caddy's eyes seemed to be penetrating Sammy. Even the tone of Bumper's speech was something off kilter. He spoke slowly, almost in a mechanical, far-off way. Sammy began to see his friend as demented.

"My God, Dennis, I don't know who did what in this . . . but to kill her?"

"She kept calling me Quasimodo, over and over. I . . . I just lost control."

Sammy was aware that Bumper had a temper, but he never thought his friend capable of flying into a murderous rage. Not knowing what to say, Sammy just continued to listen.

"Not only that," continued Bumper, "it gets worse. Judith admitted to me that she had a boyfriend on the side, Sammy. It was the husband and the boyfriend who both ruined her . . . God only knows what they had her doing."

"Good Lord, Dennis . . . "

"I'm sorry now for doing what I did to Judith. After thinking about it, I came to realize that she was a victim of the other two. It was those two bastards. They deserved what they got."

"What did they get?"

"They got the same as Judith."

"You killed them too?" asked the astonished Sammy.

"Yeah, weren't you listening? The husband and the boyfriend are the ones who caused all this trouble, so I had to stop them before they could ruin others like they did Judith."

It was vividly clear that Sammy's friend was of unsound mind. Now on edge, Sammy was afraid of saying something that might cause his friend to turn on him. Not quite sure how to handle the situation, Sammy opted to feign understanding in order to keep Bumper calm.

"I hear you, Dennis."

"You're my best friend, Sammy. I need you to help me now."

"What can I do?" asked Sammy nervously.

"Let me finish telling you what happened. I beat Judith's brains in with a golf club in her own house," confessed Bumper. Sammy found his friend's candidness chilling. "She just wouldn't quit calling me Quasimodo."

Bumper now feared that Sammy's recalling his conflict with Judith would give a transfusion to his friend's rage. He swallowed hard before nervously trying to steer the conversation elsewhere. His attempt was to no avail.

"I just saw red and snapped, Sammy. Later when I calmed down, I got to thinking more clearly. It finally occurred to me that Judith was morally corrupted by outside forces."

"I see . . . outside forces being her husband and her boyfriend."

"Exactly," confirmed Bumper. "They were the cancer, so I did to them what you do with all cancers."

Sammy gulped at the analogy. "After Judith, I knew that I had to take care of the boyfriend, which I did. I got him in his Manhattan office. And then today, I caught up with the plastic surgeon. It's his blood I got on me."

At this point just one thought entered Sammy's mind: *What am I going to do if Dennis goes off?* "Dennis, do you think you might want to talk to someone better equipped for what you're telling me . . . you know, professional people who can help you?" asked Sammy, treading lightly. "You just can't go on like this."

Bumper could see that his friend had become frightened. "Relax, Sammy. I know you're scared. You don't have to be. Everything is all right now. The bastards who ruined Judith got what they deserved, and that's that. I have no ill will toward anyone now."

Finding Bumper's calmness to be eerie, Sammy smiled weakly. His strategy was now singular. He would do whatever he had to in order not to upset Bumper.

"I'm here for you, Dennis," said Sammy softly. "You know that."

"I know, Sammy. That's why I came to you for help. I knew you would understand."

"Of course I understand."

"I'm glad that it's all over . . . all the killing, I mean."

"Dennis, you have no idea how relieved I am to hear there will be no more killing." Sammy paused for a moment to watch Bumper begin eating his sandwich. "I think I need a real drink. How about you, Dennis?"

"That's a good idea, Sammy."

Sammy rose from his seat at the kitchen table and removed a bottle of whiskey from one of the kitchen cabinets. He returned to the table with the bottle and two empty glasses. As they drank, Sammy continued to wrestle with how to proceed with Bumper.

"What can I do for you, Dennis?" he finally asked.

"I want to see Father Billy and confess my sins."

The stimulant Bumper consumed seemed to further mellow him, which was a good thing. There eventually came a point when Sammy mentioned the police.

"I know I have to give myself up, Sammy . . . and I will. But first I want to cleanse my soul. Will you talk to Father Billy for me? I really need him now. I want him to hear my confession. Once I do that, I can turn myself into the cops with a clear conscience."

Sammy was greatly relieved to hear this. "Of course I will, Dennis. I think that's exactly what you need to do." After some more talk, Bumper began dozing off at the table. "Do you want to rest awhile?" asked Sammy.

"I'm just gonna close my eyes for a minute," replied Bumper.

While his friend slept, Sammy poured himself another drink. It wasn't long before Sammy placed his own head down on the kitchen table. The only difference between him and his friend was that he couldn't sleep.

9

Three Murders,
One Perp

THE DETECTIVE SQUAD COMMANDER overseeing the Doctor Vanidestine homicide was a highly respected forty-nine year old gravel-voiced veteran who was well known to department brass. A tall educated woman who dressed well, she projected a professional image.

The lieutenant was a taskmaster who insisted that the detectives under her command stand apart from those in other squads. She relied on high productivity to accomplish this. All of the investigators working for her were expected to be arrest oriented. This was for the purpose of statistically showing more arrests annually than any other detective squad in the city, regardless of size.

Those in the department hierarchy were ardent supporters of the squad commander. Lots of arrests gave them something to boast about. The brass also loved the fact that the lieutenant managed to control overtime while turning in outstanding arrest numbers. This was recognized as no small achievement.

The squad commander was rewarded for her diligence and leadership with a promotion that earned her a captain's salary although a lieutenant. In the world of civil service such promotions were few and far between.

If the lieutenant had one shortcoming it was her dependence on cigarettes. A chain-smoker, she reeked of cigarette smoke, as did her private office. The squad commander was puffing away when someone came knocking on her office door.

"Just a minute!" she shouted.

The squad commander quickly put out the butt and hid the ashtray in her desk drawer. She then turned on the standing fan. Although the state-imposed restrictions on smoking indoors for businesses and private offices wouldn't go into effect until years later, the lieutenant recognized that the practice of smoking indoors was fast losing acceptance.

"Who might you be?" asked the lieutenant after opening the office door.

"Sergeant Markie from the Chief of D's office," announced Markie, flashing his shield. "This is Detective Von Hess."

"Come in."

Once granted access to the office, Markie conveyed his purpose for being at the squad. He made it a point to mention that he was there on the order of the chief of detectives, who had been notified of the plastic surgeon's murder. Experience had taught Markie that dropping the chief's name early went a long way when dealing with detectives and squad commanders.

"But I didn't request any support on the Vanidestine homicide," said the squad commander.

"Vanidestine is important to the police commissioner, or at least he was," advised Markie.

The sergeant went on to explain that Doctor Vanidestine had been the target of a harassment campaign. The squad commander found this information interesting.

"Do you know who was harassing the doctor?" asked the precinct squad boss.

"The doctor suspected the caddy who worked at his Staten Island golf club," replied Markie, "a guy by the name of Dennis Bumper."

The lieutenant sent for the squad detective who caught the

plastic surgeon's murder case, advising him to bring along the Vanidestine homicide folder. The case agent was a pot-bellied, salty man with large circles under his eyes.

"The victim was stabbed in the neck on the street," informed the lieutenant, addressing Markie. "Did you talk to this fellow Bumper about the harassment allegation?"

"No," replied Markie.

"Why didn't you?"

"The complainant called us off. He thought our talking to him without proof would inflame the situation."

"Oh, I see. Well, we have a few witnesses in our case who were able to get a good look at the perpetrator. One gave us a partial plate of the Yellow Cab that the perp drove off in."

"He jumped in the back of a cab?" asked Markie.

"No, he got behind the wheel and drove off."

"We ascertained that no taxicabs had been reported stolen in recent weeks," injected the precinct detective assigned to the case. "I'm still working on trying to figure out who the cab belongs to."

"Can we get the partial plate?" asked Von Hess. "Maybe we can help."

"What's the chief's big interest in this case again?" asked the precinct squad commander.

"He had no big interest," replied Markie. "Things are slow right now, and the chief likes to keep us busy," explained the sergeant.

"Let them have the partial plate," directed the squad commander. The detective wrote the partial plate number on a piece of paper and handed the paper to Von Hess.

"Was any weapon recovered?"

"Yes, a bayonet was recovered at the scene. The crime scene unit lifted prints off the murder weapon. We're thinking that maybe the perp is a veteran, a reservist, or in the National Guard. This case shouldn't be too difficult for us to solve," noted the lieutenant.

"How could you be so sure of that, Loo?"

"Our witnesses all stated that the perpetrator has a humpback, so that'll really narrow things down for us."

Before Markie could react to this statement, another precinct detective interrupted the meeting by entering the squad commander's office.

"We've got that meeting with the community council, Loo," reminded the detective.

"I know. I'm ready to go," advised the squad commander, rising from behind her desk. She then turned to address Markie:

"We all have to go to this meeting, so we have to put the Doctor Vanidestine case on hold for a while, Sarge."

"No problem, Loo. What can we do?"

"You guys read through the folder. We haven't made a family notification yet. Maybe you can start there."

"Very good, Loo . . . and there is one other thing."

"What's that?"

"Just so you know, Dennis Bumper has a humpback."

* * *

WHEN MARKIE AND VON HESS ARRIVED at the Staten Island home of Judith Vanidestine, they expected to find a grieving widow. Instead, they found a police seal placed over the front door of the house. Markie turned to look at Von Hess with puzzlement. Both investigators knew that a seal on the front door of a property meant legal protection for the belongings inside the house. What was confusing to the detectives was what caused the seal to be there.

"I don't get it, Sarge," said Von Hess. "Why is there a seal on the door? According to the reports in the homicide folder, the plastic surgeon lived here with his wife."

"I got no idea, Ollie. Let's go knock on some doors."

As they began inquiring as to the whereabouts of Judith Vanidestine, the detectives found themselves receiving information they were previously unaware of.

"What happened to that poor woman was just terrible," advised the wife of an architect who lived opposite the

78

Vanidestine family. "This was the first time anything like that has ever happened in this neighborhood."

"Well, what exactly happened, Ma'am?" asked Von Hess.

"You mean you don't know?"

"Please enlighten us," replied Markie.

"Judith Vanidestine was found murdered by the mailman."

"The mailman murdered her?"

"No, no, no . . . the mailman was the one who found the body. She was beaten to death with a golf club."

It took only a second for Markie and Von Hess to digest this revelation. "Do you know if they happened to arrest anyone?" queried Von Hess.

"I don't think so," replied the neighbor. "I doubt it."

"What makes you doubt it?"

"I doubt it because I haven't read anything about an arrest in the *Staten Island Advance*. That paper knows everything about what happens on Staten Island."

"That's what I've always heard," said Von Hess. "Thank you, Ma'am."

* * *

MARKIE AND VON HESS POSTED their superiors at headquarters. After doing so, they responded to the Staten Island squad that was tasked with investigating the Judith Vanidestine homicide. Once there, they conferred with Detective Jessica Winters and Lieutenant Jake Nightshade, her squad commander. The investigators from headquarters imparted what they knew of the Manhattan homicide of Doctor Vanidestine.

What came as news to Markie and Von Hess was that Judith Vanidestine had been having an extra- marital affair with a wealth advisor named Martin Tamor. The Staten Island squad commander communicated that Judith was believed to have been murdered shortly after returning from a Florida golf trip with Tamor. He explained that this information was gathered after tracing the dead woman's activities just prior to her death.

79

"Did you talk to Tamor, Loo?" asked Markie.

"We tracked him down," advised Nightshade. "Tell the good sergeant, Jessica."

"I went to Tamor's office in Manhattan and found that he had been murdered at his desk," said Detective Winters.

"One thing is for sure," noted Nightshade, "with the husband, wife, and boyfriend all getting whacked, there had to be some kind of a common denominator."

"It would seem that way," agreed Markie.

"So the question becomes who and why?" said Von Hess. "Revenge, money, drugs—it could be anything."

"What about jealousy?" asked Detective Winters.

"Yeah, even that, Jessica. I don't see us having a guy who kills randomly on our hands," said the squad commander.

"What do you think, Ollie?" Markie asked.

"As I see things, there are a couple of ways to look at this, Sarge. One is the relationship between Judith, her husband, and the boyfriend, right?"

"That's right," agreed Nightshade, "a triangle, but their all whacked."

"Then we got a cabdriver who figures in the murder of Doctor Vanidestine." This statement got the attention of both Lieutenant Nightshade and Detective Winters.

"There was a Yellow Cab parked in front of the Vanidestine home at the time Judith Vanidestine was believed to have been murdered," advised Detective Winters. "And we lifted fingerprints off the golf club in Judith's homicide."

"Do you know who the prints came back to?"

"Dennis Bumper. He's a caddy."

"It's looking like the caddy is our man," announced Markie. "Did a taxicab figure in the wealth advisor's homicide?"

"No, but a witness in Tamor's office remembered two things distinctly," advised Nightshade.

"What's that?"

"The bad guy had a humpback and he identified himself as Dennis Bumper."

"That cinches it," declared the sergeant. "We got ourselves a perp."

"Why don't you guys go to the golf club and see where we can find this guy," said Nightshade. "I'll personally coordinate with the two Manhattan squads that caught the plastic surgeon and wealth advisor's homicides. Me and the other two squad commanders need to get together so we don't start tripping all over each other with this thing."

"Do you want us to take the caddy in if he happens to be at the golf club, Loo?"

"If he's there, yes, but don't go out looking for him yet. I want to talk to the other squad commanders first."

"What about me, Loo?" asked Detective Winters, feeling left out.

"You keep working on your other cases, Jessica. Let the boys from headquarters do the labor. You'll have plenty to do later. You're the one who'll be making the pinch at the end of the day."

"What do you make of all this, Ollie?" asked Markie when the two were alone.

"This is beginning to really smell like there could be some kind of jealous lover thing going on with the caddy, Sarge."

"That's exactly what I'm thinking," agreed the sergeant.

10

Closing In

IT BEING A CHILLY WINTER DAY, there was little activity at the Staten Island golf club. Markie and Von Hess made their way down the long road that led to the large visitor parking area. Just a handful of cars occupied spaces. The sergeant buttoned his black overcoat and tightened his scarf to protect against the brisk wind. Von Hess, feeling the cold, donned a hat and raised his overcoat collar.

"Brrrr," the detective uttered. "It's cold as hell out."

"You gotta get a scarf, Ollie. If you protect your throat, you'll never get sick," preached the sergeant.

"I will, Sarge, when you start wearing a hat."

"I haven't any need to wear a skimmer. I still got all my hair."

By remaining quiet, Von Hess, who was showing slight signs of thinning on top, conceded his boss had a point. The detectives entered the main building in search of someone in charge. The first person they came upon was a man on a ladder. He was painting the multicolored ceiling.

"Excuse me. Where is the boss?" Markie yelled upward.

The worker looked down from his perch on the ladder and shook his head. His hunched shoulders indicated that he didn't understand English.

"Does anybody here speak English?"

The worker, appearing puzzled, again looked at the sergeant perplexed. He then pointed, indicating that they should head in a direction.

"C'mon, Ollie, he's sending us down the hall."

The detectives eventually located the manager's office. The man in charge was trim, in his late thirties, and wore his blond hair close cropped. The green blazer, blue V-neck sweater, white shirt, and olive tie gave him the appearance of an aging preppy.

"May I help you?" asked the manager.

Upon being informed of the identity of the two NYPD detectives, the manager took on a look of concern. The presence of the police at the golf club could only mean trouble, and trouble translated into grief for someone charged with operating the club.

"What can I do for you, gentlemen?" asked the club manager nervously.

"We'd like to talk to you about one of your caddies," announced Von Hess. "His name is Dennis Bumper. He works here, correct?"

"Why, yes, during the season. He's not here in the winter. Is he in some kind of trouble?"

"Will he be coming by here at all?" asked Von Hess, not responding to the question.

"I doubt it. He has no reason to come by."

"Can you let us have his phone number and address?"

"I'm sorry, but I'm not permitted to release that information."

"This is police business."

"Even so, I'm afraid I can't do that. I can't violate club policy."

"I see," said Markie. "What's the policy of the club regarding that painter you got out there?"

"Why, what do you mean?"

"Is he legal and on the books? I mean, we are talking policies, aren't we?"

The manager got Markie's drift. He rose from his desk and walked over to a standing file cabinet. After leafing through some folders, he produced the address and telephone number requested.

"Do you happen to have a picture of Dennis Bumper?" asked Von Hess.

The manager removed from his desk an envelope containing photographs taken over the past summer. Among these was a group photo of several club workers. He handed the photograph over to Von Hess.

"This is Dennis," said the manager, pointing out Bumper.

Von Hess displayed no overt reaction after viewing the photograph that reflected Bumper's humpback. Saying nothing, he passed it to Markie. The sergeant looked at the photograph, remaining stone-faced.

"Let me ask you something," said Markie, addressing the manager. "Have you had any problems with the guy with the bum back?"

"Why, no . . . he happens to be an excellent caddy. He's very much in demand by members."

"What can you tell us about him?"

"I know he's a bachelor and a very private man. I've always gotten the impression that he's a religious man."

"What gave you that impression?"

"Well, frankly, I only say that because everyone else does."

"So you haven't received any complaints about him?"

"I've never received a complaint about Dennis from anyone."

"Was he cozy with any club members?" Von Hess asked.

"I don't understand . . . "

"I mean, was the caddy friendly beyond the caddy-club member norm," clarified the detective.

"As far as I'm aware, everything has been kept on a professional basis, Detective."

"Do you know if Dennis Bumper drives a taxicab?" asked Markie.

"Why, yes . . . as a matter of fact I know he does. He drives a cab here when he comes to work."

"Have you heard from him lately?"

"No."

84

"Does Bumper have a locker here?"

"Yes . . . why?"

"I was just wondering."

After leaving the golf club, Markie telephoned Lieutenant Nightshade at the Staten Island squad. He informed the squad commander that he secured an address, telephone number, and photo of Dennis Bumper that revealed the suspect's humpback. Nightshade indicated that he would post the precinct squads' commanders in Manhattan accordingly.

"It may make sense to get a warrant so we can look inside Bumper's locker at the golf club, Loo," suggested Markie.

"I'll take care of that, Sarge. You go find this guy Bumper before he hurts somebody else."

"Do you want us to go and get a photo ID from the Manhattan witnesses?"

"No, we got enough to grab Bumper. We'll end up doing a line-up anyway."

"Everything is going to be run out of your squad here on Staten Island?"

"Yeah, the other squad commanders agreed that I should spearhead this thing since the Judith Vanidestine homicide came first."

"Very good, we'll head over to where he lives in Brooklyn and see if we can scoop up the perp."

* * *

THE INVESTIGATORS FROM HEADQUARTERS parked their unmarked police vehicle in close proximity to Dennis Bumper's Brooklyn residence. Their hope was to spot the suspect walking on the street. Detective Von Hess turned up the car heater to maintain a comfortable level of warmth. As the hot air circulated, the detectives chatted. After awhile the heat became a bit much. Von Hess cracked the car window to let some cool air in. He feared the excessive heat inside the car would make him drowsy.

The snow that began to fall was sticking. As the white flakes began to cake the windshield, Von Hess activated the wiper. Neither detective was looking ahead to dealing with the inches of snow being predicted to fall on the city.

After a couple of hours of sitting in the snow-topped car, Von Hess offered to get a couple of containers of coffee. On his walk to the store, the detective noticed a Yellow Cab parked on the street. He reached into his pocket to remove a slip of paper. On the paper was the partial license plate given to him by the Manhattan detective assigned to the plastic surgeon homicide.

After wiping the snow from the cab's plate, the detective believed he had located the suspect's vehicle. Von Hess tried to open the door of the taxi without success. Unable to access the vehicle, the detective abandoned his coffee run and hurried to his own vehicle to post Markie of his discovery.

"He's gotta be either in his apartment or holed up someplace nearby," said Markie.

"I can cover the taxicab while you stick here at the residence, Sarge."

"That won't work, Ollie. You'll just freeze your ass off if Bumper doesn't surface."

"We could rotate every half hour . . . "

"No, that won't do. What we need is another car out here."

"So what's our next move?"

"The snow may pick up throughout the day. If that's the case, I can't see Bumper driving anyplace. Let the cab sit."

"How about we get a little pro-active, boss? We could go knock on the perp's door . . ."

"Let's just give it a little longer before we do that. I'm also tired of this waiting around." Forty minutes later the detectives decided to move in.

Finding the entry door to the suspect's building open, Markie and Von Hess entered. They stopped to examine the metal mailboxes. After going through the names on the boxes, they identified the mailbox assigned to the wanted man. Von Hess peeked through the holes to see if there was mail in the subject's box.

"The box is letter free, Sarge."

"Let's see if we can get into the main part of the building, Ollie."

Von Hess attempted to slip the interior door lock with a credit card. Fortunately, as he was doing this a tenant happened to be exiting the building. The detectives wasted no time in passing through the open door.

The investigators tiptoed up the stairs to the front door of Bumper's apartment. Upon arriving, they assumed positions on opposite sides of the entryway. They did this to avoid being in the direct line of fire in the event of any gunplay coming their way from inside the apartment. Markie placed his ear to the door and listened carefully for signs of activity.

"If he's in there, Ollie, he's being quiet as a church mouse," whispered the sergeant.

"If he's in there, he might have killed himself, Sarge."

"I don't smell anything, do you?"

"He might not be ripe yet. Should we try knocking on the door, Sarge?" Receiving the go ahead, Von Hess rapped on the front door of the apartment. "What now, boss?" he asked after receiving no response to his knock.

"Let's see if any of the neighbors can tell us anything."

The very first apartment canvassed was found to be occupied by a young woman in her thirties who answered the door in her bathrobe. Fully covered, all she said was "Come in" after the detectives identified themselves.

Without entering the apartment, Von Hess inquired about her possibly having seen Dennis Bumper. She replied by extending a second invitation to the detectives. "Maybe you better come on in," she said softly. She then opened the white terrycloth robe she wore. Her broad smile was inviting. The opening to her apartment door was then widened.

Markie and Von Hess looked at each other and smiled. They remained stationary, taking in the free show being afforded them. They ultimately declined the woman's offer and moved on.

"I'm wondering if the whole joint is full of psychos," declared

Von Hess. "Maybe we should try and find the super, Sarge."

They located the super in the basement of the building. He was a man of middle age who lived on the first floor with his family. When questioned, at first he was reluctant to speak to the investigators. Eventually coming around, he described Dennis in simple terms.

"He's a nice guy," said the super. "Very quiet. He keeps to himself."

Queried further, the super explained that Dennis was the sort of person who never pestered him with calls for service as some other tenants did. The super went on to suggest that the investigators speak to a tenant who was a close friend of Bumper. He proceeded to accompany the detectives to the apartment of Sammy Angelo.

"Who is it?" the voice from within the apartment called out.

"It's me, Sammy, the super."

"What do you want?"

"I'm here with some detectives. They want to talk to you."

Sammy discreetly signaled for Dennis Bumper to seek refuge in a rear bedroom. The sight of the two detectives at his front door clearly made Sammy nervous.

"What's this all about?" asked Sammy after opening the door to his apartment.

"These are detectives; they want to talk to you," advised the super, who then returned to his duties in the basement.

Sammy began nervously fidgeting before being asked even a single question. When he spoke, his sentences came out cautiously, and his lips could be seen quivering. To the experienced detectives it was obvious that Sammy knew more than he was willing to reveal.

Trapped in the rear bedroom, Bumper strained to listen to what was being said at the front door. His fear was not of being arrested; he knew that outcome was inevitable. He had long prepared for it. At issue was the timing of him being taken away in custody. Of paramount importance to him was having time to formally repent within an official forum. Yet, even with his desire to cleanse himself by expressing remorse in a traditional religious setting, Bumper couldn't prevent himself from feeling that his victims deserved the fate they had met. If he were truthful, he'd confess that he'd do it all over again.

As Von Hess continued his questioning, Markie shifted his position so he was able to look over Sammy's shoulder into the apartment. What he saw was revealing. Seeing two glasses on separate end tables in front of the television spoke volumes, as did the Coke cans alongside the glasses. Markie also took notice of the framed photo of the pope that hung from a wall.

The sergeant then turned his attention to Sammy, focusing on the small, black leather pouch attached to his belt.

"What's in the pouch?" asked Markie.

"Only my rosary beads," replied Sammy, opening the pouch to reveal its contents.

"Do you live alone in this apartment?"

"I do."

"And you haven't seen or heard from your friend Dennis Bumper. Is that right?"

"That's right, sir."

"You do realize that if you do anything to aid or abet your friend, you'd be leaving yourself open to problems, don't you?" asked Von Hess, reminding Sammy that there could be ramifications for harboring Bumper.

"What kind of problems?"

"Let me ask you something," said the sergeant, changing the subject. "So you always carry around that pouch on your belt?"

"I do," answered Sammy, who nervously reopened the pouch.

Seeing the beads once more gave Markie the idea that the good guy-bad guy routine might be appropriate.

"I think we have a holy roller here, Ollie," announced the sergeant bluntly.

"I guess you could call me that," acknowledged Sammy. "I'm not ashamed of my faith."

"The sergeant doesn't see the big picture," injected Von Hess, picking up on his cue to be the good guy.

"I don't? All I know is that any true Christian would look to help us."

"Mr. Angelo is gonna cooperate, Sarge. He's just in an awkward position."

"Forget it, Ollie. He's just a nominal Christian."

Sammy was looking downward in apparent shame. While Markie's remark got him thinking, Sammy remained adamant in his silence when it came to the whereabouts of Bumper.

"Can I use your bathroom?" asked Von Hess, creating an excuse to legally get deeper into the apartment.

"I'm sorry, but the bathroom is out of order."

"You should get it fixed," advised the sergeant. "You never know when nature will call. Well, look, if you see your friend or hear from him, be sure to give us a call." Markie then handed Sammy his business card. Before leaving the floor, he placed a matchbook cover in an erect position against the door to the caddy's apartment.

"What are you doing, Sarge?"

"If the matchbook cover gets knocked over, we'll know someone was in or out of the suspect's crib, Ollie. I saw that done in a movie once."

The detectives were convinced that Sammy knew exactly where Bumper was. They didn't rule out the possibility that their man might actually be in Sammy's apartment.

The detectives again went looking for the super. When they found him in the basement, Markie informed the super that there was a problem in Sammy Angelo's bathroom.

"He never notified me about it," commented the super.

"I'm just saying what he told us," said Markie. "If you happen to see his friend Bumper, give me a call. There is a big reward on his head, so take my card."

"There is?" asked the wide-eyed super. "How much is the reward?"

"About five grand," replied the sergeant, who was not being truthful.

"What did he do?"

"Never minds that; it's police business. All you have to do is call me if you see him."

Once outside, Von Hess felt like asking the sergeant about making the false promise of a reward. He decided against doing so.

"If he's in there, at some point he has to come out of that house, Sarge."

"Yeah, If Bumper comes out, we'll grab him. If his friend comes out, one of us will follow him to see where he goes. There's a chance that the friend might lead us to the perp. Who know, maybe the super will give us a call."

As it turned out, the detectives ended several tours of surveillance feeling disappointed.

11

Father Billy

FEELING THAT THE DETECTIVES WERE GETTING CLOSE, both Sammy Angelo and Dennis Bumper were more anxious than ever to get in touch with Father Billy. Their reasons differed. Bumper saw the religious figure as a pathway to the pearly gates. Sammy saw him as someone who could help alleviate the burden of having to harbor Bumper.

Despite his desire to meet, Bumper decided it prudent to wait until things cooled off before reaching out to the priest. He was afraid that showing his face on the street at this time might lead to his being apprehended before he had the chance to see Father Billy. Sammy had little choice other than to go along with this decision.

The two friends had no idea as to Father Billy's true identity. Long before Father Billy surfaced in Sunset Park as a parish priest, he had lived life as Ross Holt, a man with a checkered past. Holt, who had been abandoned at birth, was the adopted son of a married Ohio couple.

Mrs. Holt, more than anything, wanted to have a baby. Unable to conceive, she pressured her husband until he halfheartedly consented to her looking into adoption options. Mr. Holt, a frugal man, tended to look at things strictly from an economic perspective. No children meant that he would have no added expenses. This was an upside that suited him just fine.

Sensing her husband's reluctance to be involved, Mrs. Holt made it clear that they were going to adopt a baby or else. Not thrilled at receiving an ultimatum, the husband vehemently protested. The ensuing ruckus ended with Mr. Holt either conceding to his wife's wishes or facing divorce proceedings. The thought of dividing his assets with his wife gave the husband heart palpitations. To protect his interests, he went along with the adoption decision.

The prospective parents soon learned there was more to adoption than they thought. Listening to friends, they went to an attorney with expertise in acquiring babies. When the lawyer conveyed that there was an available infant in the Midwest, Mrs. Holt was thrilled. Her joy was short-lived once the back story was revealed.

Mrs. Holt didn't feel good about taking a baby from a sixteen-year-old mother who had gotten into trouble with a drifter who was passing through town. Mrs. Holt felt guilty taking advantage of an unsophisticated youth who might later regret her decision to give up her child. Mr. Holt solidly supported his wife in this. The thought of taking in a stranger's child never sat well with him in the first place.

"We're better off forgetting about it," said the husband. "The baby's old man could be a junkie for all we know. The kid could have all kinds of problems. Do we need this?" he asked his wife.

In the end, the couple parted ways with the attorney. Mrs. Holt next turned to a nonprofit adoption agency that was considered a more legitimate resource. The interview process to determine eligibility soon ran into a snag when it was made clear that there were few infants of the couple's preference available. The agency representative emphasized how they had to be selective in order to do their best by those being placed.

"Doing right by our babies is demanded by our generous benefactors," pointed out the agency representative. "After all, it is their generosity that helps keep us afloat."

Mr. Holt interpreted this as a shakedown. Irked at the prospect of having to spend money, he rose from his chair with the intention of chucking the whole adoption idea.

"Where are you going?" asked Mrs. Holt.

"Let's go," announced the husband.

Mrs. Holt turned to the person representing the agency. "Could you give us a moment alone, please?" she asked, smiling politely.

"I'm not leaving here without a baby," declared Mrs. Holt when alone with her spouse. Her bulging eyes sent a convincing message that she was determined in her position.

"Can't you see that we're getting shook down by these people?"

"No one is shaking us down!"

Mr. Holt eventually yielded to the pressure exerted by his wife once she again started to throw around the word divorce. The couple resumed their conversation with the agency representative. This second go culminated in the couple agreeing to adopt a four-year-old boy the agency had been having difficulty trying to place.

Mrs. Holt was more than satisfied with the new addition to her family. The future father, on the other hand, was underwhelmed by having to take care of the little boy named Ross.

* * *

THE CURLY HAIRED ROSS HOLT never felt warmly received by his new father, who lacked interest in the boy. When in a disagreeable mood, Mr. Holt took out his bad humor on the child. He would often launch a sneaky swat to the back of the boy's head. This always occurred when Mrs. Holt wasn't around.

The effects of an abusive father were soon evident in the behavior of Ross. When of school age, Ross amused himself at the expense of those incapable of defending themselves. An out-and-out bully, his idea of fun was pulling the wings off butterflies or blowing up ant colonies with a firecracker.

When caught trying to remove the shell of a pet turtle, Mrs. Holt patiently explained to her son that a turtle's shell includes bones and nerve endings that a turtle needs to live and function. When the youth expressed no sign of remorse, his mother was appalled at his lack of sensitivity. It was at this juncture that Mrs. Holt admitted her son needed professional help.

"I'm not spending another dime on that pint-size Frankenstein," said Mr. Holt adamantly.

"We have to do something . . ."

"Let's see if we could ship him back to the agency that stuck us with him." The suggestion was one that the mother didn't find dignified enough to entertain.

Life rolled along with Mr. Holt continuing to abuse the boy. When Little Frankenstein grew big enough to stand up to his father, he was asked to pack up and leave. At sixteen, Ross was out of the house. He took up residence with a sympathetic social deviant several years older than he was. Under his friend's tutelage, Ross began engaging in criminal activity that primarily consisted of theft. He made just enough from his thievery to get by.

At twenty, Ross found himself cornered in a barn at the point of a shotgun by the father of an underage girl he had impregnated. Forced into marrying the seventeen-year-old, Ross was compelled to work at a real job. Living with his in-laws, Ross was hired at the Ohio steel plant where his father-in-law was foreman.

Two years hadn't passed before the responsibilities connected to being a family man became more than Ross could endure. His sleep was often interrupted by a recurring nightmare. Ross saw himself being consumed by a boa constrictor. With the lower half of his torso inside the snake, he watched in terror as the rest of him was gobbled up.

Waking up in a cold sweat convinced Ross that a change of venue was necessary. He decided the time had come to escape his current marital arrangement. Over the next two days Ross gathered whatever money he could get his hands on. In the middle of the night, he abandoned his family and job without ever looking back. He stopped running when he reached New Mexico. It was as good a place as any to start anew.

In New Mexico Ross managed to find work as a custodian for a small church. It was there that he was befriended by a parish priest not much older than he was. The two became friendly to where the priest taught Ross how to speak Spanish fluently. Ross would often have dinner at the rectory where he and the priest would converse in his new second language.

Although the parish was a poor one, Ross could see that the priest wanted for nothing, thanks to the the generosity of the parishioners. Churchgoers would ask the clergyman to dinners at their home and to whatever family festivities arose. Ross noted that businesses rarely charged the cleric for their services or products. The rectory was staffed by part-time workers who saw to the priest's meals, laundry, and miscellaneous needs on a daily basis. The nefarious Ross came to see religion as a vehicle that could be manipulated to his advantage.

Ross began to pay more attention to how things worked. He made it his business to learn as much as he could about the duties of a priest. A fast study, he was confident he could bluff his way through hearing confessions, administering last rites, and performing marriages. Ross was in the midst of mastering how to conduct Mass when the unexpected happened.

The sudden death of the parish priest due to a heart ailment was viewed by Ross to be a gift. His being the first to discover the priest dead at his office desk in the rectory was fortuitous. Ross stared at the crucifix on the wall and thought, *You sure do work in mysterious ways.*

Thinking fast, Ross didn't procrastinate in seizing the opportunity before him. With the rectory worker occupied elsewhere, Ross relieved the dead priest of his identification and money. He then hid the dead priest's body in an office closet that he was able to lock.

Ross then made it known to the rectory worker that the priest had stepped out and wouldn't be back until later in the evening. He then snuck into the priest's bedroom and rifled the dead man's belongings. After acquiring the priest's credentials and whatever cash was around, Ross absconded. Armed with a new identity, his destination was New York City.

* * *

MASQUERADING AS THE LATE CLERGYMAN, Ross found a parish in the Sunset Park section of Brooklyn that was in dire need of a priest to support its elderly pastor. The pastor, a sixty-five-year veteran of the priesthood, welcomed the bilingual priest into the fold. In his haste to find help, the senior priest neglected to follow the established hiring procedures.

Ross went on to popularize himself in the parish as Father Billy. In this guise, Ross made it his business to identify parishioners with money believed to be most susceptible to bilking. Once he familiarized himself with the inner workings of things, the bogus priest began tapping into the money market accounts that were set aside for the church. From these funds he treated himself to such material things as a new watch and ring.

The cunning impersonator was astute in recognizing that true believers were likely not to question a priest. Sporting a winning smile as Father Billy, Ross gladly listened attentively to those in need of attention. He'd provide advice and gracefully raise his right hand to discourage the offering of a gratuity while, at the same time, extending his lowered left hand to scoop in the cash.

The fraudster used his bilingual ability to win over many in the primarily Hispanic parish. His words of encouragement, blessings, and an occasional general absolution went far in influencing the people to part with their money. One person targeted was a stressed-out cartoonist named Santiago "Sammy" Angelo. Also on Ross Holt's radar were two siblings known as the Perez sisters.

Thanks to the largesse of Sammy Angelo and the Perez sisters, Ross accumulated enough funds to realize many of the things he previously couldn't afford. The fruits of his chicanery included excursions to Toms River, New Jersey. Located far from the borough of Brooklyn, the Jersey Shore was a relatively safe

97

venue for him to drink, gamble, and womanize without the likelihood of being recognized. To transport himself to Toms River, Ross would usually borrow the car belonging to the Perez sisters.

Before heading to Toms River one Friday afternoon, Ross was summoned to the home of an elderly man on his death bed. The son of the dying man, who had reached out to the rectory, was the owner of a thriving travel agency. After administering the last rites to the father, Ross approached the son, expecting the customary gratuity.

Before producing any money, the son asked to be granted a general absolution for himself. Ross sized up the business owner as a knock-around sort of guy who would know how to be appreciative. After being granted the request, the businessman conveyed that he was short on cash, adding that he was very grateful. Before leaving the house, Ross was given a winning off-track betting ticket, known as an OTB ticket, as a thank you. Seeing the large amount of money won, Ross realized that he'd have to identify himself to the OTB cashier for tax purposes.

Looking to circumvent the tax bite connected to cashing such a large winning ticket, Ross was in need of a resource to cash the ticket for him. He mentioned this need to the business owner.

"For the sake of appearances, I really can't cash this ticket myself," Ross advised.

"I understand, Father. I know someone who will cash the ticket for you. He's an old man with no reported income. The only thing, you'll have to give him ten percent of the ticket."

"I can do that."

"Go to the OTB parlor on Court Street with the ticket," said the son. "Look for an old man called No Tax. You can't miss him because he can't raise his head off his chest."

As suggested, Ross went to the Court Street OTB parlor in search of No Tax. As indicated, the octogenarian wasn't hard to find due to his physical handicap. Attired in the garb of Father Billy, Ross approached No Tax, who was sitting on a wooden milk box in front of the OTB parlor.

"Excuse me. Are you No Tax?" asked the phony priest.

The old man raised his eyes to see who was addressing him. Taken aback at the sight of a priest, No Tax nodded slowly in the affirmative. "What can I do for you?" he asked, leery at being approached by a religious figure.

"I was told that you cash winning tickets?"

"Who told you that?"

"Is that really important?"

"Well, how much is it for?"

"Seventeen hundred dollars . . . The ticket belongs to a disabled parishioner who can't go outdoors on his own," explained Ross. "He . . ."

"I don't need an explanation," said No Tax, cutting Ross off. He still hadn't made up his mind whether he was going to get involved.

"You do cash tickets, don't you?"

"Maybe I do, maybe I don't."

No Tax was a sick man himself. Having been diagnosed with an illness that left him with just a short time to live, he still wasn't about to take a chance on someone he didn't know. No Tax asked Ross to produce identification. After reviewing the impersonator's credentials, No Tax still had his doubts. "Are you from around here?" he asked.

"My parish is in Sunset Park. Everyone knows me there; I'm Father Billy."

"You do know that what you're asking me to do is . . . irregular, don't you?"

"Sometimes a man has to do things in order to help others."

The old man had been around long enough to know that he wasn't dealing with a legitimate man of the cloth. No Tax also was relatively certain the ticket holder was no cop, believing that a cop wouldn't go to such lengths to bust him. Suspecting that something wasn't kosher made doing business with a stranger seem safe, so No Tax cashed the ticket in return for his standard fee.

* * *

99

NOW FLUSH WITH CASH, the religious imposter wasted no time celebrating in Toms River with a waitress he had gotten close to. The two had met in the South Jersey diner where Gloria worked. Finding her attractive, Ross struck up a conversation with Gloria. She had a tough look about her that appealed to Ross, who preferred such types. The two really hit it off once Ross suspected that the red-headed Gloria shared his vices. Ross saw usefulness in the waitress. Before they reached Gloria's bedroom, Ross got to the truth. It turned out that Gloria's checkered past was as larcenous as his was.

Gloria confided that she had served two years in prison for grand larceny. Since Ross had never been sentenced to any serious time in jail, he found this to be impressive. Gloria explained that she had been working as a personal assistant for a very rich ninety-two-year-old woman. Their relationship soured after her employer took exception to Gloria addressing her by her first name. This, coupled with the employer's refusal to give Gloria a pay raise, set their course in a downward spiral. Gloria, who had the authority to use her employer's credit card to pay bills, grew spiteful. She began helping herself by making unauthorized purchases for her own benefit.

The tale of Gloria's arrest, and her ability to do time, convinced Ross that she possessed the moxie required in a good criminal associate. As Ross saw it, together they could improve upon his Father Billy scam. With this in mind, Ross revealed himself to Gloria. When the idea of their joining forces was broached, Gloria was receptive.

"You really think we can make some real money at this?" she asked.

"Gloria, if we combine forces, we can't miss."

"What makes you so sure?"

"I'm sure because we think alike."

Gloria looked deeply into the eyes of Ross, who returned her look with the same intensity.

"You know, I'm no good," she said in all seriousness.

"I know that. Neither am I. That makes for a good partnership."

"Do you want me to call you Ross or Father Billy?" she asked. It was Gloria's way of saying she was all in.

"When we're alone, Ross is fine."

"Where do we begin?"

"First thing we're gonna do is get you to quit that job you got and move you into the rectory in Brooklyn with me."

"What'll I do there?"

"You'll work as my assistant."

"How will that look?"

"The rectory has independent living quarters for you. It'll be a nice, cozy setup."

"What do I do about my apartment here in Toms River?"

"Keep it. We'll come to Jersey whenever we want and continue to do the things we've been doing."

"But what about the real priest, doesn't he live in the rectory?"

"Yeah, but he's half senile. He goes along with whatever I say."

"Are you sure about all this?"

"Relax, we're gonna have a sweet thing going, Gloria," assured Ross, sensing her skepticism. "See that Bentley I'm driving?"

"Yeah . . ."

"It belongs to a couple of sisters who have lived together in the same house for over sixty years. Those two are loaded, and they're just the start. There are lots of old people like them to be plucked over in Brooklyn."

Gloria expressed herself with a moderate embrace that left some doubt as to her total buy-in.

"You have to understand one thing, Gloria. We gotta be a little careful in Brooklyn. To the people there, we gotta appear to be strictly in a business relationship."

"I know; you don't have to tell me."

Ross didn't bother to answer his cell phone when it went off. After the caller had time to leave a voice mail, Ross listened to the recording. Seeing the frown forming on his face caused Gloria to become curious.

"Who was it?" she asked.

"Some guy I know from church. He's been calling me. He wants to talk to me about a problem his friend is having. "

101

"What does he expect you to do?"

"I listen and give advice. It's part of my Father Billy gimmick," advised Ross. "It gets me in close to the churchgoers. That's key in getting into their pocketbooks."

"They actually give you money?"

"Yeah, you'd be surprised. They give it to me or the church. Either way, I collect."

"That's incredible," declared the impressed Gloria.

"You want to know something? Sometimes I actually earn the payoff."

"I don't follow you . . ."

"Take this guy Sammy who just called me. He was ready to jump off a building when he first came to me. I boosted his confidence with a pep talk and saved his sorry ass. Now the guy loves me. It's only a matter of time before I put a real dent in his money."

"Then shouldn't you have taken his call?"

"He's not going anyplace. I'll call him back later."

When Ross finally got around to returning Sammy Angelo's call, Sammy began explaining his predicament. He started from the beginning with his friend Bumper's infatuation with Judith Vanidestine.

"If the woman is married to a plastic surgeon, she must be very wealthy," commented Ross, interrupting Sammy.

"I suppose so, Father."

"Has our friend the money to, ahh, compete with a plastic surgeon?"

"Dennis has no money, Father. He lives paycheck to paycheck. As I was saying, the problem is . . ."

"Dennis isn't being very realistic, is he?"

"He needs help, Father. He was blinded by love." Sammy had to be careful with what he said since Bumper was standing at his side. "That's why I'm reaching out to you. Dennis respects you, so he'll listen to you. He wants to come over and . . ."

Since Bumper had no money to entice him, Ross had no interest in getting involved. He cut Sammy short.

"I can't do that right now. For the time being I think it's best that you let this situation play out, Sammy. In time, your friend will realize the futility in it all."

"But Father . . ."

"Give it time. Call me in a couple of weeks. We'll revisit it then."

"What did he say, Sammy?" asked the anxious Bumper.

"He said he can't come by."

"Is that all he said?"

"He said that I should call him in a couple of weeks."

12

The Perez Sisters

IN ORDER TO CONVINCE GLORIA of the value in his Father Billy scam, Ross Holt intended to use his relationship with the Perez Sisters as an example of how the dubious duo could easily make money. Ross was certain that once Gloria began reaping financial benefits, she'd never question any plan he cooked up.

The Perez siblings were unique in that they were lifelong residents of the Sunset Park section of Brooklyn. They continued to live in the four-family row house after the death of their aged father, the single parent who raised them.

For many years the patriarch eked out a living as a chef in a Spanish restaurant. Complications in his life surfaced when his wife ran off with a coworker on the overnight shift at the factory where she worked. The absence of his spouse left the chef having to shoulder the responsibility of raising two small children alone. This domestic setback left the father so cynical that he soured on romance altogether.

The jadedness of their father resulted in the siblings living a sheltered life. The single parent entered his daughters into a convent after high school. Finding such a life too restrictive, the young girls begged to return home after two years. The sisters, who never married, never again moved out of the family home. It could be argued that the strict religious teachings they received had something to do with their lack of romantic entanglements.

Things improved financially when the family patriarch created a new cookie. While the snack he came up with didn't do well when it came to human consumption, it turned out to be a smashing success with the family's pet poodle. Listening to the advice of a veterinarian, the chef made a couple of adjustments that made his product pet friendly in terms of edibility. Thus, along with the veterinarian's investment, Eat-O Dog Snacks was born. The product turned out to net the Perez family and the vet a fortune.

Riches only caused the father to tighten his hold on his daughters. The patriarch became more vigilant than ever when it came to paramours. As far as he was concerned, anyone taking an interest in his daughters was looking to penetrate the family fortune.

Mr. Perez was never one to flaunt his wealth. His preference was to live moderately with his daughters in the Sunset Park home. Things remained this way until the patriarch died at the ripe old age of ninety-two. The sisters, who never had to hold a job, had devoted their lives to taking care of their father.

Blessed with strong genes, the sisters looked younger than the sixty and sixty-one years of age they were. They mostly cooked their own meals, did their own food shopping, and even made it a point to cut coupons. Their big treat came on Sundays when they would have an early dinner at a local restaurant. Sometimes they took in a movie after dinner.

The sisters lived together in the lower duplex of the family home. The top two floors were rented to tenants. One tenant was a woman who made her living as an international photojournalist. Due to the nature of her work, she was constantly traveling to such far-off places as Spain, Thailand, and Bali. Her frequent absences made her the ideal tenant as far as the sisters were concerned.

The other tenant was a robust sixty-seven-year-old retired seaman everyone called Captain. The Argentina born Captain was an exceedingly tanned man with a hook nose and deep lines that ran across his forehead. An avid pipe smoker, the Captain's persona was one of unquestionable masculinity. He was a welcomed presence in the house because the Perez sisters felt safe with the Captain around. This was particularly true of Millie Perez.

The Perez sisters lived vicariously through the seafaring man they saw as worldly. Many evenings the Captain could be found with his landlord(s) in their living room having drinks. These social interactions were something the Perez sisters looked forward to. To them, the Captain's exciting tales of the exotic lands he visited were thrilling. He brought to life the places they had only experienced through books.

Down deep, both sisters knew some of the stories had to have been somewhat embellished. If factual, the Captain would've been a cross between Sir Francis Drake and Jack London's Wolf Larson.

The Captain saw Millie Perez, a devotee of yoga, as the more appealing sister. The two came to reach an understanding that included Millie occasionally opening her bedroom door to her tenant. To avoid adverse speculation, their intimacy was carefully guarded. In a public setting there was no indication the two were involved in anything more than an amicable landlord-tenant relationship. Only Millie's sister had knowledge of her carrying on with the Captain.

Arlene Perez, who lacked a love connection, was starved for one. At her late stage in life she had grown desperate enough to get aggressive in her quest for a significant other.

Both Millie and Arlene, regular churchgoers, lived comfortably off their inheritance. They generously donated money to worthy causes and adhered to religious teachings as best they could. They became more involved in the church after meeting Father Billy, the new priest attached to the house of worship they attended.

Following Father Billy's reminder that it is better to give than to receive, the sisters began turning over their late father's valuables to the parish priest. Ross Holt, posing as Father Billy, gladly took the property, assuring the sisters that he'd distribute the items to those most in need.

Aside from his money, the one thing the sisters kept was their father's only true luxury item, a 1965 maroon Bentley. Whenever the sisters took to the road in the vehicle, attention was sure to follow them. While the Perez sisters continued to live with discreet modesty, being human, they didn't mind being noticed every now and then.

* * *

ONE EVENING WHEN THE CAPTAIN came downstairs to visit the Perez sisters, he was surprised to find they had company. The retired seaman smiled politely when introduced to the young priest who was sitting in the Captain's regular station in the parlor. The sight of the priest consuming a brandy didn't escape the tenant. Sitting in the chair next to Father Billy was Gloria, the priest's new assistant. The Captain believed the two to be about the same age.

The Captain couldn't help feeling that he was being intruded upon. *This is my time*, he thought. Making the best of the situation, the Captain cloaked his disappointment.

As the evening progressed, Gloria started to show signs of intoxication. Her nasty side appeared as she found something negative in every topic discussed. In an effort to lighten the mood, the Captain commenced a narrative pertaining to a treacherous voyage he had taken a number of years back. He told of outrageously fierce waters in which he faced waves of almost impossible proportions.

"There was nothing in this world more hazardous than what I faced that day in the Drake Passage," declared the Captain. "Why, I thought I was a goner . . ."

In middle of his story, Father Billy's assistant interrupted the Captain midsentence. "Aw, c'mon, Captain . . . who are you kidding?" said Gloria. "No waves can go that high."

"Some can go as high as forty feet," responded the Captain stiffly. "As I was saying . . ."

"Oh, how can that possibly be?" questioned Gloria, preventing the tenant from continuing his story.

"The Drake Passage is the most powerful convergence of seas," declared the Captain. "Weren't you taught in school about how high waves can get? You did go to school, didn't you?"

Gloria took the Captain's remark personally. "I learned enough in school to recognize baloney when I hear it," fired back Gloria. "Popeye couldn't make his way through what you're talking about . . . even with his spinach!"

Gloria's laughing at her own comment infuriated the Captain.

"A landlubber like you couldn't take a day on a rough sea," said the Captain, responding with his own brand of rudeness.

"So you think I couldn't take it. Let me tell you something—the only thing I can't take is this cock-and- bull story you're peddling," shot back the offended Gloria, pulling no punches.

Father Billy looked at Gloria harshly. He hoped his piercing eyes would register with Gloria that he wanted her to be quiet. The Captain gave a similar look to Millie Perez, only he expected Millie to weigh in on his behalf.

"You haven't a clue . . ." began the Captain.

This time he was interrupted by Father Billy, who was attempting to restore civility. "I can only imagine the courage required under such conditions, Captain."

"It took nerves of steel," advised the tenant.

"Where was it that you said this happened, Captain?"

"Somewhere around the South Fulla-Shit Islands," piped up Gloria before the Captain could reply.

Gloria's response pushed the Captain over the edge. "That's the South Shetland Island of Antarctica, you goddamn moron!" shouted the Captain. His outburst set off an exchange of hostile words that were riddled with profanities.

The combative tone of the guests was finally addressed by Arlene Perez, who expressed outrage over the foul language being hurled in the presence of a priest. Echoing Arlene's displeasure was Millie, who came down particularly hard on the Captain, ordering him out of her home.

The Captain, now humbled by what he considered to be Millie's mutiny, backed off. He was astute enough to realize the potential consequences of his conduct if he were to continue his rude behavior. The last thing he wanted to do was run the risk of jeopardizing his relationship with his landlords. The Captain wasted no time making amends with profuse apologies. He even apologized to Gloria for his coarse conduct. When no one responded to his remorse, the Captain made his exit as gracefully as possible.

"Gloria, haven't you something to say to our hosts before we go?" asked Ross, using his best priestly voice.

"Yeah, I do. I'm very sorry, ladies. Please forgive me. I know I should have let the old bastard just tell his story." With that, Ross and Gloria left the Perez home.

On their way back to the rectory, Ross verbally laced into Gloria for her placing him in such an awkward position. Gloria swore that she would never drink too much again when in the presence of a mark Ross had lined up.

* * *

ALONE IN HIS APARTMENT, the Captain remained upset. His anger slowly returned as he began to dwell
on the upsetting interaction that had occurred in his landlord's home. Not knowing what to do to calm himself, he thought a drink might help.

The Captain opened the door to the cabinet over the kitchen sink, thinking he might open the good bottle of rum he had been saving for a special occasion. He looked at the bottle he held in his hand for close to a minute. He finally decided against opening it after thinking Gloria didn't warrant wasting a good drink over.

There was something in the Captain's gut telling him that things weren't kosher with Gloria and Father Billy. He felt that a true priest would never align himself with someone like the sharp-tongued Gloria.

The whole situation . . . it just don't smell right, thought the Captain.

While the Captain was upstairs in his apartment stewing and Gloria was being lambasted by the priest impersonator, the Perez sisters remained angry at both parties. While there wasn't much they could do about Gloria, the Captain was a different story. They put their tenant on the back burner. They agreed to invite him back into the house—if he behaved himself—after the passing of a month.

When the Captain saw Gloria driving the Perez sisters around in their family Bentley, he was furious. As if that wasn't disturbing enough, he then began seeing Father Billy and his assistant going about in the car together, unaccompanied by either sister.

"I never even rode in that car," bitterly barked the Captain, speaking aloud to only himself.

Watching from his upper-floor open window one day, the Captain noticed that Gloria was making a lot of motions with her hand while talking to the sisters in front of the house. It appeared to him that Gloria was directing the sisters to do something.

The longer he observed Gloria's interactions, the better the Captain was able to recognize the comfort level the priest's assistant had when engaging the Perez sisters. He now suspected that Gloria was behind the chilling of his once warm relationship with his landlords.

The Captain's suspicions reached new heights after he received a telephone call from Gloria. She advised him that she was authorized by the Perez sisters to inform him there would be a 30-percent increase in his rent. The Captain, upset at hearing this, abruptly hung up the phone. He then immediately hustled down the interior flight of stairs and down the outside stoop to the Perez's front door. His intention was to discuss the rent increase with the sisters directly.

To his surprise, Gloria, who had anticipated his arrival, opened the door. Attired in casual wear and slippers, she seemed quite at home in the Perez house.

"Oh, it's you," Gloria said, as if surprised. Her feigned innocence didn't fool the Captain.

"I'm here to see Millie."

"She's not available right now. What is it you want?"

"Where is Arlene then?"

"She's with Millie."

"Well, where are they?"

"What is it you want, Captain?"

"I want to hear from them why I got such a big jump in rent."

"I can answer that for you. They were unaware of what the going rate is."

"And you put them wise, I suppose," accused the Captain.

"I only apprised them of the going rate for apartments these days."

"So you told them to raise my rent . . ."

"All I did was advise them of the going rates," repeated Gloria. "After all, it's only fair. Everything has gone up—taxes, gas and electric, water . . . everything has skyrocketed."

"So you're in the real estate business now," declared the Captain. "I thought you were helping the priest save souls."

"Is that all, Captain?"

"I'll tell you what, Gloria. My business is with the sisters, so I'll come back later to straighten this out with them."

"I'm afraid tonight isn't a good night," said Gloria. "We're having company. Father Billy is coming over to hear confession." Gloria could see that the information she conveyed disturbed the Captain. She decided to rub it in. "After that, we're all going out for dinner at a new Spanish restaurant in Manhattan."

Thinking fast, the Captain came up with an excuse to speak to the sisters. "Millie wanted me to take a look at the bathroom upstairs. The faucet is dripping."

"You needn't bother about that. I'll be arranging for all house repairs for the Perez sisters from now on."

That statement gave the Captain pause. "I thought you worked for the priest at the rectory . . ."

"I do, but Father Billy wants me to do all I can to look after Millie and Arlene."

111

"I see. So that's how it is," said the Captain. In his frustration, he began to walk away.

"Oh, Captain, one last thing before you go . . ."

"What's that?"

"I think I may be able to help you regarding your rent increase."

"Why would you want to help me?" asked the Captain with suspicion.

"Since you are a senior citizen and a longtime tenant, I suppose I could convince the ladies to forget about the rent increase . . . providing I had a good reason to do so."

"What would a good reason be?"

"Let's just say if it was in my interest, I could look after yours." The Captain now understood he was being shaken down.

"What if I just go tell the sisters about what you're trying to pull here?"

"What if I were to tell them that you've been taking liberties with me?" said Gloria, smiling evilly.

"What liberties?"

"Use your imagination."

"Whatever you say, Gloria," said the Captain, accepting defeat for the moment. "How much is it gonna take?"

"By the way, I wouldn't mention our little arrangement to anyone, Captain," advised Gloria, once they had arrived at a satisfactory number.

* * *

AFTER THE CAPTAIN LEFT, Gloria was exceedingly pleased with herself. She now had a modest cash revenue stream that would be coming her way monthly. The negotiation with the Captain was one she had no intention of mentioning to Ross Holt, her crime partner. When the two spoke on the telephone later, they discussed the roof strategy Ross came up with.

"When I get there, I want you to bring up the importance of making repairs to the roof, Gloria," instructed Ross. "You can start by telling them how you heard about a roof caving in someplace in the Bronx and killing people."

"Okay . . ."

"I'll volunteer to go up on their roof to see what kind of shape it's in," explained Ross. "When I come down, I'll say the roof needs repairing. Once I have them convinced that they need to call in a roofer, you volunteer to make an appointment to have one come over."

"What if nothing is wrong with the roof?"

"Don't worry; there will be."

"All right," agreed Gloria.

"You tell them you have a relative in the roofing business, so you could get them a cheaper price if they pay in cash. You get the idea."

"Sure."

"Then on the day the roofer comes, you take Millie and Arlene someplace that'll keep them busy for a couple of hours. I'll stay behind to wait for the roofer. When you get back, I'll say that the roofer came by and said a whole new roof is needed."

"How much money are you going to ask for?" Gloria asked.

"Ten . . . no, make it twelve grand. We'll tell the sisters that it has to be cash."

"What if they want to pay by check?"

"They won't. We'll tell them they'll get a big discount if they pay in cash."

On the day the roofer came to look at the roof, Ross, attired in his white collar, was there to let him in. Ross accompanied the roofer to the roof to assess what work needed to be done. After examining the condition of the roof, the bogus priest was advised by the roofer that the skylight needed tending to. In addition, there were a couple of minor repairs that required attention.

"How much is this going to cost?" asked Ross.

"I'll give you a good price, Father. Say, six hundred dollars?"

"I'm prepared to pay you in cash."

This remark caused the roofer to chuckle. "Okay, Father," he said, "then I'll make it five hundred."

113

When the time came for Gloria to ask the siblings to withdraw money for the roofing work that was to be performed, both Millie and Arlene balked at first. The resourceful Gloria managed to soften their position by explaining the costly litigation involved if the roof ever came down and hurt one of the tenants. The real convincer came when Ross, as Father Billy, personally weighed in. He clinched it when he pointed out to the sisters that making house repairs for the safety of their tenants is the Christian thing to do.

The day the work was performed, the Captain was home. When he heard voices in front of the house, he looked out the window in time to see the roofer receive the five-hundred-dollar cash payment for the work he performed,

So Father Billy is handling their money now, thought the Captain as he watched the roofer get in his truck and drive off with his team. When Ross turned to go back inside the house, he did so while counting the remainder of his money. The wad of cash he was holding impressed the Captain.

Why, there is enough there to choke a horse, thought the Captain. The sighting of the long green was enough to further spark the tenant's suspicions.

13

No Tax Johnny

SPENDING DECADES AROUND LAWBREAKERS enabled No Tax to recognize a shady character when he met one. His brief interaction with Father Billy at the OTB parlor was enough to convince him that, priest or not, the man in the white collar wasn't on the level.

After collecting his fee for cashing Father Billy's winning OTB ticket, No Tax Johnny Layton had some financial breathing room. This was a temporary condition. Streetwise with a big appetite for gambling, he quickly blew through most of his bankroll and found himself once again hard-pressed for money.

For decades, No Tax made his living working for mobsters. Failing health now prevented him from being employable. Unfortunately, his lifelong labor came with no benefits to fall back on. Regardless of his current situation, his was a career choice that came with no regrets. When self-reflecting, he'd admit to himself that he wouldn't have changed a thing. He'd align himself with the same gamblers and low-level gangsters all over again.

No Tax plodded through life without ever having reported any income. Seeing a way to use this to his advantage, he headquartered himself at a neighborhood Brooklyn OTB parlor where he engaged in cashing winning tickets for a fee. The money collected for his service was barely enough for No Tax to make ends meet.

The dropped-head syndrome that afflicted No Tax prevented the senior citizen from lifting his chin off his chest. This had become the least of the senior citizen's problems. Pancreatic cancer had invaded his body. His only complaint at this stage was that the disease had made walking difficult for him.

No Tax lived modestly in a one-bedroom apartment in a rundown, multistory building not far from the OTB parlor. Aware that he had a short life expectancy, No Tax focused on the one item he had on his bucket list: he wanted to accumulate enough money to be put to rest beneath a black marble headstone positioned between a pair of life-size patrolling black panthers.

In order to fund his bizarre desire, No Tax put the word out that he was open to any opportunity that would generate income. A low-level criminal he knew came through with a proposition.

"No Tax, I got a deal for you," said the low-level mobster.

"Yeah?"

"Yeah, and it's a piece of cake. All I need you to do is take a ride with one of my guys. It's a one-day thing."

"What kind of ride?"

"I got a load of hot videos that I gotta get delivered. All you gotta do is sit alongside the driver."

"I'm interested . . . but why do you need me?"

"Having a geezer like you riding shotgun in the van is good insurance for me. It'll protect my investment," explained the associate.

"I don't follow you. . ."

"If some ambitious cop decides to make a traffic stop, he ain't gonna get too nosy if he sees an old buzzard like you on board."

"I'm your boy," said No Tax, signing on. "How much are you paying?"

"Does two-hundred and fifty bucks sound right?"

"Could you make it three-hundred and fifty?"

Once terms were reached, the two men shook hands. Neither

man foresaw the possibility of the poor health of No Tax coming into play.

* * *

THE TRANSPORTERS OF THE GOODS were engaged in a pleasant conversation as they journeyed to their first destination when, without warning, No Tax went silent in the middle of a sentence. Seeing that the old man had turned pale, the driver pulled to the side of the parkway that led to Long Island.

"Are you okay?" asked the driver, poking the shoulder of No Tax. Receiving no response, he repeated his question with greater amplification. With No Tax still unresponsive, the driver began shaking the older man. Just as the driver was beginning to panic, No Tax began to come around.

"I don't know what the hell happened to me," uttered the passenger. His voice sounded shaky due to having entered uncharted waters.

"Are you okay?"

"I . . . I think so, but I can't see out of my left eye," answered No Tax.

"Did you get something in it?"

"No, nothing like that, I . . . just give me a few minutes."

"That eye going on the bum ain't good. You better go see a doctor about that."

"I'm already up to my ass in doctors," lamented No Tax. "Hey, hold on. Things seem to be clearing up."

The sudden blast of a siren to their rear ended their conversation. "Oh, shit, the cops," said the driver.

"They probably think we broke down," said No Tax, who was now more like himself.

"Let's hope."

The highway patrol officer approached the driver's side of the vehicle and tapped on the window. "Is everything okay?" he asked. The officer had a spit-and-polish, no-nonsense look to him, which was typical of those assigned to the highway unit.

"Everything is fine, Officer," said the driver of the van. The operator's nervousness presented a red flag to the officer.

No Tax closed his eyes and let out an audible exhale. He sensed that trouble was coming. The van operator's fidgeting and quivering lips were giving them away. Further complicating things were the visible track marks on the driver's hands. They were the telltale signs of a junkie.

"What have you got in the back of the van?" asked the officer. When the driver began tripping over his words, the highway cop called for backup.

When police backup arrived, the officer had the driver and No Tax step out of the van. After finding a loaded handgun under the driver's seat, the law enforcement officer placed both men under arrest. The apprehension led to the police confiscating the van and the swag videos.

When one of the backup officers noticed a video that interested him, he picked it up to read the synopsis on the back cover of the plastic case. Thinking of pocketing the video, the officer opened the snap-close plastic case to check the condition of the video. No one was more surprised than No Tax when small plastic bags containing white powder was discovered inside some of the video cases.

* * *

THE APPEARANCE OF NO TAX WORSENED by the time he arrived at the precinct. When asked by the arresting officer if he wanted to go to a hospital, the elderly prisoner declined the offer of medical aid. The officer tended to believe No Tax when he claimed that he had no knowledge that the video cases contained heroin. Because of his credibility in explaining his ignorance, No Tax was extended whatever courtesy possible by the officer. Under the circumstances, that didn't amount to much. No Tax was still booked and charged with possessing drugs and a gun.

After being strip-searched, No Tax was photographed and fingerprinted. Once the arrest papers were prepared, the prisoner was placed in a cell where he would remain until it was time to be transported elsewhere. While the arresting officer was processing the operator of the van, he stopped every so often to personally look in on the aged prisoner.

No Tax sat alone on the cell bench looking down at his shoes. He was deep in thought. After having contemplated his predicament, he lifted his eyes to look through the black bars that restricted him. The thought of possibly dying in jail depressed him. Even more depressing was the possibility of not having a headstone and two life-size panthers protecting his gravesite.

Being held under lock and key removed any hope of No Tax getting his hands on money. Since he was nearing his end anyway, he decided to try and cut a deal with the authorities by turning informer.

The next time the arresting officer came by the cell, No Tax made his decision to cooperate known. After some preliminary questioning, the officer concluded that the senior citizen had useful information pertaining to the death of a prominent attorney.

The officer recollected reading about how Attorney Marvin Butterworth was found dead in a Manhattan hotel room as a result of autoerotic activity. The lawyer's unusual death had been well- publicized in the newspapers at the time. After the officer conferred with precinct detectives, the Manhattan investigator charged with investigating Butterworth's death was notified. Within an hour, the Manhattan sleuth was present at the Brooklyn precinct to interview No Tax.

The visiting detective listened attentively as No Tax revealed his connection to Butterworth. When the name of an ex-detective called Fishnet was implicated, the interviewing detective was taken aback. There was only one Fishnet.

Since Fishnet Milligan was recognized throughout the department as a hero detective, the Manhattan investigator was reluctant to be involved in a probe that could result in getting Fishnet in trouble. Recollecting the interest in the Butterworth death that was expressed by members of the chief of detective's office, the detective saw a chance to shift responsibility elsewhere. The investigator put in a call to headquarters.

Markie, who strongly suspected Fishnet of being a criminal, jumped at the chance to speak to No Tax.

"C'mon, Ollie, we're going to Brooklyn," said Markie.

"What about Dennis Bumper, Sarge? I thought we're working on the caddy case."

"We still are, but this is a chance for us to get something on Fishnet."

"But what if Bumper takes off?"

"If Bumper is taking off, then he is probably already gone. We'll swing by the house to see if that taxicab is still parked on the street."

Seeing that the cab hadn't been moved, the detectives proceeded to Bumper's residence.

"I'll check the mailboxes, Sarge," said Von Hess.

"Was there any mail in his box?" Markie asked when the detective returned to the car.

"Yeah, Sarge, Bumper's got mail in his box."

"Let's get over to that squad where the snitch is being held. We'll come back here later and see if it's still there."

When they arrived at the squad room where No Tax was being held, they found the elderly prisoner waiting for them in a small office. He was sipping tea while handcuffed to a bar that was affixed to the wall.

"So what did Fishnet Milligan have to do with Marvin Butterworth?" asked Markie.

"Hold on a second," said No Tax. "I'll level with you guys and tell you everything, but first you have to assure me that I'll get what I want."

"What is it you want?" asked Von Hess.

No Tax expressed his desire for a headstone and two life-size panthers above his final resting place. Von Hess saw this as insanity. Markie saw it as a small price to pay if it enabled him to put Fishnet Milligan behind bars.

"We aren't exactly in the business of burying people," noted the sergeant.

"I already have a spot waiting for me in Cypress Hills Cemetery," advised No Tax. "My parents were real decent people. They took care of all that years ago, Sarge. I'm coming down the home stretch now, so all I'm looking for is the stone and the two panthers."

"Done . . . if you got something good to tell us," announced the sergeant suddenly. Markie's abrupt agreement came as a surprise to Von Hess.

"I want something official . . . in writing," said the distrusting No Tax.

"What you're getting here is way out of the realm of normal," advised Markie. "There is no getting something like this in writing, so that ain't happening. I'm giving you my word of honor that I'll see to it that you get your headstone and panthers, and my word is something that I don't give often."

"You expect me to take your word?"

"That's right," voiced Markie, not budging. "Either that or forget it."

No Tax studied the dead serious Markie closely. The sergeant's intensity caused the prisoner to think that maybe the sergeant was a man who could be trusted. Since there were no other offers on the table, No Tax signed on.

"Okay, Sarge, we got us a deal. I got just one question: what did this detective do to you?"

"What are you talking about?"

"You got a big interest in him. I thought Fishnet was supposed to be this big hero with you guys."

"Yeah, I know," stated Markie tartly. "Let's leave it at that. Start talking to us about Fishnet and Butterworth."

"Okay, Sergeant, don't get excited. You know, I never actually met Butterworth. I was told he looked something like me."

"Who told you that?"

"Fishnet told me."

"And . . ."

"He paid me to rent a room in Butterworth's name at the Bixby Hotel in the city."

"Who paid you?" asked the sergeant, who pitched forward in his chair. "Give me a name." Markie was anxious to hear Fishnet's name coming from the lips of No Tax.

"I already told you."

"Tell me again."

"I forget his exact name. I only remember him as Fishnet. He was the detective who got in that big shootout with Red Harris that time. It was in all the papers."

The investigators went on to learn how Fishnet Milligan paid No Tax to acquire the false identification necessary for the old man to secure a hotel room while impersonating the attorney, Marvin Butterworth.

"What was the purpose of this?" Von Hess asked.

"I wasn't privy to that. All I know is that I later read about how Butterworth was found dead in a sicko way in the hotel room. I figured he must have been clipped."

Because the information being provided was coming from a prisoner facing incarceration, more investigative work would be required. Before concluding, Markie had Von Hess take a photograph of No Tax. The sergeant briefly thought of telephoning his superiors at headquarters to apprise them of what he'd learned about the well-known lawyer's autoerotic death. He then changed his mind, figuring that he'd be ordered to concentrate only on the Dennis Bumper homicides. He decided to keep the information he gathered from No Tax to himself and work on both cases simultaneously.

* * *

MARKIE AND VON HESS RESPONDED to the Bixby Hotel where they questioned several hotel employees. This proved fruitless. Even showing a photo of No Tax to the hotel employees was a dead end.

Surprisingly, no one recollected seeing No Tax at the hotel. The detectives had thought for sure that the dropped head of No Tax would be remembered by someone at the hotel.

The hotel manager proved to be cooperative. Research of hotel records indicated that the room taken under the name of Marvin Butterworth was paid for in cash. This was in sync with what No Tax had advised. When queried as to who authorized the cash transaction, the manager admitted to approving the cash payment. When pressed by the detectives, the manager specifically recalled approving a cash payment for an elderly man with a neck problem.

Von Hess produced the photograph of No Tax. The manager identified No Tax as being the man who paid for the room in cash.

"You must have known that a man turned up dead in that room the next day, correct?"

"Of course, Sergeant," answered the manager.

"Well, didn't you see that the dead man was a different guy than the man who booked the room?"

"Why, no . . . I never got to see the deceased man. I only saw them carry the body away. By that time he was all covered up."

"Did you see Butterworth's picture in the papers?" Von Hess asked.

"Why, no, I didn't."

When finished at the hotel, the detectives went to check on Bumper's taxicab in Brooklyn. Seeing that it was still there, they drove to where Bumper lived. Once again, Von Hess checked Bumper's mailbox. This time the box was empty.

"He's around then, Ollie. Let's stick here on the house and see if he comes out." This proved fruitless. Once again, Markie and Von Hess ended their tour with no sighting of Dennis Bumper.

* * *

THE COOPERATION OF NO TAX went far in how he was treated in court. Since No Tax wasn't thought to be a flight risk due to his failing health, he was released after being arraigned. The following day, Markie and Von Hess went back to conducting surveillance at Bumper's residence. They took note that there was no mail in his mailbox. They discussed what could be done in their effort to apprehend Dennis Bumper.

"We could put mail in his mailbox, Sarge, and wait to see who is picking up the mail," suggested Von Hess.

"Yeah, that's an idea. Let's give it another day or two before doing that. Let's swing by the apartment of the old man when we're through here, Ollie."

"Whatever you say, Sarge."

When the detectives arrived at the apartment of No Tax, they could see that the cancer-stricken man was failing.

"Ahhh, what can I say. It's the ballgame," said the ailing No Tax.

The detectives couldn't disagree based on what they could see. Aside from not being able to raise his head, No Tax was now finding it a tremendous strain to make his way around his apartment. Trips to another room had become a journey for him. Thinner and more haggard, Von Hess could see the cooperator was in desperate need of cleaning up.

"He looks terrible, Sarge," whispered Von Hess. Markie just nodded.

"I heard you," said No Tax. "You think you're saying something I don't know?"

"How about we help clean you up?" asked Markie. "You'll feel better."

"I can't . . ."

"Sure you can. C'mon, we're gonna help you get washed up. Once you're clean, Detective Von Hess is gonna shave you and give you a haircut." After the ordeal of being cleaned and groomed, No Tax was spent.

"You look a hundred percent better," declared Von Hess, admiring his handiwork as a barber.

"I don't feel any better," said No Tax. "I gotta go to the recliner." The detectives walked No Tax over to the chair in which he slept. "When are you guys gonna lock up that detective?"

"We're still working on that," replied Markie. "We need to gather more information. Can you think of anything else that might be useful?"

"Here are the papers you'll need for Greenwood Cemetery," said No Tax, ignoring the question. He passed Markie an envelope that contained the necessary documents.

Markie put the envelope in his jacket pocket without opening it. "Now, let's hear what else you can tell us about Fishnet."

"I told you everything."

"Who made up the phony credentials for you?" asked Von Hess.

"Do I have to tell you that?"

"Yeah, don't worry about telling us. We're not looking to pinch anyone. We just want to be able to support what you told us."

"His name is Vega," advised No Tax. "He lives over the luncheonette at Smith and Wyckoff."

"Are you sure you can't think of anything else that might help us?"

"Not about the Butterworth thing, but I can tell you about a con artist posing as a parish priest if you want."

"Let's hear it," Von Hess said, expressing an interest.

"I cashed a winning OTB ticket for a hustler who passes himself off as a priest," advised No Tax. "Trust me; this guy ain't no priest. If he is, he's a crook in a white collar."

"What's his name?"

"He calls himself Father Billy. He's supposed to be attached to a church in Sunset Park. That's all I know about him."

"That's enough," said Von Hess. Someone pretending to be a priest was an offense the detective took personally.

"You know I'll be dead soon," said No Tax, looking at the detectives with sad eyes raised upward. "Did you get me the stone and the panthers yet, Sarge?"

* * *

AFTER LEAVING THE APARTMENT OF NO TAX, the detectives discussed the old man's health. Not being sure of how long No Tax would last caused some fret.

"Let's hope this guy lasts long enough for us to put a case together," commented Markie. "We're gonna need him as a witness."

"I don't know, Sarge. He's pretty frail."

"Yeah, I know. Anyway, I need to go shopping, Ollie."

"What for, boss?"

"I gotta get a headstone and a couple of bargain basement black panthers."

"Do you know anybody in that business?"

"Yeah, I got a favor coming from someone in that racket."

"What about the cost?"

"I'm gonna stop by Fitzie's bar and put him to work on that. He could be pretty resourceful when it comes to raising money."

"How do you figure that, Sarge?"

"I'll ask him to do me a favor and start a fundraiser. He'll run a fifty-fifty and raffle stuff off. He's raised money before, so he knows how to do it."

"Do you think No Tax will be perceived as a good cause?"

"To some people he will be, Ollie. You know that loan shark who conducts his business in Fitzie's joint?"

"I know who you mean . . ."

"Well, he's been operating out of that bar without getting taxed a dime. He'll pitch in once Fitzie tells him that I'm in need of a favor. I've been looking the other way for years when it comes to that guy."

"What if he balks?"

"He won't. He's not stupid. He knows I'll get the precinct to put some pressure on him if I have to. I doubt it'll come to that."

After some back and forth, an agreement was reached. The loan shark committed to fronting a Cadillac automobile and a two-bedroom condo in Florida as prizes. The car would be borrowed from a mob- connected dealership and the condo from a real estate developer with similar ties. The loan shark would arrange for the raffle to be promoted by unions his crime family did business with.

The understanding called for the raffle to be rigged. The winners were to be predetermined associates of the loan shark who would discreetly return the vehicle to the dealer and not seek any claim regarding the Florida condo.

A final stipulation was that once the costs of the gravestone and panthers were met, the remainder of the money generated would be split between the loan shark and Fitzie on a 65-35 basis in favor of the loan shark. The details of the agreement never reached the ears of Markie, who had no interest in anything beyond making good on his promise to No Tax.

14

Time to Pay the Piper

THE MORE TIME PASSED the more anxious Dennis Bumper became. After Markie and Von Hess came to Sammy Angelo's door the fugitive started to feel the law breathing down his neck. Bumper thought it be not to leave his friend's apartment. While not sure how long it would take for things to cool off, Bumper intended to stay put until he felt forgotten. When the time was felt to be right, he would have Sammy again reach out to Father Billy. The wanted man was more determined than ever to avoid being taken into custody until after he had the opportunity to confess his sins.

"Let's hold off on calling Father Billy, Sammy," said Bumper.

Sammy was dismayed at his friend's change of heart. "Why? I thought you wanted to confess your sins, Dennis?"

"I do, but if they pick me up, who knows if I'll ever get the chance to see Father Billy. More than anything, I want to go to jail with a clean soul."

This news was a bit of a setback for Sammy, who desperately wanted his friend out of his apartment so he could receive the professional help he needed. Since he didn't have it in him to betray Bumper, Sammy resigned himself to harboring his friend for an undetermined period.

The men saw to it that every precaution was taken. Sammy would retrieve Bumper's mail in the middle of the night when no one was around. He ordered food to be delivered to the apartment instead of going out for it. On Sunday, they watched Mass together on television. While their isolation came with stress, the one good thing was that Bumper seemed to be mentally in check. All Sammy could do was hope this peaceful patch would last until Bumper thought the time was right to contact Father Billy.

As figured, the homicides committed by Dennis Bumper began to fade as a priority with the passing of time. The detectives in the various squads continued to catch new cases that required their attention. These distractions left less time for them to concentrate on Bumper. The caddy murders were eventually put on a shelf, pending further developments. A wanted card was out for Bumper. This development gave Markie and Von Hess the latitude to do other things.

* * *

NO LONGER HAVING TO CONDUCT SURVEILLANCE, Markie and Von Hess put time into finding the forger who provided No Tax with the documents necessary to impersonate the late attorney, Marvin Butterworth. Since there were no pressing matters to attend to, they were able to engage in this with the approval of their superiors.

The forger was an unimpressive man who wore thick, round glasses that were long out of style. The vintage cardigan sweater he wore was black with brown elbow patches. The soft-spoken criminal agreed to cooperate once he was assured he'd escape arrest if he told of his role in the Butterworth caper. His statement supported the account previously provided by No Tax.

The detectives contacted a Manhattan assistant district attorney they had a history of getting along well with. The ADA vividly recalled working with Markie and Von Hess in prosecuting the psychopathic serial killer Everett Skidmore in what came to be known as "The Case of the Cross-Eyed Strangler." The ADA was receptive to meeting with the investigators.

The prosecutor, who was known to enjoy a cocktail after work hours, met with the detectives at a bar and restaurant located a short distance from her One Hogan Place office in lower Manhattan. After ordering a round of drinks at Forlini's on Baxter Street, the ADA was brought up to speed concerning their suspicions surrounding the death of Marvin Butterworth.

Hearing the name Butterworth, who was known to have been a top-tier attorney, went far in gaining the prosecutor's attention. This, and her faith in the detectives, caused the ADA to seriously entertain the assertion that Butterworth's apparent autoerotic death was no accident. Correcting an injustice involving someone like the prominent Butterworth was an opportunity for the prosecutor to catapult her career to greater heights.

As the ADA digested the details, she recognized the possibility of foul play. Like the investigators, she found it hard to fathom that Marvin Butterworth, at his advanced age, would engage in bizarre sexual behavior in a hotel room. Butterworth's having been the attorney for Fishnet Milligan and his late wife was a factor that needed to be considered when searching for a possible motive. Once learning that Fishnet's wife died under unusual circumstances in a Pennsylvania quarry, the ADA was sold. However, concerns did exist.

"I have to be honest with you," advised the ADA. "Even with No Tax and the forger, making a case against a retired hero cop who was shot in the line of duty is going to be challenging."

"So we're just gonna let that son of a bitch walk away from this?" Markie asked, referring to Fishnet.

"No, I can't in good conscience let that happen," replied the prosecutor. "Get me all the paperwork on the Butterworth case and let me review it."

The ADA went on to examine all available documents. She also conferred with the medical examiner before arriving at the decision to prosecute Fishnet for homicide. While not optimistic in gaining a conviction, the ADA was, nevertheless, willing to push ahead. Sensitive to having a losing prosecution on her record, the ADA intended to do her utmost to attain a plea bargain, regardless of how generous the offer to the defense had to be.

Markie was delighted when Marvin Butterworth's death was reclassified as a homicide. Sharing in his joy, although to a lesser degree, was Von Hess. The one person who wasn't thrilled was the detective originally assigned to investigate Butterworth's death. He didn't like being involved in the messy affair of a former detective, rogue or not, being brought to justice.

The precinct detective was compelled to accompany Markie and Von Hess to the office of the ADA. Once there, papers were drawn up, and an arrest warrant was signed by a judge. Armed with the warrant, the three detectives set out to arrest Fishnet for the murder of Marvin Butterworth.

"How do you want to do this, Sarge?" asked the precinct detective.

After thinking it over, Markie replied, "You call Fishnet and tell him to call his attorney. Let him know he has a case against him and that his attorney has to surrender him to the precinct squad."

"Righto, Sarge."

Markie wanted to humble Fishnet. By getting Fishnet to wave the white flag and surrender himself, the sergeant was hammering it home that he had won, and Fishnet had lost.

* * *

WHEN IT CAME TO MATERIAL THINGS, Fishnet had everything he wanted. He lived stylishly in a posh

131

West Village townhouse, had plenty of spending money, and was able to live large off the inheritance he received after killing his wife. The cunning former law enforcement officer had successfully manipulated things so that the Pennsylvania quarry deaths of his wife and her lover appeared to be accidental.

Sticking to the accidental death formula, Fishnet masterminded the murder of Marvin Butterworth. With Butterworth, Fishnet's motive was not of a financial nature. The lawyer was eliminated because Fishnet believed Butterworth suspected him of being behind the quarry homicides.

Without ever having discussed the subject with Butterworth, Fishnet nevertheless felt vulnerable with the attorney alive. To assure Butterworth's silence, Fishnet had placed the attorney on an incredibly generous retainer. Fishnet's largesse was always intended to have a shelf life.

Once the death of Marvin Butterworth was behind him, Fishnet settled down to try his hand at other things. One of his interests was to further the career of an aspiring actress he met at the Dancing Elf, a 10th Avenue bar-restaurant in the Manhattan Theater District. Through chicanery, the onetime sleuth was presented to the young waitress as a theatrical powerhouse who could help realize her career ambitions. Believing Fishnet to be what he claimed, the impressionable Cheryl Arbuckle was amenable to his advances.

Fishnet, who was a dead ringer for the late actor Clark Gable, could be quite the charmer when he wanted to be. His way was to make the targeted love interest feel as if she was the only woman who mattered.

Fishnet strong-armed a friend of his late actress wife who possessed the necessary connections to advance Cheryl. Thanks to the pressure applied on the Maestro, Cheryl was able to secure a role in a new play. To the budding young actress, Fishnet's arranging this was the equivalent of his being able to walk on water.

* * *

FISHNET WAS STUNNED WHEN HE was telephonically notified
that there was a warrant out for his arrest. The former detective
had committed so many wrongful acts that, at first, he was
baffled as to what charges he'd be facing. When informed that
he was looking at a homicide charge, the phone went silent.
Fishnet began thinking of the homicides he had perpetrated.
The one thing that didn't require any thinking was Fishnet's
need to lawyer up.

Fishnet had the funds to hire a highly experienced criminal
lawyer to handle his defense. A former federal prosecutor, the
attorney was known to be an aggressive bulldog in court. His
style was an effective one. The onetime college football player
was a barrel-chested man with a booming voice that matched
his burly appearance. Guilt or innocence mattered little as long
as the attorney was being generously compensated.

"So what's our strategy?" asked Fishnet when meeting with his
attorney at his law office.

"We're going to have to surrender you to the precinct
detective as requested," advised the lawyer. "At your
arraignment, I'll try to get you out on bail."

"What are my chances of that?"

"Let's just hope we get a reasonable judge."

"Look, hoping is a crap shoot. I got plenty of money, so put it
to work. I'm looking for a sure thing over here."

The attorney was taken aback by Fishnet's bluntness. While
surprised, he was not offended. He paused for a second and
then looked Fishnet straight in the eye. Feigning to be
perplexed, the defense attorney pretended not to know what
his client was talking about. It was the attorney's patented
reaction to things illegal, immoral, or unethical.

"Let me do the strategizing," the lawyer finally said. "I'll tell
you when you need to worry."

Fishnet let it go at that.

"I think we understand each other," said Fishnet. "You go
make it happen."

The attorney, siding with caution, refused to assume any
acknowledgment of what Fishnet was talking about. He didn't

have to. Fishnet knew that the cash in the envelope he had slipped the defense attorney was enough for the lawyer to compromise whoever he had to.

15

Fishnet's Trouble

DENNIS BUMPER MADE CAUTION A priority as he began to feel the noose tightening around his neck. So not to be seen he avoided the windows in the apartment he was hiding out in. When speaking to his friend Sammy Angelo the two conversed in a low voice in order to prevent someone from overhearing them from the hall.

"I think that things might have settled down, Dennis," said Sammy. "Maybe I'll go to a store. It'll give me a chance to see if there are any cops around."

"No, Sammy, don't do that. Let's give it a little more time. Let's leave here once we make arrangements with Father Billy."

"Do you want me to call him?"

"No, not yet, let's wait a little longer." Bumper picked up on the frown projected by his friend. "Don't be mad at me, Sammy. I just want to be careful. In another week we'll reach out to Father Billy."

"I'm not angry, Dennis," said Sammy, not wanting to do anything that would set his disturbed friend off. "You can stay here for as long as you want."

At this juncture Sammy was beginning to wonder how much trouble he was going to be in with the law. When finally called to task by the authorities, he intended to defend his harboring

Bumper by claiming that he acted out of duress. It seemed plausible to him that anyone would naturally fear for his life when around a killing machine like Bumper.

* * *

FISHNET MILLIGAN WAS DETERMINED to conceal his true feelings. With his attorney at his side, he braced himself as he entered the police station. Surrendering to waiting detectives was embarrassing for sure, but he'd take whatever was being thrown at him with his chin up. He was intent on keeping his wounds invisible.

"Buck up," whispered Fishnet's legal representative, who knew better. "It'll be okay."

"Don't worry about me," said Fishnet with his typical bravado. "Nobody is getting the satisfaction of seeing me sweat."

Fishnet walked into the detective squad room with his head held high. He immediately scanned the room in search of a familiar face. Glad at not recognizing anyone, he turned his attention to the working conditions.

Nothing much had changed since his days in the squad. The beat-up desks were shared by detectives who worked opposite shifts from each other. The wastepaper baskets were close to overflowing, candy bar wrappers could be found on the floor, and blistering paint was visible overhead. The walls were marked with dirt spots and required a fresh coat of paint. Areas of the floor were in need of repair.

"What a dump," Fishnet declared to his attorney out of the side of his mouth. He had gotten used to the finer things.

The attorney didn't respond. Instead, he announced his identity and asked for the detective that his client was scheduled to surrender to. After being summoned by a coworker, the detective in question emerged from another room with Markie and Von Hess. Seeing his nemesis caused Fishnet to wince.

"I might have known," said the former detective, looking directly at Markie.

Fishnet locked eyes with the sergeant in a way that made the hostility between the men obvious. The former detective stood defiantly tall with his shoulders pulled back. *The son of a bitch is probably getting off in his drawers*, thought Fishnet, who was thinking of Markie.

After being printed, Fishnet was photographed. This put him in closer proximity to the desk where Markie and Von Hess were stationed. The former detective couldn't resist making a snide comment.

"So you finally got around to framing me," accused Fishnet, addressing Markie. "Well, enjoy yourself while you can, because I'm gonna beat this phony rap you cooked up."

Fishnet's macho bluster was a defense mechanism to conceal his actual concern over facing the possibility of long-term incarceration. Fishnet's attorney, looking to avoid a scene, intervened.

"Let's do our talking in court," announced the lawyer curtly.

At the subsequent arraignment, Fishnet's attorney put forth a convincing argument as to why his client should be released on bail. The mouthpiece cited Fishnet's years of dedicated service as a member of the police force. He emphasized how his client had been seriously wounded in a gunfight while attempting to apprehend a notorious gangster. The lawyer made mention that his client was an affluent man with roots to the community. He cited this as proof that Fishnet was no flight risk. In the end, the judge granted the defendant reasonable bail without conditions.

Fishnet's lawyer had no intention of enlightening Fishnet as to how, through an intermediary, he was able to pass cash to the judge. The attorney preferred that all favorable results be attributable to his courtroom brilliance, rather than corrupt tactics.

Trouble surfaced for the defense when the judge assigned to the case was involved in a vehicle accident. The serious physical injuries he sustained prevented him from continuing his duties. As a result, a new judge was assigned to preside over Fishnet's murder trial. The installation of the new judge, one with unflappable integrity, was a setback that put the case's outcome in question.

* * *

FISHNET SAT IN THE COURTROOM stone-faced. Hard as he tried, he couldn't cloak the bitterness within him. His face tensed with anger as the prosecutor cast him as evil incarnate during her opening statement to the jury. Fishnet called upon the one reliable resource capable of blocking out the verbal attack. He transported himself to his world of fantasy, this time seeing himself as an avenger.

Fishnet's mental fantasy saw him kidnap both the ADA and No Tax Johnny Layton. He held them captive on a secluded Long Island beach with their hands and feet bound. He then buried them up to their necks so all that could be seen was two heads sticking up from the moist sand a few feet from the ocean.

Fishnet positioned the doomed pair a yard apart so they could communicate with each other as they faced the incoming tide as it drew closer to them. The defendant sat at the defense table with a silly smile on his face as he envisioned two round heads being swallowing up by the seawater. Strangely, Markie didn't figure in Fishnet's wild fantasy.

When Fishnet returned to reality, he turned his attention to those sitting on the jury. It was not an encouraging sight. To a person, those in the jury box were sitting up straight and paying close attention
to what the ADA was saying to them. Fishnet interpreted that as a bad sign.

"I ain't got a chance in hell with this crew," the defendant said in a very low voice.

"Shhhh," whispered the defendant's attorney as he elbowed his client.

Fishnet next commenced his analysis of the judge, who seemed to be nodding approvingly as the ADA addressed the jury. This observation caused the defendant's stomach to start giving him trouble. *It's hopeless,* Fishnet thought, shaking his head pessimistically.

"Hey, what the hell did you do to me over here?" the defendant asked, turning to his attorney.

"Shhhh," replied the lawyer, again hushing his client.

The defense attorney then pushed a yellow legal pad and pen across the table to the defendant, suggesting that Fishnet take notes. He hoped that would quiet his client. Fishnet took the pen and began to doodle.

When the defender noticed that his client had drawn a disgusting picture involving the judge and the ADA, he quickly took the yellow legal pad from him. He then hurried to place the offensive material in his briefcase before others saw it.

Fishnet knew that he had to take matters into his own hands in order to save himself. With an offensive to launch, Fishnet began having some really dastardly thoughts.

"Are you okay?" asked the defense lawyer.

"I'm fine," replied Fishnet. Let me have that pad back."

"Try to keep it decent this time," he instructed.

Out of the corner of his eye the attorney monitored what Fishnet was putting on paper. He wasn't writing words. Instead, he again began drawing. This time he sketched an old man with a bent neck stepping off a cloud, only to fall into a bed of high flames within what could only be interpreted as the depths of hell. The lawyer didn't want to know the significance of the sketch.

"It'll soon be our turn to address the jury," announced the lawyer.

"Okay," said Fishnet in a way that seemed devoid of caring. The defendant's nonchalance gave his lawyer an inkling that his client was up to something.

"Hang in there. Once I get a crack at this jury things won't seem so grim."

Fishnet didn't respond to his lawyer's comment. All the attorney could do at this juncture was wonder what was going on in his client's mind. He had no idea as to the depths of Fishnet's treachery. The cool facade of the defendant was that of a man planning to embark on a path that would leave nothing to chance in the courtroom.

* * *

FISHNET ENDEAVORED TO ASCERTAIN one thing before parting ways with his lawyer after court. He wanted to confirm that without No Tax Johnny Layton in the equation, the case against him would collapse. After some discussion, the defendant received the answer he was looking for.

"Let's face it; it looks like I don't have a shot with these jurors," Fishnet stated to his attorney once outside the courthouse. "And this judge we got ain't about to help us, right?"

"Don't be so pessimistic; there is always a chance," replied the lawyer. "Remember, we only need one juror to see our side."

"Yeah, well, it's my neck, not yours. Without the right judge playing ball, things are iffy." Fishnet's attorney shrugged. He couldn't dispute the point.

"At least you're out on bail, so try and enjoy the weekend," finally replied the lawyer, attempting to put a positive spin on things. "As for me, I'll be working on fine-tuning your defense," added the attorney.

"The old man, No Tax, he's our big problem, right?"

"Yes, he's their key witness. His credibility will determine how much trouble we have."

"It kills me how an old prick like that, a degenerate gambler and liar his whole life, can be counted on to tell the truth," said Fishnet with disgust.

"I intend to tear him apart on the stand. But, to be upfront with you, there is one major concern with that approach."

"What's that?"

"Some of those jurors might sympathize with a sickly senior citizen if I get too tough."

"But he's the only guy saying I was involved in the homicide, right?"

"Yes. The prosecution is going to use him to link you to Butterworth's death."

"You know that for sure?"

"Yes. I have a good source in the DA's office."

"Well, that old prick would lie about his mother for a buck," declared Fishnet. "Ask your good source what they're paying No Tax to get him to say what they want to hear. I bet they're hiding him, right?"

"No, it's my understanding that he's home. He's supposed to be a very sick man."

"Do you think they got a guard babysitting him?"

"I have no idea."

"Find that out from your snitch."

The defense lawyer ignored the request. "There is another witness the prosecution has," he said, changing topics.

"And who is that?"

"I don't know his identity yet, but apparently this witness can testify that he was paid to make up bogus credentials in the name of the murder victim."

"So what happens if the old man cashes in his chips?"

"That's the best thing that could happen. If he were to go before he gets to take the witness stand, your troubles would be over."

"That's just what I was figuring."

"I think it comes down to how much of a gambler you are."

"I ain't," replied Fishnet.

"Then you might want to seriously consider trying to make a deal."

"What kind of a deal?"

"You plead guilty in return for a reduced sentence."

"Yeah, well, you can forget about that," stated Fishnet firmly. "Let's just wait and see. You never know what can happen."

"Be aware of one thing," warned the lawyer. "If you wait, and if the prosecution starts to gain traction, the less generous their offer will be. You need to consider that."

"Yeah, I get it. Let me think about this over the weekend."

"Okay."

"And do me a favor; go find out right now if the old man has a baby sitter keeping an eye on him."

"Is that important?"

"I just want to know for my own edification."

"I'll find out, but I wouldn't get any ideas about approaching him with money to alter his testimony. That could backfire on you big time."

"I'd never do such a thing," assured Fishnet with a straight face.

Once his attorney ascertained that No Tax was living alone in his apartment without protection, Fishnet was cheered. His good spirits carried over to the koi that swam happily in his townhouse backyard pond. Once home he tossed the little pellets of fish food into the pond, the former detective spoke to his little friends in a melodious voice that was soothing.

"Pretty soon you folks are going to have company," said the former detective. He was planning to purchase another koi to add to the ranks. The new addition was going to be named after No Tax.

When done in the backyard, Fishnet went inside the house to map out a plan to kill the prosecution's main witness against him. He reconciled this homicidal intention by looking at the murder as a necessary step in order to maintain his liberty. In time, he came to justify murdering No Tax by referring to the intended slaying as the mercy killing of a sick old man.

* * *

MARKIE AND VON HESS HAD FOUND TIME to stop by the court for a few minutes before the session broke for the weekend. The detectives entered the courtroom unnoticed, slipping into the last row of seating directly behind the defense table. From his vantage point Markie noticed, for the first time, how pronounced Fishnet's ears were.

Although aware of Fishnet's uncanny facial resemblance to the late actor Clark Gable, Markie never picked up on this particular similarity. Finding Fishnet's ears to be something of interest, he pointed this out to Von Hess.

"Hey, Ollie, did you ever notice Fishnet's big ears?" whispered Markie. "The guy could fly away with those flappers."

Von Hess smiled at the remark. "He's got his hair cut short now, Sarge. That's probably why they're so noticeable."

Markie next turned his attention to the judge, a woman of middle age who spoke as would someone with a higher education. Her sentences were brief, direct, and authoritative. Markie sized her up as the no-nonsense type with the flexibility of steel. These attributes met with the sergeant's satisfaction because it meant that Fishnet was unlikely to receive any breaks.

The jurors also met with Markie's approval. Satisfied that things were going well, the team from headquarters departed the courtroom a short time after arriving. By the time they were outside, it was clear to Von Hess that his boss was in exceedingly high spirits.

"I'm feeling pretty good about this, Ollie," said the sergeant. "Since we're off tomorrow, how about we stop off for a drink after work?"

"Where were you thinking of going?"

"I'm thinking of calling up my girl and asking her to meet me at Fitzie's. Why don't you come along?"

"You've gotten pretty cozy with this new girlfriend, haven't you?"

"Yeah, so far we've been getting along. Are you up for Fitzie's?"

"I'll have to pass, Sarge; three's a crowd."

The real reason Von Hess declined the offer was that he already had plans. He intended to nose around Sunset Park in order to get a line on the questionable priest who had No Tax Johnny Layton cash his winning OTB ticket.

Before leaving work, Von Hess telephoned his wife to let her know that he wouldn't be home at the usual time. Mrs. Von Hess was used to her husband's erratic hours, so there was no protest. "Where are you going?" she asked.

"I'm just stopping off for a drink."

"Are you going with Al? You know how I feel about that. He's a single man . . ."

"Relax, will ya. I'm not going bouncing with the sergeant. I have to check something out. Don't worry; I'll be home early."

"So where are you going?"

"The O'Hara and Mercato Lounge; it's a gin mill in Sunset Park."

"Why there?"

"Remember that priest I told you about?" Von Hess was referring to Father Billy, the man No Tax voiced suspicion of.

"Yes . . ."

"I'm going there because I want to see what I can find out. It's a popular neighborhood joint."

"Oh, I thought you forgot all about that."

"There is no way I can do that."

"I really don't see why you need to get involved."

"Hey, can I just sit on my hands and let people get away with making a monkey out of the church?"

"No, I suppose you can't. It's not in your makeup. Just be careful . . . and don't forget to come home."

144

16
A Big Surprise

SAMMY ANGELO WENT DOWNSTAIRS in the early morning hours to check Bumper's mailbox. Attired in his pajamas and slippers, he walked on his tiptoes so as not to draw attention to himself. Sammy was at the mailboxes when the building super, an early riser, exited his first-floor apartment, carrying trash to be put out. He couldn't help but see that Sammy had just opened Bumper's mailbox. The super pretended not to notice.

"Hey, Sammy, I thought I was the only guy who got up this early," said the super in a matter-of-fact way.

"I couldn't sleep," replied the tenant.

"I thought you might be away. I haven't seen you lately."

"I'm home. I haven't been feeling well."

"Sorry to hear that. Let me know if you need anything," said the super as he exited the building with the trash.

Sammy quickly emptied Dennis Bumper's mailbox before heading back to his upper-floor apartment. Once inside, he placed his friend's mail on the kitchen table and looked through his own. Seeing nothing important, he went to the refrigerator for something to drink. After pouring himself a glass of orange juice, he stepped into the living room to look in on Bumper, who was sleeping soundly on the couch.

After letting out a deep sigh, Sammy finished his juice and retired to his bedroom. When he awoke several hours later, he found Bumper having coffee at the kitchen table.

"Good morning, Sammy," said Bumper. "Did you sleep well?"

"Yeah, I slept fine," replied Sammy, not being exactly truthful. He hadn't been sleeping well since he began harboring Bumper. "You got mail, Dennis."

"I saw it. It's from The Meow Mission. They're looking for a donation. I usually send them a couple of bucks."

"I never heard of them . . ."

"They take care of stray cats."

Sammy nodded without responding. He was wondering if there was a mission to take care of stray killers like his friend.

* * *

OVER A DOZEN HANDGUNS WERE amassed by Fishnet throughout his law enforcement career. Of those, just two .38 caliber revolvers were legally registered, the service gun he carried when he was on patrol and his off-duty snub-nose detective special. The other weapons in his possession were taken off criminals during his police career.

When on the force, if Fishnet came across an illegally carried weapon he fancied, he'd pocket it and let the lawbreaker go. Over time, his arsenal came to include revolvers, automatics, a German Luger, and even a derringer. Fishnet's collection wasn't restricted to guns. He also accumulated a number of brass knuckles, switchblades, and other items designed for violence.

Since the former detective lived alone, the concern of being victimized via a home invasion was always in the back of his mind. Never wanting to be caught unprepared, he put himself at ease by hiding guns throughout his house. A gun could be found in his bathrooms secreted within one of several towels stored on a shelf. Another was placed inside an old toolbox in

146

the cellar. The living room, kitchen, spare bedrooms, and so on were all home to a readily available, loaded firearm.

The off-duty detective special was the weapon Fishnet regularly carried on his person after retiring from the force. His other legal gun, the service revolver, was kept in the top drawer of the end table next to his bed. Knowing that these two weapons could be traced back to him, he dismissed them as being appropriate for the dastardly deed he had in mind. In considering his authorized firearms, a thought came to him: *I wonder if they're gonna get around to making me surrender these guns because I got pinched?* He was unsure of the current police procedure under such circumstances. *I guess I'll just have to wait and see.*

Fishnet eventually decided not to use a gun to kill No Tax. He felt that the noise created by a firearm might increase his chances of getting caught. After a review of his weapons collection, he whittled down his options to a dagger and a crack hammer. He opted to go with the dagger, finding bludgeoning to be too messy a proposition.

Once armed with the dagger, Fishnet drove to the Brooklyn off-track betting parlor in a quest to find his prey. Since the octogenarian was known to be a degenerate gambler, the ex-detective was hoping that, sick or not, No Tax couldn't avoid the temptation to place a bet.

Fishnet parked his car near the gambling den and waited in the hope of spotting his man. After two hours, Fishnet got tired of waiting. Contemplating what to do, he decided that it would be too risky to ask a police resource for help in ascertaining the home address of his intended victim. Having someone in the department, active or inactive, capable of linking him to No Tax would be reckless. This left the former detective to his own resources.

Fortune came when Fishnet recognized a low-level junkie drug dealer exit the OTB parlor. When on the force, Fishnet would routinely shake down the thirty-five-year-old doper when funds were low.

As Fishnet approached, the addict quickly tried to walk off in the opposite direction to avoid him. The druggie only halted when Fishnet pulled him back by his collar. Unaware that Fishnet was no longer on the force, the junkie offered no complaint to such rough treatment. His holding several decks of heroin in his pocket was the reason for his acceptance of being manhandled.

"Hey, man, where are you running to?" asked Fishnet. "I want to talk to you."

"Look, business is real bad today, Detective," whined the drug-dealing addict.

"Relax, we're good. I just need a favor," said Fishnet calmly.

"You want a favor from me?"

"Yeah, that's all. I'm looking to cash a winning ticket. Have you seen the old guy with the messed-up neck around today?"

"Nah, he ain't been around."

"You know who I mean, right?"

"Yeah, I know—the old man. I ain't been seeing him around lately."

"Do you know where his crib is?"

The addict shrugged as he responded. "Uhhh . . . I dunno, man," he said.

By looking away and avoiding eye contact, the addict gave himself away. Fishnet knew he was holding out. Fishnet produced a one hundred dollar bill and held it up to the junkie's face.

"You see this C-note? It has your name on it," advised the ex-detective, "if you tell me where No Tax lives." The answer came without hesitation.

"He lives on Pacific Street between Smith and Bond."

"C'mon, let's take a ride. I want you to show me."

"I dunno, man . . ."

"C'mon let's go," ordered Fishnet firmly, not taking no for an answer. The promise of an additional hundred removed all resistance.

* * *

THE AILING NO TAX SPENT his time in his rent-controlled apartment, waiting to die. When he wasn't hoping to drift off peacefully in his sleep, he was watching television. His physical decline prevented him from doing much else. Aside from his neck and cancer issues, the senior citizen now suffered from an aching lower back that compelled him to sleep in a recliner. The one good thing about this was that, when positioned all the way back, the tilted chair made watching television easier.

Then there were the thigh pains he had to contend with. Walking had become so difficult that No Tax only left the recliner when he had to. The stinging aches coming from his upper legs demanded that he stay off his feet whenever possible. The combination of his ailments left No Tax hesitant to venture beyond the confines of his apartment.

While still a defendant in the drug case, the prosecutor's office decided to put off prosecuting the matter for as long as possible. The hope was that No Tax would live long enough to testify against Fishnet and expire before having to face justice in his own case.

Day in and day out, No Tax lounged around his apartment in a white terrycloth bathrobe. Beneath his robe he wore red-and-black flannel pajamas. Thick, white socks were worn to keep his feet warm. When removed, the stench from his bare feet was substantial. As a result, he rarely took his feet out of the socks and slippers he wore.

Since shaving and showering had become a chore for No Tax, they became a part of his routine that he tended to neglect. Hygienically speaking, this left the senior citizen with a lot to be desired.

The run-down building No Tax lived in was mostly inhabited by people with problems. Some had criminal pasts, some had psychiatric issues, and others were substance abusers. Practically all were economically challenged. It was an environment that kept No Tax on the alert, day and night. Sickness was one thing, but the possibility of facing a violent end via a home invasion was quite another.

In answer to his safety concerns, the octogenarian slept with the television on. In fact, it was on twenty-four hours a day. The volume was set high so the noise emanating from the old black-and-white set would send a message to outsiders that someone was home in the apartment. The television also served as a form of company for No Tax, who was always armed. He kept a loaded Saturday night special in the pocket of the bathrobe he never took off, even when sleeping.

Taking things day by day, No Tax managed to cope with his unfortunate situation. He found some comfort in Markie's promise to arrange for a headstone and walking panthers to patrol his gravesite. At least that was something.

* * *

FISHNET DECIDED THAT AN AFTER-MIDNIGHT intrusion into the apartment of No Tax would work best. In preparation for the homicide he intended to commit, the ex-law enforcement officer went shopping. He spent Saturday morning at a costume store looking for the few things he needed to alter his appearance. He purchased putty to give himself a bulbous nose. He thought wearing a black eye patch and a mustache would be a nice touch, so he bought those as well. Fishnet then moved on to pick up a cheap, black, double-breasted peacoat and black skull cap from a thrift shop.

Before emerging from his townhouse at midnight, the former detective had transformed himself into something akin to a pirate. Satisfied with the look, Fishnet proceeded to the Brooklyn residence of No Tax. He wasn't surprised to find the front door to the seedy building open. After checking the mailboxes, he ascertained the apartment number of his intended victim.

The ex-detective slowly crept up the stairs. Due to the hour, he didn't come into contact with anyone in the building. *So far, so good*, thought the intruder as he made his way to the apartment.

Hearing voices coming from the apartment of No Tax gave Fishnet pause. He placed his ear to the door, trying to ascertain what was being said. He became sure that the voices stemmed from either a radio or television. Fishnet ever so gently tried the apartment door. Finding it locked, he reached into his coat pocket for his lock picks.

No Tax, a light sleeper, was alerted by the sound of someone tampering with the door lock. He inched up in his recliner while removing the Saturday night special from the pocket of his bathrobe. At the ready, No Tax waited in silence with his gun trained at the front door.

Fishnet opened the door a crack before entering. The television screen provided a grayish blue light that lit the apartment. Assuming that No Tax was fast asleep, Fishnet tiptoed in. After carefully closing the door behind him, the assassin produced his dagger. Once No Tax heard approaching footsteps he fired his first round.

The old man's shaking hand caused the bullet to find a home in the wall to the right of Fishnet's shoulder. The noise of the blast threw Fishnet into a panic. Fearing for his life, he bolted toward the front door to flee the apartment. The quivering hand of No Tax discharged a second round that made its way through the smoke caused by the first gunshot. This last bullet also failed to hit its target. Far off the mark, the round struck the hanging picture of the octogenarian's late mother. The sound of the second blast lit such a fire under Fishnet that it caused him to fall several steps down the stairs in his haste to get away. Surprisingly, he was unhurt as a result of the tumble.

When he reached the street, Fishnet glanced at the upper windows of the building he had exited. Satisfied that there wasn't a sniper positioned at a window, he walked briskly around the corner to his parked car. On the drive home Fishnet disposed of his disguise items by dropping them out of the car window as he drove.

By the time he got home, Fishnet felt physically drained. Before turning in, he made himself a stiff drink to ease his mind. The ex-detective found himself with no choice other than to take a risk and make a second attempt on the life of the witness slated to testify against him. By hook or by crook, No Tax Johnny Layton had to die. It seemed like the only way for Fishnet to remain a free man.

17

Rum Loosens the Tongue

WHILE MARKIE'S MAIN INTEREST rested in the prosecution of Fishnet, Detective Von Hess was drawn to something of an equally personal nature. Although Von Hess was far from being a religious fanatic, he was protective of his faith. On the surface it would seem that he was in tune with the basics. He dutifully recognized church weddings as the only legitimate way to enter into matrimony. He attended Mass and observed holy days of obligation when possible. He believed only those in the state of grace were entitled to receive communion. Since he drew the line at going to confession, it was years since the detective made the trip to the altar to partake in the body and blood offering.

Having been educated in the parochial school system, Von Hess endeavored to live his life adhering to the Ten Commandments. He figured that by observing the religious precepts he'd warrant a place in heaven, while those who failed to measure up to the standard were doing so at their own peril.

The thought of someone passing himself off as a priest for questionable purposes was distasteful to Von Hess. For this reason the suspected priest impersonator, as described by No Tax Johnny Layton, needed to be investigated.

Von Hess commenced his probe on his off time. Recognizing the value of alcohol when it came to loosening lips, Von Hess began sniffing around the Sunset Park watering holes. He made headway at his first stop, the O'Hara & Mercato Lounge, an establishment that catered to a predominately blue-collar clientele.

The lounge was a popular gathering place that boasted of having the finest assortment of intoxicants. The lively songs blasting from the jukebox most evenings was a sure-fire way to draw in those passing by on the street. An added attraction was the Friday night 50-50 drawing, which guaranteed the happiness of some lucky customer.

By the time Von Hess arrived, the daytime crowd was reduced to a just a few elderly leftovers. These were primarily folks who had no one at home waiting for them. An atmospheric change came when the bar transitioned to younger men and women who stopped in after work. The presence of a younger crowd jazzed things up considerably.

Von Hess, who always stood erect with his shoulders back, had assumed a position mid-bar. The trench-coat-wearing veteran detective stood out for his military-like appearance. The bartender immediately took notice of the stranger, pegging him to be the gumshoe he was. The only question in the mind of the bartender was *NYPD or a fed?*

Von Hess was acknowledged with a nod by the stout man tending bar. His wrinkled brow, ruddy complexion, and large circles under his eyes gave him a tired look. These characteristics were indicators of a lack of sleep, overwork, or excessive drinking. Most likely it was a combination of all three.

"What'll it be?"

"Gin and tonic," said Von Hess.

After mixing the drink, the bartender placed it in front of the newcomer. "Do you work in the precinct?" he asked, looking to ascertain his customer's employment status.

"No," replied Von Hess. He wasn't surprised at the question; he knew he looked like a cop.

"Do you live in the area?"

"No."

"Then what brings you in here?"

"What, am I taking up too much room?"

"Oh, no," said the bartender, backing up. "I was just curious, that's all. All the cops from the precinct come in here. Vets and the boys in blue are always welcome to stop by."

Von Hess noted the American Flag that hung prominently behind the bar. "I can see that," he said, pointing to the flag. The detective, whose trench coat was unbuttoned, made his middle available for viewing when he pointed.

"You were a Marine?" asked the bartender, spotting the detective's Marine belt buckle.

"I was. How did you figure that out?"

"Your belt buckle jumped out at me," explained the bartender. "And your detective ring didn't exactly make you a mystery."

"You don't miss much, do you?"

"I like to know my customers. Are you here for a drink or are you in here on business?"

"I'm trying to get a line on someone."

"Maybe I can help you. Who are you looking for?"

"I'm not really looking for anyone. I'm just attempting to verify something. Have you ever heard of a priest called Father Billy?"

"Yeah, I think I heard the name someplace," said the bartender. "Let me check with some of the old- timers. These guys in the late innings are all church regulars. They figure it'll get them in good with the man upstairs."

After a few minutes the bartender returned. "See that old guy sitting at the end of the bar with the hook nose? He's your man. Everybody calls him Captain."

"He knows Father Billy?"

"That he does, and just so you know, he's no fan."

"Did he say why?"

"Nah, I try not to get into any negative shit with customers."

"I hear you. Do me a favor and send him a drink on me."

After the bartender delivered the drink, he returned to Von Hess. "The Captain said to tell you thanks. He wants to know why you bought him a drink," advised the bartender, laughing.

"What's so funny?

"The Captain thought you were trying to pick him up."

"He did?"

"Yeah, that's pretty funny. Anyway, I spoke to him, so you can go over and talk to him. He's expecting you."

Von Hess left his station to go over to where the Captain was seated at the bar.

"Thanks for the drink, mate," said the Captain. "The bartender said you were a detective."

"That's right, I am."

"He said you're asking about Father Billy. Is that right?"

Von Hess nodded. "What can you tell me about him?"

"You came to the right guy, Detective. I can tell you plenty. What did you say your name was?"

"Von Hess."

"Let's sit in the corner back there where we can talk privately, Von Hess. As long as you're buying, we have a lot to talk about."

Once they were seated at a table, the Captain began to share with Von Hess what he knew about Father Billy.

"It's like this," began the Captain, "Father Billy showed up at the parish one day out of nowhere. Then all of sudden, bingo, like a pirate he boards ship and takes over from the old priest we got."

"What happened to the old priest?"

"He's still around, but he's on the back burner cooling down," said The Captain, gulping down his drink. He then pushed his glass forward toward Von Hess, indicating he wanted a refill.

"What kind of drink is that?"

"I'm having rum, neat."

After picking up a round at the bar, Von Hess returned to the table. "Cheers," he said, placing the double rum in front of The Captain. "Tell me more about Father Billy."

"I'm convinced the guy ain't a-hundred percent on the level. He's got a way of worming himself in with people and then taking advantage."

"Can you give me an example?"

"Yeah, for instance take my landlord, the Perez sisters. They're real nice people. Father Billy and that woman he's in cahoots with got them both buffaloed good."

"You're losing me . . . what woman?"

"Father Billy's got a young wench who works at the rectory with him. They're taking advantage of the old people. They turned my landlord against me."

"Do you know if Father Billy gambles?" asked Von Hess, thinking of the No Tax connection.

"I can't say one way or the other," advised the Captain, adding, "I did see him holding a wad of cash that could choke a horse. My guess is he got it from the sisters."

"When was that?"

"I saw him with the cash when he paid off the roofer who fixed the roof on my landlord's house."

"Where was the landlord?"

"I think they were out someplace."

"Doesn't your landlord live in the house?"

"Both sisters live in the house. You gotta understand, these two sisters are naïve. They come from money, so they've been sheltered their whole lives."

"Would you say that the sisters are elderly?"

"They ain't too bad as far as being old. They just can't see through these slippery bastards. It wouldn't surprise me if the son of a bitch is no priest at all."

"What makes you suspect that?" asked Von Hess,

The Captain went into detail about his suspicions of the Perez sisters having fallen under the control of Father Billy and Gloria. He also explained his being shaken down by Gloria. The story conveyed was enough to convince Von Hess there was nefarious activity afoot.

"So believe what I'm telling you. Those two over in that church ain't any good."

157

"The woman working with Father Billy, what's her name?" asked Von Hess.

"Gloria. I don't know her last name."

"Did they ever try to get close to you?"

"Not in a pig's eye!" replied the Captain with bitterness. "They know they can't sucker me. Besides, I ain't got a pot to piss in. It's the wealthy people like the Perez sisters they go after."

"But you said you were paying Gloria money . . ."

"Yeah, well, she got me over a barrel on that. I'll figure out how to fix that once I get close to Millie again."

"Millie is one of the Perez sisters?"

"Yeah, we used to be real tight, if you get my drift."

"The sisters have money?"

"Are you kidding? The Perez sisters are filthy rich."

"Tell me again about Gloria wanting money from you."

"She talked the sisters into raising my rent. Now I have to pay Gloria cash to keep the rent increase from happening."

"You pay in check or cash?"

"No more checks. I gotta give the rent money to Gloria in cash, plus something for her. Can you imagine? That Gloria is collecting the rent for the Perez sisters now. I don't know what kind of deal they got going with that."

"And you saw the priest with a wad of cash paying off a roofer?"

"Yeah, he had enough on him to paper a wall."

"Do you know what roofing company?"

"I do. Their truck had white with gold lettering on the side that said, 'Berry Roofing Company'."

After gathering all he needed to know, the detective rose from his chair to buy a final drink for the Captain. He returned to the table with a double straight rum.

"Thanks, Captain, you've been a big help. Here, take my card. If you notice anything else fishy, give me a call."

"What are you gonna do?"

"I intend to talk with the Perez sisters."

"Do me a favor, will ya, and keep my name out of it. I'm still on Millie's shit list."

"No problem. We never spoke."

* * *

VON HESS WANTED TO BE SURE THAT Father Billy and Gloria were engaged in criminal behavior before contacting the detectives working out of the Sunset Park Precinct. The veteran detective didn't even bring Markie into his confidence at this early stage.

On his day off, Von Hess went to the roofing company that did the work on the Perez house. The firm, located in Maspeth, Queens, operated out of a small storefront office. Since there were no company trucks to be seen in the area, Von Hess correctly assumed that the Berry Roofing Company was a mom-and-pop business.

Upon entering the storefront, the detective was greeted by a middle-aged woman who seemed to be the only office worker. Seated behind her desk, from the waist up she appeared to be a robust woman. She projected the confident look of someone of high status within the company. The glasses she wore low on her nose added to the look.

Von Hess figured her to be the owner of the business or, perhaps, a relative of the owner. A glance at her desktop confirmed his suspicion. A nameplate in bold lettering read as follows:

ELOISE NATALIE BERRY, CEO

"May, I help you?" Ms. Berry asked. "I'm a detective from police headquarters, Ma'am," stated Von Hess, producing his gold shield. "Can I have a minute of your time?"

"Oh!" said the woman, startled at the presence of a detective. "Is there something wrong?"

"Everything is fine, Ma'am. Are you in charge here?"

"Yes, I'm Eloise Berry. I'm the owner."

Seeing the concern on her face, Von Hess again assured her again that everything was fine. "I'm just here to verify something, Ma'am."

Von Hess explained, in part, what his purpose was. He then asked to see the invoice for the work performed at the Sunset Park residence of the Perez sisters. Unable to find the invoice in question, Ms. Berry grew flustered.

"I have no record of such work, Detective. You probably have the wrong company."

"No, I have the right company, Ma'am," said Von Hess. "You have a company truck with your name printed on the side in gold letters, right?"

"Well, yes."

"How many trucks do you have?"

"We just have one."

"Who performs the work?"

"My husband and a couple of helpers go out on the jobs."

"Maybe your husband forgot to turn in the invoice."

"I suppose that's possible, but it's unlikely."

"Where is your husband now?"

"He's out looking at a job."

"See if you can get him on the phone. I'd like to talk to him."

"He never answers his cell phone when he's working."

"Where is the job?"

"I don't exactly know. He just told me this morning that he was going to Steinway Street in Astoria to give someone an estimate. Do you have a card? I'll have him call you."

"I'll come back later, Ma'am."

After leaving Berry Roofing, Von Hess proceeded to Steinway Street in the belief that he stood a good chance of spotting the company truck. Fortunate in locating the vehicle, he parked his car and sought out Mr. Berry for questioning.

Berry was taken aback by a detective approaching him. At first he failed to acknowledge that he performed the roof repairs in Sunset Park because he feared there might be tax implications by admitting that he accepted a cash payment.

"Look, Mr. Berry, I already know you were there," said Von Hess. "I have a witness that can attest to that. Don't be worried. You have no problem with the law."

"Well, er . . . wait a second. I do seem to remember doing some work there now."

"Who did you deal with?"

"I dealt with a priest who was representing the property owner."

"He paid the freight in cash?"

"Look, Detective, I'm just a small business. I don't want any trouble. I declare all the money I make on my taxes, only this time seeing it was a priest . . ."

"Relax, I have no interest in any of that, Mr. Berry," advised Von Hess. "I'm not obligated to tell the IRS anything, so what you tell me in that regard stays between us." Berry was relieved to hear this.

"Okay, with that settled, what do you want to know?"

"What kind of work did you perform at the Perez house?"

"We made repairs to the roof."

"Was it a big job?"

"No, not at all. We just did some minor patchwork."

"Did you generate an invoice detailing the work you did?"

"No, I was paid in cash, so there was no invoice."

"Who paid you?"

"I already told you: I dealt with a priest. He paid the bill. For God's sake, you aren't going to drag him into anything are you?"

The investigator ignored the question. "How much were you paid?"

"I got five hundred bucks."

"Do you know if the priest had a lot of money on him?" asked Markie.

"As a matter of fact he did. How did you know that?"

"I have my sources. How much would you say he had on him?"

"My guess is about five or ten grand, maybe more. It was hard to tell."

"Maybe it would be a good idea for you to put that work you did on the books," advised Von Hess.

"I thought you said this was between us," said Berry, taking exception at what he perceived to be a double cross.

"It is as far as the IRS goes. But you may have to appear in court down the road as a witness. You might be asked to produce the invoice."

18

Street Justice

SAMMY ANGELO PRETENDED TO BE watching the news on television. Out of the corner of his eye he could see Dennis Bumper enter the bathroom. After a minute, he rose from his chair to place his ear to the bathroom door. Listening to the shower water running told him that his chance had arrived. He then nervously looked at the telephone that rested atop an end table in the living room.

Several times he reached for the phone, each time aborting his intention to telephone Father Billy. In Father Billy, Sammy would have a responsible partner in figuring out what to do with his disturbed friend. Sammy's lack of nerve to pick up the telephone cost him his chance.

He who hesitates is lost, thought Sammy, recalling the adage.

Fear of the psychopathic Bumper was too much for Sammy to overcome. There was no telling how Bumper would react if Sammy took it upon himself to reach out to Father Billy without his friend's approval. As frustrating as it was, Sammy resigned himself to waiting for Bumper to give him the green light to call the bogus priest. He hoped it wouldn't be too much longer.

When Bumper exited the bathroom, Sammy smiled, pretending that all was fine. Once Bumper was dressed, the two men sat at the kitchen table. Over coffee, Sammy broached the subject of calling Father Billy to arrange for Sammy's confession and subsequent surrender to the law.

"You know, we're supposed to be getting snow at some point over the next few days, Dennis."

"Are we really?"

"That's what they're saying on television. That might be a good thing."

"What do you mean?"

"If we get a lot of snow, I can't see the cops going out looking for anybody. That might be the right time for us to call Father Billy."

"You may be right about that, Sammy. Let's see what the weather looks like when the snow comes."

"Sure, Dennis, whatever you say."

Bumper's being amenable to calling Father Billy if the weather was foul gave Sammy hope. Bumper's best friend took out his rosary beads and began praying for a snowstorm.

* * *

ARLENE, THE ELDER PEREZ SISTER, was a true romantic who never gave up the hope of meeting someone to share her life with. Leaving nothing to chance, Arlene made it a habit to always try and look her best in the event of a chance encounter with a prospective suitor. Although not a yoga enthusiast like her sister, Arlene still managed to maintain an impressive figure for her age.

When the doorbell rang, Arlene peeked out the front window to see who was there. Seeing a man who was age appropriate caused her to quickly pin up her hair with a hairpin. She then flattened out with her hands whatever wrinkles existed in the clothes she wore. Arlene didn't have to worry about applying makeup. That was already a part of her daily routine.

"Ms. Perez?" asked Von Hess when Arlene came to the door.

Arlene's eyes widened as she looked up at the tall detective. *My goodness, what a handsome man,* she thought, *and all dressed up like a gentleman!*

"Yes, I'm Ms. Perez," answered Arlene.

"I'm Detective Oliver Von Hess, Ma'am," said the investigator, who wasted no time in producing his credentials.

"Do come inside, Detective," invited Arlene, smiling broadly.

As a man who knocked on many a door, Von Hess instantly sensed that Arlene was in the market for companionship. Since reaching a certain age, the well-preserved detective was finding himself in demand by women close to his own years.

"Thank you, Ma'am," said Von Hess.

"So what can I do for you? Ah, what did you say your name was, Detective?"

"Oliver Von Hess."

"Oliver Von Hess . . . what a lovely ring that has to it," said Arlene pleasantly, secretly thinking of how melodious the name Arlene Perez Von Hess sounded.

Arlene's smile reminded Von Hess of a comment Markie once made about women: "Ollie," he had said, "'when it comes to women, we're just a tool to scratch an itch. Once satisfied, we go back on the shelf until next time."

"I just need to have a word with you and your sister, Ma'am," said Von Hess. "Is she home?"

"No, I'm afraid not. Millie is out just now," replied Arlene. "Sit down and tell me what this is all about."

Von Hess took a seat in the living room. "Are you sure I can't get you something, Oliver . . . coffee, perhaps?"

"No, thank you."

Detective Von Hess went on to inform Arlene of what he knew about Father Billy and Gloria, his accomplice. Arlene listened attentively, temporarily forgetting her romantic inclinations.

"I can hardly believe this! Father Billy said the man put on a whole new roof . . . to the tune of, oh, I don't even want to say how much!"

"I'm sorry for that, Ms. Perez."

"Please, call me Arlene. Besides all the money my sister and I have given them, they're always asking to borrow our car."

"Do you have a record of how much you've given them?"

"Yes, we do. My sister and I are very careful about that. Our accountant insists that we keep accurate records for tax purposes."

"That's a very good thing to do."

"And listen to this, Oliver!" Arlene exclaimed as a thought came to her. "Father Billy suggested that we amend our will to help out the church and those less fortunate!"

"You didn't do that, did you?"

"No, but we were thinking of it. What do you propose we do, Oliver?" Her question came across as if she were an innocent damsel in distress.

"Don't worry," said Von Hess soothingly. "Let's start by you and your sister making a list of whatever those two got from you. Once there is an accounting of how much you are out, I'll go to the precinct and talk to one of the detectives."

As he spoke, a look of happiness began to form on Arlene's face. Von Hess had now graduated in Arlene's eyes to a knight in shining armor.

"Do you have a business card to give me, Oliver?" The detective wrote his cell number on the back of his business card and handed it to Arlene. "Oh, you're not from our precinct?" Arlene asked, noticing a Manhattan work address on the detective's card.

"No, Ma'am. I'm from headquarters." Von Hess then provided a brief explanation of how he came to be involved.

"But you'll come to the house if I really need you, won't you, Oliver?" asked Arlene hopefully.

"Sure I will."

"What do we do about Father Billy and Gloria in the meantime?"

"For now, just make up an excuse to avoid them. Don't worry, Ma'am. I'll be getting back to you. You start working on that list."

He's such a gentleman, thought Arlene wistfully after the detective left.

Since Von Hess was so accommodating, Arlene sensed that a romantic spark existed between the two. After sleeping on this notion, she became convinced of it.

VON HESS WAS LOOKING AHEAD to spending a quiet evening at home. There was nothing he relished more than being in his own house enjoying the company of his family. The little things people took for granted, such as a home-cooked meal and someone to share things with, were greatly appreciated by the detective.

It was understandable why Von Hess savored the tranquility of his home. The excitement of dealing with criminals had lost its appeal. It had become taxing. He tired of refereeing squabbles and having to put up with, at times, an irrational public. Yet he soldiered on, exercising the self-control necessary to do his job. What few knew was that behind the calm facade of Von Hess existed a savagery capable of equaling the violent behavior of those he was tasked with monitoring.

The detective was contentedly sitting on a love seat alongside his wife, watching a movie after dinner. At peace, he held his wife's hand as if they were a couple of young lovers. There was no need for conversation. The union of their hands said it all. Simple as it was, the assurance that they were there for each other made them both happy.

The movie selected by Mrs. Von Hess was a sentimental tearjerker. Von Hess hated this genre because it embarrassed him to be caught shedding a tear. His preference was something more macho; westerns, war movies, and hard hitting film noir being more to his liking. However, since it was his wife's turn to choose the flick, the detective went along with her selection without complaint.

The children who still lived at home were out and about doing things that young people do. This allowed Von Hess the quiet time to kick off his shoes and place his feet atop the footrest without distraction. Then his cell phone went off. He didn't recognize the exchange of the incoming call.

"Hello . . . Von Hess speaking."

"Oliver?"

"Who is this?" asked the detective, not recognizing the voice.

"It's me, Arlene Perez. You do remember me, don't you?"

"Oh, yes, sure I do Arlene," acknowledged the surprised detective. "What's up?"

"My sister and I have a problem, and we don't know what to do . . ."

"What's wrong?"

"Father Billy is coming over in an hour for the keys to our car. He wants to borrow it for the weekend!"

"Why didn't you tell him that you needed the car?"

"My sister spoke to him, not me. That's not all, Oliver. Millie said he asked her for another cash donation. It had something to do with the church needing some electrical work."

Von Hess turned to look at his wife. His shrug indicated to her that he had to entertain the caller. This imposition and the fact that the imposter was continuing his impersonation of a priest didn't sit well with the detective. Truth be told, it made his blood boil.

"What did your sister tell him?"

"Hold on a second. I'll put Millie on the line."

"Hello . . . Detective?" asked Millie.

"What happened, Millie?" asked Von Hess.

"Father Billy asked me for five thousand dollars!" declared Millie, who sounded quite upset.

"Five thousand bucks!" declared the detective. "You've got to be kidding."

"He's done this before, and we were stupid enough to give him the money. He knows we have money. The other one, Gloria . . . she even suggested that we keep lots of cash in the house in case of an emergency. They think we're Fort Knox."

"Unbelievable . . ."

"He's due to come over in an hour, and we don't know what to do. After what you told Arlene, we're afraid to deny them. They may be dangerous."

Arlene, seeing that Millie was getting upset, took the phone from her sister. "Oliver, can't you come over and help us deal with this?"

168

"I'm sorry, but I can't come over right now, Arlene."

"But you said . . ."

"I know what I said, but unfortunately I'm tied up right now. I intended to talk to the precinct detective squad for you on Monday morning."

"So what are we supposed to do?"

"I can't tell you what to do, Arlene. You folks need to decide that on your own. All I can say is that I wouldn't give them a damn thing."

"I don't think we feel safe denying them," advised Arlene. "We'll just have to give them the money and the car if you aren't coming over," she said. Her disappointment was evident in her voice.

"You can call 911 or simply don't answer the door," suggest Von Hess.

"I'm afraid they'll break down the door. As far as 911, we'd rather deal with you."

"If you do give them the money, add it to the list of what you already gave out."

"I will, Oliver." Arlene's voice sounded almost like that of a disappointed child.

"I'm sorry, Arlene, but let me ask you something: where do you keep your car?"

After providing the location of the garage, Arlene was asked the type of vehicle.

"We have a maroon Bentley."

"Pretty swanky," commented the detective.

"It's been in the family for years."

After hanging up the phone, Von Hess felt too restless to remain idle. His annoyance at someone impersonating a priest reached the point where he felt the need to do something. His deciding to leave his house caused him to grow ornery. The detective announced to his wife that he was going out. When Mrs. Von Hess questioned her husband as to where he was going, he responded, "To work."

Mrs. Von Hess was long accustomed to sudden changes. Their relationship, while exceedingly close, was one in which her husband's job was a priority. Mrs. Von Hess was conditioned not to ask too many questions. Since she trusted her husband implicitly, where he was going and what he was doing was considered his business. This was a formula that contributed to their marital longevity.

* * *

VON HESS HAD ENOUGH of the bogus priest. He was irritated to the point where he felt compelled to confront Father Billy personally. In preparation for the showdown, the off-duty detective went to his bedroom to remove his revolver from the dresser drawer. He also dug out a pair of handcuffs. He debated whether to take along his blackjack. He opted to do so in the event things got really nasty.

Von Hess donned a dark blue crewneck sweater over the black turtleneck he wore. The sweater aptly concealed the five-shot detective special that hung from his belt. He slipped the blackjack in the side pocket of his overcoat. Von Hess sported a gray tweed newsboy cap worn low on his brow to protect against the chill. Before leaving the house, he made sure to kiss his wife goodbye.

"No jacket and tie?" she asked after receiving a peck on the cheek.

"Not necessary," answered Von Hess. "I'm sorry to have to run out and leave you like this, but duty calls."

"Don't worry about me. I won't be alone for long. The kids will be coming home soon enough."

The detective drove to the garage where the Bentley was housed. He arrived in plenty of time to assume a surveillance position. The detective perked up after spotting a man carrying an overnight bag entering the garage. Beneath the man's coat the white collar of a priest was visible. It was obvious the man was Father Billy. Curious about the overnight bag, the detective decided to shadow his man to see what he was up to rather than immediately approach him.

Von Hess followed the Bentley to the parking lot of a nearby church. He waited patiently for the Bentley to emerge from the lot. When it did, Von Hess could see that the passenger seated next to the driver was a female. Von Hess correctly assumed the woman to be Gloria.

Von Hess tailed the Bentley to an apartment house in Toms River, New Jersey. After double parking in front of the building the subjects entered with their luggage. Von Hess noticed that the Bentley's engine was left running. He waited, intending to confront Father Billy after he returned to park his car.

The detective's plan was altered ten minutes later when the subjects emerged from the building together. The priest impersonator no longer wore his white collar. Under his black overcoat a bright red shirt could be seen.

Turning his attentions to the woman, Von Hess saw that she, too, had made an apparel adjustment. Gloria now wore a waist-length black leather coat with a fur collar. Her pants, believed to be jeans, were clearly tight-fitting.

Ross Holt had made the trip to the car with a walk that could best be described as a strut. That irked Von Hess, who saw his cockiness as the pinnacle of arrogance. The detective resumed his surveillance. He followed the pair into a high-end waterfront restaurant that featured live music.

"May I help you?" asked one of the restaurant staff, seeing that Von Hess was milling around the reception area.

"I'm just looking to see if a friend of mine is here."

"What's the name? I'll check the reservation list."

"Never mind, he's not here," fibbed Von Hess after spotting the subjects sitting at a table.

The pair seemed not to have a care in the world. This annoyed Von Hess. The detective returned to his vehicle and waited in an area that had a clear view of the Bentley. It was close to two hours later when the couple left the restaurant. By now the detective's patience had run thin.

Having consumed several drinks caused Father Billy's swaggering to be more pronounced. Von Hess watched closely as the bogus priest and Gloria made their way to the Bentley.

The detective resumed his rolling surveillance, turning his headlights off as he neared their apartment house.

The passenger got out of the Bentley alone and entered the building while the driver began looking for a place to park. The empty streets were very dark, giving the off-duty detective an advantage. When Ross Holt finally found a place to park, Von Hess double parked his own vehicle. Prepared to confront the impersonator, Von Hess got out of his car and waited for his man to walk by him.

"Hey, fella . . ." Von Hess called out.

Ross, having consumed a good deal of drink, now seemed unsteady on his feet. He continued walking without bothering to look at the detective.

"Hey, I'm talking to you!" called out Von Hess to Ross, who was now several steps beyond him. Again the detective's overture went ignored.

Von Hess, in his haste to catch up with Ross, slipped and fell to the ground. Peeved at tearing his pants at the knee, the detective lost it. Without considering the consequences, he charged up behind Ross and spun the bogus priest around to face him. This caused Ross to fall to lose his balance. The impersonator, believing he was under attack, rose to his feet and threw a punch at the detective.

After dodging the haymaker, Von Hess drew his blackjack. With a swift backhanded swipe he struck Ross on the mouth with the deadly weapon. The blow dropped the fraudster, causing him to strike his head on the cement. Furious at how things escalated, Von Hess took his wrath out on the dazed Ross.

"You son of a bitch, you," said the frustrated Von Hess, as he again jacked Ross. This time home was the assault victim's left eye area.

It was the trail of blood that freely flowed that caused the detective to back off. He failed to notice his victim's eye begin to swell to the size of a plum. "Now look at what you made me do," hissed Von Hess.

The detective was committed to going all in. He quickly looked in all directions. Seeing that the street remained deserted, he rifled the assault victim's pockets. Von Hess stuffed the large amount of cash he removed from Ross into his own pocket. He then rushed to his car and fled the scene.

Having settled down during the ride home, the detective began experiencing tremendous guilt for his actions. It had been many years since he let his temper get the better of him to such a degree.

* * *

WHEN ROSS HOLT FINALLY CAME AROUND, it took him a few minutes to realize where he was. Groggy, he could feel the cold ground beneath him. He gradually became aware that something terrible had happened to him. The throbbing in his head was intense. As his head became clearer Ross began to do an accounting of his injuries.

The assault victim slowly rose to a sitting position. His lips were swollen and numb. His tongue felt something floating inside his mouth. He let out a groan after spitting out two of his teeth. Ross then worked his tongue around his mouth in search of the holes where those teeth once rested. Soon afterward he realized that there was something terribly wrong with one of his eyes.

Oh, no! Ross thought, after gently touching the large purple bubble that filled his left eye socket.

Although unsteady, Ross managed to rise to his feet. Slowly, he made his way back to his girlfriend's building. He didn't realize that blood was still oozing from his head. When he got to Gloria's door, she was aghast at the site of her paramour.

"Oh, my God!" Gloria shouted upon seeing the condition of her crime partner. "What happened?"

"Somebody bushwhacked me."

"Who?"

"I never even saw the guy; he snuck up on me from behind."

"Why?"

"How the hell do I know why?" he answered sharply.

"You need to go to a hospital . . ."

"No, no hospital. That'll lead to questions. If this gets out, it could ruin everything I got going. I can't take the chance of exposure."

"Your front teeth . . ."

"Yeah, I know; they got knocked out."

"And look at your eye!"

"I know, I know."

"Even your head is bleeding."

"My head is bleeding too?"

"There is blood all down your back . . ."

"Get me a couple of towels," directed Father Billy. "And wrap a clean dish rag around some ice." When Gloria returned, she began wiping the blood off the charlatan's head while he held the ice pack against his damaged eye. "Does it look like I need stitches?"

"I'm not sure."

"If you're not sure, then I don't need any."

"But you'll get a scar."

"My hair will cover it."

"How do you feel?"

"I don't know. Get me some Advil," answered the assault victim.

With the help of the Advil, the impersonator felt a wee bit better. "Let's get back to the rectory while it's still dark, Gloria. You'll have to drive."

"You need to rest."

"I'll sleep in the car. I can't hang around here like this."

"But people will see you back in Brooklyn."

"No they won't, I'll stay in my room. You'll cover for me."

Ross slept in the car all the way back to the church parking lot. When the Bentley was shut off he woke up, finding himself stiff and achy.

"We're here. How are you feeling?" Gloria asked.

"I need some more Advil."

"I'm worried about that eye."

The fraudster checked his left eye in the mirror attached to the car visor. "It's just a bad black eye. It'll heal. But I'm gonna have to see a dentist to plug up these holes in my mouth. That'll cost me a few," he complained.

"Don't worry. We'll get the money from the Perez sisters," said Gloria confidently.

When Ross went to check his money he realized it was gone. "Did you take my money, Gloria?" he asked.

"No . . . don't you have it?"

"Son of a bitch!" he declared bitterly. "So that was it. I was robbed!"

"Everything is gone?"

"Yeah, all I got left is a little cash at the rectory. But I don't get it. If it was a robbery, why wasn't my watch and gold chain taken?"

"I don't know. All I do know is that we have to tell these people here in Brooklyn something," advised Gloria, "if they start asking questions."

"I'll come up with something. Get me inside the rectory."

"What happens when people see you?"

"They won't. I told you, I'm staying out of sight in my room. You can field my calls."

"What'll I tell everyone?"

"What the hell do I know?" barked the bogus priest. "Tell them I had an accident or tell them I got the measles. Just have a story for them."

"All right, don't take it out on me," said Gloria defensively. "I wasn't the one who rolled you."

"Will you just get me into the rectory?"

"You want me to return the Bentley?"

Father Billy nodded weakly. "Put it back in the garage and get the keys back to the sisters."

19

Like-Minded

DETECTIVE VON HESS had difficulty sleeping. As someone who had spent his entire life following the rules, the assault he had perpetrated weighed heavily on his conscience. Being a resilient man, regardless of how much remorse he felt, he soldiered on. When daybreak came, he set out on a course he needed to follow.

The detective double parked his car in front of the Sunset Park home of the Perez sisters. The sound of the car door closing echoed loud enough to travel through the one inch of open window in the Captain's upper floor apartment.

The Captain, an early riser, went to the window to investigate. He arrived in time to see Von Hess place something in his landlord's mailbox. *That's the detective from the O'Hara & Mercato Lounge*, thought the Captain. *What's he up to?*

The Captain's curiosity got the best of him. After Von Hess drove off, the Captain went downstairs to see what was placed in the mailbox. The feel of the sealed envelope caused him to wonder further. Seeing that the envelope was only held closed at the center with a small piece of Scotch tape, he decided to peek. After carefully lifting the flap, he was astounded to see that the envelope was stuffed with cash.

The Captain took charge of the money and returned to his apartment. Since he believed the sisters might still be sleeping, he waited before going to see them. This also gave him time to count the money several times over.

* * *

MILLIE PEREZ WAS SURPRISED when Ross Holt's crime partner stopped by to return the keys to the Bentley so soon.
"The car is back in the garage, Millie," advised Gloria.
"It is?"
"Yeah, and it needs to be gassed up."
"Why didn't you get the gas?"
"There wasn't time for that. Father Billy was hurt terribly. He's in bad shape."
"Oh . . ."
"He's gonna need money to help meet his medical expenses. He told me to see you about a loan."
"I don't know . . ."
"Look, he needs the money to fix his face," Gloria stated forcefully.
"But we just gave him money, Gloria."
"That's gone."
"Oh, I don't know about more money . . . what happened to him?"
"He was mugged," barked Gloria, saying the first thing that came to her mind. Millie found her elevated voice to be intimidating. "You're not going to turn your back on him when he needs you—are you? He may lose an eye!"
"Oh, dear . . ."
"He's going to need money to fix his teeth too. And his head was opened up."
"Well, I'll have to talk to Arlene," said Millie, stalling for time.
"You do that . . . you go and talk to your sister. I'll be back later to go to the bank with you."
After Gloria left, Millie went to the second floor of their duplex to talk to her sister.

177

"What's wrong, Millie?" Arlene asked, seeing that her sister looked distraught.

"They want more money," Millie announced grimly. "Gloria said Father Billy was mugged. Now they want money to cover medical expenses."

"Not a penny more!" declared Arlene. "Enough is enough. I'm going to call Oliver. He'll know what to do."

"That detective of yours hasn't done a thing for us yet."

"Oliver won't disappoint us."

The sisters were still debating the diligence of Von Hess when the Captain rang the doorbell. "Let me answer the bell," said Millie. "Oh, come in, Captain," greeted Millie after opening the front door. She was glad to see him.

Her invitation took the Captain aback. "You're not mad at me anymore?"

"Oh, stop. I was never really made at you. Come on in."

"What's wrong? You look worried."

"You're not going to believe what's going on."

"What happened?"

"It's a long story. I'll put on some coffee."

"It's been a long time since we've had coffee together, Millie," said the Captain.

"I'll get it," volunteered Arlene, who had entered the room. "Explain to the Captain what's going on."

While Arlene got the coffee, Millie went on to explain that Father Billy and Gloria were fraudsters. Not surprised to hear this, the Captain nodded with understanding. He was surprised to learn of all the money the sisters had already given to Father Billy and Gloria. When informed of the bogus priest being assaulted and mugged, a knowing look came over the Captain. Things were slowly starting to make sense to the wily old sailor.

"Did they get much?" asked the tenant.

"They took all his money, or I should say, our money," replied Millie.

"Was he hurt?"

"His head was opened up," chimed in Arlene from the sink area. "He lost teeth, and he may even lose an eye, according to

Gloria." The Captain listened with suspicion. He wondered about the teeth being knocked out, an eye and head injury, and the money loss. "My friend, Detective Von Hess is helping us with this situation," added Arlene as she handed the Captain a mug of coffee. "He was the one who alerted us to what those two were all about."

A satisfied look came over the face of the Captain. Since he had seen Von Hess put money into the mailbox, the Captain formed the opinion that the detective must have beaten and robbed the fraudster.

"I never trusted those two landlubbers from the start," declared the Captain. "I'm glad to see that you two girls finally got wise."

"Well, maybe I should call Oliver," Arlene announced, rising from her chair.

"Just a second, Arlene, I have something here for both of you," said the Captain. He then produced the envelope containing the money that Von Hess had placed in their mailbox. "I believe someone wanted you to have this."

Arlene took the envelope and opened it. "What's all this?" she asked as she began to thumb through the cash. "Why, this is even more money than we gave Father Billy," declared Arlene.

"Where did you get all this money from?" asked Millie.

"I saw you had mail in your mailbox, so I took it in for you."

"Who could have put it there?"

"The lord works in mysterious ways," commented the tenant, who had no intention of sharing all he knew. The last thing he wanted to do was cause a problem for Von Hess, who he suspected of having settled the account, in spades, with the phony priest.

While Millie remained in the dark, Arlene didn't require things to be spelled out for her. She, too, was able to piece together parts of the puzzle. The only difference between the Captain and Arlene was that the Captain arrived at his conclusion based on what he saw. Arlene was influenced by wishful thinking. She convinced herself that Von Hess, due to a romantic interest, wrestled the Perez money back from the clutches of Father Billy.

Arlene spent all day thinking about Detective Von Hess. She was so taken by the belief that Von Hess extended himself for her that she forgot all about Gloria having asked for more money.

* * *

LATER THAT DAY MILLIE PEREZ packed a bag. Stressed over having to deal with Gloria and Father Billy, she needed to remove herself from the situation. Her escape was in the form of spending a couple of days with a girlfriend in Maryland. Not wanting to leave Arlene home alone, Millie pleaded with her sister to accompany her on the motor trip.

"Why don't you come with me, Arlene?"

"The weather is iffy, Millie. Now they're saying that there is a chance we might be getting snow later."

"We have plenty of time. The drive is only about four hours, and we haven't taken a trip together in ages. Why don't you just pack a bag while I go to the garage and get the car?"

"No, you go, Millie. I'll stay home and watch the house."

"I hate to leave you alone to deal with this mess."

"I'm not alone. Besides, the Captain is upstairs if I need anything, so go along, dear."

"Promise me you won't let those two awful creatures in the house . . . and don't answer the phone."

"I won't."

"And don't give those two crooks any more money. If I need to talk to you, I'll call the Captain, and he'll let you know."

"That's fine, Millie."

"All right then, I guess I'll be going. I'll be home in a couple of days."

Unbeknownst to Millie, her sister couldn't have been happier with her leaving. An empty house offered Arlene the privacy necessary to entertain Detective Von Hess—if she could get him to come by.

* * *

VON HESS ENTERED THE Sunset Park Precinct detective squad alone. To his good fortune, the precinct investigator was an older gumshoe he knew. He was a fair-complexioned man with a head of bushy, white hair. Of average height and stocky, he wore thick, black glasses that pronounced his pale coloring. A smattering of dandruff could be seen on the shoulders of his black suit jacket.

"Mad Dog Switzer!" shouted Von Hess enthusiastically.

"Ollie!" Switzer acknowledged with equal enthusiasm. "Are you still around? I thought you were long retired."

"Nah, they're gonna have to carry me out. What about you?"

"I'm sticking around for the duration too," replied Mad Dog. "My wife passed away last year. We never had any kids, so this job is all I got to keep me busy."

"I'm sorry to hear about your loss."

"Hey, life goes on."

"You like working the chart?" asked Von Hess, changing topics. "I always found the turnaround tours to be murder."

The veteran detective nodded and smiled. "I got those squared. I stay with a lady friend who lives in the precinct. I put her husband away for ten years, so she's grateful. She thinks I did her a big favor."

"So you're still pitching . . ."

"I hold my own, but the marathon days are long over."

"I'm glad to have run into you, Mad Dog. I need a favor."

"What is it?"

"Are you working alone?"

"Yeah, the boss if off on Sundays and Mondays," answered the precinct detective, "and my partner is on vacation. So what's the favor?"

Von Hess explained to the detective the situation involving the fraudsters who were taking advantage of the Perez sisters. He conveyed his suspicions that there were likely other church parishioners who were being victimized. Von Hess specifically detailed the roofing scam used to bilk the Perez sisters out of

thousands of dollars. Fortunately for Von Hess, Detective
Switzer thought as he did when it came to the church. As a
result, he was receptive to taking up the matter.

"So this bird works in collusion with a squeeze that lives in the
rectory with him, Ollie?"

"That's about the size of it, Mad Dog. How is that for balls?"

"Unreal."

"Anyway, everybody in the parish knows him as Father Billy.
His crime partner girlfriend is named Gloria."

"We can't let them get away with pulling this shit."

"That's just the way I see it," commented Von Hess.

"You know, back in the day what would happen to these two
miscreants. Why they . . ."

"I know," said Von Hess, cutting Switzer short. "I know." Von
Hess didn't want to go there.

"Ahh, there is a lot of law in the end of a nightstick, Ollie."

"You'll work on this then?"

"Sure I will. Did the sisters prepare a complaint report yet?"

"Not yet, but I'll see that they do."

"Do that. Tell them to come to the precinct and ask for me. I'm
here all day today and again tomorrow. After that, I'll be
swinging out for a couple of days off."

"Thanks, Mad Dog. It's been good seeing you again. I'm gonna
go see the complainant now. She's been calling me about this,
so I know that she'll be good to go."

"Did you talk to the monsignor or anyone in the diocese about
this, Ollie?"

"No. The only person I spoke to is you."

"Well, don't worry about a thing. I'll take a personal interest in
this."

"One thing I have to tell you about the Perez sisters, Mad Dog.

"Yeah, what's that?"

"I get the impression that one of them is man hungry."

"What does she look like?"

"She's nice enough."

Upon hearing this, Mad Dog looked toward the ceiling, flapped
his arms and began howling. Von Hess, who knew Mad Dog to

be something of a character, could only shake his head and laugh.

20

Any Port in a Storm

DETECTIVE VON HESS TELEPHONED THE Perez house to let Arlene know that he'd be there in an hour. Thrilled at hearing this, Arlene wasted no time in transforming herself in a way that was designed to seduce the law enforcement officer.

After washing her hair, she let her tresses sprout wildly. She believed it gave her a look of reckless daring. Arlene doctored her face with lipstick, eyeliner, and other items used to beautify. The black turtleneck top she opted to wear pronounced the positive and concealed her aged neck. Her dark pants complimented her body, and the shoes she chose were glossy black with short heels. Lastly, she generously perfumed herself.

When the doorbell rang, Arlene peeked out the window to see who was there. Seeing Von Hess at her doorstep, she took a deep breath and answered the door.

"Detective Von Hess!" said Arlene with true enthusiasm. "How nice it is to see you again. Come in, Oliver."

Arlene's bubbly demeanor was such that Von Hess didn't need to be told that she was happy to see him. The detective noticed something different about Arlene. She seemed to be more attractive than he recalled.

"I just came from seeing a detective I know at the local precinct about this Father Billy business. He said that he'll take the case and investigate the matter."

"That's wonderful, Oliver. Thank you."

"You and your sister are going to have to go to the precinct and file a complaint report about how you were bilked out of your money."

"Millie is away, and she won't be back for a few days," said Arlene.

"I see, well, I don't think you both need to file the complaint. I can take you to see the detective right now; he's working. Do you have an accounting of what you lost?"

"Yes, my sister and I took care of that. I love that you're going with me, Oliver. I hate doing anything alone, don't you?"

Von Hess wasn't sure how to read Arlene, who seemed to be batting her eyes as she spoke. "Well, why don't we head over to the precinct now," suggested the detective.

"Of course, I'll get my coat."

On the drive to the precinct, Von Hess and Arlene seemed to be having two separate conversations. The detective spoke of bringing a fraudster to justice while his passenger kept circling back to matters of a more personal nature. By the time Von Hess returned Arlene home after speaking to the precinct detective, she knew all about her love interest's family life. In return, she revealed that she had never been married, had no children, and loved to dance. She also injected the substantial inheritance she came into after her father died. In short, Arlene made it clear that she was baggage free, financially independent, and available.

"Come in, Oliver, and I'll fix you a nice lunch," offered Arlene once they arrived back at the Perez residence.

"Oh, no thank you. I have to get home."

"Oh, come on. It's the least I could do after all you've done. We can have a drink. I certainly can use one."

"It's kind of early . . ."

"Scotch?" she asked.

"Well, maybe just one."

Arlene had the detective sit on the couch in the parlor while she went to the liquor cabinet and removed two bottles. The scotch was for Von Hess, the wine for her.

Arlene poured the scotch into a four-ounce Waterford crystal glass. She then poured herself some wine. Taking a seat alongside the detective on the couch, she got close enough for their legs to rub against each other.

The close proximity caused Von Hess to get a bit nervous. Smiling as she spoke, Arlene unbuttoned the detective's overcoat, urging him to remove it and get more comfortable.

"What's all this pampering about?" asked Von Hess, who wasn't used to such aggressiveness.

"It's a thank-you for a fine man who went above and beyond to help me and my sister."

"Well, look, Arlene, I only . . ."

"Drink up, Oliver," said Arlene, cutting off the detective.

Von Hess took the glass as told and began drinking. During their subsequent chit-chat, Arlene made no mention of Father Billy or the fraudster's lady friend. After finishing his drink, Von Hess rose from the couch to leave.

"I guess I should be going," he said. "Thanks for the drink."

"What's the rush, Oliver?" asked Arlene. "We still have to have our lunch. It'll only take me a second to fix something. Have another drink while I get lunch."

After consuming the second scotch, the detective began to settle in. When Arlene returned with the sandwiches, she sat even closer to Von Hess. When she began leaning into him, the detective began to weaken. This development wasn't lost on Arlene, who could see that she was making progress in her seduction.

Arlene rose to put on some Elvis music. When "Are You Lonesome Tonight" began playing, Arlene took Von Hess by the hand, inviting him to dance.

"I can't dance," said Von Hess, pulling his hand back.

"Oh, come on. I'm not going to bite you, silly," insisted Arlene, tugging at her guest's jacket sleeve.

Von Hess complied and rose to his feet. The meshing of their bodies as Elvis warbled stimulated the libido of both parties. At the conclusion of the song, the shorter Arlene continued to hold on to Von Hess. She looked up into the detective's eyes in a wanting way, waiting for him to make his move. It was an expectation not to be met. Von Hess mustered the resolve to suddenly step away from Arlene, clear his throat, and announce firmly that he was leaving.

"I guess it'll take another round," said Arlene.

"I appreciate the offer, but I really do have to leave."

"What about our lunch?"

"No, I'm afraid I have to go."

"But Oliver . . ."

"Sorry, Arlene, but I'm heading out. Good luck with the Father Billy situation."

The sad look on Arlene's face was evident as Von Hess headed out the front door. The detective felt a little bad about that, but he remained unwavering.

"Oliver, wait a second. You didn't give me the name of the plastic surgeon you mentioned in the car."

Von Hess reached into his jacket pocket and handed Arlene the business card of Doctor Gordon Vanidestine. Vanidestine's card was one of the many he kept in his coat pocket.

"I only met this Doctor Vanidestine once, but he's supposed to be a top man in his field," advised the detective. "Good luck, Arlene."

Von Hess felt a buzz when he hit the fresh air. During the ride, the detective briefly wondered what an interlude with a woman other than his wife would have been like.

* * *

THE CAPTAIN, WHO HAD HEARD THE MUSIC coming from the landlord's digs, took up a position by his upper-floor window. From his perch he patiently watched the street below. When he saw Von Hess leave the building, he grew curious as to what the detective was doing back at the house. Deciding to find out, the Captain ventured to his landlord's front door.

Arlene, thinking that Von Hess had returned, rushed to open the door. Seeing that it was the Captain, Arlene turned glum. In her disappointment she blurted out, "Oh, it's only you."

"Yeah, it's just me. Your sister told me to look in on you." The Captain immediately noticed Arlene's change in appearance. "What happened to you?" he asked.

"Why, nothing happened, Captain. Is there something you need?" asked Arlene.

"Oh, no, I don't need anything. Like I said, your sister wanted me to let you know that I'm home if you need anything."

"Yeah, everything is great with me," answered Arlene halfheartedly.

The Captain, looking over his landlord's shoulder, was able to see the open bottles and Arlene's partially filled wine glass. "Were you having a party with that detective?"

"Do you know Detective Von Hess?"

"That I do—better than you think."

The smell of intoxicants combined with Arlene's revised look had an influence on the Captain. Arlene's wild hair, although graying, reminded him of his long-ago trysts with Marshanda, an Indonesian woman he had gotten intimate with when his ship dropped anchor in Komodo Island. Marshanda, the descendant of a convict who had been exiled to Komodo, had tried to pick the Captain's pocket. In a strange sort of way, the Captain viewed both Perez sisters as women who picked pockets legally via rent payments.

"How do you know him, Captain?"

"Why don't we have a drink, Arlene," suggested the Captain, "and let me fill you in."

After the Captain consumed several rums, he began to get flirtatious. Arlene only needed a few wines to start thinking things over. While the Captain wasn't Von Hess, he was there. There was no need for Elvis. It was a case of any port in a storm.

21

Time to Make Tracks

SAMMY ANGELO FELT more under pressure in his apartment than did his friend, Dennis Bumper. How Bumper could sleep peacefully every night after murdering three people was beyond belief to him. *It's like he hasn't a care in the world,* Sammy thought. Unlike his homicidal friend, the stressed-out Sammy wasn't able to sleep well.

Sammy spent the night monitoring the televised weather reports. Impatient for snow to come down, he grew restless. When the snowflakes started, Sammy was exceedingly happy.

"Should I call Father Billy now, Dennis?" he asked.

"No, not yet. Let's see if the snow accumulates," replied Bumper. "You know, Sammy, I've been meaning to ask you something about Digger."

"What's that?"

"Digger's going to need someone to look after him when they put me away. You'll look after him for me, right?"

"Yeah, Dennis, I'll take care of your hamster as if he was my own."

"Feed him fruit and vegetables; he loves those. And don't forget to give him lots of water."

"No problem."

"You could even give him a hard-boiled or scrambled egg. He likes nuts also."

Sammy saw irony in the word "nuts." He thought it an apt description of his friend.

"Don't worry, Dennis, I'll take good care of Digger." As Sammy conversed with Bumper, he came to feel that the time was right to take a bold step and broach the subject of his friend's state of mind. "Dennis, I've been thinking—you probably do need some professional help."

"I know I do, Sammy." Bumper's reply was surprising to his friend, who was relieved over the acceptance of his suggestion. "When the time comes, you'll go to the police station with me, right?"

"Sure I will, Dennis. I'll go there with you now if you want," said Sammy, who was looking to take advantage of Bumper's willingness.

"Did you forget? I have to go confess my sins to Father Billy first . . . remember?"

"Oh, that's right. We have to do that first."

"Do you think that Father Billy will be willing to come with us to the police station after confession?"

"Of course he will. I'll call Father Billy now, okay?"

"Thanks, Sammy."

Sammy truly hated the thought of seeing his friend spend the rest of his life behind bars. From what he understood, the cruelties of doing time in a prison were many. Unfamiliar with exactly how the court system worked, Sammy could only hope that Bumper would be placed in the hands of professionals trained in mental illness.

"Besides spiritual guidance, I think you're gonna need a good lawyer too," suggested Sammy.

"I'm not too concerned about having a lawyer, Sammy. I'm willing to accept the consequences for what I did. All I want to do is confess my sins. After that, what will be, will be."

"Sure, Dennis," said Sammy softly, pitying his friend. "I think that cleansing your soul is a great idea."

"See if you could get Father Billy now."

Sammy wasted no time in reaching out to Father Billy telephonically. Sill in fragile condition from the beating he sustained at the hands of Detective Von Hess, the bogus priest didn't answer his phone. His calls were being fielded by Gloria.

Sammy was informed by Gloria that Father Billy was in no condition to speak to anyone. She explained that the imposter sustained injuries that rendered him incommunicado for the time being. When Sammy inquired as to the cause of the injuries, Gloria was evasive. She only committed herself to conveying that the fraudster was in the process of healing.

Sammy persisted, impressing upon Gloria the importance of his speaking to Father Billy. He tried to explain that he was faced with a dire situation that required immediate attention. Gloria, exhibiting little empathy, made it clear that Father Billy wasn't available. "Father Billy has his own problems," she bluntly said.

"I understand, but . . ."

"Look, if you're in such a big hurry, you can see another priest."

Surprised at Gloria's abruptness, the disappointed Sammy had no alternative other than to accept her decision to terminate their conversation. To his dismay, this meant that Sammy would have to continue to harbor his homicidal friend until Father Billy was well enough to receive visitors.

"Sorry, Dennis, but it looks like it's gonna take a little more time before you get to see Father Billy," advised Sammy.

"What happened?"

"He had some kind of an accident."

"What kind of accident?"

"I don't know; the woman didn't say."

"Then I'll have to stay here with you until we can get to see Father Billy," said Bumper.

"I suppose that's all we can do."

Bumper sensed that his friend was lukewarm to the prospect of extending their arrangement.

"I hate to put you out, Sammy, but I can't stay in my own apartment. That's gonna be the first place the cops are gonna be looking for me if they decide to come around. I'm safer here with you."

* * *

AFTER GLORIA CONFERRED WITH ROSS HOLT, the impersonator instructed her to call Sammy Angelo back and see if she could get some money out of him. She immediately complied.

"You know, Sammy, I forgot to mention that Father Billy needs to borrow money badly to help offset the cost of his medical bills. He would appreciate you helping out."

"Doesn't he have insurance?"

"Not enough to cover all his injuries. He needs extensive dental work, an operation on his eye, and lots of other things. I'm sure I can get Father to meet with you in a couple of days when he's feeling a little better . . . especially if he can count on you for a loan. Father said that you'd be okay with me asking you to contribute."

"He can count on me," said Sammy. "But I need Father Billy to talk to my friend Dennis as soon as possible."

"Of course," assured Gloria. "Father Billy will see your friend the day after tomorrow. That'll give you time to get together the loan we need."

"How much do you want?"

Gloria was surprised at how willing Sammy was to part with his money. As a result, she aimed high.

"I'd say about $10,000. Can you float that?"

"I'll have it for you," replied Sammy without hesitation.

"Please bring it in cash."

"You want it in cash?"

"The doctor insists on cash."

"I never heard of such a thing."

"The doctor is going through a divorce," said Gloria, thinking

192

fast. "He needs to hide income."

* * *

FORGETTING WHERE HE WAS, Ross Holt began shouting out a series of expletives. Hearing the profanities, his girlfriend rushed to the rectory bathroom to see what was wrong. She found her agitated crime partner standing in front of the mirror, holding a shaving brush.

"What's wrong?" Gloria asked. She could tell just by looking at him that the fraudster was in an ornery frame of mind.

"It's taking forever for the water to get hot."

When the water finally heated up, the charlatan placed his lathering bowl under the faucet. Once the scented cake of soap warmed, Ross began to vigorously rub his shaving brush into it to create a thick lather. He peered into the mirror as he began to apply the suds to his face. Raising the razor, he paused to run his tongue along his fattened lips. He found the path to be a mountainous one. Causing further distress was the eye that was hidden behind a discolored, bulbous swelling. The hideous slit across the center of the swelling disheartened Ross to a point where he questioned why he was bothering to shave in the first place.

"Aw, there ain't any purpose," he declared. "I'm gonna look like shit whether I shave or not."

"Why are you crying about now?" asked Gloria.

"Look at my face. It's gonna take forever for me to heal," lamented the imposter. "And I still have to find a dentist to fix me up."

"We'll find someone in the parish who will take care of it."

"Nah, that won't work. I gotta go to a dentist someplace far away or else face the locals asking me questions about how I got banged up."

"I've just been telling people you were mugged without providing details."

"Don't they ask when and where?"

"I don't give them a chance to. I just change the subject."

"Well, I'll have to come up with something to tell them."

"Say it was traumatic and that you'd rather not talk about it."

"Yeah, maybe that'll work. Do you hear that bell ringing? How come nobody is answering the door?"

"There is no one here in the rectory but us."

"Where is everybody?"

"The priest went to see the Christmas show at Radio City with the cook. They got free tickets from the guy who owns the travel agency."

"What about the woman who works in the office here?"

"Everybody is off."

"Why is that bell still ringing?"

"Let it ring. Whoever it is will go away."

"I got a splitting headache. Get me a beer, will ya?"

"Take some Advil."

"I already did. Now go get the beer." Gloria went to fetch the beer. To Father Billy's dismay, she returned a few minutes later empty-handed. "Where's my beer?"

"We're out. The priest probably polished it all off. That old man's got a wooden leg."

"He's a freaking sink!" barked the religious impostor. "The guy would drink kerosene. Do me a favor and go out and get some beer."

On her trip to the store, Gloria passed the church located alongside the rectory. She was stopped by an elderly churchgoer who occasionally served as an usher at Mass. He informed her that a detective from the local precinct was at the rectory door ringing the bell a few minutes earlier.

"How do you know the detective was from the local precinct?"

"I recognized him," replied the citizen. "Detective Switzer has worked in the precinct for years. Everybody knows him. They call him Mad Dog. Here, look . . . he gave me his card."

This revelation startled Gloria. "Did he say what he wanted?"

"I don't know. He just told me to do him a favor and call him the next time I see Father Billy."

"Did he say what for?"

"He just said it was a police matter."

"Oh, I think I understand," said Gloria, who was thinking fast. "Let me have the detective's card. I'll call him."

Gloria rushed back to the rectory to inform her crime partner that the law was looking for him. She then showed her cohort the detective's business card.

"I don't like this, Gloria," said Ross, forgetting all about the beer he wanted. "Start packing. We're taking off."

"Where are we going?"

"I'm not exactly sure yet, but we're not staying here."

"Do we have to leave?" Gloria asked. "We have a sweet thing going here."

"Look, if we got a detective sniffing around, we definitely have to book. I'm not taking any chances."

"But you're not sure what the detective wants . . ."

"Give me your phone," Ross said abruptly, losing patience. Reading off the detective's business card he dialed the cell phone of the Sunset Park detective.

"Hello, Detective Switzer?"

"Speaking."

"I'm the priest from Sunset Park. People are telling me you want to talk to me."

"Father Billy?"

"That's right, Father Billy. What's on your mind, Detective?"

"I'd like to come by and talk to you, Father. Are you at the rectory now?"

"No, I'm driving up to my sister's house in Connecticut," fibbed Ross. "I'll be there for a few days."

"Where are you in Connecticut?"

"What's this in reference to, Detective?"

"I need your help in clearing up a small matter. I'll explain everything when I see you. When are you returning home?"

The sham priest immediately became suspicious. Not buying what he was told, he played along. "I can see you at the precinct when I return. What day and time works best for you."

"Can you come to the precinct on Thursday evening?"

"That's fine, Detective. I'll be there around seven."

"Is your assistant, Gloria, around?"

"Why, no, I'm not sure where Gloria is right now. She's on a holiday as well."

"Can you bring her along when you come to the precinct, Father? She may be a help to us as well."

"I think that could be arranged. I'll see to it that we both make ourselves available."

After the bogus priest and the detective set up their appointment to meet at the Sunset Park Precinct, the imposter hung up the phone.

"If that guy thinks I'm sap enough to walk into his trap at the precinct so that he can pinch me, he's nuts!"

"Where are you going?" asked the visibly nervous Gloria.

"Start thinking in terms of *we*, baby. He wants to see you too."

"What'll we do?"

"Don't worry; it's a big country. Maybe we head out West someplace, or down South."

"What about money?"

"We still got some, but we're gonna need more. Start packing."

"Don't forget—we still have to collect from the Perez sisters and Sammy Angelo," reminded Gloria.

"We'll get it."

Once packed, the larcenous duo went directly to the Perez house, which was walking distance from the rectory. The impersonator's plan was to influence the Perez sisters by having them take a look at his battered face. He intended to claim that he needed money right away for an operation to save the vision in his traumatized eye.

When Arlene Perez answered the bell, she only opened the door a crack. She gasped at the sight of the badly bruised imposter. Father Billy's appearance only made Arlene more distrustful of him. Since the Captain was with her, she felt safe enough to open the front door.

Despite not being invited into the house, Ross and Gloria invited themselves inside. Ross brushed against Arlene as he made his way into the foyer. He was followed by Gloria.

"Where's Millie?" asked Gloria.

"Millie is away on a trip," answered the homeowner. "If you

don't mind, I'm not up to company. I'm not feeling very well."

"We'll leave as soon as you help us out," said Gloria, taking a defiant stand. "Did you get the money?"

At this point the sham priest intervened. "Gloria is upset, Arlene. You have to excuse her. As you can see for yourself, I'm in pretty bad shape and in need of medical attention."

"Maybe you need to go to the hospital, Father," suggested Arlene, who could see that Ross was frail.

"You don't understand. I've already been to a hospital. A nurse gave me the name of a specialist, a top man in his field who can save my eye. I've already made the necessary arrangements. Time is of the essence, and I need to get moving. You're gonna have to lend me your car."

"I'm sorry, but I don't have the car. Millie has it."

"Oh, well, just give me the money. I have to pay the doctor. I'm afraid you're going to have to loan me more cash than anticipated, Arlene."

Arlene's facial reaction made it obvious to the fraudster that she was reluctant to part with any more money.

"It'll only be a loan, Arlene. You and your sister are the only people I know who have the kind of money required."

"Since when does a specialist work for cash?" chimed in the Captain, who had been listening from another room. The entry of the tenant into the conversation took the fraudsters by surprise. The Captain projected a skepticism that was troubling to Ross.

"If it's any of your business, offering cash was the only way we could get the doctor to see us immediately," voiced Gloria snippily. "We have to fly him in from out of town."

"Maybe you should talk this over with your sister, Arlene," suggested the Captain, ignoring Gloria's comment.

"I could never loan any of our money, regardless of why, without discussing it with my sister," said Arlene, taking her cue from the Captain. "I'm sorry."

"Now listen, Arlene!" shouted Gloria, who was tired of all the talk. "Father Billy needs some financial help, so you call your sister and get the okay or just go and get the money."

"Just who the hell do you think you are?" asked the Captain heatedly. "You ain't coming in here and giving orders to nobody!" thundered the Captain. In true seaman style, he was fully prepared to mix it up.

Tangling with the Captain was the last thing Ross Holt was up for. "Excuse Gloria, folks," said the imposter weakly. In no condition to battle, he sought to defuse things by excusing himself from the fracas. "Gloria hasn't been herself lately. She's worried about my health and is terribly upset. We'll come back at a better time, perhaps when Millie gets home." Ross looked at the Captain and smiled humbly. He then took Gloria by the arm and hustled her out of the house.

"Are you nuts, Gloria?" asked Ross once outside.

"You said we need the money, didn't you?" asked Gloria.

"C'mon, Gloria, take the blinders off. Can't you see that the tenant is wise to us? He's probably got Arlene calling that detective right now."

"So now what are we supposed to do?"

"We're gonna scram out of here right now. If Arlene starts talking to the cops, they're gonna be coming for us," pointed out Ross. "But we ain't gonna be around."

"Where are we going?"

"We'll have to go back to your apartment in Jersey. We'll be safe there."

"How do we get there?"

"We'll have to take a train to Manhattan and take a cab from there."

"Why don't we just take car service from here?"

"That's no good. If they're looking for us, they're liable to check the local car services. If they do that, the driver will be able to tell them where he took us. C'mon, we gotta get a move on."

"What about our collecting money from Sammy Angelo?"

"We'll have to put that off. We'll take our chances and come back to Brooklyn to see him once things cool down. Besides, I'll feel a little better by then."

22

Fishnet Gets Lucky

FISHNET WASN'T SURPRISED WHEN his attorney phoned him. He expected to hear from his legal representative once word reached the lawyer about the murder attempt on No Tax. The attorney called for an emergency meeting to discuss the situation. The meeting was held at Fishnet's townhouse.

The lawyer communicated to his client that he had been in contact with his source at the District Attorney's Office. He conveyed that the ADA prosecuting his case was highly concerned about the illegal entry into the apartment of No Tax. He noted that the prosecutors were convinced that the purpose of the intrusion was to kill their witness. Fishnet's attorney concurred with this belief. Although his suspicions were definite, the defense attorney fell short of actually accusing his client of any involvement.

"What do you know about that," said the former detective. "I guess the old man pissed somebody off."

"Don't you realize the magnitude of what I just told you?"

"So somebody went into the old man's house. What has that got to do with me?"

"Somebody tried to kill the witness against you in the Marvin Butterworth case," clarified the lawyer, with emphasis.

"Well, what do you expect from me?" Fishnet asked. "I had nothing to do with it."

"Don't you realize how this appears, how it will impact a judge and jury? They're going to figure you had every reason to try and kill that old man."

"Look, I'm paying you big money to do my worrying for me. You're the bright lawyer, not me."

"I'm trying to tell you that they're going to be going for your throat now." The directness of this statement gave Fishnet pause. "When that pathetic old man gets on the witness stand, forget about it. Look, I'm your lawyer, and I'm telling you no jury in the world is going to doubt his sincerity."

"What evidence is there that I had anything to do with going after No Tax?" asked Fishnet. "Besides, I've been home all weekend."

"Have you proof of that?"

This comment got Fishnet thinking. He wanted to convey how No Tax had taken a shot at him, but he knew he couldn't. "Look, instead of asking me questions, why don't you just tell me what our next move is."

"You're not going to like what I have to say . . ."

"Don't worry about what I like, just give it to me straight."

"My advice is not to take any chances by going to trial. Let's try and make a deal."

"You're saying that I should cop a plea?"

"Give me the green light to talk to the District Attorney's Office. Seeing you're a hero detective and all, maybe I can swing a reasonable plea deal."

"And I get to go to the can for how long?"

"That'll be up to the judge."

"But she's supposed to be a hanging judge."

"The way things stand, it's either we shoot for a deal on the Butterworth case or run the risk of you coming out of prison with a white beard down to your ankles."

"You got twelve people on that jury. Can't you get to one?"

"I don't engage in any shenanigans," replied the lawyer with a straight face. "Besides, the other side will have their antennas up for something like that."

"So you think if I go to bat, I'll lose in court?"

"I'm afraid there is a good chance of that outcome."

"Start negotiating with them," said Fishnet reluctantly. "But do me a favor . . . don't be too hasty in coming to terms. Try to string it out for as long as you can before agreeing to anything."

"We can't afford to waste time."

"Just do what I'm asking you to do," said Fishnet, losing patience. The former detective wanted the time necessary to try and come up with a way to silence No Tax once and for all.

* * *

FISHNET WAS NOW UNDER pressure to kill No Tax. After failing once, he knew a second go at it wasn't going to be easy. Try as he might, he was unable to arrive at a suitable plan. This compelled him to consider other options. Since he had the financial wherewithal, the ex-detective considered what life would be like if he absconded. With this in mind, he researched a book in the townhouse library for potential venues.

Fishnet thought that Montenegro in the west-central Balkans was a place to consider because he couldn't be extradited from there. While reading up on Montenegro, the former detective briefly slipped into his fantasy world. He saw himself at peace, smoking a cigar, and sipping coffee at a luxury resort in the ancient fishing village of Sveti Stefan. After his pleasant daydream, he returned to his research.

Fishnet was disappointed after reading that Montenegrin was a difficult language to master. *Ahh, who the hell wants to be around all those ethnic beefs they got over there anyway,* he thought, abandoning Montenegro altogether as a place to settle. *Maybe I need an island not too far away.*

After more research, Fishnet discovered Cuba. The Clark Gable lookalike soon envisioned himself in Cayo Largo, an island south of the mainland noted for its nude beaches. The male beachgoers in his fantasy were all exceptionally endowed. His feeling of inadequacy left Fishnet chatting up the free- spirited women while remaining in his swim trunks.

Fishnet's interest in Cuba soon evaporated once he found out about the mosquitoes. *I'd go to the can before I let a bunch of them bugs gobble me up,* he thought. Rather than wish the pests away and continue to dream on, Fishnet continued to search for the ideal place to flee.

When he tired of this, he pondered how things would be for him in prison. Aware that incarceration could present a difficult time for a former member of law enforcement, he struggled to find a way to make the best of things if that was to be.

It eventually dawned on Fishnet that jail could be made tolerable for someone with money.

What am I worried about? Fishnet thought. *I could buy all the protection I need in the can! I'll spread enough green around to have every tough guy and screw in the joint in my pocket.*

Fishnet began thinking of how he'd survive if incarcerated. Halfway through his thoughts he caught himself. "What am I, nuts altogether?" he asked himself aloud, suddenly turning aggressive. "I ain't going to jail for nobody! I'll kill that old bastard, even if I have to die doing it!" As things turned out, Fishnet's worry was for naught.

* * *

THE ATTEMPTED ASSASSINATION of No Tax advanced his physical decline. When the bullets he fired at the intruder failed to strike the intended target, he lost confidence in his ability to defend himself. Feeling vulnerable, he examined his hands for steadiness. They were shaky.

Although hit with a new felony charge for unlawful possession of a loaded gun, the District Attorney's Office intervened on his behalf. Since No Tax was a witness in a murder trial, it was arranged with the police department for him to be issued a desk appearance ticket for the offense. This meant that the ailing octogenarian was free to remain home until he was to appear in court. No longer possessing a gun, No Tax took to carrying a kitchen knife in his bathrobe pocket.

No Tax had little tolerance for the cold. He consumed great quantities of hot tea in an effort to neutralize his constant chill. This was a remedy that came with frequent trips to the bathroom.

What's the use, the witness thought, finding the bathroom runs to be a monumental inconvenience. *It's only a matter of time before I start peeing in my drawers.*

No Tax reached for the kitchen knife he kept on his person, thinking the time had come to permanently put an end to his misery. His life was spared when he heard someone knocking on his front door.

Wary since the intrusion, he nervously shouted, "Who is it?"

"It's Sergeant Markie. Open the door," came the reply.

Hearing Markie's voice cheered the old man. It broke the monotony—at least temporarily.

"What's the password?" No Tax asked, mustering up a semblance of humor.

Markie and Von Hess both shook their heads. "Your Aunt Tillie's fat ass," answered the sergeant. "Are you letting us in or what?"

"Hold your horses. I'm coming."

No Tax opened the door and then turned around without saying anything. Once inside the apartment the detectives could see how difficult it was for No Tax to get around. They also noted that the odor in the apartment was repulsive.

"What have you got for me?" asked No Tax, falling into his recliner. He saw that Von Hess was carrying a large brown paper bag. The ailing man had been receiving goodies delivered by the detectives, courtesy of the District Attorney's Office. The ADA prosecuting Fishnet wanted No Tax kept happy long enough to take the witness stand.

"Milk, juice, cherries, plums, vanilla ice cream, and yogurt," replied Von Hess.

"Did you bring the pineapple yogurt? That's the one I like."

"Yeah, I got you the pineapple."

"We threw in a couple Hershey bars for good measure," injected Markie.

"Thanks."

"Don't thank me. Thank the DA's office. So how are you holding up?"

"I feel like shit."

"I'm not surprised. The place stinks of it," said Markie. "I'm gonna open a window to get some air in here."

"Don't do that. I'm freezing as it is," protested No Tax.

"We'll shut the window when we leave."

"Then get me that other blanket over there," said the sick man, pointing to a small table.

"Oh, by the way," said Markie, "I have a surprise for you."

With a second cover over him, No Tax pushed back in the recliner that doubled as his bed. "What's that?"

"Take a look at this." The sergeant produced two photographs. One was of two life-size walking black panthers. The other was of a headstone.

No Tax looked at the photographs and smiled. "You did a real good job, Sergeant," he said softly.

"How about we help you clean up, No Tax?" suggested Von Hess softly.

"You'd do that for me?"

"Sure, why not."

"I don't know if I'm up to it. I'm afraid of falling."

"Don't worry about that. We'll be right here with you," assured Markie. The sergeant then turned to Von Hess. "Ollie, go to the cellar and see if you can find a scrub brush and bucket."

"Scrub brush!" barked No Tax, thinking Markie was serious.

"He's kidding," advised Von Hess. "Come on," he added, taking No Tax by the arm to help him up from the recliner.

After his shower, No Tax put on fresh nightwear. He was then shaved by Von Hess, who also cut his hair. The aftershave that was applied, while inexpensive, had a pleasing enough scent.

By the time No Tax returned to his recliner, he was exhausted. The chill coming from the open window caused No Tax to complain that he was cold. Markie lowered the window, leaving just the slightest opening.

"Better?"

"Will you close the damn thing?"

"Okay," agreed Markie, closing the window tight. "This guy who tried to kill you—are you sure it wasn't Fishnet?" asked the sergeant.

"I couldn't tell you one way or the other."

"He was about the right size?"

"Height and weight-wise he was about the same, but that's it. The guy who came in looked nothing like Fishnet."

"Too bad you missed when you took those shots at him."

"Yeah, it all happened so fast that I couldn't really aim the gun properly. What do you think is gonna happen in my gun case?"

"I wouldn't worry about that right now, old-timer."

"Yeah, I see what you mean. I probably won't be around for it," No Tax said. He then closed his eyes.

"You rest yourself," said Markie. "We'll stop by from time to time to look in on you."

No Tax raised his hand a couple of inches off the armrest of the recliner and waved slightly. "Lock the door on your way out," he said, closing his eyes.

Thirty minutes after Markie and Von Hess exited the building, the octogenarian made his exit from this world. When word reached the detectives from headquarters that No Tax died in his sleep, Markie and Von Hess began shaking their heads. Markie's head shook not in grief but in disgust.

"Can you believe it, Ollie? The old man's gone. And with him goes the case against Fishnet."

"Maybe our cleaning him up was too much for him, Sarge."

"Nah, it was just his time, Ollie. At least he went out smelling like a rose."

"Yeah, I suppose that's something."

"All I can say is that friggin' Fishnet must have been born with a horseshoe up his ass," declared Markie. "He slipped through the net again!"

FISHNET'S ATTORNEY WAS ecstatic upon learning that the case against his client had collapsed. This was the kind of news the lawyer wanted to deliver to his client in person.

The attorney phoned Fishnet and asked, "Can you meet me for a drink?"

"Now?" asked Fishnet.

"Yes, right now."

"I don't know," replied Fishnet. "I'm working on something pretty important at the moment."

"There isn't anything more important than you meeting me right now."

"What are you talking about?"

"Just meet me in an hour at Brother's, the bar down the block from my office. I have some news for you."

Fishnet wasn't happy at being pulled away from attempting to square root the murder plan he was trying to put together. "All right," he finally conceded. "See you there in an hour."

"One other thing before we hang up . . ."

"What?"

"Plan on our straightening out once you get here."

"You want more money?"

"Yes."

When Fishnet arrived at the tavern, he found the attorney seated at the bar, nursing a martini. Fishnet figured that since the lawyer was asking for payment, he was going to step away from the case. Down deep, Fishnet disliked all lawyers. He viewed them as crooks with an education.

"So what's the big news?" asked Fishnet. The onetime detective broke into a broad smile once told that the homicide charges against him in the Marvin Butterworth case had been dropped due to the death of No Tax. "I caught a break," Fishnet happily declared. "How did he croak?"

"My understanding is that his heart gave out."

Fishnet began laughing out loud. "If this doesn't take the cake," he said. "The bum's ticker did what an assassin couldn't!

This calls for a celebration." When the next round of drinks was delivered, Fishnet raised his glass and said, "Here's to No Tax," and then he clicked glasses with his lawyer. "The old bastard ended up doing the right thing after all."

"By the way, speaking of the right thing, did you bring your checkbook?"

"Sure, sure . . . what do I owe you?" asked Fishnet, who was in the best of humor. The attorney presented an invoice from the breast pocket of his suit jacket. Fishnet was surprised at the fee reflected on the printed document. "Are you sure this is right?" asked the client. "I thought it would come out to more than this." Fishnet immediately wrote a check and gave it to the attorney. "I guess this squares us."

"Not quite," answered the lawyer, slightly smiling. He then wrote a number on the back of a white napkin and passed it to Fishnet. "This is the balance . . . payable in cash," announced the lawyer.

Fishnet looked at the number written on the napkin. Although it was excessive, Fishnet agreed to settle the account with a cash payment. "I'll have it for you tomorrow." Since Fishnet had inherited plenty of money, he didn't bother to dicker.

23

Big Ambitions, Big Treachery

SAMMY ANGELO GOT OFF THE phone looking glum. Gloria had just informed him that Father Billy needed to put off their meeting for an undetermined length of time. She offered no explanations as to why, saying she would call in a week or so. Before hanging up, she reminded Sammy to make sure to have the money on hand for when they finally did get together.

Bumper, seeing that something wasn't right, inquired as to what was wrong with his friend. Sammy explained that Father Billy was unable to meet with them as planned.

"What happened?" asked Bumper.

"The woman didn't say. She just said that it'll be a while before we could meet with Father Billy," replied Sammy.

"So where does that leave us?"

"They're gonna call us next week."

"That's okay, Sammy. We didn't get much snow this time anyway."

"Yeah, I know."

"I heard on television that a snowstorm may be coming. Let's pray that it comes when Father Billy is finally available."

"Yeah, let's pray for that, Dennis."

* * *

WITH HIS COURT TROUBLES behind him, Fishnet once again turned his attention to his girlfriend, Cheryl, a waitress turned stage actor. Cheryl, who had no idea of Fishnet's legal troubles, had proven herself to be a talent in the role he helped her secure. Cheryl's performances were good enough for her to be the understudy to the lead.

The lead, who resided in Westchester County, had been receiving favorable notices. This frustrated Cheryl, who believed that, if given the opportunity, she could turn in a superior performance.

"Did you see this story about the lead in your show?" asked Fishnet as he sat in Cheryl's apartment reading a trade paper.

"I saw it," said Cheryl tersely.

"Based on this buildup, I figure the guy who wrote it must be banging her."

"No, she's just good in the role," acknowledged Cheryl, adding, "I have to give her that."

"What's wrong with you?" asked Fishnet, detecting an attitude in Cheryl's voice.

"I'm frustrated."

"What over?"

"I should be the one playing the lead."

"C'mon, you're still a rookie."

"Maybe so, but that role is perfectly suited for me. All I need is a chance to show what I can do."

"You don't have to sell me, baby. I saw you up there on stage. You got plenty of presence."

"I have more than just presence." Fishnet shook his head and chuckled at Cheryl's remark. "You doubt that?" she asked.

"I'll say this for you, sweetheart. You got confidence."

"I have talent," corrected Cheryl.

"Yeah, well, according to what I'm reading, so does this other gal."

"Oh, please. The whole cast knows that I'm more suited for that role. Everyone says so."

"So why did she land the role and not you?"

"Oh, I don't know. What I need is a good manager, or agent, or somebody who can advance my career."

Hearing this caused Fishnet to think. "Let me ask you something: what exactly does a manager do?"

"A manager controls everything for a talent."

"What's everything?"

"All aspects of an entertainer's career, things like business dealings and stuff like that."

"So the business manager deals with all the big shots then—even the producers?"

"I think so."

"Well, you just got yourself a manager, baby."

"Who is that?"

"Me."

"What do you know about being a manager?"

"I knew enough to land you a role in that play, didn't I?"

"You tricked me into believing you were a big presence in the theater," pointed out Cheryl, who had eventually learned that Fishnet had misrepresented himself when they first met.

"But I delivered, didn't I—and ain't that what counts?"

"I suppose so," Cheryl acknowledged, unable to pose a rebuttal.

"You bet I did."

"Okay, so you're a budding Enzo Baffi."

"Who is he?"

"Mr. Baffi is a prominent movie producer who is searching for a fresh face to star in his new film. Everyone is out of their mind over his new project."

"He's a big deal then?"

"The biggest . . . people in the industry would kill for a part in his new movie. Everyone knows that Mr. Baffi's a star-maker. Why, Mr. Baffi is just about the last word when it comes to movie projects."

Cheryl's frequent referral to the producer as 'Mr. Baffi' bothered Fishnet. It suggested that Baffi was held in a higher regard than he was. The impact of Cheryl affording the producer this kind of respect was vexing enough for Fishnet to retaliate with a tart comment.

"Will you stop with the Mr. Baffi already," said Fishnet.

"Everyone calls him Mr. Baffi. He's a very important man."

"Why is that—because he's got money? Well, I got news for you; I got plenty myself."

"You don't understand how preeminent he is. He hires and fires everybody. The scriptwriters, the director, the crew members, the actors . . . I mean everybody. He handles all the money."

"Okay, so he's got all the juice," Fishnet barked. "I get it."

"Mr. Baffi also understands the creative side of the business," explained Cheryl.

"And you think this hotshot wants to feature *you* in a movie?" asked Fishnet, now wanting to burst Cheryl's bubble. Cheryl found his pessimism insulting.

"I never said that! But now that you mentioned it, why wouldn't he want me?"

"C'mon. He doesn't even know who you are," said Fishnet. His words were meant to be cutting.

"I know that," conceded Cheryl. "If he only did know me, Mr. Baffi could take me to another level."

Cheryl's statement gave the ex-detective pause. Fishnet's mind began to race as he began to see an opportunity for himself. *If this bitch really possesses the talent she believes she has, then maybe I got a play to make in the game*, he thought.

"I have a question, and give it to me straight, Cheryl. Are you a hundred percent certain you'd be better in the top role in that show than the other woman?"

"I'm two hundred percent certain."

Assuming this to be true, Fishnet had a direction to pursue. The ex-detective coveted the respect that Enzo Baffi was being afforded. It was the one thing his money couldn't buy. The thought of having people in awe of him became the most

211

desirable thing he could imagine. Baffi enjoyed a status that Fishnet wanted and was hell bent on attaining.

Fishnet was determined to enter into a business relationship with Enzo Baffi. In aligning with the producer, the onetime detective believed he'd have a clear path in gaining the respect he desperately wanted from those interested in the world of film and stage.

Why, once I'm established as a player in this entertainment racket, thought Fishnet, *I'll use these celebrities to get close to all the big shots. I'll work it so I'll have these politicians and business executives begging me to introduce them to their favorite entertainers. But first, I have to get this hotshot producer to notice Cheryl.*

Fishnet let no grass grow under his feet. He immediately set out to convince Enzo Baffi that Cheryl was a terrific talent with great potential. To accomplish this he needed to secure her a position in the limelight. The scheme Fishnet concocted was as ruthless as any he had ever orchestrated.

* * *

FISHNET STOOD IN THE SHADOWS outside the theater one evening, waiting for the star of Cheryl's show to leave for home. His purpose was to establish what the actor's routine was after finishing work.

When the actor emerged from the theater, at first Fishnet didn't recognize her. He was surprised to see how plain she looked in street clothes. Fishnet trailed his prey on foot to the nearby garage where her car was parked. Wanting to see the type of vehicle the actor drove, he waited outside the garage for her to pull out. His work for the evening was over once he ascertained the plate number of the actor's white BMW.

The following morning Fishnet telephoned a private investigator he knew. The two had worked together years prior as detectives. The PI, who subscribed to the DMV database, provided Fishnet with the name and home address connected to the registered owner of the BMW. As Fishnet hoped, the vehicle was registered to the actor in question.

Fishnet proceeded to the actor's Westchester County residence. He found her house to be just off a dead end. From a safe distance, the former sleuth could view the premises with the aid of binoculars. Fishnet emerged from his car and walked to the residence to get a closer look at the property. He noted that three wide marble steps led to the entranceway. Once armed with all he needed to know, Fishnet returned to the city.

Fishnet stopped by an auto repair shop located in the precinct where he used to work. He engaged the owner of the shop in a pretext conversation that resulted in him being advised that Tufoil was the most effective industrial lubricant on the market. After some coaxing, the business owner agreed to part with a bottle of the lubricant.

"Be careful not to spill this stuff," cautioned the business owner. "If you do, you'll end up falling on your ass. It's very, very slippery."

"Thanks, I'll remember that," replied Fishnet with a cocky wink.

That evening Fishnet returned to the Westchester residence of the actor a short time before his intended victim was expected to arrive home. Fishnet poured the Tufoil on the three marble steps that led into the house. After doing that, he returned to his vehicle that was parked a safe distance away. With the aid of his binoculars, he was able to maintain a view of the residence.

Fishnet lit a cigarette as he waited for the white BMW to pull up to the house. When it did, the former detective could see that the actor wasn't alone. Exiting the BMW with his target was a large male of roughly the same age as the actor.

"Now who the hell is this?" Fishnet asked himself aloud. *It could be her old man*, he thought. Fishnet watched closely as the couple exited the vehicle. "Hah, hah, hah!" laughed Fishnet as he watched the big man tumble atop the much smaller woman, who was the first of the pair to slip and fall. When neither was able to rise to their feet, Fishnet knew his mission had met success. Leaving the two wailing in pain on the doorstep, Fishnet drove back to his Manhattan townhouse a satisfied man.

Fishnet had covered his tracks well enough not to be worried. He had worn the brim of his hat low and had placed a black scarf around his mouth to conceal his face. Before arriving in the vicinity of the target's residence he had taken the precaution of placing black electrical tape over two of the plate numbers on his vehicle.

The subsequent Westchester County Police investigation indicated that foul play was involved. Since the actor's male companion also sustained injuries, he was eliminated as a suspect. As a result of the tumble, the companion sustained injuries that included a fractured hip and a broken arm.

The police inquiry as to who was responsible for putting the lubricant on the steps produced no suspects. The victims were as clueless as the police.

***

FISHNET'S GIRLFRIEND WAS overjoyed at her good fortune. The understudy couldn't stop herself from gleefully dancing about her apartment. Being notified that she was to assume the lead in the play was the greatest of news. Overcome with elation, she never thought to consider the unfortunate woman who sustained two broken ankles as a result of her fall in Westchester County. The possibility of foul play never entered the realm of her thoughts.

Fishnet calmly sat in a chair studying the high-energy Cheryl as she carried on gleefully. He wondered how his girlfriend could be so dense. *How can she not realize that I created this opportunity for her?*

* * *

AS IT TURNED OUT, CHERYL'S stage performance exceeded expectations. Her reviews were even better than those of her predecessor. With Cheryl's overnight triumph came a development that the actor never imagined possible.

Cheryl was shocked when she received an invitation from Enzo Baffi's secretary to join the producer for an after-performance dinner to discuss an opportunity. The secretary conveyed that Baffi had heard about her theatrical triumph and wanted to speak to her about his new movie. Perceiving the invite as her ship coming in, Cheryl enthusiastically accepted without giving a thought to Baffi's reputation as a notorious womanizer.

When warned by a coworker about the producer's rumored sexual proclivities, Cheryl fluffed it off as just talk. When Cheryl informed Fishnet telephonically that she'd be unable to see him after her theater performance, he wanted to know why.

"Enzo Baffi asked me to dinner."

"Is that so?"

"Yes, Mr. Baffi heard about my performance and wants to see me about his new movie! He wants to talk about it over dinner."

"Yeah, I'm coming to that."

Cheryl was puzzled by his remark. "What do you mean?"

"C'mon, wise up. He's probably looking to get into your pants."

"Oh, stop it. You can be so crude sometimes."

"Well, whatever the reason, you could forget it. You're not going to any dinner without me being there to represent your interest."

"I am too going! This is my big chance, and I'm not going to blow it." Cheryl's adamant stance caused Fishnet to back off. "Don't you realize how important this is? We're talking about Mr. Baffi wanting to see me!"

While this was what Fishnet had planned, things were moving a bit too fast for him. The ex-detective wanted to control the action at his pace.

"What about what's important to me, Cheryl?" asked Fishnet.

"I know what's important to you. It's getting a little when you get horny," replied Cheryl sarcastically.

"You got a short memory, baby. I'm the guy who got you on first base—remember that. Without me, you're still serving hamburgers."

"I do remember, and I appreciate that. But sitting down with Mr. Baffi is the opportunity of a lifetime for a young actor."

"Go have your dinner with Baffi, Cheryl," said Fishnet, modifying his opposition. "Find out what he wants. And don't appear too anxious. All you gotta do is be patient and remember that I'm working behind the scenes for you. I'll propel your career like nobody's business," promised Fishnet. "There ain't anyone in this entertainment racket who can out-fence a guy like me."

"So now you're a producer?"

"Soon to be, baby, soon to be. You're swimming in deep waters," declared Fishnet. "And I'm just the guy who knows how to talk turkey with the sharks. I'll get you everything you want."

As Fishnet spoke, Cheryl recollected that when they first met, Fishnet pretended to be someone of prominence in the theater. She couldn't get around the fact that, as Fishnet often reminded, he delivered on his promise to get her a part in a play. For that reason, and the emotions that came with their being romantically involved, Cheryl believed in Fishnet.

"How do you plan on accomplishing that?" asked Cheryl softly.

"Don't worry about how, baby. Just leave everything to me."

"Okay, should I call you tonight after dinner?"

"You don't have to. I'll be waiting at your apartment for you. By the way, how old is Enzo Baffi?

"He's about 60."

"How does he look?"

"I've only seen pictures of him in the newspaper. He seems okay for his age, I suppose. Why do you ask?"

"Your manager needs to know everything, baby—everything."

While Cheryl was at dinner, Fishnet studied up on the power structure in the world of entertainment. The knowledge he gained verified everything Cheryl had told him. The notion of a producer controlling the purse strings and having the authority to hire and fire people captivated Fishnet.

Why, it all comes down to pure domination, thought Fishnet. *Once I get in position to start calling the shots, they'll all be bowing to my power.*

As Fishnet made himself a sandwich while waiting in his girlfriend's apartment, his mind drifted off to his other world, as it often did. In this fantasy, everyone admired him for the power he wielded. They all respectfully referred to him as "Mister."

24

A Golden

Opportunity

ENZO BAFFI WAS BORN IN Manhattan to an Italian father who came to America from a small town in southern Italy. Settling in East Harlem, the father secured work as a cleaner in a Midtown Manhattan hotel. It was there that he first met his wife, the daughter of a barber who worked in the hotel barber shop. Once he was accepted as a member of the family, the barber taught Enzo's father the hair-cutting trade. In time, the pupil went on to open his own barber shop on 10th Avenue, just a few blocks west of the Theater District.

The senior Baffi was the chatty sort who possessed a knack for making friends with his customers. One friendship he formed was with a Broadway actor who came from the same town in Italy as he did. Through this customer Enzo's father learned that, with some experience, he stood a chance of earning a little money by playing small ethnic roles in the theater.

Influenced by the perceived glamour and money connected to theatrical performances, both of Baffi's parents joined a small Greenwich Village acting troupe that put on amateur productions. This paved the way for young Enzo to develop an affinity for the arts.

A good student, Enzo attended The Julliard School, a private performing arts conservatory. Further education in both film and stage resulted in Enzo conducting his own workshops. He then graduated to creating, directing, and producing shows. Destined for success, Enzo went on to gain great fame.

Even at the age of sixty, Enzo remained a well-proportioned man who fell somewhere between handsome and average. He wore his hair slicked back without a part. Enzo tended to walk stiffly, taking measured steps without moving his arms.

A natty dresser, Enzo favored expensive, custom-made clothes. The cigarettes he smoked were housed in a gold-plated case with round, emerald studs that bore his initials. The cash he carried was held together by a diamond money clip, which was a far cry from the rubber band used by his father.

On the surface, Baffi was the picture of success. He owned homes and had a wife and family to be proud of. Somehow, he had managed to accomplish all this while concealing a demented side that would make the devil himself shudder.

* * *

CHERYL ARBUCKLE WALKED SIDE BY SIDE WITH Enzo Baffi as they made their way to Gallagher's Steak House on West 52nd Street. Baffi's dinner date adjusted her stride to get in sync with his. When not engaging with Cheryl, the producer's eyes stared straight ahead, oblivious to those he passed on the street.

Baffi was sincere in his desire to cast Cheryl in his new film. However, his interest wasn't purely professional. Since the actress was young and beautiful, she also appealed to his perversions, which were extensive.

Traveling to the restaurant on foot was all part of the cunning Baffi's seduction plan. He made it a point to stop in front of a store window, as if interested in what was being displayed. In reality it was a ploy to plant a seed in Cheryl's mind as to what a good pairing they made. As they gazed into the glass he casually remarked, "We look good together."

En route to the eatery, Baffi praised Cheryl's professional ability. He also incorporated flowery references to her beauty. His flattery was met by a receptive audience. The evening wind cooperated by furthering the tone set by the producer. The breeze blew the scent of Baffi's aftershave in Cheryl's direction. It was a strong fragrance that, along with the producer's confidence, triggered a slight romantic spark. By the time they had reached their destination, Cheryl had made up her mind that in order to meet her goals, if necessary, she would be his for the taking.

Seeing how well Baffi was received at the restaurant furthered Cheryl's awe. As an established name with a reputation for being a generous tipper, the producer rated special treatment.

"Your usual table, Mr. Baffi?" asked the maître d'.

"Yes, please."

"Allow me to order for us, Cheryl," said the producer, once seated.

Cheryl found Baffi to be a fascinating conversationalist with a vast knowledge of many things. Even his awareness of the trivial was interesting. He spoke of the restaurant's cofounder, Helen Gallagher Solomon, a former Ziegfeld girl, as if they were close.

"Did you actually know her?" asked Cheryl.

"Yes, my dear," said the producer. "In our industry, if traveling in the right circles, one gets to meet many people."

"Are you originally from Manhattan, Mr. Baffi?"

"Please, call me Enzo."

"Well, all right . . . Enzo."

"Yes, I'm a product of East Harlem. Does that surprise you?" Cheryl didn't know how to respond to his question. "Many people are surprised at that," he added.

The two went on to chat about their respective childhoods. The serial seducer made no reference to his wife and children, nor was he queried about them. In some ways Baffi reminded Cheryl of her ex-detective boyfriend. However, unlike Fishnet, the producer concealed his iron fist in a silk glove.

As charmed as Cheryl was, she never lost sight of the fact that Enzo Baffi was nothing more than a means to an end. While Baffi was attractive in his way, her heart remained with Fishnet. Nevertheless, Cheryl was prepared to loan herself to someone who could do her the most good professionally. It was a sacrifice she was willing to make.

* * *

AFTER DINNER, CHERYL ACCOMPANIED the producer to his penthouse for a nightcap. The special treatment extended by the building staff was another example of the type of life Cheryl wanted for herself.

It was at this point that Cheryl came to learn something of Baffi's wife and children. His explaining how they resided full time in his California home didn't interest Cheryl one way or the other. Her indifference pleased the producer. It signaled that things were likely to progress nicely.

"Why, my dear, your celebrity will be such that your photo will hang alongside those gracing the walls of the best restaurants in the Theater District," assured Baffi.

"But how can you be so certain, Enzo?"

"I create stars, my dear. I've accomplished great things with others who possess half your professional ability. Never doubt my ability to guide your career to the heights."

"I believe you," answered Cheryl with a timidity that conveyed to the producer the time was right to make his move.

"Come, let me show you the view from the bedroom, my dear," said Baffi. Cheryl, being led by the hand, followed willingly.

It was well into the wee hours of the morning when a car arrived to take Cheryl home. During the ride, her head was filled with thoughts of how she was now destined to be a big star.

* * *

FISHNET SAT IN HIS GIRLFRIEND'S apartment watching TV. He

ceased channel surfing when he came upon a documentary about African predators. He watched with interest as a hyena was being gobbled up by several lions. While most would have sympathy for the chewed-up hyena, Fishnet remained unfazed. He dismissed the brutal spectacle as being a simple question of the survival of the fittest.

At the conclusion of the documentary, the former detective began watching a movie. By the time the two-hour flick ended, he began to get impatient as he awaited Cheryl's arrival home. He drew upon his imaginary world to help pass the time.

This installment of fantasy saw the Gable look-alike as a famous producer. He was holding court at a VIP table inside a trendy nightspot while sitting with a bevy of Penthouse Pets who were celebrating the birthday of one of the girls. The red velvet rope that sectioned him off from other patrons made it clear that he was a man of importance.

"Who wants to be in my next picture?" Fishnet asked.

The echoing cries of "Me! Me! Me!" brought a satisfied smile to the daydreamer as he gazed off, deep in thought.

The fantasy was so delightful for Fishnet that it proved to be his longest fantasy ever. It concluded with him accepting an Academy Award for his contribution to the motion picture industry.

As more time passed, Fishnet began to get angry. There came a time when his interest in hearing about how Cheryl's dinner went professionally with Enzo Baffi became secondary. He wanted to know exactly what she was doing that was keeping her out so late. The thought of calling Cheryl's cell phone crossed his mind. He soon dismissed the idea, not wanting to show his jealousy.

Fishnet's ire manifested itself when Cheryl finally arrived home. Quick as a cat, he sprang from his chair and confronted his girlfriend the minute she entered the apartment. Without a word being exchanged, the former detective hauled off and slapped Cheryl's face hard.

"Did you have a nice time?" Fishnet asked, his teeth now clenched tight.

Cheryl raised her hands to protect against another blow. In Fishnet she now saw her father. He, too, had slapped her face when, as a teenager of sixteen, she came home late. She eventually came to justify both assaults as gestures of love coming from caring men who worried about her safety.

"Where the hell were you?" hissed Fishnet, his anger red hot.

"I'm sorry. I should have called you," apologized Cheryl. "The time just got away from me, I . . ."

Cheryl's explanation was cut short by Fishnet's advance toward her. Anticipating a second blow, Cheryl continued to cover her face. The second slap never came.

"Tell me everything you did tonight," ordered Fishnet, now wanting to hear all the details.

Fishnet stood in judgment as Cheryl articulated the events of the evening in the low voice of a youth who had behaved naughtily. When her narrative concluded, Fishnet had just a couple of questions.

"What did you think was going to happen once Baffi got you up to his penthouse?"

Cheryl offered no answer other than to say, "I know."

"So you went with him anyway," Fishnet said accusingly.

"What else could I do? Can't you understand? He's going to make me a star! Isn't that what we both want?"

"Didn't I tell you that I was going to make you a star?"

Cheryl sighed heavily before responding. "Do you really think I enjoyed going with that old man?" she asked, hoping to see signs of understanding. "Can't you see that was the fastest way for us to make things happen? Mr. Baffi is established, filthy rich, and can propel my career."

"I have plenty of money myself," reminded Fishnet, who disliked not being the top man in all areas.

"But Mr. Baffi has all the important connections. You have to see how much respect people have for him. He has huge power. He could be good for me—for us." The words "respect" and "power" got Fishnet's attention. "Enzo doesn't mean a thing to me," added Cheryl, "I'm just another notch on his bedpost."

Fishnet looked at Cheryl and nodded approvingly as the wheels began to turn in his head.

"You're absolutely right, baby. Guys like him have romances that always run their course. It'll be all over as soon as the next skirt comes along. By that time, I'll have what I want." Fishnet's comment, while puzzling, did show that he was thinking ahead.

"I don't understand."

"You will, baby. Once I get my hooks into him, I'll end up the guy with the power and juice."

"What are you planning on doing?"

"I'm planning on making you a star, baby. Enzo Baffi and me are gonna be partners."

Cheryl's mouth dropped open at hearing this. "How. . ."

"Don't worry about how, baby. What you have to do now is let that sucker know that I'm your business manager. Be sure he knows who I am. Make it clear that, moving ahead, everything goes through me."

"But that could turn him off and undermine my chances."

"Not a shot of that happening. Trust me; I know my poker. I'm gonna make you a screen queen."

Fishnet maintained such a strong emotional hold on Cheryl that, even after assaulting her, she believed in him. As someone susceptible to strong, confident personalities, the blinded Cheryl found in Fishnet her ideal. She viewed any attention she received from him, be it kind or cruel, as an indication of his love. Seeing that Fishnet had calmed down, she got around to addressing his brutal treatment of her.

"You slapped me."

"Because I'm crazy in love with you, baby," lied Fishnet, knowing exactly how to play her. "I got worried that something might have happened to you. I just went nuts." Cheryl accepted this explanation because it was what she wanted to hear.

"I want you to promise me that you won't ever do that again," Cheryl said.

"Did I hurt you?" asked Fishnet, not agreeing to anything.

"I'll live."

"Let me ask you something, baby."

"What?"

"I'm just curious. What is this producer like in the sack?"

"You're not going to believe this."

"Try me."

"It took my giving him a golden shower to get him excited."

"Are you serious?"

"Yes. It's something I'd rather not think about."

"Well, now ain't that something," said Fishnet, who looked pleased. He now saw himself armed with leverage. "Come over here to Papa Bear," he said happily. "It's time for us to kiss and make up."

25

A Beast at the
Door

FISHNET WENT TO SEE THE MAESTRO at the apartment the
violin virtuoso shared with his lover, Pascal. The couple
detested Fishnet, who they considered a beast who had once
been married to a dear friend and late actress known to both
men. The Maestro knew the actress professionally. Pascal,
bisexual, knew her intimately. Both the Maestro and Pascal had
the displeasure of experiencing Fishnet's dark side firsthand.

Fishnet first met the Maestro and Pascal at a party thrown by
his late wife at her townhouse, the same townhouse that
Fishnet later inherited. At the time of their first meeting, Pascal
was the resident boy toy of Fishnet's future wife. Recognizing
how good Pascal had it, Fishnet decided he wanted to assume
Pascal's role of a kept plaything. To accomplish that end, the ex-
detective resorted to skullduggery.

Fishnet displaced Pascal by making it appear that the kept man
had stolen from his benefactor. After physically ejecting Pascal
from the townhouse, Fishnet was free to successfully pursue his
future wife without competition.

Once ousted, Pascal fell on hard times. After a short tenure at a Bowery flophouse, Pascal finally found a soft landing in the apartment of the Maestro, a man he had been intimate with many years prior when he was young and hustling older men of wealth.

The last time Fishnet visited the Maestro was when he persuaded the octogenarian to lend a hand in securing a stage role for his girlfriend, Cheryl. It had taken heavy-handed tactics to gain the Maestro's cooperation in assisting Cheryl. The violinist—and his lover—both had good reason to fear and detest the ex-detective.

When Fishnet arrived at the Maestro's apartment, he could hear the sound of violin music emanating from behind the closed door. Since the instrument wasn't being played well, Fishnet assumed it was one of the Maestro's students who was producing the sound.

Fishnet checked his watch. Seeing that it was five minutes to the hour, he decided to wait until the lesson would likely be over. His wait in the hall was interrupted by Pascal returning home from an errand. Pascal, many years younger than the Maestro, was something of a dandy. He presented a dapper appearance in his cream-colored, double-breasted overcoat.

"Hello, Pascal. How have you been, pal?" asked Fishnet in a wise-guy, sing-song way. "Nice coat. I see the old man has been good to you."

"What are you doing here?" asked the nervous Pascal. "I thought your business with the Maestro was over."

"Is that any way to greet a friend?"

"We're not friends, Mr. Fish," answered Pascal, who only knew Fishnet by the name Shepherd Fish. The alias was assumed prior to Fishnet inheriting his great wealth from his late wife.

When the door to the apartment suddenly opened, their conversation was curtailed. A youth of about fourteen exited, carrying a violin case. The boy passed by the men without acknowledging either of them. Fishnet held the apartment door open while addressing Pascal. "Shall we?" he asked, inviting Pascal to step into the apartment.

"What is the meaning of this, Pascal?" thundered the excitable Maestro. "Why are you bringing this ruffian into our home?"

"Easy," said Fishnet, closing the apartment door. "We got business, Pop."

"I didn't invite him in, Maestro," explained Pascal defensively. He was about to clarify matters when he was suddenly silenced by the unwelcome visitor.

"Take a seat in the corner over there, Pascal, and take a load off. Me and Pop got business."

"We have no business, Mr. Fish," said the Maestro with firmness. "I don't approve of you or your methods. Now, please get out of my house at once!" demanded the Maestro.

"Ain't you being a little reckless now, Pop?"

Fishnet took a menacing step toward the old man. His serious look made it clear that mayhem might be fast approaching. The Maestro placed his hand to the front of his neck. He recalled the pain he endured from the time Fishnet twisted the loose flesh that hung from his throat. The violinist retreated two steps.

"You stay away from me," said the wary Maestro, the force in his voice now diminished.

"Maybe we should at least listen to what he has to say, Maestro," pleaded the cowardly Pascal, who was hoping to avoid violence.

The Maestro looked at Pascal. Seeing the concern in Pascal's face caused the violinist to concede his disadvantage. He decided it prudent to hear Fishnet out.

"Well, what is it you want?" asked the octogenarian. "I have a student scheduled to come by in twenty-five minutes, so get to the point quickly."

"Don't sweat it, Pop. Our business ain't gonna take long."

"Please stop calling me Pop!"

"Sure, Maestro, sure," said Fishnet, appeasing the violinist. "All I want is for you to give me an introduction to Enzo Baffi."

"I don't know anyone by that name," fibbed the Maestro.

"Don't give me that crap. You artsy guys all know each other."

"I said that I don't know him," insisted the Maestro.

Fishnet looked around the apartment for something to frighten the Maestro with. He walked to the kitchen and removed a steak knife from the tray next to the sink. He then walked over to the window blinds and cut off a length of cord. Wrapping an end of the cord around each hand he approached the Maestro.

"Maestro!" shouted the anguished Pascal. "For God's sake tell him that you'll do what he asks!"

Fishnet looped the cord around the Maestro's neck and lifted, bringing the much shorter man up on his toes. Feeling the coarseness of the cord beginning to tear into his throat, the Maestro relented, admitting his familiarity with the producer. Once released, the violinist dropped back onto his flattened feet. With one hand the Maestro held his throat. With the other he took the telephone Fishnet handed him and dialed Baffi.

"Enzo, it's the Maestro speaking."

"Maestro!" answered Baffi energetically. "How are you, my friend? It's been a while."

"It has been a while."

"How is Pascal? I assume you are both well."

"We're fine. Now let me tell you why I'm calling."

Baffi had tremendous respect for the Maestro. It was the virtuoso who had been there for the producer when he was an unknown starting out. Being at the top of his game at the time, the Maestro opened doors for Baffi that might have otherwise been impossible to open. This consideration was something Baffi never forgot.

The producer, once understanding that a friend of the Maestro sought an introduction to him, agreed to a meeting.

"Will you be joining us, Maestro?" asked the producer.

"Oh, no, no, no. Mr. Fish will be attending alone."

"Well, let's us do lunch or dinner one day soon. Bring along Pascal."

"Yes, of course. Let's do that."

"There now, was that so hard, Pop?" asked Fishnet after the Maestro hung up the phone. "After all, what the hell are good friends for?" The Maestro held his tongue. Fishnet then turned to Pascal, giving him a nod before leaving the apartment.

Once the Maestro was certain that Fishnet had left the

building, he immediately called Enzo Baffi and explained that Mr. Fish was a dangerous man who was not to be trusted or taken lightly. The Maestro strongly advised his friend to listen but to avoid getting involved with him in any way.

When Baffi queried the Maestro as to why he had facilitated an introduction to such a disreputable character, the Maestro failed to be completely honest. His explanation was brief and revealed little. All he could commit to saying was that existing conditions necessitated the introduction. Baffi could tell that his old friend was ill at ease talking about Mr. Fish.

"Why, exactly, does he want to meet me?"

"He didn't say."

"Tell me, my dear friend, is this meeting really necessary?" asked Baffi.

"Enzo, would I call you if I had other options?" replied the Maestro. "Please, do me this favor. Just meet with this beast, but don't get involved."

The producer honored what he felt to be an obligation to his old friend. He assured the Maestro that he would be more than prepared when meeting Mr. Fish.

Enzo Baffi did not rise to the heights he had attained by being a fool. After hanging up with the Maestro, he contacted his personal trainer, a man who had wrestled professionally. The trainer agreed to be on hand with another bruiser when the producer was to meet with the mysterious Mr. Fish.

While Enzo Baffi embraced the importance of self-protection, the potential for peril was something he didn't shy away from. He held an odd attraction for violence. The satisfaction he received from it was as bizarre as his love of golden showers.

* * *

THE FIRST THING FISHNET NOTICED when he entered the Broadway office of Enzo Baffi was the two burly men who sat in the reception area. They were tough-looking characters, the type you didn't see often. Their ears were cauliflower, a deformity of the outer ear associated with old-school boxers

230

and wrestlers. Fishnet wondered if the men were there for his benefit. If yes, it meant that the Maestro must have crossed him. Fishnet approached the woman seated at the reception desk. An older woman attired in a black business suit, was Baffi's private secretary.

"I'm here to see Mr. Baffi. He's expecting me."

"Are you Mr. Fish?"

Fishnet smiled at being referred to by the alias he had been using. "Yeah, that's me."

"One second, please," said the secretary. She telephoned the producer to let him know his visitor was outside his private office. "Mr. Baffi said you may go right in, Mr. Fish," said the receptionist.

Fishnet nodded his thank-you and headed toward the door that led to the producer's office. Out of the corner of his eye he glanced at the two burly men seated in the reception area. Taking their cue from the secretary, the security people rose from their seats and followed Fishnet into the private office. At that point, Fishnet knew for certain they were there for him.

That friggin' Maestro must have given this producer an earful about me, thought Fishnet. *Just wait until I see him again.*

Fishnet pressed his hands against his overcoat. The feel of the .38 caliber revolver he carried reassured him. It was his equalizer. In the event of trouble, he was prepared.

Fishnet's first impression was that Enzo Baffi looked pretty good for his age. Baffi's impression of Fishnet was also favorable. The producer was surprised to see how much the former detective resembled Clark Gable. Since Baffi was a Gable fan, Fishnet's likeness to the late movie star was beneficial to him.

"Wait outside, gentlemen," said Baffi, addressing the bodyguards. "I'll call you if I need you."

"Whatever the Maestro told you about me, you gotta take with a grain of salt," said Fishnet, mincing no words. "Our friend is starting to lose it in his old age."

"Have a seat, Mr. Fish. I was only warned that you could be a dangerous man," said the producer bluntly. Baffi's unblinking

231

eyes and taut mouth made it clear to Fishnet that the producer was no milquetoast.

"I don't know about me being dangerous. I'm what I like to describe as passionate."

"That's a quality we share, Mr. Fish. I'm also a passionate man. So tell me, why has the Maestro formed such a low opinion of you?"

"Because I go after what I want, and the Maestro is an old man who scares easy," replied Fishnet.

"I find your honesty admirable, Mr. Fish. You say what you want without worry of offending."

"The way I see it, every man puts his pants on one leg at a time," stated Fishnet, indirectly putting Baffi on notice that he was not intimidated by him.

"That's true, but some of us get to wear wool pants in the winter, while others wear them in the summer," countered Baffi. "In any event, the Maestro is a dear friend who helped me early on in my career. How do you happen to know him?"

"He was a friend of my late wife. You may have heard of her. She was pretty well-known on the stage."

Baffi was taken aback when Fishnet dropped the name of his late wife. The producer knew her to have been both an heiress to a fortune and a well-known theatrical presence. This revelation erased some of the concern the producer initially had about his visitor.

"So what brings you here, Mr. Fish?"

"I'm Cheryl Arbuckle's business manager . . . and boyfriend. She probably mentioned me to you."

"Cheryl Arbuckle?"

Fishnet didn't appreciate Baffi's feigning ignorance of Cheryl. The producer's pretending not to know who Cheryl was prompted Fishnet to be shockingly direct.

"Yeah, Cheryl—the girl who plays the lead in that hot play. You know who I mean. She's the babe you like to have piss on you."

"Oh, I see," voiced Baffi with coolness. The producer now suspected that his visitor might have come to his office out of jealousy. "Let's keep this civil, Mr. Fish," said Baffi, his tone now cold. "Those two gentlemen out front are here for a reason. Let's not necessitate their joining us as we have our little talk, shall we?"

"That's fine with me, Enzo."

Baffi stiffened at being called Enzo by someone he now considered an uncouth lout. He wasn't used to such familiarity from those he considered beneath him.

"Most people call me Mr. Baffi."

"Okay . . . Mr. Baffi."

"So am I correct in assuming that my evening with Cheryl prompted you to seek an audience with me, Mr. Fish?"

"I can be very open-minded when it comes to Cheryl . . . as long as we're doing business together."

"What business do you see us doing together, might I ask?"

"I see us as partners in Cheryl."

"I have no need for a partner—or for Cheryl. I have no use for anyone who comes with complications."

"This ain't complicated," said Fishnet. "All I want is to have my name listed next to yours as the producer in the movie you're making. My goal is to have everyone recognize me as a power in the movie industry. You can help me make that happen."

"You're joking, aren't you?"

Fishnet responded with questions of his own. "You want funny? How about your wife and kids finding out how you get off on young girls pissing on you? That would be a riot on the home front, wouldn't it?"

"So this is a shakedown!" exclaimed Baffi.

"Let's just call it a negotiation. You play ball with me, and we both win. You get what you want, and I get what I want."

"And money?"

"I'm not after money." Fishnet's remark took Baffi by surprise. "And if I don't agree to this?"

"Then you got no Cheryl for your picture and no Cheryl to piss on you. And you gotta deal with people snickering at a slime-ball pervert whenever you enter a room. No big shot wants that, does he?"

Baffi mentally weighed his options before speaking. Knowing that golden showers were only the tip of the iceberg when it came to his preferences, he thought it wise to appease Fishnet.

"No, I suppose not," replied the producer. "Perhaps we should discuss this in a less official setting, Mr. Fish. Are you available to come to my penthouse for a drink this evening?"

The invitation presented one of those rare occasions in which Fishnet wasn't totally sure of himself. He didn't know where Baffi was coming from. He accepted the drink invitation with the understanding that the get-together would be held in a safer venue. Fishnet suggested the two meet at his own townhouse.

That evening the two men reconvened at Fishnet's townhouse. After some back and forth, they struck a deal. It was agreed that Fishnet would be the associate producer on the movie Cheryl was to star in. In return for this designation, Fishnet agreed to keep the producer's embarrassing secret.

Their agreement stipulated that Fishnet would be permitted on the set but not be allowed to offer any professional contributions. He was also not to receive financial compensation. This worked for Fishnet because all he was after was the notoriety and perceived power that came with the position.

As a result of reaching the compromise, a certain comfort level existed that enabled the men to talk in a more civil fashion.

"It was unfortunate what happened to the lead in Cheryl's show," said Baffi.

"Shit happens," replied Fishnet.

"I suppose it does," agreed Baffi. "I often wonder who may have greased those steps."

"She probably pissed somebody off. Anyway, it's none of my business . . . curiosity killed the cat."

"Just to be clear, my friend, do you have a problem as far as my continuing to have relations with Cheryl?" asked the producer.

"No problem at all, Enzo. Cheryl can water you down anytime you want." The devious smile on Fishnet's face caused the producer to despise his new business associate even more than before.

"By the way, for my own edification, just how flexible is Cheryl?" asked Baffi.

"What do you mean, Enzo?"

"I'm a man of assorted enjoyments. Would she be open to experimentation in nontraditional forms of gratification?"

This guy is one sick puppy, thought Fishnet. "Let me put it this way, Enzo . . . anything goes with Cheryl if she's being fast-tracked to being a movie star."

"You can be assured of that. Cheryl has that something extra that will come through to filmgoers."

Fishnet found this encouraging. *If this guy knows his business, there is no telling how big Cheryl can be*, he thought. *Why, once I get smartened up, I'll build my own empire!*

Along with Fishnet's great optimism came a concern. When alone, Fishnet came to the disturbing conclusion that it was possible Cheryl might get so big that she wouldn't need him anymore. To prevent that outcome, he knew that he had to come up with a way to lock her in. He thought of the one way to protect his interest: *I gotta marry the bitch!*

26

Money Talks

BACK AT THE APARTMENT in Toms River, Ross Holt did lots of thinking. Bothered by Gloria's behavior at the Perez residence, he was of the opinion that his paramour crime partner had become more trouble than she was worth. He decided that, once he collected money from Sammy Angelo, he'd slip away and start anew in another state, solo.

Thanks to the multitude of senior citizens in the Sunshine State, Ross saw Florida as, possibly, the ideal venue to continue his Father Billy scam.

Several days after arriving in Toms River, Ross received a call on his cell phone. It was Sammy Angelo inquiring as to when the bogus priest would be available to meet. Angelo's voice came across as tense, smacking of someone desperate. This was encouraging to Ross, who equated distress with the potential for commanding more money.

"You sound all wound up, Sammy. What's wrong?"

"I'm worried, Father. When can you see my friend, Dennis?"

"Soon, I'll get to you soon. I need to see you as well. You know my medical situation, right?"

"Yes, I'll have the money you need for that when you come, Father."

"Thank you, Sammy. Remind me of the problem with Dennis."

When Sammy finished conveying how his friend Dennis Bumper was in deep trouble due to having committed several murders, the conversation went silent.

"Father, are you there?" Sammy asked.

Not sure if he heard right, the fraudster sought clarification. "Did you say several murders?"

"Yes, Father. Dennis went off the deep end and snapped. He killed three people."

Again the phone went silent, this time until Ross regained his composure. "Why would he do such a thing?"

"It was over love, Father. He just went totally insane."

"Where is he now?"

"Dennis is in my apartment with me. He's in the next room watching television."

"Are you crazy too?" blurted the bogus priest. "Why didn't you call the cops?"

"He's my closest friend, Father. He's docile now that he got all the anger out of his system."

"How can you be so sure?"

"I'm sure because he's staying with me in my apartment."

"Well, what does he want with me? He's not angry with me, is he?"

"Of course not, Father. He needs you."

"What does he need me for?"

"Dennis wants to make his peace before turning himself into the police. He wants you to hear his confession before he turns himself in at the police station. He wants us to go with him when he gives himself up."

Fat chance of that happening, thought Ross. The situation being complicated caused the priest impersonator to back off.

"This is really a police matter, Sammy."

"But I'll have the money you need, Father . . . all in cash like you wanted. I mean, I can even give you another five or ten thousand for your trouble. You may need a nurse or something after they fix you up."

The offer of additional money was too tempting for Ross to walk away from. "Are you sure that Dennis isn't dangerous?"

237

"Thank God, he's been himself, Father."

Ross proposed a date to meet with Sammy Angelo and Dennis Bumper. Sammy indicated that Bumper preferred to meet around the time the blizzard was being forecast.

"Why then?" Ross asked.

"Dennis feels the cops will be busy dealing with the snow." Ross believed this to be sound thinking for reasons of his own.

"Dennis is going to need a good lawyer, Sammy. I know of an excellent criminal attorney, but he's going to need money for his services up front. Can you rustle up another five thousand on top of the extra ten?"

"I can cover that, Father."

This guy's crazier than his friend, thought Ross. "Are you sure you can get your hands on that kind of money?"

"I keep more than that in my house, Father. I came into enough money to cover whatever it takes."

"You did?"

"Yeah, I inherited money from a rich relative. I took care of him when he got sick. I was his only living relative here in America."

"What kind of work did your uncle do?"

"I'm not really sure. He was a little shady, so everything he left me was in cash. Do you think that having a priest standing with Bumper before a judge might convince the courts to place Dennis in a hospital, Father? He needs the help of trained professionals."

"I'm sure of it, Sammy. When did your poor uncle die?"

"About six months ago."

How about this little shit, thought Ross. *He's been holding out on me all this time!*

"I'm surprised you never mentioned your uncle to me before, Sammy."

"My accountant told me to keep the money I got to myself."

"Oh, did he? What else did he tell you to do?"

"He said I should live off it."

"I see. Well, we can't have Dennis continue to flounder in a state of sin. You two plan on meeting me at the church the day after the storm. Let's say at 1 p.m. I'll make arrangements with

238

the lawyer. Bring the money with you."

"We'll meet you at the rectory?"

"No, not the rectory, I said the church. I'll be waiting inside the first confessional booth. After I hear confession, you give me the cash, and I'll go see the lawyer with the money while you and your friend wait in church for me to return with the lawyer. Dennis will be safe in the church."

After the con man hung up with Sammy, he rose from his seat to give his girlfriend a big hug.

"What was that all about?" asked Gloria.

"I'm gonna need a car so I can pick up the money in Brooklyn. What about your sister?"

"What about her?"

"She's gotta loan me her car."

"Not a chance."

"What if we pay her good?"

"Well, that may be a different story. I'll go see her."

* * *

GLORIA'S RELATIONSHIP WITH her sister had chilled since the time Gloria was imprisoned years ago. Gloria's incarceration was considered a great embarrassment to her sister. Adding to the decline in their relationship was Gloria's constant borrowing of money from their parents. The sister saw each bank withdrawal as an attack on her inheritance.

Gloria anticipated having a difficult time convincing her sister, who lived within walking distance, to loan out her car. She decided to come as close to the truth as possible when explaining to her sibling the need for the vehicle. Gloria conveyed that her priest friend was going to need her car to pick up several boxes of religious articles and then transport the boxes to his Brooklyn rectory the following day. The sister scoffed at the very thought of Gloria having a priest friend.

"Since when do you have a priest friend, Gloria?"

"What's so strange about that?" asked Gloria defensively. "I go to church."

239

"When did that start?"

"Since I got out of jail," replied Gloria. "You always think the worst of me."

"Okay," said the sister curtly. "Let's just drop it. I'm not loaning anybody my car."

"But this is for the church . . ."

"Didn't you hear the weather forecast? They're expecting heavy snow."

"He's a careful driver."

"Why doesn't the priest just rent a car?"

"I don't know. Father Billy hasn't the money for that. I promise you, he'll have the car back the day after he borrows it."

"What's your connection to this priest?"

"He's helped me a lot . . . in a spiritual way. I've been working with him at the rectory in Brooklyn. With his guidance I've been able to clean up my act," said the untruthful Gloria. "When was the last time I had to mooch money from Mom?"

"I don't know about this, Gloria. I mean, after all, I don't even know this person."

Gloria sensed that her sister's resistance was diminishing. "I told you he's a priest. When was the last time I bothered you for anything? Just do me this one favor, will you? I swear you'll get your precious car back tomorrow night."

Admittedly the older sister, who was a self-employed graphic designer, hadn't heard of any problems with Gloria of late. After some further questioning, she finally relented.

"Okay, it's against my better judgment, but I'll loan you the car. Just remember, I expect you to have my car back the day after I give it to you," advised the car owner. There was no mention of payment for use of the vehicle.

Gloria telephoned her paramour on the walk home to advise Ross that she'd be there in a few minutes. When Gloria was asked how much she had to promise her sister for use of the car, she informed her lover that it would cost him three hundred dollars. Ross, who was not in a position to quibble, forked over the requested sum.

27

Watching the Weather

IT WAS ANNOUNCED ON TELEVSION that the city was well-equipped to deal with the substantial amount of snow that was being predicted. Depending on whom you were, this bulletin had varying degrees of relevance.

For most adults snow was an inconvenience. For Sammy Angelo, the coming storm was great news. It meant he and Bumper would be meeting with Father Billy at the Sunset Park church the day after the snow fell. Bumper was finally going to have the opportunity to confess his sins and then surrender to the law. As for Sammy, he'd be free of the fret connected to harboring his friend.

"It won't be long now, Dennis," Sammy announced happily. "The snow is definitely coming."

"That's great," Dennis answered in a low voice. His response seemed to lack enthusiasm.

"What's the matter? Aren't you happy?"

"Yeah, I'm happy," replied Bumper, "but I'm gonna miss not being able to hang around with you."

Sammy's mouth dropped after hearing this. He was concerned that Bumper might be having a change of heart.

"Seeing Father Billy and turning yourself in is the right thing to do, Dennis; you know that. You can't change your mind now. After all, Father Billy is coming off a sick bed to help you."

"Yeah, I know that. I didn't change my mind. I just hope we stay in touch once they put me away."

"Don't worry about that, Dennis. I swear by all that is holy that I'll come see you regularly wherever you are."

* * *

ARLENE AND MILLIE PEREZ WERE at a point in their lives where they dreaded snowy weather. For the sisters, a substantial accumulation meant work. Since the time Millie broke her arm years ago due to slippery conditions while walking to a corner store, both siblings restricted venturing outdoors until pathways were established by the homeowners.

"Maybe the forecast is wrong," said Arlene. "They've been wrong before."

"Oh, let's hope so," voiced Millie.

"The city said they planned to close the schools. If it does snow heavy, at least that'll make the children happy."

"Remember when we used to build a snowman as kids?"

"I do, Millie. That was fun, wasn't it?" answered Arlene, thinking fondly back on her youth. "Even shoveling the snow out front with Papa was fun in those days."

"Not anymore. Shoveling is a lot of work now. Thank goodness we have the Captain around to pitch in and help us."

"Yes, it is," agreed Arlene, secretly wishing that Detective Von Hess was around to help out. Ever since their encounter, she thought of the detective. Several times Arlene picked up her phone to call Von Hess, only to change her mind.

* * *

WITH THE WEATHER SITUATION BEING A CONCERN, Fishnet

wanted no problems at his townhouse. He contacted a young handyman to come and clean the boiler in the basement. He also made arrangements for the handyman to clear the snow from his property once it stopped falling.

When the worker finished on the boiler he was paid in cash and offered a cold beer. As the man consumed the beer, Fishnet noticed he was wearing a spanking new gold wedding band.

"Newly married?" Fishnet asked, making conversation.

"Three months."

"Congratulations. You had a time?"

"Excuse me?" asked the handyman, who didn't understand the question.

"Did you have a big party?"

"No, we had no money for that. The priest, he took good care of us. We didn't have to do none of the stuff you usually have to do to get married."

"I don't follow you . . ."

"My wife was pregnant, so we were in a hurry. The priest understood and married us real quick in the rectory. We were in and out in fifteen minutes."

"And you got a marriage certificate?"

"Oh, yes, right after he married us. He even got the witness for us and everything.

"You had just one witness? I always thought you needed two."

"No, we only had one. Father Billy had the woman who works for him in the rectory be the witness."

"And that's all there was to it?"

"Yes, the priest made it very easy. The only thing is that I had to pay him in cash."

I suppose cash can grease any wheels, thought Fishnet, who now believed the priest had probably gone into business for himself.

"Where is this rectory, my friend?"

"It's near where I live in Sunset Park."

Providing he could come to terms with the priest, Fishnet saw a way to ensure his control over his girlfriend Cheryl. *If I can get this Father Billy to play ball, he could go through the motions of performing a phony marriage ceremony,* thought Fishnet. *Once Cheryl thinks we're married, I'll own her....and still be free to walk away clean anytime I want.*

"Sit down and have another beer, my friend," invited Fishnet, who wanted to hear more about Father Billy.

* * *

FISHNET'S GIRLFRIEND HAD BEEN in the greatest of spirits ever since being awarded the starring role in Enzo Baffi's new movie. She could hardly believe that Fishnet landed her the choice role in the producer's film. Her boyfriend's ability to deliver on his promises never ceased to amaze Cheryl.

The actor locked her arms tightly around the finagling ex-detective. Her vice-like embrace came complete with emotions. The tears shed were not unwelcomed by Fishnet. The former detective stroked the back of Cheryl's head in a calming fashion as they continued to hold each other. When Cheryl looked up into Fishnet's face, he saw the innocence of a grateful child.

"Stick with me, baby," he said, looking deep into Cheryl's eyes. "We're perfect for each other. Just look how things have been breaking for you."

"It's like a dream come true."

"Never stop betting on me, baby."

"You're amazing."

"It's all about having the right technique. But there is one thing about this Enzo Baffi that you're gonna have to go along with."

"What's that?"

"Has he called on you yet?"

Cheryl stiffened. "What do you mean?" she asked.

"He's got that kinky side that you'll have to satisfy for a while. It'll be just a temporary thing."

"You mean I have to keep giving him golden showers?"

"Yeah, just look at it like paying your dues." Cheryl's expression turned glum.

Fishnet believed Cheryl's dismay would be reversed once he proposed marriage. The unexpectedness of his proposal totally flabbergasted Cheryl, who was still digesting the news of her having to carry on with the producer. While Cheryl had strong feelings for Fishnet, she was reluctant to commit to marriage. The former law enforcement officer, sensing Cheryl's apprehension, immediately put her on the defensive.

"You don't want to marry me?" he asked, pretending to be heartbroken. "After all I've done for you?"

"It's not that I don't want to marry you, only everything is happening so fast for me right now. Planning a wedding is not a simple thing for me at this time," explained Cheryl.

After some further dialogue, Fishnet was satisfied that all Cheryl needed was time to think his proposal over.

"Sure, baby, I understand. This is a big step, so take some time to sort things out. But remember, I ain't the kind of guy who hangs around waiting forever."

28

The Super Snitch

THE SUNSET PARK SUPER WAS ENGAGED IN a row with his wife over money. Rather than argue he thought it better to leave their apartment before the dispute escalated. He took refuge in the basement of the building where he maintained a small work station that consisted of a desk and chair that had been left behind by a tenant who had moved.

The super lit a cigarette and began to ponder his financial situation. He opened the top drawer of the desk and removed the business card that was given to him by Sergeant Markie. Tempted by the reward that he was led to believe existed, the super recollected seeing Sammy Angelo at the mailboxes. He struggled to remember if the mailbox of Dennis Bumper was actually opened by Sammy. He concluded that it was.

Seeing a way that might ease his economic distress, the super gathered his tools and proceeded to Sammy Angelo's apartment. He paused to listen at the door before knocking. Certain that he heard voices coming from inside, he tapped on the front door. Suddenly, the voices abruptly went silent.

"Who is it?" Sammy asked.

"It's me, the super."

"What's up?" asked Sammy after partially opening the door.

"Are you having a problem with the bathroom?"

"No. What gave you that idea?"

"Those detectives who came around, they told me you did."

"I don't know where they got that idea from," said Sammy, appearing nervous. "Did they come around again?"

"No, they just came by that one time."

"Did they say what their business was?"

"No, they just asked for you."

"Did they ask for anyone else?"

"No, just you," fibbed the super.

"Oh, okay. Anyway, there is nothing wrong with the bathroom."

"They're saying we got some big snow coming our way."

"Yeah, I heard," said Sammy.

The super went on to make several visits to Sammy's floor throughout the evening. The sounds he overheard through Sammy's front door convinced him there was someone in the apartment with Sammy. Based on what he heard, he believed that Sammy's company was Dennis Bumper. The super telephonically passed this information on to Sergeant Markie. He also reminded the investigator of the reward promised

* * *

WITH HIS FORMAL ATTACHMENT to Enzo Baffi established, Fishnet made time to expand his knowledge in order not to appear artistically ignorant. The former detective devoured portions of the encyclopedia that pertained to the theater and filmmaking. He had even boned up on some of the literary classics.

As his education developed, Fishnet took to casual behavior that he suspected Enzo Baffi of engaging in. During evenings alone in his townhouse, Fishnet took to lounging around in a wardrobe that consisted of a shark-colored smoking jacket, silk pajamas, and leather burgundy slippers.

Fishnet had just poured himself a brandy before assuming his place on the cushioned chair near the fireplace in his townhouse. On the end table next to him was a large crystal ashtray that held the cigar he fired up.

Over his drink, Fishnet began reading *Of Mice and Men* by John Steinbeck. The American classic was just one of the dozen books he picked up at Barnes & Noble. His peaceful tranquility was interrupted just before midnight when his cell phone rang. It was his girlfriend Cheryl.

Fishnet was a bit annoyed at being interrupted by the late-night phone call. Things got ugly when a sobbing Cheryl began conveying what a beast Enzo Baffi turned out to be.

"Back up and take a breath, Cheryl," instructed Fishnet. "Now start from scratch and tell me what happened," he said after achieving a degree of calmness. The information communicated by Cheryl was disturbing enough for Fishnet to seek retribution.

"Where are you now, Cheryl?"

"I'm on my way home. Can you come over?"

"I'm not even dressed," explained Fishnet. "I'm in my pajamas. Besides, snow is in the forecast."

"It's not snowing now . . ."

"It's coming; they just can't pinpoint exactly when."

"Can I come to your house?" asked Cheryl. The shakiness in her voice was convincing. Fishnet knew he was needed.

"Yeah, you might as well. Come on over."

Fishnet threw the book he was reading down in anger. He disliked being distracted.

When Cheryl arrived at the townhouse, Fishnet couldn't get over his girlfriend's troubled appearance. Her hair was tousled, and the tears she had shed caused her eye makeup to leave long, black streaks leading to her cheeks. Cheryl looked like she'd been put through hell.

"Now tell me again exactly what happened," said the former detective, his concern genuine.

Cheryl's look turned wild. It was clear to Fishnet that a fierce fire had been lit within her that would never go out. "Enzo is a human monster! The things he made me do . . . It just sickens me to talk about it!" That was as far as Cheryl got before breaking down in tears.

"Calm down," said Fishnet softly. He placed his arms about her gently to console her.

Fishnet's efforts at soothing gained traction enough for Cheryl to convey her horrid experience. As the report of the despicable perversions unfolded, Fishnet listened without expressing emotion. By the time Cheryl concluded her account, Fishnet knew Baffi's behavior required stern answering. The horrors inflicted by the producer were revolting, even to a callous man like Fishnet.

"I just can't go on like this," announced Cheryl between sobs.

"You won't have to be alone with that pervert again. I'll see to that. But your movie career, you can't just throw it away."

"Career or no career, I can't continue with Enzo. I know it'll probably be over for me professionally, but I can't go through another minute in that black room of his."

"What black room?"

"There is a room in his penthouse that he keeps locked. The walls and ceiling are painted black. It's like a dungeon," Cheryl explained. "The only lighting is red, and he's got . . ."

"Save it, baby. I don't need you to draw me pictures."

"I want nothing to do with him!"

"Okay, take it easy, Cheryl. He didn't kill you. This is a bad situation; I'll give you that. But let's not bite our nose to spite our face. I know exactly how to handle this sicko."

Cheryl was astonished at Fishnet's words. "How could you be so indifferent?" she asked her boyfriend.

"I'm not indifferent, baby—just calculating."

Fishnet intended to punish Baffi for Cheryl's sake while, at the same time, maintaining the three-sided professional relationship they had. Failure in this respect was not an option. His inability to mend the torn relationship could result in Fishnet's own personal ambitions being derailed.

"You can't expect me to continue on with this son of a bitch?"

"No, baby, that romance is over. But you're not throwing away your career over a setback."

Fishnet's comment only served to inflame Cheryl. "A setback!" she shouted.

"All right, call it whatever you want. Your beef ain't with me, it's with Enzo." Fishnet's remark gave Cheryl pause. She began to look at him quizzically in silence. "Trust me; don't you worry about a thing," assured Fishnet. "You'll never have to endure any misery with that bastard again. That's my promise to you, and you can take that to the bank."

"What are you going to do?"

"Don't you worry about what I'm gonna do. Enzo is the guy who should be doing the worrying. I'm gonna go see him."

"What are you going to say to him?"

"Never mind that, baby. You just make yourself comfortable and stay here tonight. Have a nightcap and then go to bed. You'll feel better after getting some sleep."

Once Cheryl was asleep, Fishnet wasted no time in taking action. After dressing, he wrapped the newspaper that had been delivered to his home around a twelve-inch lead pipe that had been stored in the townhouse cellar. He then placed the pipe inside the large interior pocket of his overcoat. Fishnet then proceeded to Enzo Baffi's penthouse.

When Fishnet arrived at Baffi's building, the first thing he did was slip the deskman enough cash to assure his cooperation. The payoff resulted in Fishnet learning that Enzo Baffi was at home. It further gained him access to the elevator that led directly into the producer's penthouse. The deskman made an entry in a log book kept at the lobby desk. The entry indicated he had stepped away to use the restroom.

The producer was reviewing an old contract when the unannounced intruder stepped off the elevator and into his apartment. Baffi looked at Fishnet without displaying any overt sign of emotion. He long ago had conditioned himself to never express surprise at anything. He believed that appearing unflappable was always to his advantage, regardless of circumstances.

"How did you manage get up here unannounced?" asked Baffi casually.

Without offering a reply, Fishnet briskly walked to where the producer was seated. In a flash, he viciously swung the newspaper that contained the lead pipe. The force of the blow striking Baffi's thigh caused him to roll off his seat and onto the floor in pain.

As Baffi yelped, Fishnet administered a second blow with the pipe. This was a lighter one that tapped the side of the producer's head. Thanks to the pipe's paper packaging, no blood was drawn. A fist-sized lump began to form just above Baffi's ear. Fishnet then stood over his dazed victim and began to slap the producer's face mercilessly with both hands until it turned apple red.

When the attack ceased, Enzo Baffi was left curled in a ball. Fishnet removed the newspaper casing and placed the cold lead pipe flush against the side of the producer's nose. Baffi's eyes bulged, expecting to be struck again.

"Please, no more," sputtered Baffi.

"Listen to me good, sweetheart," said Fishnet, using his most intimidating tone. "From now on we have
a new deal. You're gonna keep your filthy mitts off Cheryl. Do you understand me?"

"Yes," uttered the producer feebly.

"And we're gonna make her a star without any side benefits coming to you. Get me?"

"Yes."

"And our partnership is now 50-50 in everything that concerns Cheryl—and that includes money. Am I coming through to you, or do you need more convincing?"

"Yes, I understand," replied Baffi in a barely audible voice.

"Say it so I can hear you!"

"We're going to be 50-50 partners in everything that concerns Cheryl—including money," echoed Baffi.

"Because I'm telling you now, hot shot, if you renege, go to the law, or ever touch Cheryl again, I'm coming back, and you ain't gonna be no pretty boy no more. So do we understand each other, partner?"

"We do," answered the terrified Baffi.

"Say it louder!"

"WE DO," repeated the producer as loud as he could. His

words came out cracked.

"Good, we'll be talking again soon to work out the details. I'll get us a lawyer to finalize things. It'll be my treat. Oh, one other thing, you sick prick. From now on, when you need to talk to Cheryl, you go through me. Follow that formula, and you'll stay healthy. Get me?"

The producer weakly nodded his understanding. Fishnet considered administering a kick to Baffi's testicles as a farewell gesture before leaving. He then decided against it. *No sense in overreacting*, he thought.

* * *

THE WHITE-HAIRED MAESTRO waddled when walking. Penguin shaped, the octogenarian virtuoso looked small strolling alongside Pascal, his taller and younger lover. The musician's uncertainty was evident on his face as he came to an abrupt halt in front of the twenty-four hour pharmacy. He stood in silence on the sidewalk, massaging his chin. Pascal recognized this to be something the Maestro did only when pondering something of importance.

"Why are we going to see Enzo?" complained Pascal. "We shouldn't be out in this cold. Doesn't he know it's going to snow?"

"I'm sure he has his reasons for summoning us, Pascal."

"What did he say?'

"He didn't say why he wanted to see us. He just insisted that we should come right over."

"Perhaps he has an opportunity for you?"

"I hardly think that. His tone was far too forceful for good news."

"Do you think it could have something to do with that brute you introduced him to?"

"That's exactly where my concern lies," admitted the octogenarian. "I warned him to keep his distance from Mr. Fish. I only hoped he listened." The Maestro was referring to Fishnet, a man he only knew by the name of Fish.

"Maybe I shouldn't go with you to see Enzo," said Pascal, hoping not to get involved. "It might be prudent for me to stay far away from whatever business exists between you, Enzo and Fish." Pascal's fear of Fishnet far overshadowed any sense of loyalty.

"We must remain united, Pascal. We can't abandon Enzo after introducing him to that menace," announced the Maestro. "Come inside this pharmacy with me."

"What do you need from the pharmacy?"

"Enzo asked me to pick up two Ace wraps and a heating pad."

"What does he want those for?"

"I don't exactly know, Pascal," answered the Maestro. "We'll just have to wait and see."

"If he's had a problem with that maniac Fish, we should stay away, Maestro."

"Buck up, Pascal. Fish should have no quarrel with us because I did what he asked."

When the Maestro and Pascal arrived at the penthouse, they were staggered by the producer's condition. Baffi was sitting on a couch holding an ice pack to the side of his head. When he rose from the couch, he winced from the pain emanating from his battered thigh. Upon closer inspection it was obvious to the visitors that Baffi's eyes were glassy. This was caused by the producer having self-medicated.

"My God, Enzo!" declared the Maestro, appalled at his old friend's appearance.

"Did you bring me the Ace wraps?" asked the producer. "I need them for my leg."

"Enzo, what happened?" asked the Maestro.

"It was your friend, Fish. This is how he negotiates!" The Maestro offered no response. "He smashed my thigh with a wrench or something, and he practically fractured my skull! Feel over my ear."

Both the Maestro and Pascal gasped after feeling the huge lump over the producer's ear.

"You need to go to a hospital," said Pascal.

"No, no hospital. I can't afford unfavorable publicity," said the assault victim.

"But why did Fish do this to you?" questioned Pascal.

"He's muscling in on my business, that's why. He cut himself in for a 50-50 partnership in his whore girlfriend. He expects me to make a star out of her."

"Has the girl any talent?" asked the Maestro.

"Yes, Maestro, that's the pity of it, she does. But I can't be affiliated with a barbarian like that."

"I warned you about that monster," pointed out the Maestro.

"You did. I'm not forgetting that. But it was you who introduced him to me in the first place!" reminded Baffi. "But that makes no difference now; the damage is done. Help me wrap my thigh—and be gentle."

"Your upper leg is all discolored. There might be something broken inside."

"I don't think so; it just aches. I just took something for the discomfort."

After wrapping the producer's thigh, the three men decided that a cup of tea laced with brandy would do them well. While Baffi wasn't one hundred percent himself, he was still able to think clearly.

"That son of a bitch can't be permitted to dictate to us," declared the producer.

"What do you suggest we do, Enzo?" asked the Maestro.

"We need to rid ourselves of him, once and for all."

"We?" asked Pascal nervously.

"Like it or not, we're in this together, Pascal," said the Maestro.

"An animal like Mr. Fish is not going away on his own," stated the producer. "He'll milk us for all we're worth, be it our money, our connections, or whatever."

"That's right," the Maestro concurred.

"He beat me because he wanted more," pointed out the producer, leaving out the meaty part of the story.

Neither the Maestro nor Pascal had any idea of the goings on in Baffi's black room. They knew the married producer was a notorious womanizer, but they had no inkling of his erotic proclivities. Enzo Baffi was regarded as a gentleman of the highest caliber, a celebrated producer with a stellar reputation. The Maestro and Pascal gave no weight to how Baffi handled his paramours. Paying out hush money was considered an accepted method to remedy a potentially ugly scandal.

"So what do you propose we do about Mr. Fish, Enzo?

"Since he seems to already have plenty of money, I can't think of anything that would deter him."

"Perhaps we should notify the authorities," suggested Pascal.

"No, no, no. That will never do," replied the producer. "That's the very thing we don't want. The ensuing publicity would be damaging to us all."

"I agree with Enzo, Pascal. Whatever we decide to do must be done quietly."

Since Pascal was living off the Maestro, he was in no position to disagree with his benefactor. At this point he sat quietly, keeping his thoughts to himself.

"I see us left with only one option," said Baffi in his most serious tone. "We need to rid ourselves of this menace once and for all. I'm speaking of liquidation, gentlemen."

"You can't mean that," said Pascal, unable to refrain from reentering the conversation.

"Enzo is right, Pascal," said the Maestro, stroking his own throat. He vividly remembered how Fishnet twisted the flesh on his neck. "Did you forget what he did to you, Pascal?"

Pascal was now reminded of how he was dislodged from his cushy niche in the townhouse that was then owned by Fishnet's late actress wife. In those days he was the man of the house, living in luxury as a kept plaything. Pascal's bitterness was renewed as he remembered how Fishnet orchestrated things to make it appear as if he had been stealing from his past benefactor.

Pascal grew further vengeful while recollecting how he had been reduced to living in a Bowery flophouse after Fishnet physically ejected him from the townhouse. The thought of Fishnet assuming Pascal's role in the townhouse and ultimately marrying the heiress-actress was enough for Pascal to reconsider his position.

"You two are absolutely right," declared Pascal. "The animal needs to be eradicated, once and for all!"

"We're in agreement then," concluded Baffi. "Now we need to decide on how to dispose of Mr. Fish."

"Should we hire someone to do the dirty work?" asked Pascal.

"Then we'd have to find someone capable," advised the producer. "That could be tricky."

"I don't like that idea," chimed in the Maestro. "The more people we involve, the greater the chance of our own exposure."

"What then, Maestro?"

"We'll have to do it ourselves."

"Do you have a suggestion as to how?"

"I'm not exactly sure, Enzo. We'll need time to flesh this out."

"We could poison him," suggested Pascal.

"No, that's too much like a 1940s murder mystery," said Baffi. "I've thought this over. I believe I've come up with a good way to kill off Mr. Fish."

29

Snow Time Is Show Time

THE SNOW WAS STILL COMING DOWN when Arlene Perez looked out her window. She was preparing for the snow and the work that was to be done.

"Get out your boots, Millie," said Arlene. "It's supposed to come down heavy."

"That's what they said last time," said Millie, who returned from her trip without incident.

When the snow finally came, the siblings got out their boots, gloves, and shovels. By the following day the snow had finally stopped falling. Arlene went directly to the sidewalk to create a path for pedestrians to walk on when passing their house. Millie shoveled her way from the front door to the trash barrels that stood within the gated area.

As the sisters worked, the Captain emerged from the top of the stairs with his own shovel in hand. He began to clear the steps and place salt down to prevent slipping. Arlene and Millie weren't surprised to see their tenant pitch in. In fact, they'd have been surprised if he hadn't.

Once the clearing of snow was completed, the three workers entered the house for a bite to eat. Over coffee and a meal, Millie thought of how lucky she was to have the Captain as a tenant. The old seaman, having had both sisters, also considered himself to be fortunate.

As opposed to the others, Arlene didn't feel as lucky. She still yearned for Detective Von Hess, a prize that had, thus far, evaded her. As she drank her coffee she thought of how she needed to be proactive if she were to ever get close to the lawman.

* * *

THE THREAT OF TREACHEROUS ROADS wasn't going to deter Fishnet. He had it on his mind to make arrangements to marry Cheryl, and nothing was going to prevent him from moving forward with his plan. The reluctance his intended expressed when it came to getting married did nothing to diminish his confidence. The former detective possessed great faith in his persuasive ability when it came to Cheryl.

Having forgotten his gloves, Fishnet began to feel the sting in his reddened hand as he wiped the snow off the windshield of his car.

Fishnet resigned himself to facing challenging streets and extended travel time. It was a price he was willing to meet in order to get together with the Brooklyn priest who presided over the quickie marriage of the handyman who had cleaned his townhouse boiler.

The roads were beginning to clear when the ex-detective made his way to his Sunset Park destination. His pockets housed enough cash to lubricate any squeaks that might arise from the proposition he intended to make to Father Billy, who he believed to be a pliable member of the cloth.

Fishnet pulled his car in front of the fire hydrant a few feet from the rectory. After ringing the rectory doorbell he waited under the building's green awning for someone to come to the door.

A well-spoken, gray-haired woman of about sixty answered the bell. She was a local resident employed by the church. Wearing a modest skirt and black sweater, she seemed a very proper fit for her role. Her hair was worn in a neat bun, and her glasses hung in front of her chest from an adjustable eyeglass strap.

As the two conversed through the open door, Fishnet noticed the rubber fingertip grip that was affixed to the woman's thumb. *A greasy thumb*, thought Fishnet.

Fishnet wasted no time in explaining his purpose. After listening politely, the woman advised that Fishnet's request for an audience with Father Billy was impossible at this time. She conveyed that the priest wasn't present at the rectory.

"Are you saying he ain't around, period?"

"I'm saying he isn't home right now."

"Where is he?"

"I haven't seen Father Billy," she replied before adding, "so I can't tell you when he'll be available for consultation."

In answer to Fishnet's insistence on meeting with Father Billy, the woman told him to come back later in the day. She strongly recommended that he call prior. The persistence of the former detective went unabated. He now asked the woman to call Father Billy on his cell phone.

"Oh, I couldn't disturb him unless there was an emergency," she advised. The certainty in her reply was irking to Fishnet. The woman employed at the rectory reminded him of a prim and proper aunt he always disliked.

"Well, give me his number, and I'll call him."

"I'm afraid that's out of the question. I suggest you call the rectory later."

As he continued to debate the point, a car pulled up. Fishnet noticed a man in a religious collar was behind the wheel. "Who is this guy?" he asked.

"Why, here's Father Billy now," said the woman happily, pointing to the religious imposter. Ross slowly exited the car he had borrowed from his girlfriend's sister. When the rectory worker saw the condition of the fraudster's face, she gasped. "Oh, my goodness, what happened, Father?"

"I had a bad accident," he answered without going into detail. "Do me a favor and park the car in the church lot for me."

"But your face . . ."

"Never mind my face. Just take the keys and park the car."

The woman rushed inside the rectory to get her coat. Upon returning, she announced Fishnet's purpose.

"This gentleman is here to speak with you, Father," she said before hustling off to park the car.

"I'm sorry, but I'm not open for business today," said the con man, addressing Fishnet. "I'm not receiving any visitors until tomorrow. Come back then."

Fishnet looked with curiosity at the beaten face of the man wearing the white collar. "What happened to you, Father? Did you run into a train?" he asked bluntly.

"Not quite," the phony priest sharply replied. "Come back tomorrow for whatever you want. I'll be available then."

Based on the dismissive response of Ross, the former detective's antennas went up. It caused Fishnet to question the legitimacy of Father Billy.

This guy can't be what he's cracked up to be, thought Fishnet. *Who is he kidding? Somebody gave him a going over!*

"Just a second, Father," said Fishnet, stopping Ross from entering the rectory. "We got business to do." The remark gave Ross Holt pause. "I was talking to somebody who told me that you could perform a rectory marriage for me, Father."

"Now look, this ain't a good time. Come back tomorrow and we'll talk about that."

"I'm here now, Father, and I'm willing to pay you for your time." As expected, this got the attention of the bogus priest.

"What did you say you needed?"

"I want one of your rectory specials . . ."

"Just a second," said Ross as he cut Fishnet off to take the car keys from the returning secretary.

"What do you mean by a 'rectory special'?"

"I want to get married fast. You know, in and out."

The two men knowingly looked at each other as only two crooks could. At this point the man posing as Father Billy knew he had encountered someone who was onto him.

"Who was it that referred you to me?" Ross asked.

"You married the guy who cleaned my boiler."

"What was his name?"

"Look, Padre, you got nothing to worry about with me. How about we go inside and work something out. I have the cash to fatten you up good."

The repeated mention of cash was all the incentive the charlatan required. "What you're asking for isn't a cheap proposition, my friend."

"I didn't figure it to be."

"Maybe we do need go inside to talk this over," said the religious imposter.

Once inside the rectory, the two men sat in a small private office to discuss terms. In short order they arrived at a financial understanding.

"I can give you the paperwork right now if you have the cabbage," said Ross, abandoning all pretenses.

"No good. We gotta go through the motions of a half-ass ceremony. The bride has to think it's on the level."

"Well, how soon can you be available?" asked the bogus priest. "I got some pressing business, so I have to move this along. Can you come back later today?"

"That won't work on my end," advised Fishnet. "I'm gonna need a few days, so let's make it near the end of next week."

"Hmm, I see," stated the disappointed religious fraudster. "Well, whatever works for you will be fine. But I'll need a retainer if I'm expected to be available for whenever you call."

"Sure, Father," said Fishnet, shaking his head in amusement. He then handed over a generous allotment of cash to the fraudster. "You'll be ready to go whenever I call, right?"

"Yes. In New York State, the church has the official authority to fill out the marriage certificate, and there is no government involvement."

"Okay, save the song and dance. You made the sale. Figure on hearing from me sometime next week, Padre. You'll have the witnesses on hand?"

"Yeah, that's no problem. I'll have people present to witness things."

Since he knew he was dealing with an out-and-out con man, Fishnet had no hesitation in making it clear there would be consequences should the bogus priest fail to live up to his end of the bargain.

"But just so we understand each other," said Fishnet, "if you cross me, those lumps you got are pimples compared to what you'll be getting."

"There is no need for that kind of talk, I assure you."

"No, let me assure you, Padre. You screw me, and your next negotiation will be with the undertaker."

"We understand each other," assured Ross, who had no intention of ever seeing Fishnet again. "You look familiar to me. Are you sure we haven't crossed paths before?"

"No, we haven't met before," said the Clark Gable lookalike. "People make that mistake about me all the time."

* * *

MOTIVATED BY THE TIP RECEIVED from the building super, Markie and Von Hess once again jumped into the homicide cases involving Dennis Bumper. They directed their attention to the apartment building where part time caddy lived. While travel was still difficult, the roads were quickly being plowed by the Sanitation Department.

The detectives set up not far from the front of Bumper's apartment building. Since the snow had concluded earlier that morning, visibility was clear from the vehicle they were in. Markie sat up straight when a man who exited the building began turning his head in all directions, even upward. He was obviously on the lookout for a police presence.

"Someone just came out, Ollie," alerted Markie.

"I got him," replied Von Hess.

The man was dressed in a black down jacket, jeans, and blue ski cap. At first, Markie and Von Hess thought the man might be Bumper. Once they realized the man had nothing wrong with his back, they dismissed that thought.

"It could be Bumper's friend, Sarge," said Von Hess, passing the binoculars to Markie.

"That's exactly who it is" said Markie, now having a closer look.

"Stay with him Ollie," instructed Markie. "I'll stay here to keep a visual on the front of the house in case the subject pops out."

Von Hess got out of the unmarked car and proceeded to shadow Sammy Angelo on foot. Sammy was on his way to the bank to withdraw extra money. While he had plenty of money in his apartment, he wanted to be sure his home stash was replenished after paying Father Billy. Sammy trucked along without realizing that he was being followed by Von Hess, who trailed him from the opposite side of the street.

The detective waited outside while Sammy was in the bank. When Sammy was told by the bank manager that the money requested wouldn't be available until the following day, he frowned. This delay was the last thing he wanted to hear. Depressed over this, Sammy returned home.

"What happened?" asked Markie when Von Hess slipped into the passenger side of the unmarked police vehicle.

"He went into the bank and spoke to somebody for a while and then left. I'm gonna turn up the heat, Sarge. I'm freezing."

"You warm up, Ollie. I'll run out and get us a couple cups of java," advised Markie.

* * *

ONCE BACK IN HIS APARTMENT, Sammy explained to Bumper that he had completed his business at the bank.

"Didn't you say you had enough money here in the house?" asked Bumper.

"I did, and I do. I just had to take care of something," said Sammy.

"Are you gonna call Father Billy?" Bumper asked.

"I already did. We're confirmed to meet him at the church as scheduled. It's not gonna be much longer now, Dennis."

"Did you see any cops when you went out?"

"Not a one, Dennis. All I saw were people shoveling."

"Did you see the super out there?"

"No, he shoveled out front already, so he's probably resting."

The two men then worked out a plan. It was decided that when it was time to go to the church, Sammy would leave the apartment first. Once he reached the street, he would scan the area for signs of law enforcement. If all was clear, Sammy would then telephone his home and let it ring just once. That was to be Bumper's signal that it was safe to leave the apartment.

The two would then proceed to the church cautiously. Bumper would follow Sammy, who would be leading the way at a distance of just under half a block. In the event that Sammy sighted the police, his signal to his friend would be bending down as if lacing his shoe. This gesture would be Bumper's cue to conceal himself by ducking in between two parked cars, after which he would hastily make his way to the church from a different direction and wait.

Assuming he reached the church without incident, Bumper was to enter the confessional with Father Billy. After confessing his sins, he would then go to the altar at the front of the church to make his penance. Upon completion of the required prayers handed down by Father Billy, Bumper would reconnect with the religious imposter and Sammy. Sammy would then pay Father Billy who, in turn, would contact his lawyer friend to arrange the surrender of Bumper to the authorities

* * *

MARKIE WAS THE FIRST TO NOTICE that Sammy again exited his apartment building. "Here we go again," said the sergeant, alerting Von Hess that Sammy was again on the move. "He's standing in front of his building."

"I see him, Sarge."

264

"He's on his cell phone. Hold it a second . . . He's walking off while on the phone."

"Do you want me to get out and tail him on foot, Sarge?"

"No, I'll do it this time. You keep an eye on that building in case Bumper is in there and decides to come out."

Once Sammy was a distance away, Markie emerged from the unmarked car to pursue him on foot.

Just as Markie was about to close the car door, he heard Von Hess call out to him.

"Hold it a second, Sarge," said Von Hess, who was looking through the binoculars. "I think Dennis Bumper just came out of the apartment house. Take a look, Sarge." Von Hess then passed the binoculars.

"That's him, Ollie," confirmed Markie. "He's going in the same direction as his friend. Let's follow in the car," said Markie, now back in the unmarked vehicle.

"Do you want to take him down now?"

"No, not yet, Ollie. Let's follow them and try to take them in a place where they can't make a run for it. I'm not looking to get into a foot race in the snow with these assholes."

* * *

BUMPER HUSTLED TO CATCH up with Sammy when things looked like smooth sailing. Together the friends trucked their way in the snow to the church. When they got there, they spotted Father Billy exiting the rectory, which was located alongside the house of worship. The bogus priest was with a man who looked familiar. The man with the priest impersonator was Fishnet, the Clark Gable lookalike. The imposter and the ex-detective were exchanging goodbyes while standing under the rectory awning.

Sammy and Bumper ventured forward to let the religious imposter know that they had arrived. The detectives observed the four men assembled under the awning from their unmarked car, which was stationed on the opposite side of the avenue.

"Are you seeing what I'm seeing, Ollie?" asked the surprised sergeant. Markie was baffled at seeing his elusive nemesis Fishnet in the company of the men he and Von Hess had been pursuing.

"What the hell is Fishnet doing with this crew?" asked the detective, who was equally shocked.

"I only wish I knew how these guys all fit in the same puzzle."

"Me too," replied Von Hess, who was mostly concerned at seeing the religious imposter he had battered in the mix.

The relationship between Markie and Von Hess was one in which they exchanged many secrets. But the savage attack on Father Billy was not a confidence Von Hess was willing to share. His reason for keeping the assault he perpetrated in the shade had nothing to do with the detective's concern that Markie would hold him accountable. After all, Von Hess had been witness to Markie's own acts of nastiness over the years. Von Hess held his tongue because he was ashamed of what he had done. Admitting to such a vile act, especially to a former Marine like Von Hess, would be a personal embarrassment. His preference was for the incident to remain buried.

Since Markie was so consumed with the presence of Fishnet, it took him a while to notice the battered face of the priest, who he assumed was a legitimate man of the cloth.

"I don't get any of this, Ollie. That priest looks like he got his ass handed to him," said the sergeant, looking at the quartet through the binoculars.

"This is the church with the priest that No Tax told us about, Sarge," revealed Von Hess.

"Then there has to be something crooked going on here. Just look at how banged up the priest is," said Markie. "This is the guy you reported to the precinct squad, right?"

"Yeah, Sarge, that's him. Do you want to move in on Bumper?" asked Von Hess, looking to avoid further questions.

"Hold on a second, Ollie. It looks like the party under the awning is breaking up."

* * *

WITH ROSS HOLT'S FAREWELL with Fishnet interrupted, the phony priest directed Sammy and Bumper to the church by pointing to the house of worship.

"Go inside," said Ross. "I'll be right in." Once they walked off, Fishnet and the fraudster parted ways seconds later.

As Fishnet proceeded to his vehicle, he suddenly stopped in his tracks after noticing the unmarked police car on the opposite side of the avenue. Recognizing Markie and Von Hess caused Fishnet to become uneasy. He thought the law was there for him. Expecting a bad time, Fishnet's eyes remained trained on Markie. The guilty-minded Fishnet wondered if Markie had finally come up with evidence to prove his criminal activity.

When Markie and Von Hess exited their vehicle, Fishnet anticipated a confrontation. The former detective didn't waver under the intensity of the moment. Rather than cower, the Gable clone stood erect in the snowy street to his fullest height with his chest puffed. His look was one of defiance.

Bring it on, you son of a bitch, thought Fishnet, who had no intention of showing any sign of weakness. The tenseness was broken when the investigators began walking in the direction of the church. It was at this point that the rogue former detective realized the law wasn't there for him.

Fishnet turned just in time to see the bogus priest enter the church. Standing his ground, Fishnet waited to see what the detectives were going to do. When Von Hess entered the church, Fishnet knew that the bogus priest's scamming days would likely be coming to a close.

Markie, who had intentionally paused at the top of the church steps, bit on his lip as he turned to look back at Fishnet. As he entered the house of worship, he had but one thought: *I'll get that bastard one day if it's the last thing I ever do!*

* * *

IT HAD BEEN A LONG TIME since Markie had been inside a church. The odor of incense brought back memories of his youth. That was a time of good deeds and regular observance of Mass. The sergeant shook his head at the realization that he had long been stripped of his innocence.

The detectives watched Bumper embrace his friend prior to his stepping into the confessional the priest had just entered. *Can you beat this,* thought the sergeant as he turned to face Von Hess. In answer to Markie's look, the detective expressed himself with a slight shrug.

The detectives moved in on Sammy as he sat in a pew praying for his friend. The price of Sammy's loyalty was now at hand. The detectives moved in to arrest him on an offense they'd figure out later. Even if the charge didn't stick, Sammy's being arrested would be an apt punishment.

Sammy, who recognized the law enforcement officers, soon found himself sandwiched between the two detectives who entered the pew from opposite ends. He sat openmouthed while being discreetly handcuffed behind his back. He offered no resistance.

"What's that priest's name?" whispered Markie.

"He's Father Billy."

Sammy's reply caused Markie to look at Von Hess, who nodded to show he heard Sammy's answer.

"Sit tight and be quiet," advised the sergeant. Sammy gulped. Not knowing what else he could do, he began to pray in silence. Since he was rear cuffed, he was unable to make use of the rosary beads he always carried.

Markie pointed his thumb to the confessional. The gesture was a signal for Von Hess to place his ear to the enclosed stall. Von Hess was positioned in time to overhear Dennis confess to the three murders he had committed. The veteran detective was impressed by the seemingly sincere remorse expressed by Bumper.

When Bumper exited the confessional, he walked into the waiting handcuffs of the law. The bogus priest, hearing what was transpiring outside the confessional, quietly remained in place. He was hoping that Bumper's problem excluded him.

Despite having two prisoners in tow, Markie didn't forget about the fraudster taking refuge within the confessional.

"There's an open case on this supposed priest in this precinct, right, Ollie?" asked Markie.

"There is, Sarge."

"Then let's make it a three-bagger. Get his ass out of the box, Ollie," directed the sergeant. Markie's true motive in taking Ross Holt into custody was to find out where Fishnet fit into the picture.

Von Hess opened the door to the confessional, reached in, and pulled the imposter out by his arm.

The three prisoners were transported to the Sunset Park detective squad where they were placed in a cell while things were being sorted out. Markie notified headquarters of the arrests. He then apprised Lieutenant Nightshade, the Staten Island detective squad commander. Nightshade, in turn, notified the other squad commanders.

This series of notifications resulted in the case detectives assigned to the Bumper murders all making their way to the Sunset Park squad. Upon their arrival, Markie and Von Hess turned over the prisoners to their custody for processing. Deciding which of the responding detectives would be the first to arrest Bumper for homicide was something that had to be worked out by the respective squad commanders.

As far as the bogus priest was concerned, Ross Holt belonged exclusively to Detective Mad Dog Switzer of the Sunset Park squad. It was Switzer's responsibility to address the crimes committed by the imposter who had bilked parishioners while posing as a priest.

Once Markie and Von Hess gave their statements to an assistant district attorney, they headed back to their headquarters office. Their conversation on the ride to Manhattan was light.

"Did you hear what that psycho caddy said, Sarge?" asked Von Hess.

"What did he say?"

"He wanted to know who was going to take care of his pet

hamster." Markie offered no reaction. "What's wrong, Sarge?"

"It pisses me off how that wannabe priest clammed up when I asked what he was doing with Fishnet."

"He's just a flimflammer, Sarge."

"I know that, Ollie. I just want to know the connection for my own edification."

"Yeah, I guess that would be interesting," agreed Von Hess.

"I'd also like to know who kicked his ass for him."

"He wasn't talking, Sarge," said Von Hess, anxious to let it go at that.

"A black eye, teeth knocked out, and a knot in the head ain't no accident, Ollie. That spells a beating in any man's language." Von Hess didn't add to the conversation. He didn't want to go there.

30

Cell-Shocked

IT WAS AGREED AMONG the squad commanders that Detective Winters of the Staten Island squad would be the arresting officer for Bumper and Sammy. They reached that decision because the homicide of Judith Vanidestine was the first to have occurred.

Bumper sat handcuffed to a metal chair in the main area of the squad room. Seated at the desk alongside him was Detective Winters. As the detective was occupied going through the papers she needed to prepare, Bumper studied her. In comparison to the other investigators, Winters seemed to have a nice way about her. Considering his crimes, Bumper was surprised to see how civil she was to him.

Bumper noted that police work in general didn't appear to be overly demanding. Everyone seemed to be happy at their job as they went about their duties. Bumper began to wonder what it would have been like to have been a cop.

When the prisoner tired of analyzing the police, his attention was drawn to the condition of the office. *Nothing to write home about*, he thought. *These metal desks are really crappy.*

When the time came to be interviewed, Bumper was placed in a small, private office, where he was given his Miranda warnings. He was then queried by the investigators assigned to the murders he was charged with committing. To the satisfaction of all concerned, Bumper proved to be an agreeable prisoner willing to answer all questions in a straightforward fashion. He admitted to committing each murder. He provided a full account of his killing spree, as well as his motives for the slayings.

The detectives couldn't have been more pleased with how things were turning out. Their cases were wrapped up into a neat package with Bumper's signed confession being the bow.

There came a point when Bumper expressed concern over his friend, Sammy Angelo. He made it his business to explain to the detectives that he had acted alone in the commission of the murders. He emphasized that Sammy Angelo played no role in the heinous acts he perpetrated. Bumper further indicated that the same was true of the man he knew as Father Billy.

The case detective in the homicide of Judith Vanidestine explained to Bumper that Sammy's harboring him constituted a crime.

"Do you understand what I just explained?" Detective Winters asked.

"I do. Is Sammy being charged with a felony?" asked the prisoner.

"No, I believe it's just going to be a misdemeanor," replied the detective from the Staten Island squad. "But I'll have to figure that out later."

"Does this mean Sammy might have to go to jail?"

"That depends on his record. Was he ever arrested before?"

"No, Sammy was never in trouble."

"If this is his first arrest, then they'll probably go easy on him."

Hearing this made things a little easier for Bumper. When taken back to the main squad room he glanced over at the cell where Sammy was being housed. He looked at his friend with sadness as the two made eye contact.

"Why was the priest arrested?" Bumper asked, addressing Winters. "What did he do?"

"I don't know what his case is all about," replied the detective. Winters called across the room to Detective Switzer, who was sitting at his desk filling out the arrest paperwork on Ross Holt, the religious imposter. Alongside Switzer sat Ross, who was cuffed to a chair.

"Hey, Mad Dog, could you come over here for a second?" When Switzer came over, he was asked about the status of the prisoner who had been posing as Father Billy. "What's the story with your collar?"

"He's a con man," advised Switzer. "Him and his girlfriend have been swindling the people in this community left and right."

"He was never a real priest then?" asked Bumper, injecting himself into the conversation.

"If he's a priest, then I'm the tooth fairy, pal," answered Switzer.

Bumper's flash temper was activated after hearing this. He began to show signs of rage as he excitedly called out to Sammy, who remained alone in the cell waiting his turn to be processed.

"Sammy!" shouted the harried Bumper. "They're saying that Father Billy was never a priest!"

"I heard, Dennis," replied Sammy. "He tricked us."

Ross, having heard the conversation between Bumper and Sammy, shook his head. *These have to be two of the dumbest bastards in the world*, he thought.

Bumper now centered his attention on Ross Holt. He stared at Ross with a frightening scowl on his face. His free hand was balled into a fist as he worked hard to contain his rage.

"I haven't been forgiven at all!" Bumper suddenly blurted. He was addressing no one in particular, while all the time looking at the bogus priest. In his state of agitation, Bumper rose to his feet. He began furiously trying to pull his handcuffed hand free from the arm of the chair. Bumper, with eyes bulging and face contorted, was a scary sight to behold.

"Sit back and settle down," said Detective Winters sternly as she pushed the prisoner back down into his seat. The other detectives jumped to their feet, ready to assist in subduing the angry prisoner.

Being pushed by Detective Winters had an effect on Bumper. Her touch caused him to pause. Seeing it was Winters, who he had come to like, Bumper listened to her soothing voice as she began to speak calmly to him. The detective assured Bumper that he would be meeting with a legitimate man of the cloth at the earliest opportunity, which went far in settling the disturbed prisoner. This later proved to be the lull before the storm.

Bumper had no personal animosity toward any of the detectives he had encountered. He accepted that they had a job to do. His venom was strictly reserved for Ross Holt. The face of Ross was imbedded in his mind's eye. This was not a good place for anyone to be. Since Bumper already had killed three people and had yet to confess his sins to a legitimate priest, the murderous psychopath felt he had nothing to lose by adding another victim to his homicide list.

When she finished processing Bumper, Detective Winters placed her prisoner in the cell located in the squad room. She then took Sammy Angelo out of the same cell and began working on his arrest processing.

From behind bars, Bumper quietly monitored Ross Holt as he was being processed by Detective Switzer. Bumper's seemingly passive behavior concealed his evil intentions. His desire for religious forgiveness for his sins was on hold until the bogus priest met his comeuppance. Bumper saw no sense in repenting twice.

With things under control, the detectives assigned to the murders committed by the caddy got around to posting their supervisors back at their individual commands. Of the three, it was the detective in the Doctor Vanidestine case who put things most colorfully.

"The sicko who clipped the plastic surgeon is as cold as ice, Loo," said the detective. "He admitted to knifing the doctor, and did so without a shred of regret. The guy gives me the willies."

"Did you get a signed confession?" asked the squad commander, who was lighting up her last cigarette.

"Definitely, I got it all in writing with his John Hancock."

"Are you finished over there?"

274

"Yes, I'm on my way back to Manhattan now to take care of business on our side of the water."

"Good job. On your way back bring me two packs of Marlboro Lights."

The squad commander in the Martin Tamor homicide, when told by his detective that the prisoner had signed a full confession, wasn't interested in hearing details. Knowing that the prisoner admitted to bludgeoning the wealth manager in his office was sufficient.

"Okay," said the squad commander. "Get back to the office and take care of what needs to be done over here."

* * *

BUMPER'S CHANCE FOR REVENGE CAME after the Manhattan detectives left the precinct. Their departure left Detective Winters and Switzer in charge of the three prisoners.

The cell that housed Bumper was ample enough to accommodate many prisoners. It was located just a short distance from the desks where Ross Holt and Sammy Angelo were being processed. Bumper, alone in the cell, peered through the iron bars at Ross. While he sympathized with his dear friend Sammy, the object of his undivided attention was Ross Holt.

After conferring with an ADA telephonically, Detective Winters issued Sammy a desk appearance ticket (DAT). This enabled Sammy to be released from custody under order to appear in court at a future date. Sammy's clean record was a consideration in the DAT determination. Bumper was happy to see his friend cut loose.

Neither detective thought it odd when Bumper began exercising in his cell. Prisoners were known to do this on occasion. In Bumper's case, he was limbering up for the assault he was preparing to unleash.

Bumper's opportunity to administer his own brand of justice came when Detective Winters needed to take a few minutes to tend to a personal matter.

"Mad Dog, I'll be right back," said Winters. "Do you mind keeping an eye on my prisoner?"

"No problem," replied Switzer.

Once he finished his paperwork on Ross Holt, Switzer made the mistake of placing his prisoner in the same cell where Bumper was lodged. Bumper froze like a jungle cat preparing to pounce on its prey. His eyes began to dance as he watched Ross enter the cell. With his eyes remaining on Ross, Bumper listened for the click that would indicate that they were locked in.

Once Mad Dog Switzer was back at his desk Bumper went into a low crouch and began to slowly advance toward the conman. Ross, seeing that something was definitely wrong with Bumper, moved to the far end of the cell. As the caddy neared, the imposter positioned himself in a corner of the cell. As Bumper continued to slowly advance, Ross began calling out for help. With nowhere to retreat, Ross stepped atop the cell bench and began to desperately kick at the lunging Bumper.

All efforts by Ross to protect himself proved futile. The much stronger Bumper took hold of the imposter and threw him to the ground. With his hands tightly around his victim's throat, Bumper began to squeeze. Ross frantically tried to peel away the madman's fingers to prevent strangulation. Ross was beginning to fade as the life was being snuffed out of him.

Hearing the ruckus coming from the cell, Detective Switzer rushed to see what was going on. Switzer wasted no time in entering the cell to put an end to the mayhem. Once in the mix, the detective found that he was unable to restrain Bumper through authorized means. He was compelled to resort to unorthodox methods.

The veteran detective removed the metal knuckles from the interior pocket of his jacket. Back in the early days of Switzer's career, an officer carrying brass knuckles or a blackjack wasn't unusual. Luckily for Ross, it was a habit the old-school detective never discontinued.

Switzer clobbered Bumper with enough force to put an end to the strangulation. As the blood flowed freely, the dazed prisoner required a second punch in order for him to take his hands off Ross. Losing consciousness, Bumper fell in a heap atop Ross. There was no need for Switzer to administer a third blow.

The detective had no sooner rear cuffed Bumper when he heard Detective Winters voice over his shoulder. "Mad Dog!" she shouted. "What the hell did you do?"

"Your prisoner tried to kill mine."

"But all the blood . . ."

"He had to be stopped," said the panting veteran.

"My prisoner is going to need stitches," declared Winters, who questioned the degree of force used.

"Relax. We'll take them both to a hospital, get them fixed up, and that'll be that," barked Switzer. "Don't make a federal case out of this."

31

Doing Time

DENNIS BUMPER WAS SENT TO SERVE his time at the Attica Correctional Facility, home to some of the worst violent offenders. At first, Bumper was placed in a special unit at Attica that kept him in his cell for many hours a day. He was let out four hours each weekday to participate in special programming and one hour for recreation. Once he was diagnosed as stable, Bumper was moved into the prison's general population.

Bumper was fortunate to have a loyal friend like Sammy Angelo. Sammy's visits to the prison meant a lot to Bumper, as did the letters he received regularly. Hearing from Sammy always came with tidbits of local gossip. Bumper found receiving up-to-date information on people and things he was familiar with to be uplifting.

During one of Sammy's visits to the prison he informed Bumper that he was planning to spend several months overseas to visit relatives in Italy. Bumper's frown made it clear that he wasn't happy to hear that. Things lightened a bit when Sammy assured his friend the time would soon pass.

Without Sammy's visits, Bumper quickly grew melancholy. His depressed state of mind was noticed by other inmates. One prisoner in particular, perceiving Bumper's moping as weakness, began persecuting Bumper with disparaging remarks pertaining to his humpback. It was a situation destined for a bad outcome.

Things began coming to a head when the abusive inmate started referring to Bumper as Quasimodo. Unaware of the impact his provocation was having on Bumper, the prison bully persisted after being warned to cease with the name-calling. The continued reference to the Victor Hugo character triggered a violent response from Bumper that no one in the inmate population thought he was capable of.

When he finally snapped Bumper attacked his tormenter in the prison yard. He unleashed a barrage of powerful blows in quick succession that felled his man. Caught totally by surprise, the antagonist had no opportunity to get set and defend himself. Once downed the inmate was savagely pummeled before being rescued by a team of corrections officers.

Much to the bully's humiliation, the sound trouncing he received became the talk of the prison. His inability to make a fight of it was highly embarrassing to the bully. With himself now open to ridicule, the inmate felt the need to retaliate in order to restore his tarnished reputation. Plainly put, he was now gunning for Bumper.

As a result of the fight, Bumper was returned to the prison's specialized unit for further evaluation. He remained there for quite awhile, eventually being returned to the general population after again being deemed mentally fit.

Bumper's return was what the prison bully had been waiting for. He wasted no time in taking steps to salvage his damaged image. When closure finally came, it arrived at a high price.

Bumper was sitting quietly in the prison library reading the Bible when the bully took his revenge. The former caddy never heard his assailant creep up behind him. Bumper winced from the pain caused by the shiv that entered his lower back. The second jab with the handcrafted cutting instrument resulted in Bumper letting out an agonizing groan that broke the library silence. Those present looked on as the assault continued. There was no intention on the part of anyone to intervene in what was viewed as a private squabble.

Bumper sustained two additional stab wounds in rapid succession. One penetrated the area of his spinal cord. Bumper might have been fortunate in his bleeding to death. Had he survived, the once lovesick caddy would have permanently lost his ability to function below the point of injury to his spine.

With no next of kin to claim the deceased inmate's remains, Dennis Bumper ended up being placed in a plain wooden casket. Stacked three deep in a trench, he was buried in a prison cemetery.

* * *

THE LAW PROVED NOT to be too harsh on Sammy Angelo. The remorse he expressed when before the court was perceived as genuine. Leniency prevailed. Even those of the sternest nature were hard pressed to ignore the tears that flowed down the face of Bumper's friend. The fact that Sammy had no prior arrest history further influenced the decision of the court.

In return for his plea of guilty, Sammy's punishment consisted of performing community service. Even a novice in the workings of the criminal justice system like Sammy recognized the good deal he received. Once his community service was behind him, Sammy took the long vacation he told Bumper about.

Ever the loyal friend, Sammy thought of Bumper while in Italy. Once in the old country Sammy visited Venice, Florence, and Rome. He especially enjoyed visiting the Vatican in the hope of seeing the pope. Sammy departed Italy with a special gift for Bumper that was in memory of Padre Pio, who had been beatified by Pope John Paul II in 1999. Padre Pio, an Italian priest, inexplicably bore the wounds of Christ. He exhibited the stigmata for most of his life.

Sammy felt like a new man when he returned home. Treated well by his relatives overseas, he looked ahead to making a return trip the following year. After unpacking, he went through his mail to see what bills needed paying. After separating out the important correspondence, he was surprised to have received no communication from Bumper.

Once settled, Sammy went to the super's apartment to collect Digger. After letting the super know that he was home, he slipped him some money for taking care of the hamster in his absence. Sammy then headed to his own apartment with the caged Digger. On his way, he wondered what was wrong with the super, who seemed to have an attitude after receiving the money. *I gave him plenty of money*, thought Sammy. *How much does her think he's entitled to?* Sammy had no idea that the super was still bitter over being deceived by the police department's Sergeant Al Markie. Markie had promised the super a reward for snitching. It was a reward that never existed.

Sammy turned on the radio to listen to some music while he cleaned Digger's cage. Afterward, he went shopping for food. By the evening hours, jet lag had set in. Exhausted, Sammy nevertheless found the energy to write Bumper before turning in. In his letter to Bumper he made reference to the Father Pio gift he had for him.

Sammy mailed the letter the following day. In the communication he let his friend know that he would be visiting the prison the following week to see him. Not receiving a response from bumper caused Sammy to wonder if something was wrong. Anxious to find out, he pushed up his visit to Attica. Upon arriving at the prison, he learned of the violent death of Dennis Bumper. Sammy was stunned by the news.

Once back home, Sammy slipped into a severe state of depression. To cope, he turned to drinking. The bender he went on lasted several days, concluding when Sammy collapsed on his bed due to his intoxication. When he finally came around, he felt awful. This translated into his entering his first phase of recuperation. Rising only when absolutely necessary, it took a full two days before he began to regain his form.

Sammy went through this period without nourishment, drinking only water. When Sammy finally pulled himself together, he remembered Digger. When he saw the hamster's cage vacated, he began to search for the pet. This proved to be unfruitful.

Sammy wrestled to recall the last time he had encountered Digger. He did have a vague recollection of feeding the hamster but possessed no recall as to the specifics of that. It remained an enigma to him as to whether he left the door to Digger's cage unsecured.

It was the odor of death that finally led Sammy to Digger. He found the hamster behind the kitchen trash basket. The pet was caught in a mouse trap. Flushing Digger down the toilet was an aquatic send- off that Sammy took no pleasure in. It depressed him that his final connection to Dennis Bumper had been swept away in the water that led to a sewer.

Exhaling deeply after disposing of Digger, the Holy Roller briefly thought of returning to the bottle. The smell coming from the intoxicant was all it took to persuade Sammy not to partake in further drink. He knew his stomach could never take it. The whiff alone caused him to come close to getting sick.

Sammy carried on by throwing himself into volunteer work at the church. He took part in feeding the needy and performing other church services he felt suited for. These activities led him to offer his support to a local hospital. The gig at the hospital turned out to be as personally rewarding as the one at his church.

It wasn't long before Sammy became a well-known face at the hospital. Members of the Security Department, as well as other staff members, all got to know Sammy as a well-intentioned do-gooder. This familiarity enabled Sammy to travel about the hospital freely. It was not uncommon to see him, rosary beads in hand, praying at the bedside of an ailing patient.

With his hospital routine established, Sammy had a purpose. There were times that he'd reflect on his departed friend. Once such reflection of Bumper occurred in 2002 when Padre Pio was canonized by Pope John Paul II.

32

Life Goes On

ROSS HOLT STOOD BEFORE the judge at his arraignment with the injuries he sustained still evident. He used his poor physical appearance to his advantage. In order to generate sympathy, he walked with a shuffle and stood stooped. Ross stretched his neck upward whenever the judge looked his way. He did this so the purplish strangulation marks on his throat were visible. Whenever spoken to, Ross replied in a raspy whisper. He made sure to leave his mouth open wide to display the gaping holes where his teeth once were.

Regardless of his physical decline, Ross remained astute mentally. His first impression of the legal aid lawyer assigned to represent him was an unflattering one. He was unimpressed due to the attorney's youth. This caused Ross to assume that the young lawyer lacked the experience necessary to save him from prison.

The risk of facing a maximum prison sentence of fifteen years made Ross amenable to a plea bargain. To his surprise, the legal aid attorney representing him proved far more capable than initially thought. Ross didn't hesitate to accept the sentence offered in return for his guilty plea. *Doing a few years is better than doing fifteen*, thought the flimflammer.

Incarceration was going to come with challenges for Ross. This was something he knew. Posing as a man of God was the sort of activity that was likely to put him afoul of those inmates who took their religion seriously. He needed a plan.

Ross pondered this as he peered out the window of the bus that was transporting him to the Green Haven Correctional Facility. He sat quietly, alone, with his arms holding his elbows in an effort to offset the morning winter chill.

As the unheated bus steadily moved along, Ross stared out the window at the scenery. His mind was active as he searched for answers. He came to convince himself that not implicating Gloria in his criminal activities was something in his favor. *That'll prove to people that I'm a standup guy,* he thought.

The true motive Ross had for shielding his accomplice was purely self-serving. Gloria was protected only because the imposter knew he was going to need someone on the outside to do his bidding while incarcerated.

Once confined to a cell, Ross began to experience bouts of paranoia. The beatings Ross received prior to entering prison had shaken his confidence. He was uncertain in his ability to protect himself behind bars.

Ross proceeded cautiously as he navigated his way through the prison system. Exposure to the inmate population came with a learning curve. One of the first things he learned was to keep his mouth shut until he acclimated to what was accepted behavior in his new environment.

Ross diligently began studying those around him. In doing this he came to understand how important strategic alliances were behind bars. What struck Ross was the degree of respect afforded to the institution's resident tattooist. To those prisoners fond of the ink, the tattooist was an important man. Upon realizing this, Ross set out to make friends with the jailhouse artist.

By forming an alliance with the tattooist, Ross figured that he'd be able to step under a protective umbrella. To accomplish this end he sought out the cooperation of Gloria, who he viewed as a lifeline. What Ross hadn't foreseen was how the dynamics with his paramour accomplice had changed. He came to find out that Gloria's interest in him had waned.

Gloria feared going back to prison more than anything. She saw her Toms River apartment as a safe haven—as long as Ross didn't open his mouth to the law. But there was no guarantee of this. Gloria blamed Ross for all of her problems. Her resentment led to Gloria losing all interest in him. When Ross finally got around to reaching out to Gloria, their telephonic reconnection was laced with hostility.

"What do you want?" asked Gloria, her bark making it clear she was upset with Ross.

"What do you mean what do I want?" asked Ross. "It's me."

"I know who it is. What do you want?"

"What's with the attitude?"

"You got me into this mess!" she accused, as she shouted into the phone. "I don't know if the cops . . .

She caught herself and ceased talking midsentence. She remembered that in jail telephone calls might be monitored.

"I'm in Green Haven; what do you want from me?"

"What do YOU want from me?" Gloria countered.

"I want you to come and visit me."

"You can't be serious . . ."

"Look, I'm in the can. It ain't even easy for me to get at a phone in here. This ain't exactly a picnic I'm on."

"You have enough phones there. I'm no stranger to doing time, remember?"

"So how have you been?" asked Ross, changing the subject.

"How do you think I've been? I had to give my sister money so she could get her car back. It was towed!"

"You paid the freight?"

"Who do you think ended up paying for it?"

"Look, forget about the car. Just come to the prison and see me."

"Do you know how far that is from here?"

"Never mind how far it is, just get up here. I'll fill you in on the setup I got in mind when I see you."

"Yeah, sure," said Gloria, appeasing Ross. She had no intention of going to see him in jail.

Gloria set a date to visit Ross just to get off the phone with him. Having had enough of Ross, she saw him more as a liability than as someone advantageous to her well-being.

Gloria's failing to show up at the prison sent a disturbing message to Ross. His subsequent calls to Gloria went unanswered. No calls, no letters, and no visits, in effect, neutered Ross. He reacted to this by turning foul. He began leaving Gloria cryptic messages on her cell phone. These were veiled threats of exposing her whereabouts to the authorities. The bluff he was running gained no traction.

Gloria, having given up on Ross, tossed her cell phone into the river. She also began scouting for employment out of the New York-New Jersey area. Having access to whatever cash she and Ross had amassed, she considered relocating to either Pennsylvania or Delaware. Her goal was to be long gone before Ross was released.

Ross felt trapped. Unable to run away from his trouble in the middle of the night as he did when leaving his family behind in Ohio, he had to stay put and find a way to make things tolerable. This reality caused his imagination to run wild. He began envisioning the most horrible of prison atrocities happening to him. Feeling vulnerable, prison was starting to become hell on earth for Ross.

Desperate for security, Ross became more determined than ever to get close to the prison tattooist. Believing that money was the greatest of all connectors, Ross hit upon an idea that seemed a perfect solution. After reading something of interest concerning Charles Ponzi, an infamous con man who created the Ponzi scheme, he struck up a conversation with the tattooist. When the tattooist expressed ignorance of Ponzi, Ross explained how Ponzi scammed investors into putting money into businesses and then used some of this newly invested money to pay off prior investors.

The tale of Ponzi was received by the intellectually limited tattooist with mixed interest. However, the door was now open to further discussion. Ross switched direction and explained the scheme that he perpetrated while posing as a priest. This was something the tattooist, an atheist, could relate to. He began asking questions. Ross knew he had struck the right chord.

"I have a way of making a score from right here in the can," declared Ross.

"How do you plan on doing that?"

"There are a lot of chumps out there, and I got the perfect mark to start off with. All I need is a partner."

Ross explained his scheme to the tattooist. The plan called for the tattooist to write a letter to Gloria's sister. The letter was to indicate that the tattooist was an inmate at Green Haven who knew Ross. The tattooist was to explain that he got the sister's address from an address book that belonged to Ross. The communication would convey that the tattooist was unable to get in touch with her sister, Gloria, directly.

"You'll put in the letter that I'm no good," explained Ross, "and how you want to get word to Gloria about me. You'll tell her I was talking about hurting Gloria and thought she should know."

"But won't she maybe go to the cops?"

"That's the beauty of it. Gloria is wanted, so she'll never go to the cops. We gotta let Gloria's sister know that you've found religion. That's an important piece. She has to think that this was what moved you to write her."

"She's gonna believe all this?"

"Trust me: she'll believe it because she hates me," answered Ross.

"How should I end the letter?"

"Assure her that you'll keep her posted regarding me."

"What do I say if she writes me back and starts asking about me?"

"Tell her how you're in jail because you got involved with a woman who got you hooked on drugs—no, make it booze. Say how you loved this girl deeply and that you're a victim yourself. Let her know that you have no family or friends to correspond with and that you'd love to have her for a platonic friend to write to."

"That's it?"

"No, make it clear that you no longer have a drinking problem now that you're doing time. Tell her how nice it was for her to write you and ask her if she wouldn't mind being your pen pal. Tell her that, more than anything, you need someone caring and decent to talk to during this difficult period in your life."

"I get it. Maybe I could even write her a small poem."

"We'll save that for after a few letters go back and forth."

Ross went on to explain that if Gloria's sister responded as expected, they'd work her to where they could start asking her for things like stamps, writing paper, and envelopes.

"I see. I gotta suck her in."

"Exactly," said Ross. "You gotta make her think she's the only person who understands you. We'll lay it on thick about how you wish you could have met someone like her before going to prison. Tell her that if you had someone like her, your life would have been completely different. You get the idea?"

"Is she religious?"

"Who the hells knows?" answered Ross honestly. "Maybe you even send a picture of yourself."

If things went according to the plan Ross outlined, the expectation was that Gloria's sister would be sending money and packages to the prison.

As things turned out, that wasn't the case. Gloria's sister was astute enough to refuse to take the bait. This left Ross and the tattooist disappointed but not discouraged.

If nothing else, Ross was resilient. He tweaked the introductory letter he prepared for the tattooist and began targeting random women. After sending out dozens of letters weekly, he began receiving encouraging responses. With success came expansion. In time, Ross and the tattooist began tutoring other inmates on how to cultivate romantic relationships while incarcerated.

Many of the pairings lived on after an inmate was released from jail. A number of these unions even made it to the altar, and a couple of those marriages actually took. As for Ross, he had found his jailhouse niche.

MARKIE COULDN'T LET HIS SIGHTING of Fishnet in the company of the bogus priest go unexplained. It took some coaxing, but the sergeant managed to convince Von Hess to accompany him to the prison that held Ross Holt. They took the two-hour drive to Green Haven Correctional Facility on their day off. The ride was to be a stressful one for Von Hess. He was worried that Ross might recognize him as the person who beat him in Toms River.

Ross was bewildered when told he had visitors from the New York City Police Department. His initial thought was that they were there to question him in relation to his jailhouse scam. If this was the case, he intended to cast all blame on the prison tattooist. There was also the outside possibility that the law was there to seek his help in locating Gloria, but that was doubtful. Since company was scarce, the inmate agreed to meet with the detectives.

When Ross came to learn the true reason for the prison visit, he was relieved. Equally relieved was Von Hess once it was apparent that Ross didn't recognize him. Deciding that it was in his interest to remain on the good side of the detectives, Ross was more than willing to provide a sanitized version of his meeting with Fishnet.

"How do you know him?" asked Markie.

"That's just it—I don't. The guy just dropped in on me at the rectory out of the blue," advised Ross when queried about Fishnet.

"What did he want with you?"

"He wanted me to marry him and his girlfriend."

"You actually got involved in marrying people?" asked Von Hess.

"Hey, I was playing a role."

"And he wanted you to marry him to somebody?" questioned Markie.

"Yeah, but he knew it wouldn't be on the level."

"Wait a minute; he knew you were no real priest?"

"I don't know what he knew going in. All I know is that, when he left, he knew I wasn't legit."

"Why wouldn't he go to a real priest?"

"C'mon . . . he never wanted to get married. He just wanted the girl to think they were married."

"Did you know the bride's name?" asked Markie.

"I only know her first name: Cheryl."

"And that's all you know?"

"That's it, Sergeant. I never saw the guy again after that day. I'll tell you one thing though . . ."

"What's that?"

"He's gotta be a bigger crook than me."

* * *

AS THINGS TURNED OUT, THE SCAM that Ross and the tattooist were perpetrating from jail proved to be a lucrative enterprise. The years spent pairing couples made the time Ross was serving go fast. It also improved his life during his confinement. By the time Ross was released from prison, he found himself in the enviable position of juggling several love-seekers, all vying for his attention. All Ross had to do was decide which woman in his stable was the best for him to pursue.

Ross ultimately settled on a lady from Idaho who advertised herself as a childless widow with an interest in an impressive 2,000-acre potato farm. Swayed by photos of the farm, Ross was won over by what he believed to be his chance at some big bucks. After a year of spicy letters that professed his love, Ross made his way to the Idaho farm immediately upon his release. His intent was to propose marriage. The fact that he was already married never crossed his mind.

Upon meeting his love interest, Ross found himself faced with a couple of unexpected realities. First, the prospective bride had filled out substantially from the photos she had sent him in Green Haven. Second, she appeared to be several years older than what she had claimed. However, the lucrative potato farm was accurately portrayed, so Ross was willing to overlook the deceptions.

Things began to sour once Ross was shown around the farm. During the tour of the property, the woman confessed that her interest in the business was restricted to being the assistant to the potato farm manager. This eye-opening revelation caused Ross to forget all about potatoes and Idaho. The former convict immediately departed the farm, leaving in the direction from which he had come.

Ross made his way to a local library to research what state had the most churches. His intent was to resurrect Father Billy.

* * *

ON THE DRIVE BACK TO MANHATTAN, the detectives spoke little. Both Markie and Von Hess were deep in thought. The sergeant was thinking about the information he received from Ross Holt regarding Fishnet. The question running through Markie's mind was why Fishnet would want to dupe someone into believing they were legitimately married. *That son of a bitch must have an angle,* thought the sergeant. *I wonder what he was up to?*

While Markie remained hell-bent in his pursuit to bring Fishnet to justice, the thought running through the mind of Von Hess was entirely different. Thel detective breathed easily knowing how fortunate he was that Ross Holt hadn't recognized him.

When his cell phone went off, Von Hess checked to see who was calling. When the detective didn't answer, Markie wondered why not.

"Who was that, Ollie?" asked the sergeant.

"It's nobody important, Sarge." Von Hess didn't want to say that the caller was Arlene Perez.

33

A Double Loss

IN LIGHT OF THE FATHER BILLY fiasco, the elderly clergyman assigned to the Sunset Park Parish was forced to retire. His replacement was young, ambitious, and afforded free reign in an effort to expand the congregation.

In appearance, the new priest was a trimly built, handsome man with fine grooming. A persuasive speaker, had it not been for his strong faith, the results-oriented priest could have found success in a boiler room as a salesman pressuring investors into buying fraudulent securities.

Diligent to further his mission at the church, the new priest took the time to review the recent parish contributions. He came to wonder why the donations from the usually generous Perez sisters had slackened off. He decided to investigate.

The priest's overtures to the Perez sisters were resisted. Post Father Billy, the affluent siblings were less inclined to welcome another priest into their inner circle. The sisters opted to simply attend Mass and then return home without lingering. It took the death of Millie Perez to alter that pattern.

Millie's middle-of-the-night heart attack had come totally unexpected. She never revealed to anyone that she had been experiencing chest pains ever since she shoveled the snow in front of the house. The death of her sister devastated Arlene.

The inheritance she came into did nothing to ease the grieving sibling's heart.

The Captain did his best by stepping up to offer his support in the face of Arlene's loss. A stouthearted man, the tenant accepted the death of Millie stoically. His expressing to Arlene that the final hour was all a part of living did little to bolster the spirits of the older sister. Even less soothing was the tenant's off-the-cuff remark, "Everybody has to go sometime."

Tactful or not, it was the Captain who stood by Arlene as she faced the painful process of picking out a casket, making funeral arrangements, and doing all the other unpleasant things connected to dying. For this, Arlene was grateful. Arlene's weakened emotional condition caused her barriers to break down as far as the newly assigned parish priest was concerned.

The surviving sibling acclimated to the new parish priest when he became involved in the religious arrangements for Millie. The priest's spiritual support proved to be the proper formula to win over Arlene. The clergyman attentively listened to Arlene with understanding for as long as she needed someone to talk to.

As Arlene's mental state improved, the priest began to regularly stop by the Perez house. His looking in on her greatly impressed Arlene, particularly since the priest never asked her for money in return for his thoughtfulness. Even the salty Captain, a man of a suspicious nature, had to admit that the priest seemed to be everything a clergyman should be.

Once trust was established, Arlene began to have the priest over to the house regularly. This synergy ultimately led to Arlene increasing her contributions to the church without having to be asked. Part of their platonic relationship included having dinner weekly at a local restaurant. Often this was followed by a movie.

In other ways, the Captain also secured a place in Arlene's life. With Millie gone, Arlene and her tenant came to see each other as someone available to fill a need that was mutually beneficial. The Captain, having once had a sexual encounter with Arlene, welcomed the renewed intimacy.

Even with the Captain's romantic availability, Arlene still retained a strong desire for the elusive Detective Von Hess. His clean-cut, military bearing and professional demeanor were attributes that Arlene continued to find appealing. When she and the Captain shared a bed, she fantasized that it was Von Hess making love to her. The thought went far in spicing things up for Arlene.

Arlene's desire for the detective only increased as a result of all this. Once over the death of her sister, she decided the time had come to go after what she wanted. She commenced a shameless pursuit of Von Hess

* * *

PART OF THE JOB OF DETECTIVE SILVERLAKE was to filter all incoming telephone calls to the office of the chief of detectives. When he received a call for Von Hess from a woman who refused to identify herself, Silverlake became suspicious. The detective placed her call on hold while he consulted with Von Hess.

"Ollie, I got some woman on the line who wants to talk to you," advised Silverlake.

"Who is it?"

"She ain't saying."

"Did she say what she wanted?"

"No, she just asked to speak to you."

"Did you ask her what her business was?"

"Look, Ollie, do you want to talk to her or not?" tartly replied Silverlake, who had about the same time on the job as Von Hess. In the police world, seniority entitled people to be crabby.

"Tell her I'm in the field and take a message."

When Silverlake asked the caller if she wanted to leave a message, she declined, advising that she'd call again. Over the next week, Silverlake received numerous calls from Arlene, who continued to ask to speak to Detective Von Hess. Eventually, Silverlake told the caller to either identify herself or stop calling.

Seeing the futility in her efforts to get Von Hess on the line, the caller finally relented and agreed to be more forthcoming.

"Please apprise Oliver that his friend from Sunset Park called," said the woman, leaving a call-back number.

"Do you have a name, Ms. Sunset Park?" asked Silverlake.

"He'll know who I am," said Arlene Perez confidently.

Von Hess shook his head when Detective Silverlake delivered the message. "I should have known," commented Von Hess, who had been ignoring Arlene's calls to his cell phone. "She's been hunting me down like a dog."

"So you know who it is?" asked Silverlake.

"Yeah, I do."

Von Hess felt that he had no choice other than to return Arlene's call. Realizing that her interest rested in something intimate, he promptly abbreviated their conversation by claiming that he had to run out of the office on an urgent matter. At that point Von Hess instructed Silverlake never to entertain another call from Arlene.

"If that woman calls again, I'm not in," Von Hess advised Silverlake.

"What has she got the hots for you?"

"Yeah, she looks at me like I'm a whopper....and she hasn't eaten in a week."

"What do you want me to tell her?"

"Tell her whatever you want, just don't put her through to me."

Von Hess was wary of Arlene because experience had taught him the downside of illicit affairs. He had known philandering detectives who had ended affairs only to have their dalliances show up at their precinct looking for them. The last thing Von Hess needed at his age was having a stalker on his hands.

Detective Silverlake didn't ask for a further explanation as to why Von Hess refused to accept any calls from the Sunset Park woman. Although he would have liked clarification to satisfy his own curiosity, he knew better than to press Von Hess for details. Silverlake found it hard to imagine Von Hess involved in a romantic interlude because the detective was known to be a straight arrow with a preference for one woman and one God.

Silverlake briefly wrestled with what to tell the mystery caller the next time she reached out for the detective. He decided that he would inform her that Von Hess had retired and relocated to Germany. Since Silverlake also served as the eyes and ears of the chief, he saw it as his duty to inform the chief of detectives of the situation with Von Hess.

"You never know about people, Silvie," said the chief, laughing the matter off. "It's these straight-laced guys like Von Hess that fool you."

Following the chain of command downward, the chief referred the matter to the head of his speci00al investigative squad, Lieutenant Wright. The lieutenant, who oversaw both Von Hess and Markie, passed the ball to the sergeant for rectification.

"What's going on with this woman calling up over here all the time, Ollie?" asked Markie.

"Don't tell me that house mouse bothered you with this?"

"Lieutenant Wright dropped this in my lap—so what's the story?"

When Von Hess confided in his sergeant how he became involved with Arlene Perez, Markie offered no critique. He just nodded his understanding. Having loads of faith in Von Hess, Markie instructed the detective to do whatever was needed to get Arlene Perez to cease and desist. This was exactly the latitude Von Hess wanted.

"I'll take care of it, Sarge."

"Ollie, do me a favor, will ya?

"Sure, boss, what is it?"

"Let it go with Silverlake. He's the chief's snitch; everybody knows that. That's why he's in the office. So do us both a favor and make like he never gave you up to the chief."

* * *

TO PUT AN END TO ARLENE'S PURSUIT OF HIM, Von Hess resorted to trickery. The scheme he concocted was a ploy that required the support of an accomplice. Mad Dog Switzer, the detective assigned to the Sunset Park Precinct, was the perfect fit for what Von Hess had in mind. Since Switzer had already proven himself to be agreeable, Von Hess was optimistic that he'd gain the detective's cooperation.

Von Hess stopped at a liquor store to pick up a bottle of scotch prior to arriving at the Sunset Park squad. He learned that bearing gifts went a long way with detectives when asking for a favor.

Detective Switzer was at his desk preparing a report on one of his cases when Von Hess entered the squad room. Looking up from his desk, he smiled broadly after seeing the visitor was carrying a gift-wrapped bottle in his hand.

"Hello, Ollie. What have you got there? Is it something for me?"

"You bet, Mad Dog. It's just a little something to thank you for that Father Billy caper."

"It's about time. I thought you forgot about me. What have you got there?"

"Johnny Walker."

"Did you get me the good bottle?"

"Yeah, Mad Dog, I got you the good one."

"Beautiful!" said Switzer. You know I earned it. I ended up having to save Ross Holt's life."

"What happened?"

"The guy with the humpback went bat shit in the cell and started to beat the hell out of him."

"I had no idea . . ."

Over coffee Mad Dog explained what happened to Von Hess. When done, they then discussed the predicament Von Hess was having with Arlene Perez. Sympathizing with Von Hess, Switzer asked few questions.

"Why don't you just try making her happy?"

"Forget that, Mad Dog. That ain't happening."

"Did you tell her to screw off?"

"No, I really don't want to be that callous with her. I'm looking to ease out of it gently."

"If you want my advice, you're better off easing in."

"C'mon, Mad Dog, I'm being serious about this. I need a favor."

"So what do you want me to do, Ollie?" asked the Sunset Park detective, cutting to the chase. "Do you want me to go see her and tell her to back off?"

"Not exactly, Mad Dog. I'd like you to bump into Arlene Perez on the street, you know, a chance meeting."

"Then what do I do?"

"Strike up a casual conversation with her. Then, let her know about poor Detective Von Hess. I want you to fabricate a story about my poor health."

"You want me to tell her that you're dead?"

"No, I wouldn't put it past her to check the obituaries. Tell Arlene I got cancer and had to retire. Tell her I relocated to Germany to live out my final time," instructed Von Hess, taking a page from Detective Silverlake's strategy.

* * *

ON SUNDAY, DETECTIVE SWITZER MONITORED the Sunset Park church in an effort to cross paths with Arlene Perez. Aware that Arlene was a church-going woman, he figured she was bound to show up at one of the services. The detective proved correct in his thinking. Pretending to have attended the same Mass himself, he connected with Arlene outside the house of worship at the conclusion of the Mass she attended.

"Hello, Ms. Perez," said Switzer.

"Oh, hello, Detective Switzer," greeted Arlene, surprised to see him. "I didn't know you came to this church."

"I do whenever I work days on Sunday."

"Oh, that's nice."

"I just said a prayer for poor Detective Von Hess."

"Something happened to Oliver?" Arlene asked, the concern in her voice obvious.

"I'm afraid so."

"What happened?"

"He's riddled with cancer."

298

"Oh, no!" exclaimed the shocked woman.

"Yeah, I'm afraid that it's all over for him."

"Is Oliver at home or in the hospital?"

"He retired and moved with his entire family to Germany. He's living over there with his parents."

"They're still alive?"

"Yeah, they're way up there in age, but supposedly they're in good shape. Von Hess wanted to close out his days in the old country. His parents still maintain their own home over there."

"This is so upsetting to me—poor Oliver."

"Yeah, I suppose we'll all miss old Ollie."

After leaving Arlene teary-eyed, the Sunset Park detective telephoned Von Hess.

"How did it go, Mad Dog?" asked Von Hess anxiously.

"It was a piece of cake. Arlene went for it hook, line, and sinker . . . *Oliver*."

"Cut it out with that Oliver stuff, will ya? Did she really go for it?"

"Yeah, Ollie, she did. The way she reacted, I don't think she'll ever stop wearing black."

"Thanks, Mad Dog. I owe you one, pal."

"No problem. Just don't forget; you owe me another bottle."

* * *

WHEN ARLENE PEREZ RETURNED home from Mass, she was in a state of depression. The Captain, who was stationed at his apartment window that overlooked the street, observed Arlene return home from church. Seeing Arlene out and about was a good thing because Sunday evenings had become sort of date night for them. Their understanding was that he'd go downstairs promptly at 8:30 p.m. to have drinks with his landlord.

As usual, the Captain went downstairs for his evening visit at the established time. At the sound of the bell, Arlene looked out her window to see who was at the front door. Seeing the

Captain, she frowned. She was in no mood for company, least of all intimacy.

A second ring of the bell also went unanswered. It took several of the Captain's knocks to convince Arlene of his unwavering determination to see her. *He never gives up,* thought the landlord. Relenting, Arlene went to the front door.

"Hello, Captain," she said after opening the door. Her lack of enthusiasm was unmistakable.

"What, did you go deaf?" asked the tenant.

"I was upstairs," Arlene countered.

"I thought something happened when you didn't answer the bell," replied the Captain. "What took you so long?"

"I already told you; I was upstairs doing something," she lied.

When the Captain tried to enter the house, she blocked his passage with her body. Her not stepping aside made it clear that no invitation was being extended. Not willing to simply push past Arlene, the Captain took a step back. A perplexed look came over him as he wondered what he did wrong. Undaunted, he persisted in trying to establish what the problem was. His probing was met with great annoyance.

"I'm not feeling well, Captain," said Arlene abruptly. She hoped that her clipped response would make it clear to the Captain that he should take the hint and leave.

"What's wrong?"

Arlene let out a long sigh before answering. "Look, I'll call you when I'm feeling better," she declared, rudely closing the door in the Captain's face.

The despondent landlord turned on her radio before sitting down in the lightless living room. The music was barely audible. Tucked beneath the protective shell of a navy-blue blanket, Arlene rested her head against the cushioned chair. Her eyes closed, locking out the world around her. In this moment of privacy, she entered the depths of melancholy that came with thoughts of life without Von Hess and her beloved sister.

34

Good Riddance to a Beast

THE MAESTRO WAS DRINKING COFFEE while on the telephone with Enzo Baffi. The producer was going over the details of their plot to do away with Fishnet. As the virtuoso listened carefully, he sipped coffee from his mug. While on the telephone he turned to look at Pascal, who had just entered the kitchen.

"Who are you talking to?" asked Pascal.

"Hold it a second, Enzo," said the Maestro to the caller. "Pascal, can't you see that I'm on the telephone?" asked the musician tartly. He was annoyed at his concentration being interrupted.

"Sorry," answered Pascal, who backed away. It seemed to him the Maestro had gotten into the habit of being curt with him as of late.

"Yes, we'll be fully prepared when summoned, Enzo," assured the Maestro, returning to his call.

"That was Enzo?" asked Pascal once the Maestro was off the phone.

"Yes, it was Enzo. Did you see my black onyx ring?"

"No, I told you yesterday I haven't seen it."

"You never told me that yesterday," corrected the Maestro.

"Yes I did. You're starting to forget."

"I don't forget, Pascal!" barked the virtuoso, with a burst of anger. He didn't want to hear it.

"Okay, I guess I'm mistaken," said Pascal, not looking to exasperate the situation. "What did Enzo want?"

"He just wanted to finalize our arrangements concerning that beast."

Pascal nodded weakly, indicating that he was on board in taking part in the killing of Fishnet. Pascal poured himself a glass of water and sat at the kitchen table. He nervously began thinking of his role in the murder Enzo Baffi plotted. While he wanted their target dead as much as his associates did, he was fighting off the worry connected to the risk involved.

Pascal's train of thought was broken as he heard the Maestro muttering to himself. The old man, wanting another mug of coffee, was searching the kitchen for the coffee pot.

"Where did you put the damn coffee pot?" asked the annoyed Maestro.

"I haven't had any coffee," replied Pascal.

"Well, the pot isn't in the kitchen!"

"Did you leave the kitchen with the coffee pot?" asked Pascal, rising to get himself orange juice from the refrigerator.

"Of course not, why would I do that?"

"Here it is," announced Pascal after opening the refrigerator door. "You put it in the refrigerator."

"I did not," insisted the virtuoso. "You must have put it there," he accused.

"No, Maestro, you did. You must have been so absorbed in talking to Enzo that you inadvertently put the coffee pot in the refrigerator instead of the milk."

"Oh, whatever," stated the octogenarian, dismissing the matter.

"So we're really going to do it then," said Pascal, referring to the plan to kill Fishnet.

"We're committed, Pascal. That beast has been a thorn in the side of all concerned. If we don't stop him now, he'll only surface later to make more demands on us. We must put an end to him."

"We've got to be absolutely certain that nothing can be traced back to any of us," emphasized Pascal.

"Enzo has orchestrated a well-thought-out strategy. He knows we're all too old to go to jail."

"Personally, I would have loved to see the beast run over by a car. That way he'd suffer, and it would appear as an accident— and accidents do happen."

"Oh no, Pascal, that would never do. It would require our getting a car. Besides, who among us would be willing to drive the car?"

"Oh, well, I suppose you're right," acknowledged Pascal. "Enzo's plan is probably best."

Enzo Baffi's murder plot called for the police to find Fishnet hanged in his own home. The scheme was to set a stage in which the natural assumption would be that Fishnet took his own life. Baffi intended to use a strong sedative in order to render the intended victim helpless.

The drug was supplied to Baffi by a physician friend under the guise of combating the producer's periodic bouts of depression. In actuality, the controlled substance was given to Baffi to further his romantic encounters with women who resisted his overtures. The physician provided the producer with the sedative from an allotment that came from his office stash. This meant there was no prescription involved that could be traced back to Baffi.

"Enzo knows what he's doing, Pascal. Rest assured of that. He indicated to me that enough of the sedative in a drink will put the beast to sleep long enough for us to perform our, well, let's call it public service."

"So the sedative is in liquid form, Maestro?"

"Yes. Things couldn't be simpler. All Enzo has to do is pour enough in a drink."

"Is there a foul smell to it?"

"Supposedly, it's odorless. A little salty perhaps, but other than that, according to Enzo, the beast will never know what hit him."

"Did Enzo say that we needed a suicide note? I don't remember."

"A note isn't necessary, Pascal," answered the Maestro. "People who take their own life don't always leave a suicide note. Don't fret. It'll appear as if the beast died at his own hand."

Enzo Baffi intended to use advancing the career of Fishnet's girlfriend as an excuse to get into his target's townhouse. Baffi was confident that the ex-detective would be receptive to this. The producer was going to arrive at the townhouse armed with an expensive whiskey. The drink offering was to show there were no hard feelings over Baffi's being assaulted.

If things went according to plan, the two would drink a toast to their collaboration. After a sip or two, Baffi would ask for a glass of cold water. When alone and waiting for the water, the producer would pour enough of the sedative in his victim's drink to put him out. Once Fishnet was helpless, Baffi would summon the Maestro and Pascal to come to the townhouse. Then the trio of assassins would, collectively, rid the world of the man they considered a beast.

"What if they decide to do an autopsy, Maestro?" asked Pascal.

"The beauty of Enzo's plan, Pascal, is that the beast lives alone. It'll be a long time before anyone finds him. By the time he's discovered, his system will be clear. Besides, people take this type of sedative for depression all the time."

"What about his girlfriend? Won't she be missing him?" asked the Maestro.

"Enzo will get word to Cheryl that Mr. Fish was traveling on business."

"He can do that?"

"Yes. He said his secretary can handle it."

"Enzo is a genius," declared Pascal. The Maestro agreed.

* * *

HEARING FROM ENZO BAFFI so soon after their confrontation made Fishnet leery. His antennas raised, the former detective suspected the producer might be recording their telephone conversation. Preferring to remain on the side of caution, Fishnet opted to listen rather than talk.

Baffi indicated there were no hard feelings, adding that he now saw their working together as a feasible undertaking. He suggested that the two meet at Fishnet's townhouse so he could present the ex-detective with something to celebrate their union. Fishnet was certain the producer had something up his sleeve. *What is this son of a bitch up to?* Fishnet thought, not buying into Baffi's let bygones be bygones philosophy.

"That's not necessary," said Fishnet, not letting on that he was suspicious of Baffi's motives.

"Please, indulge me. If we plan on working together, there must be a meeting of the minds. We need to reach a mutual comfort level."

"Okay, have it your way, Enzo. Are you sure you don't want to meet at your office?" asked Fishnet.

"That's too formal a setting," replied Baffi. "Besides, I have a gift for you. Now that we're partners, we need to grow closer if we are to collaborate with success."

"Is that a fact?"

"I'm being quite sincere with you," assured the producer. "If we are to be a successful team, you'll need mentoring. I'm prepared to fulfill that role."

"So you're saying you're willing to mentor me?"

"Yes, as long as you're serious about learning."

"Why, all of a sudden, are you so generous?"

"I've come to realize that it's in my interest to have you working with me rather than against me."

Either this guy is on the level, or he should get an Academy Award for his acting, thought Fishnet, who began to let his guard down.

"Believe me when I say that I've put a lot of thought into this. I suppose you can say that you beat some sense into me."

"I don't know anything about any beating," commented Fishnet, who would never acknowledge any wrongdoing over the telephone.

"Whatever," voiced Baffi. *Maybe this jerk-off does want to get together*, thought Fishnet. *If he's bullshitting me, I'll see it soon enough.* Fishnet decided to give the producer the benefit of the doubt.

"Okay, Enzo, come over to the house whenever you feel like it."

"When is a good time?"

"You can come over now if you want," said Fishnet.

"Well, how about I come by this evening?"

"Okay, come tonight. You know where I live."

"Yes. I'll see you about eight."

Fishnet wasn't taking any chances. He strapped on a brown leather shoulder holster that contained his five-shot revolver. The snub nose .38 caliber Smith & Wesson was the off-duty gun that he regularly carried when a member of the department. Fishnet donned his smoking jacket to conceal the weapon.

The producer wasted no time in reaching out to the Maestro and Pascal. Their instructions were to respond to the townhouse when called, armed with a clothesline rope and a knife.

With death in his thoughts, Baffi began to fantasize about necrophilia. While he had no desire to engage in such a perversion, it was a topic he found of interest. The idea of partaking in a sex act with a corpse was something that went even beyond his wildest black-room antics.

* * *

WHEN ENZO BAFFI ARRIVED AT FISHNET'S TOWNHOUSE, it was evident to the onetime detective that the producer had been humbled. Fishnet attributed this to the beating he had administered. Seeing the effects of the injuries he caused brought a smile to Fishnet's face. It pleased him to see that the punishment he had inflicted had staying power.

"Come on in, Enzo," welcomed Fishnet. *How does it feel to have been knocked down a peg?* he thought.

"Thank you," replied Baffi politely. It required all of the producer's theatrical skills to conceal his animosity.

"What have you got there?" asked Fishnet, pointing to the small shopping bag carried by the producer. Contained in the bag was a very expensive bottle of whiskey.

"Just a small gift to show there are no hard feelings," said Baffi. "It's a fine whiskey." Baffi then extended his hand in friendship.

Fishnet accepted the producer's hand. "I'm glad we understand each other," he said. "It makes life easier for us both."

"Since we are to collaborate on projects, I'm at peace with our getting together."

"Come on, cut the crap," said Fishnet, tired of dancing around what he saw as the obvious. "You're playing ball because you got no choice, right?"

Although taken aback, Baffi remained quick on his feet. "I'm a practical man, Mr. Fish," replied the producer. "Having just the key does me no good."

"I don't follow you . . ."

"I'll explain. I have the ability to put Cheryl, a true talent, on a course that will propel her career. In effect, I have the key to the door. You can deadbolt that door by controlling the talent's heartstrings. Under the circumstances, we need to work together if we are to advance Cheryl."

"So you need me."

"Precisely, just as you do me," confirmed Baffi.

"So what's all this talk about mentoring me, Enzo?"

"The way I see it is that you might as well know the business if we are to work together."

"You're starting to make a lot of sense to me, Enzo. Once I get the hang of things, you can retire whenever you want, and I can steer the ship."

"Before we get ahead of ourselves, let's toast our coming

together."

"Sure, have a seat. We'll crack open that bottle you gave me."

"By all means, let's do."

Fishnet smiled and walked to the cabinet where he stored his fancy drinking glasses. He poured a generous portion of the whiskey into two four-ounce glasses.

"Here you go, Enzo," said Fishnet, handing one of the glasses to the producer.

"Can I have a little water on the side, Mr. Fish?"

"Why not?" answered Fishnet, leaving the room to fetch a pitcher of water.

In Fishnet's absence, Baffi poured the sedative into his intended victim's glass. He then added additional whiskey to his own glass to make the pouring appear equal. When Fishnet returned, he placed the water pitcher and a clean glass on the small table in front of the producer.

"Bottoms up," said Fishnet. The two touched glasses and proceeded to drink their whiskey.

By the time Fishnet began to feel the effects of the sedative, it was too late for him to do anything about it. When it dawned on him that he had been drugged, Fishnet looked at Baffi in disbelief.

"White Fang had ceased eating, lost heart, and allowed every dog of the team to thrash him," voiced the gloating Baffi, quoting a line out of Jack London's *White Fang*. "Now, Mr. Fish, we dogs are having our day!"

Fishnet began to feebly reach for the gun lodged in the holster beneath his armpit. His weakened condition made the effort too monumental a task.

"Now, now, we'll have none of that, Mr. Fish," said the producer, slapping Fishnet's hand away from the weapon.

Seeing his victim motionless, the producer began to pinch Fishnet's nose harshly. When no reaction came, he began flicking his finger against the helpless man's proboscis. Fishnet was, without question, at Baffi's mercy.

"I probably could have made something of you since you look so much like Clark Gable," said Baffi. "Goodbye, you bastard . . .

and good riddance!"

The last thing Fishnet noticed was the smirk on the producer's face. Flashing in Fishnet's mind was the picture of his being discovered dead. *This can't be . . . It just can't be . . .* thought Fishnet as he began his descent into where all evil people wind up.

The producer telephoned his crime partners, instructing them to respond to the townhouse. While Baffi waited for their arrival, he picked up a newspaper that was on an end table and began working on his favorite word game. As was his habit, he first read the words at the bottom of the puzzle. He then picked a word and looked for it among a multitude of letters at the top of the puzzle. Once a word was found, Baffi circled the applicable letters. He then inked out the found word as it appeared at the bottom of the puzzle before moving on to the next word. As he progressed with the words, small ink rectangles began to form. When the game was completed, the ink rectangles had all merged to form one thick, inked-out square.

After finishing the word game, the producer began to amuse himself by placing the barrel of Fishnet's gun against the crime victim's cheek. The producer's pleasure was abruptly truncated by the ringing of his cell phone. It was Pascal.

"Where are you?" asked Baffi impatiently.

"We'll be there in a few minutes. The Maestro thought he forgot to lock the door to our apartment. We had to go back to make sure the door was locked."

"Was it?"

"Yes."

"Did he remember to bring the rope and knife?"

"We have them. We'll be there shortly."

When the Maestro and Pascal arrived, the trio of assassins carried Fishnet to where the banister turned at the top of the grand staircase that led to the second floor. Baffi looked over the rail and nodded in the affirmative. The unobstructed drop to the floor below made the location ideal for a hanging.

After cutting a sufficient length of rope, Baffi had Pascal affix one end to the banister while he made a noose out of the other end. The Maestro was tasked with tightening the noose around Fishnet's neck. The three assassins then gently lifted their victim's body and eased Fishnet over the railing.

The trio of killers looked down at their dangling victim until he gradually ceased to swing. The open-mouthed Pascal gulped at the gruesome sight of the dead man. Down deep he couldn't believe what he and his cohorts had just done.

The Maestro's tightened mouth reflected a firmer resolve. He was perfectly fine in the belief that the murder he had partaken in was justified. He looked down at the hanging man he detested with nothing short of great satisfaction.

Of the three, it was the producer who had the most unusual reaction—he ejaculated. Baffi's euphoria in committing murder fueled a new sexual thirst that could only be quenched by homicide.

While the producer collected himself, the Maestro wasted no time in taking charge of the cleanup.

"Put the whiskey glasses in the bag the rope came in, Pascal," instructed the Maestro, "and the knife too. We need to take everything with us and dispose of it."

The three men decided to depart the townhouse one at a time. It was further agreed by all parties that the murder they had committed would never be discussed again.

35

Suicide or Murder?

TO REGAIN CHERYL'S CONFIDENCE, Enzo Baffi profusely expressed his remorse over what occurred in the black room at his Manhattan penthouse. Although Fishnet's girlfriend questioned the producer's sincerity, she allowed herself to tolerate him in order to advance herself professionally. This decision was based in no small way on her faith in Fishnet's ability to keep the producer's hands off her.

Cheryl was surprised to learn from Baffi's longtime secretary that Fishnet had embarked on a road trip relative to the movie she was to star in. When the actor questioned the secretary as to why she was notifying her instead of her boyfriend conveying the news, she received an uninformed answer. The secretary advised that she was just following the instructions of her boss.

Cheryl's query as to the precise nature of Fishnet's work on the road was met with an unsatisfactory response. The secretary vaguely communicated that the job of a producer was a wide sweeping one, adding that Fishnet could out performing any number of tasks. Cheryl had no choice other than to justify the incomplete answer as something that comes with success.

Cheryl's attitude shifted to one of concern after the passing of a week. With no word from Fishnet, she grew worried,

311

wondering where he was. Her feeling was magnified when her phone calls and messages continued to go unanswered.

Having grown suspicious, Cheryl decided to go to her boyfriend's townhouse to see if he had been in New York City all along. At the townhouse she noticed that her boyfriend's mail had been piling up in the mailbox. Fishnet's newspaper deliveries littered the townhouse steps. Several rings of the doorbell produced no response. Cheryl then examined the garbage pails outside the building. Finding them free of trash, she concluded that Fishnet was, in fact, away.

You'd think that he'd at least call me, she thought, now more annoyed than worried. Further contemplation came with more thoughts. *Could something have happened to him?*

Not knowing what to do next, Cheryl telephoned Enzo Baffi. She believed the producer possessed the insights as to where her boyfriend was. Baffi had been expecting her call.

The producer claimed ignorance as to Fishnet's current whereabouts. He advised Cheryl that her boyfriend, being the unpredictable sort, could be anywhere. Baffi fabricated a story to explain Fishnet's absence. He indicated that his new partner was out looking for new out-of-town talent to appear in their upcoming movie.

"Did he say anything as to where he would be looking?" asked Cheryl.

"No, not a word my dear, he could have commenced his search for new talent anywhere," replied the producer with a convincing innocence.

Baffi's reply disappointed Cheryl, who concluded their conversation with the understanding that she intended to notify the authorities. The producer agreed to meet with Cheryl at her apartment the following morning to report Fishnet missing.

On his way to see Cheryl the next day, Baffi took a moment to stop at a newsstand to pick up the daily paper. Upon arriving, he sat in Cheryl's living room as she readied herself to go out. While waiting, the producer began working on the newspaper word game he enjoyed doing each day.

When Cheryl emerged from the bedroom, she indicated that she was nervous about dealing with the police. She asked the producer if he would make the initial overture to the authorities.

"So you'll call the cops for me, Enzo?"

"Why certainly, my dear," replied Baffi, adding, "I'll call police headquarters right now."

Baffi immediately informed the headquarters operator who he was. After explaining the situation, the operator, aware she was talking to a well-known personality, transferred the call to Detective Silverlake in the chief of detective's office.

"Chief of D's office, Detective Silverlake speaking. How may I help you?"

"My name is Enzo Baffi. I want to report someone missing."

"You have the wrong number, Mr. Baffi," said Silverlake. "You need to go to your local precinct to report a missing person."

"I can't report someone missing to you?"

"No. This office doesn't get involved in that. You have to go to the precinct."

At this point the producer immediately went on the offensive. "See here," he began, "I don't want to go over your head, but I will if I must. I'm Enzo Baffi. Do you know who I am?"

"Didn't your parent's tell you?" asked the detective, getting cute.

Baffi went on to explain exactly who he was. Now under the impression that he was dealing with a man of influence, Silverlake put the caller on hold so he could check for himself who Enzo Baffi was. Once Silverlake understood the importance of Enzo Baffi in the world of entertainment, the detective became more obliging. Silverlake knew well that people of Baffi's prominence were not shy about reaching out to someone in the department at a superior level.

"Now tell me, who is in charge over there, Detective?"

"I can take care of things for you, sir," said Silverlake. "What's the name of the missing person?"

"His name is Fish, F-I-S-H . . ."

Cheryl suddenly tugged at the producer's sleeve. "No," she said, "Fish isn't his real name. His real name is Bruce Milligan."

Unaware of this, Baffi was taken aback by the correction. "Hold on a second, Detective," he said. The producer then cupped the phone and turned to Cheryl. "When did this happen?"

"I only found out his real name when he began talking about marriage," informed Cheryl.

"Here, you better talk to the detective," said Baffi, passing back the phone.

After Cheryl provided the detective with her name, address, and relationship to Fishnet, the fact-gathering continued.

"So how long has your friend been missing, Ms. Arbuckle?" asked Silverlake.

"He's been gone for a couple of weeks."

"Has he gone missing before?"

"No."

"Has he been upset over anything or experiencing any problems?"

"No."

"Is he of sound mind?"

"Yes."

"Is he on drugs or does he have alcohol problems?"

"No."

"Did he have a reason to run away? You know, in debt or something like that."

"No," replied Cheryl. Actually, he is a very wealthy man."

"He lives with you?

"Sometimes he stays over with me."

"I see. Have you checked where he lives?"

"Of course I have. He hasn't been home."

"Do you have any reason to suspect foul play?"

"Well . . . I don't really know whether there is any foul play. That's why I called you."

"What is the business of the missing person?"

"He's a retired detective. Now he works as a producer. He was supposed to be away on business."

"He was an NYPD detective?" asked Silverlake, his interest now stirred.

"Yes."

"What's his name again?"

"His name is Bruce Milligan," replied Cheryl.

Silverlake did a double take. "Fishnet Milligan?" he asked.

"I don't know anyone who ever called him Fishnet . . ."

"Was your Milligan ever involved in a shootout?"

"Why, yes. I remember him speaking about being shot by some gangster. I can't recall the last name."

"Red Harris," declared Silverlake.

"That right. So you know my fiancé then?"

"Sure, everyone in the department has heard of Fishnet Milligan. He's a big hero around the job."

"So what can we do about locating him, Detective?"

"Let me have your callback number. I'm gonna walk this down to the Missing Persons Bureau myself, Ma'am. They work out of the building here at headquarters. I'll make sure a detective from that office calls you back right away. Don't you worry; they'll do all they can to find him for you."

"Thank you, Detective."

"No problem, Ma'am. If he got in an accident or is hurt, you'd have heard about it. The fact that you haven't heard anything might be a good thing. Remember, bad news travels fast."

True to his word, Silverlake went to missing persons after getting off the phone with Cheryl. Once there, he asked for a detective he knew who was assigned to the unit.

"Is Bloodhound working today?" asked Silverlake, addressing one of the people assigned to the office.

"Here I am, Silvie," announced the missing persons detective, stepping from behind a row of large file cabinets.

"Hey, Bloodhound, I got a case for you."

"Don't I have enough work without you giving me more?"

"This involves a missing retired detective."

After briefing the detective, Silverlake went to see the chief in his office. He knew the chief would have an interest. After being apprised of Fishnet's disappearance, the chief summoned

Lieutenant Wright, Markie, and Von Hess to his office. He then had Silverlake repeat what he knew.

"What do you make of it?" asked the chief after they were brought up to speed.

"Who reported him missing?" asked the lieutenant.

"His girlfriend and Enzo Baffi filed the missing report. Baffi's that big-shot producer."

"What's Baffi's connection to Fishnet again?" questioned Markie.

"Apparently, Fishnet is in business with Baffi," answered Silverlake.

"What's the girlfriend's name?"

"Cheryl Arbuckle."

"This is has to be the Cheryl we were wondering about, Ollie," said Markie.

"What are you talking about?" asked the chief.

"Just before we made those collars in the Sunset Park church, we saw Fishnet talking to the bogus Priest we pinched in front of the rectory," explained Markie. "The phony baloney claimed that Fishnet wanted him to perform a marriage ceremony for him and his fiancée . . . a woman named Cheryl."

"So what if Fishnet wanted to get married," declared the chief. "What's the big deal?"

"Dollars to donuts, Fishnet knew the priest was a scammer, Chief. He must be suckering these people somehow."

"Maybe, maybe not," said the chief. "All I know for sure is that this Enzo Baffi probably has the juice to give me a headache. Let's prevent that by appeasing him. I don't need a call from the commissioner or some politician."

"What do you want done, Chief?" asked Lieutenant Wright.

"Have Markie and Von Hess lend a hand to whoever caught the case over at missing persons. If something's up, I want to know about it."

"No problem, Chief," said the lieutenant. "You heard the man, Sarge."

"Did Cheryl Arbuckle mention what her business was, Silvie?" asked Markie.

316

"She didn't say," replied Silverlake.

"Who has the case in missing persons?"

"Bloodhound Kelly is on it."

* * *

THE MISSING PERSONS DETECTIVE was a veteran investigator who found a home in his assignment many years ago. Nicknamed Bloodhound for his tenaciousness, the sixty-year-old had just made the height requirement when aspiring officers had to be at least 5' 8". The passing years, coupled with back issues, had left him a couple of inches beneath that onetime requirement.

Since both Von Hess and Markie had worked cordially with Bloodhound in the past, there was no strain connected to their joining forces. If anything, they were happy to work together again.

"We're here to lend a hand on the Fishnet Milligan case," advised Markie.

"I heard, Sarge," said Bloodhound. "I got a heads up from Silverlake that you'd be coming."

"So where are we with the case?"

"I was just going over to where Fishnet lives. He owns a townhouse not far from here. Where do you suppose he got the money for a joint like that?"

"He married well," answered Von Hess.

"Do you guys want to take a ride over there with me?" Markie nodded.

When they arrived at the townhouse, the detectives concluded, as Cheryl Arbuckle had previously, that the dwelling had been unoccupied for a while. The investigators went a bit further and conducted a canvass of the neighboring houses. It was unanimous that Fishnet hadn't been seen in a while. The investigators returned to the front of the townhouse to talk over what to do next.

"He could be anywhere, Sarge," voiced Bloodhound. You know, technically, we shouldn't have even taken a case like this. The

317

guy isn't mentally challenged, so he could have just left without wanting to tell anyone. Who knows—he might have gone off someplace with a squeeze or whatever."

"That's true. Is there any business address for Fishnet?" asked Markie.

"I haven't gotten that far, Sarge."

As Markie and Bloodhound conversed, Von Hess peered through the first-floor window of the townhouse in the hope of seeing something through the slit in the wooden shutters. Unable to gain a clear view of the interior, Von Hess turned the knob on the front door. To his great surprise, the door was unlocked.

The failure of Fishnet's assassins to lock the door behind them when they fled the townhouse proved to be of benefit to the investigators. This oversight was one of two miscues the trio of murderers made.

"Look at this," announced Von Hess, pushing the door wide open.

"What did you do, pick the lock, Ollie?" asked Bloodhound.

"No, the door was left open."

"C'mon. Let's go inside and have a look-see," said Markie.

Markie and the others weren't prepared for the shock they were about to receive. Seeing Fishnet hanging by his neck from a grand staircase railing was eerie. The former detective's head was tilted in the direction of his left shoulder. The dead man's face was contorted, making the scene even more horrid.

"Is this him?" asked Bloodhound, who had seen photos of Fishnet, but never actually met him.

"Yeah, that's him," answered Von Hess in a low voice.

Markie remained silent as he looked upward at the man he so desperately wanted to put behind bars. While he had no love for Fishnet, the sergeant didn't want to see this as a finish. In a way, Markie was disappointed. He felt cheated out of the satisfaction of taking Fishnet down himself.

"It looks like a case of suicide to me," declared Bloodhound. "I wonder what demons he was fighting that caused him to do something like this."

"I never figured Fishnet for the type to take his own life," commented Von Hess. "You never know about people."

As far as the cause of death, from the onset the sergeant never believed Fishnet to be a suicide. In Markie's opinion, the dead detective simply wasn't the type to take his own life. *There has to be more to this,* thought Markie. With nothing to support his doubt of suicide, Markie kept his thoughts to himself.

"Start looking around the joint while I make some notifications," directed the sergeant when he finally spoke.

Markie's first call was to Lieutenant Wright, his superior at police headquarters. Wright was also shocked at the news of Fishnet's death.

"How did he croak?" asked the lieutenant.

"Right now it looks like he hanged himself, Loo," replied Markie, "but we're still checking things out."

"Whatever way he went, this is sure to make the papers," said Wright. "Fishnet drew a lot of attention in the press when he was on the job, so this won't go unnoticed."

"What do you want us to do over here, Loo?"

"Stick with it until you hear back from me. I'm gonna fill in the chief. I'm sure he's gonna want us involved until this thing blows over. Keep me posted, Al."

"Righto, Loo. I'll notify the local precinct squad."

"Do you want me to let Cheryl Arbuckle know, Sarge?" asked the missing persons detective when Markie hung up with the lieutenant.

"Work that out with the local squad when they get here," answered Markie. "This is their responsibility now."

Markie scratched his head as he reflected on the circumstances. Things still didn't sit well with him. Although he couldn't envision someone like Fishnet taking his own life, he continued to keep his opinion to himself.

While waiting for the other investigators to arrive, Markie picked up a newspaper that rested atop a living room end table. While scanning through the pages to pass the time, he came across the unfinished word game in the newspaper that Enzo Baffi had been working on. This was Baffi's second mistake.

The blackening out of the words at the bottom of the game jumped out at the sergeant, as did the date on the paper. *What a waste of ink*, he thought at first, incorrectly assuming that Fishnet blackened out the words.

The precinct detective assigned to the case concluded the matter to be one of suicide. He wondered why the chief of detectives wanted his people involved.

"I don't get it, Sarge. Why are you here?" asked the case detective. "I can handle this. It's an open-and-shut case of suicide."

"Now look, don't take it personal," said Markie. "Our being here is no reflection on you. The chief wants us here. He had his reasons."

"Okay, Sarge, I understand. I'm not looking to make waves."

When Von Hess had the chance, he took a moment to fill in the blanks for the precinct detective.

"Look, this ain't any ordinary retired member of the service we got here," advised Von Hess. "The guy swinging is Fishnet Milligan. He's the guy who had that big shootout with Red Harris, the gangster."

"I heard."

"Yeah, well that's why this is getting so much attention."

In the absence of a precinct squad commander, Markie stepped up to oversee things. He called in the crime scene unit. When the crime scene unit arrived at the townhouse, they cut Fishnet down and searched his body. They then dusted for fingerprints and looked for signs of possible foul play.

Markie found it most interesting that Fishnet was wearing a smoking jacket that concealed the gun he was carrying. This reinforced his suspicion that Fishnet's death was no suicide. This observation didn't escape the attention of Von Hess.

"Do you really think we needed crime scene here, Ollie?"

The precinct detective asked his question in a whisper. Von Hess shrugged his shoulders before he answered:

"I've been working with the sergeant for a long time. I know exactly how he thinks—and I understand how he thinks."

"How about clueing me in."

"The sergeant figures that anybody with a gun wouldn't go to the bother of hanging himself. Especially a guy like Fishnet."

"That's a good point. I never thought of that."

"We'll have to notify the girlfriend," said Markie, joining the two detectives.

"What girlfriend?" asked the detective from the local precinct.

"A girlfriend reported Fishnet missing," said Von Hess, adding, "Bloodhound here is from missing persons."

"That's me," said Bloodhound, extending his hand to the precinct detective.

"Let's do this," said Markie. "Bloodhound, you stay here with the precinct squad. I'll go with Ollie to talk to the girlfriend. We'll regroup later at the precinct."

36

A Chilling Thrill

CHERYL WAS AT HOME waiting patiently for an update from the detective assigned to find Fishnet. In need of moral support, she was glad to have someone at her side, even Enzo Baffi. The producer was careful to remain a perfect gentleman while alone with Cheryl in her apartment.

To pass the time Baffi worked on his favorite newspaper word game. From time to time he'd pause to look at Cheryl. Within him there was a yearning to get her in his black room again.

Baffi's lips formed a cruel smile as his mind filled with thoughts of hosting Cheryl in his den of perversion. The producer blamed Cheryl for his having to kill Fishnet. Baffi felt that Cheryl never should have revealed to her boyfriend what had transpired in his black room. But she did, and for that she'd one day pay.

The producer didn't discount the upside of Cheryl possessing the talent that would enable him to make her a star. Her professional success would add to his reputation. As another Baffi discovery, Cheryl represented the fuel that kept the producer's fame going.

Satisfied that all would be going his way once the Fishnet business was put to rest, the producer continued on with his word game. He was confident that the law would find the former detective's body at some point, declare the dead man a suicide, and that would be that.

Baffi circled the letters of each word he identified after locating it at the top of the puzzle. After doing so he inked out the identified word as listed at the bottom of the puzzle. The end result was the formation of one bold ink square when the puzzle was completed.

Cheryl sat by the telephone chain-smoking cigarettes while waiting to hear from the police department. Baffi took a break from the puzzle when he began to get hungry.

"Are you hungry, my dear?" asked the producer.

"No, I can't eat," answered Cheryl.

"I understand totally," said the producer soothingly. Baffi had a unique way of feigning great understanding. "I'll call Martinelli's. They'll send us over something to eat. As I recall, you prefer the red wine, correct?"

"They deliver?"

"For me they will," assured the producer.

"I don't think I can eat anything now."

"You can eat the food whenever you can. I'll order."

"Go ahead and order; maybe I'll have something later," replied Cheryl.

Over their meal the two discussed a number of topics, including Cheryl's career. The producer touched on his interest in planning a series of movie projects for Cheryl. He then vaguely insinuated that they would again be spending lots of time together while working very closely.

"Don't get any ideas, Enzo. I'll not participate in anything like last time," advised Cheryl, point blank. Baffi backed off, realizing that now was not the time for such a conversation.

"Of course not, my dear. Pay me no attention."

Baffi went on to smooth the waters by again apologizing to Cheryl for what he referred to as their misunderstanding in his penthouse. Experienced theatrically, Baffi convincingly put forth a fine performance as to his remorse. The producer claimed that he misread Cheryl's preferences, swearing to her that their friendship would remain strictly platonic and professional moving forward. Baffi went on to expound upon how he intended to turn Cheryl into a major motion picture star.

"Why, there is no saying what we can achieve together," said the producer. "Why, my dear, minus distractions, you have unlimited potential." Without realizing it, Baffi had said too much.

"You think my boyfriend isn't coming back?"

"Oh, no. I never said that, my dear."

"Are you sure that you're telling me everything you know about him being missing, Enzo?"

Cheryl's question hit too close to home for the producer. Baffi backtracked, attempting to fend off suspicion.

"Oh, my dear," he said with earnest, "I assure you that you know as much as I do about the disappearance. Why, I was actually looking forward to us three collaborating."

Before Cheryl could respond, the telephone rang. It was the detective from the missing persons squad. Bloodhound advised Cheryl that investigators from the Chief of Detectives Office would be coming by her apartment to speak to her. The detective made no mention that Fishnet was found hanged. After getting off the line, Cheryl was queried by Baffi.

"Who was that?" asked the producer.

"It was the detective from missing persons. He said that people from a special squad in the Chief of Detectives Office is coming over."

Hearing this was a wrinkle that Baffi hadn't expected. The Chief of Detectives Office took things to a higher level, one that was alarming to him.

"Really? What else did he say?"

"That was it."

"Perhaps I better go, Cheryl," said the producer, who was concerned over this unexpected development. He thought it prudent to distance himself from the situation.

"You're leaving?"

"I must protect my reputation, Cheryl. You understand. I'll be at my office and available by phone. Be sure to call me when the detectives leave."

324

"Sure, go," commented Cheryl, not doing a good job in concealing her annoyance. .

* * *

MARKIE PROCEEDED TO Cheryl's apartment with mixed emotions. On the one hand, informing someone of the death of a loved one was never something Markie looked forward to. On the other, he was anxious to talk to Cheryl because she'd be able to shed light on Fishnet's activities prior to his death.

The investigators did little talking during the drive. Both Markie and Von Hess were too absorbed in their own mental reflections of Fishnet to engage in chatting. Markie wasn't about to shed any tears over Fishnet's death. He felt no mournfulness because Fishnet was no friend. However, a sadness did exist within the sergeant. It was a melancholy of an unusual nature. The absence of Fishnet from the scene created a vacancy in Markie's professional life. He regretted that his mission to get Fish had now suddenly come to an unrewarding close. In a nutshell, Markie's hound-dogging of Fishnet had always been a question of good guys versus bad guys and right besting wrong. Fishnet's passing in the manner he did meant the sergeant lost in his quest for justice.

Markie knew that Fishnet had gotten away with the commission of a host of heinous crimes. His inability to prove it had always been the sergeant's frustration. The elusive Fishnet always managed, somehow, to emerge unscathed as he repeatedly slipped through the Sergeant's net. As Markie saw things, Fishnet's unlawfulness dwarfed whatever good police work or heroic acts the rogue detective may have engaged in while on the force.

As a rule, Markie's tendency was to avoid speaking ill of the dead. In Fishnet's case, this proved to be challenging. Reflecting on his nemesis caused the sergeant to talk to himself in his frustration.

"Hero or not, the son of a bitch was no good," muttered Markie.

"What was that, Sarge?" asked Von Hess, who was interrupted from his own reflections.

"Nothing, Ollie. I was just thinking out loud."

"What about?"

"Fishnet. It bothers me that we never did get him good."

"What can you do, Sarge? He was a shrewd article. Anyway, look how he ended up . . . swinging from a rope. That ain't a good way to go."

"That's true, Ollie. But I'm still curious about something."

"What's that?"

"I'd like to know exactly what the business was between Fishnet and Father Billy."

"The bogus priest said that Fishnet wanted him to perform a phony marriage."

"I know that's what he said. But I'd like to know why. Fishnet had to have had a specific purpose."

"It beats me," admitted Von Hess. "We can't even be sure that Fishnet knew the priest was a fugazy, Sarge. After all, we only got the word of a bandit telling us that."

"There's another thing, Ollie. I wouldn't be surprised if there was some kind of connection between Fishnet and that caddy's murdering spree."

"Do you really think so?"

"That phony priest was shaking hands with Fishnet with his right hand and waving to the caddy with his left, wasn't he?"

"I suppose he was, Sarge. You know, nothing would surprise me about Fishnet."

"And now the prick is dead, Ollie, and we'll probably never figure out the true story."

"Maybe dead and buried is a good thing, Sarge." Markie offered no response to this comment.

When it came to Fishnet, Von Hess didn't discount the fact that Fishnet was a bona fide hero. Fishnet's gunfight with Red Harris, the notorious mob hit man, was an act of heroism that made him a legend. That was something Von Hess respected. Even Markie couldn't take that away from his nemesis.

Aside from surviving the life threatening wounds he sustained in the gun battle, Fishnet had the resiliency to bounce back when at death's door. This too scored points in the book of Von Hess. Then there was the flowery press coverage and medal Fishnet received. This all amounted to recognition that was shared by all members of the department who flirted with danger on a daily basis. In a sense, Fishnet was proof of the bravery of everyone.

Many outside the police department also looked up to law enforcement legends. Fishnet was seen by civilians as a figure who perpetuated the positive image of those in blue, and that was good in terms of public relations.

* * *

CHERYL ARBUCKLE CLEANED OFF the kitchen table before the detectives arrived at her home. The plate Enzo Baffi had used indicated that the producer had no loss of appetite. He had eaten the food he ordered heartily. Cheryl's own plate remained untouched. She was still too upset to eat.

When Markie and Von Hess finally arrived, they appeared somber as they stood in the entrance to the apartment. Von Hess was holding his hat in his hand. This suggested to Cheryl that bad news was forthcoming. She braced herself for what she was about to hear.

"I'm Detective Sergeant Markie, Ma'am. This is Detective Von Hess. May we come in?" Cheryl stepped aside to let the detectives enter her home.

"You found him?" asked Cheryl, feeling that they did. Her words were transmitted with obvious distress.

"Yes, Ma'am, we found him. Are you here alone?"

"Yes, I am . . . so where is he?"

"I'm afraid we have some very bad news . . ."

Fearing what was coming, Cheryl got emotional. She began to tremble, causing the detectives to guide her to the couch in the living room. After being informed of Fishnet's death, Cheryl put forth a dramatic burst of grief that included tears that flowed freely.

Once Cheryl exhausted her allotment of sorrow, she slowly began to recover. She managed to keep her pain internal as she listened to all the unpleasant details surrounding Fishnet's demise. It was if she now had a room within her that stored all things melancholy.

Once the detectives communicated the facts, they proceeded to answer all of Cheryl's questions. Then the investigators weighed in with questions of their own.

"Are you okay answering a few questions?" asked Markie. "If not, we can wait."

"No, I'm all right," replied Cheryl, looking the detective sergeant directly in the eye.

"Go ahead, Ollie. You start," directed the sergeant.

Turning the questioning over to Von Hess was something Markie did when he didn't want to do it himself.

"Could you think of any reason Fishnet would take his own life?" asked Von Hess.

"Fishnet?"

"I'm sorry, I mean Bruce. Fishnet was what everyone on the job called Detective Milligan."

"Oh, so that's where the name Fish came from."

"I don't follow you."

"When Bruce asked me to marry him, he said I was destined to be the next Mrs. Bruce Milligan. Before that, I always thought his name was Shepherd Fish."

"He used an alias?"

"Bruce said it was for professional purposes. I never questioned him about it."

"You two were planning on getting married?" asked Markie.

"He asked me to marry him, but I told him I needed some time."

"How did he take that?"

"He was a very confident man. He told me to take my time and then gave me something like a minute to think about it." Recounting their conversation caused Cheryl to briefly smile.

"Was he depressed?"

"I don't think so. He wasn't the sort of man prone to

depression," explained Cheryl. "He was very strong emotionally, the take-charge sort. Besides, he had no reason to be depressed. In fact, he had everything to live for."

"He had no financial setbacks?"

"No, he was actually quite solvent."

"Was he having problems with anyone?"

"No," replied Cheryl after some hesitation. Finding her own role in the fray to be embarrassing, she neglected to reveal the Fishnet-Enzo Baffi conflict.

"Are you sure about that?" injected Markie, who sensed Cheryl might be holding back something.

"I'm sure."

"Did you know anything about his seeing a priest in Brooklyn?" asked Von Hess.

"No."

"Have you ever heard the name Father Billy?"

"No, never."

"How did you meet the deceased, Ma'am?"

"We met in a bar-restaurant on the West Side where I was working."

"You no longer work there?"

"I left there. I'm employed as an actress now, thanks to Bruce."

"He helped with that?" queried Markie.

"He knew a musician with connections. That's how I was able to get my foot in the door of the play I was appearing in. After that, everything began happening fast."

"What happened fast?"

"After securing the part, I then got to be the understudy to the lead. Then the lead had an unfortunate accident. When that happened, I assumed the lead role."

"You no longer have that role?"

"I left the play once I got an offer from Enzo Baffi to appear in his new film."

"Baffi the producer?"

"Yes . . . Enzo Baffi. He's quite famous in the film industry. The next thing I knew, Enzo and Bruce started working together. So you see, Bruce had everything to live for."

"How did your boyfriend manage to hook up with such a prominent man like Baffi?" asked Markie.

"Bruce was exceedingly resourceful."

"I understand that, but how did he get to know Baffi?"

"A musician Bruce knew arranged for the two to meet."

"What musician?"

"He was a violinist, I believe."

"Do you know the name of this violinist?"

"No. All I remember Bruce saying about him is that he was very old and highly regarded."

At the conclusion of the interview the detectives extended their condolences. As Markie walked to the door to leave, he noticed for the first time an open newspaper lying on a living room chair. The paper was opened to a word game. The boldly inked square below the puzzle jumped out at the sergeant. The unique markings were identical to the newspaper he remembered seeing at Fishnet's townhouse.

Markie turned to make eye contact with Von Hess. After doing so he raised his chin in the direction ofthe newspaper, signaling Von Hess to look there. That was the cue for Von Hess to begin probing.

"You like to do word games, Ms. Arbuckle?" asked Von Hess.

"No, I never do them."

"Well, somebody does," said the detective, picking up the newspaper.

"Oh, that wasn't me. Enzo likes to do those."

"Baffi, the producer?"

"Yes."

"When was he here?"

"Earlier today. He came to offer his support."

"Did Mr. Baffi know we were coming over, Ma'am?" asked Markie.

"Yes."

"I'm just curious about something," said the sergeant. "If he came here to support you, what made him leave?"

"He said he was worried about possible publicity. He felt that since he's so well-known, his presence might draw the interest of the press. I know what his real worry was. He was concerned that the wrong publicity could damage the effort to further my career."

"He represents you?"

"Enzo and Bruce were partners in trying to make me a star."

Cheryl went on to again tell of how her rise on the stage and subsequent offer to appear in Baffi's new movie had come about. This time her story came with more details.

"If you need any assistance, Ma'am, feel free to call," said Von Hess as the interview concluded.

Cheryl thought the detective's offer was sweet. "Thank you," she answered. "Before you go, I want
to give you something." Cheryl wrote a note on her business card. "Here, this is for you two," she said, handing the card to Von Hess."

"What's this?"

"Present my card at the box office; it'll get you two front-row seats to the play I was in. If you go, call me, and I'll get you backstage to meet the cast. But don't go for at least a week. I'll be too busy making the arrangements for Bruce."

"By the way, Ms. Arbuckle, do you mind if I take this newspaper with me?" asked Markie.

"You can have it if you want, but why?"

"I want to look over the racing selections at Yonkers," fibbed the sergeant.

Markie's true intent was to have a forensic comparison conducted between the newspaper in Cheryl's apartment and the one he saw in Fishnet's townhouse. His hope was to match the ink used in the word game, compare the writing samples and lift fingerprints.

* * *

AFTER THE DETECTIVES LEFT HER APARTMENT, Cheryl telephoned Enzo Baffi. The producer was at his office. When Cheryl happened to mention that one of the detectives left with his newspaper, Baffi got nervous. He wasn't one to underestimate the investigative abilities of the police department. The producer wanted to know more.

"What in the world would they want the newspaper for?" Baffi asked calmly, cloaking his true concern.

"One of them wanted to look at the racing section, Enzo."

"I see. Did he ask if it was your newspaper?"

"Why, he did ask me who the paper belonged to . . ."

"Did you tell him it was mine?"

"Yes. Did I do something wrong?"

"No, of course not, my dear. I just have to be careful of negative publicity. You understand."

Baffi's comment got Cheryl thinking of her own reputation. *What about my bad publicity*, she thought.

"Can you come over, Enzo?" With this now on her mind, Cheryl was in need of someone, even if it was the man she so disliked.

"Do you really need me, my dear?"

"I need help. I don't know what I'm to do first about making arrangements. Who do I call?"

"I understand fully," replied the producer. "Unfortunately, I have pressing business right now. I'll send my secretary over. She's quite capable. She'll know what to do. Okay, my dear?"

"That's fine, Enzo. Thank you."

After hanging up, Baffi stepped out of his office to speak to his secretary. As expected, the secretary was receptive. She wasted no time in going to Cheryl's apartment. With Cheryl's need taken care of, Enzo Baffi began to consider his own problems.

37

The Log Cabin Calls

ALONE IN HIS OFFICE, A TROUBLED ENZO BAFFI sat at his desk nervously tapping his finger against his cheek. He often did this when thinking analytically. Using his legs the producer pushed the chair he sat in away from the desk. After lighting up a cigarette he resumed contemplating what to do.

Baffi examined the homicide he masterminded from every conceivable angle. Included in his analysis was the potential threat posed by his two accomplices. Although the possibility was remote, the producer was concerned that the detectives from headquarters might speak to the Maestro and Pascal at some point. Their standing firm under police questioning without slipping up was worrisome.

The producer wasn't one to view things through rose-colored glasses when it came to his own carelessness. He was well aware that he had screwed up by leaving the newspaper at the townhouse.

"Me and those damn word games!" Baffi declared aloud, slamming his hand on the arm of his chair. *Those detectives took that newspaper from Cheryl's apartment for a reason*, thought the producer, *and that reason had nothing to do with horseracing!*

Baffi believed that the detectives from headquarters were

more than likely the police department's better investigators. That translated into their being more thorough. *Those detectives are bound to notice my way of working the word game in the newspaper. If they compare that newspaper to the one I left in the townhouse, they could place me in Fishnet's townhouse around the time or day of Fishnet death! They could send those newspapers out to be forensically analyzed for fingerprints, ink type, and who knows what else,* thought Baffi. *Circumstantial evidence or not, this can cause me a real problem!*

At this point the producer's mind ran amok with questions: *What if the cops take a closer look into the cause of death? Could they figure out that it wasn't suicide?*

What if they start pumping Cheryl, and she opens up about the problem I had with her boyfriend?

The producer came to the conclusion that Cheryl posed a primary threat. This required immediate rectification and that, for Enzo Baffi, equated to another murder.

Baffi found it truly unfortunate that he had to dispose of Cheryl. He considered it a pity that the time he had invested in his budding star would be for naught. A successful launch of her career would have netted him great financial dividends and added to his name. Now, that was not to be. There could be no loose ends left. It had all come down to self-survival. By eliminating Cheryl, there would be no one
to tell the tale of the imperfect relationship that existed between Baffi, Fishnet, and Cheryl.

As far as the Maestro and Pascal, they, too, posed potential problems. If necessary, their demise would come with no remorse from the producer. *What's the big loss?* Baffi wondered to himself. *One is an old man who had lived his life. The other was insignificant.*

* * *

MARKIE AND VON HESS HURRIED to Fishnet's townhouse for the purpose of retrieving the newspaper. They intended to make a visual comparison of both word games before sending them off for forensic analysis. When the detectives arrived at the townhouse, they saw that a police seal was affixed to the front door. Markie called the patrol sergeant to the townhouse for the purpose of removing the seal so he and Von Hess could enter the building.

"What's up?" asked the arriving patrol sergeant, recognizing the detective sergeant.

"We need to get back inside for a minute, Sarge," said Markie. "Then you can re-seal the door."

When Markie and Von Hess entered the townhouse, to their dismay the newspaper in question was nowhere in sight. "It was right here, Ollie," said Markie.

"Maybe it's in the garbage, Sarge."

"Yeah, maybe. Let's go outside and check."

Von Hess checked the townhouse garbage pails for the newspaper. "No luck, Sarge," he announced.

"Let's go to the precinct, Ollie."

When the investigators from headquarters arrived at the precinct squad room, they met with the squad detective who was assigned to investigate Fishnet's death. Also notified to meet them at the squad was Bloodhound, the detective from the missing persons squad.

"Did anybody happen to take the newspaper from the townhouse?" questioned Markie.

"What newspaper?" asked the precinct detective.

"The one in the townhouse. It was in the living room."

"I never saw it. Why, was it important?"

"Maybe yes, maybe no," replied Markie, who then explained the relevance of the document. "What about you, Bloodhound? Did you see it?"

"Not me. Are you saying this may not be a suicide, Sarge?" asked the confused precinct detective.

"I ain't saying anything," answered Markie. "Fishnet's death remains a suicide until it can be proven differently."

Bloodhound, who was now free to return to his office at missing persons, made his goodbyes. Before going to his car, he hurried to visit the precinct men's room in search of the newspaper in question. He had been the one who removed it from the townhouse. He entered the stall he had previously occupied while in possession of the newspaper. To his disappointment the newspaper he had wedged behind the toilet paper was no longer there.

"Ahh, rats," said Bloodhound aloud. *What are ya gonna do? Shit happens*, he thought.

* * *

ENZO BAFFI FABRICATED A REASON that called for Cheryl accompanying him to the producer's log cabin in the wilds of northern New York. She believed that she was going there to meet the director of Baffi's upcoming film.

At first, considering her history with Baffi, Cheryl expressed a reluctance to go. Baffi's having Cheryl under contract came with some obligation on her part to comply with his request. The producer's assurances that the film director and two others connected to the movie project would be there convinced Cheryl to go.

"I suppose getting away from the city might do me good," said Cheryl.

"Of course, there is nothing like the cabin to relieve stress, my dear. If you like, I'll ask my secretary to join us. I know you like her, so we'll make a holiday of it."

"She'll drive up with us?" asked Cheryl, perking up.

"No, she has some work to get out. She'll join us the second day."

"Oh, I see," said the actor, sounding disappointed. "How is the weather up there, Enzo? It must be freezing this time of year."

"Don't worry about that, my dear. Trust me—you'll find it quite toasty at the cabin."

"I'll still have to pack extra warm clothes."

"If you like. But I have a special heating system at the cabin, my dear. You'll find yourself quite warm." The producer was referring to the incinerator on his property.

336

* * *

SINCE MARKIE AND VON HESS had free tickets to see the play
Cheryl had been appearing in, they decided to go to the theater
one evening after work. Afterward, they intended to treat
themselves to dinner somewhere in the Theater District.

When the detectives arrived at the box office, Von Hess
produced the business card Cheryl had given him. As the ticket
seller read the business card, she bit down on her lip and began
shaking her head.

"Oh, dear," she voiced.

"Is there a problem?" asked Von Hess, seeing that the seller
was flummoxed.

"I'm afraid so, sir. When did you get this?"

"A couple of weeks ago. Ms. Arbuckle gave it to me. We're
detectives," added Von Hess.

"Oh, I see. Please excuse me for a moment," replied the
woman. "I need to speak to someone about this."

"If they expect us to pay for the tickets, they got a long wait,"
declared Markie. "I'm not springing for theater tickets. It's not
in the budget."

"I'm with ya, Sarge. I don't need to see anything at these
prices."

When the theater manager, a thin man in his early forties
arrived, he informed the detectives that Cheryl was no longer
with the show.

"We know that," advised Von Hess.

"I'm sorry, sir," said the manager, "but I can't admit you
without your paying for your ticket. Ms. Arbuckle has been
replaced in the show," explained the manager. "If you like, I can
provide you with great seats at a discounted rate."

"No, that's okay, thanks," said Markie. "C'mon, Ollie. Let's
breeze."

When the two detectives exited the theater, they weren't
overly disappointed. Neither detective cared much for stage

productions anyway. On their way to find a restaurant they discussed Cheryl's leaving the show.

"She must have gotten a real sweet offer to leave that show, Ollie," observed Markie.

"Day after day on the stage is probably a lot of work, Sarge. You have to always be up for it, remembering lines and so on."

"I suppose so."

"I hope she's getting over Fishnet. She probably still misses him."

Markie snickered at the thought of anyone missing the late former detective. "Missing Fishnet is like missing acne," quipped the sergeant. "You know, the whole thing still makes me wonder."

"About what?"

"You know, about Fishnet's death and that whole connection to Father Billy."

"What about Bumper, that murdering caddy?"

"And him too. Where the hell does he fit in meeting with the phony priest and Fishnet?"

"The caddy wanted to confess his sins, Sarge."

"Yeah, I know. But it's a cinch Fishnet wasn't confessing any sins. What's he doing with those people?

"Father Billy said the meetings were unrelated, Sarge."

"Is that swindler to be believed?"

"Well, anyway, there is one good thing, Sarge."

"What's that?"

"We're caught up on our cases."

"Yeah, for now."

* * *

WITH THE MURDER OF CHERYL behind him and having received no word from the authorities, Enzo Baffi felt he had some breathing room. He thought it prudent for some time to pass before addressing his concern about the Maestro and Pascal. Yet this was easier said than done. Once the producer got a taste of blood on his hands, he came to realize that, for him, there was no comparable form gratification. The urge to kill provided a thrill that led the producer with an almost uncontrollable urge to kill again.

Baffi was in his penthouse apartment preparing to go to dinner with an aspiring actress he had met at a cocktail party. This was to be their second tryst. Having passed Baffi's golden shower hurdle, the young thespian was considered primed for a visit to the producer's black room.

After dressing in evening clothes, Baffi walked to his closet to remove the overcoat he intended to wear. He opted to don the charcoal, double-breasted coat that he hadn't worn in awhile. Upon reaching the street, Baffi warmed his hands by placing them in the side pockets of his coat. To his surprise, he discovered the red silk scarf that had belonged to Cheryl Arbuckle.

"Oh, I forgot about this," Baffi stated aloud about the memento. He then raised the scarf to his nose and sniffed deeply. The aroma of Cheryl's favorite perfume brought vivid memories that excited him. He envisioned himself once again poisoning the unsuspecting woman before feeding his upstate furnace with her carcass. The article of clothing he held in his hand was the only clothing the producer didn't burn in the Dutchess County incinerator. Cheryl's jewelry had been carefully disposed of on an individual basis, a piece here and a piece there, in various waters far from his log cabin.

The producer's evening went as anticipated, with Baffi returning to his penthouse with the aspiring actor after dinner. As Baffi figured, the young woman was amenable to experiencing the producer's black room as long as her compliance came with the fast-tracking of her career.

While the events of the night should have been no different than any of the others, it somehow fell short in terms of pleasure for the producer. His black room activities had become passé. They paled in comparison to the tremendous thrill he got from firing up Cheryl in his upstate incinerator. The maniac producer had a chilling thought: *I wonder how it would have been if I had burned her alive?*

Snuffing out a life had become the ultimate power trip for Enzo Baffi, who found himself uncontrollably excited by having the life and death of another in his hands. His evil desire morphed into a craving that demanded satisfaction.

38

The Fiddle Goes Silent

WITH THE AGE DISAPRITY BETWEEN THE Maestro and Pascal being substantial, Pascal tried never to think about the day when life as he knew it would change. He shied away from discussions pertaining to life expectancy and the downside of living too long, finding them to be morbid. Since he lived in comfort with the Maestro he was able to take each day as it came, without thought of the future. When the consequences of the Maestro's longevity became a reality, Pascal was ill prepared.

The virtuoso's mental decline first surfaced when Pascal found himself having to defend against outlandish accusations that were cast by the octogenarian musician. The confused Maestro, who was now suffering from paranoia, was convinced that Pascal was out to do him harm in a variety of ways. The virtuoso had it in his head that Pascal was intentionally leaving water on the tiled floor in the bathroom for the purpose of seeing the Maestro slip and fall when exiting the shower.

Things rapidly spiraled downward as the Maestro began having trouble distinguishing the real from the imagined. The octogenarian began blaming Pascal for hiding his eyeglasses and tampering with his violin. Reluctant to disrupt their living arrangement, Pascal opted to tolerate such mistreatment.

The Maestro, being of an artistic nature, was well known for his short fuse and verbal acidity. This was especially prevalent when quarreling. When the Maestro's temper tantrums became more difficult to control, Pascal was forced to start thinking of options. In the end none he arrived at were palatable to him.

It took Pascal being struck in the head one night while asleep to convince him that things had reached a dangerous stage. The sting of the blow caused Pascal to jump up in bed. Seeing the Maestro standing over him with his violin bow in hand caused Pascal to acknowledge that his lover was in need of professional help. However, with no provisions having been made, Pascal feared that he'd end up living in a Bowery flophouse again if the Maestro was put away. As a result Pascal decided to put up with his benefactor for as long as possible.

"What did you do with my timepiece, Pascal?" asked the Maestro one morning after a restless night.

"Maestro, how many times must I tell you?" asked Pascal. "I never took it."

"I've always provided for you, Pascal, haven't I? You want for nothing."

"Yes, you have been most generous, and I've always tried to show you my appreciation as best I could."

"Then why are you stealing from me?"

"I'm not stealing from you, Maestro!" said Pascal, emphasizing his words.

And so their conversations went, only to further the Maestro's ire and to frustrate the wrongly accused Pascal. When the Maestro began freely speaking of the murder they partook in, Pascal knew he had to take steps. At the end of the day, freedom in a flophouse was far better than incarceration with criminals.

"Maestro, stop talking about that!" shouted Pascal. "We swore never to breathe a word of that. Don't you remember?"

"I swore to what?" asked the Maestro softly. His uncertainty diminished the conviction in his voice.

Pascal rolled his eyes in frustration. He made up an excuse to leave the apartment.

"We need milk, Maestro. I'm going out to pick some up. Do you want anything from the store?"

"No, nothing. Just come back with my watch."

Once out of the apartment, Pascal telephoned Enzo Baffi. When the producer was told of the Maestro's loose tongue, he couldn't have been happier. This gave the producer an excuse to remove the threat the Maestro posed, while, at the same time, fulfill his vile desire to accommodate his newly acquired thrill. Baffi immediately called for a meeting with Pascal to discuss what was to be done.

* * *

PASCAL AND ENZO BAFFI MET FOR a late-night drink after the Maestro had turned in for the night. Baffi listened without interruption as Pascal put forth the facts. When Pascal completed his narration, he waited anxiously for the producer to weigh in with a solution to the precarious situation. Baffi didn't disappoint.

"The fact that our dear friend spoke of Mr. Fish is, indeed, problematic, Pascal. This can't be allowed to continue."

"I know, Enzo. That's why I reached out to you. What are we to do?"

"The Maestro has become a cancer to both of us," voiced the producer without emotion. "You can see that, can't you?"

"Yes, of course," replied Pascal, who found Baffi's graveness chilling.

"We're left with little choice than to arrive at a way to address this disease for our own safety, Pascal. You do understand that, don't you?"

"I understand, Enzo," answered Pascal, who was under the impression that the producer was angling to come up with a way to have the Maestro institutionalized. "But the Maestro supports me. What becomes of me without the Maestro paying the bills?"

"Has he a will?"

"He has, and he's leaving everything to his favorite charity."

"There are no provisions for you?"

"A pittance . . . but in fairness to the Maestro, he made that clear from the very beginning."

"Well, we'll worry about that when the time comes. Right now we need to face the immediate danger."

"So what do you propose, Enzo?"

"The man's mind is failing him, not his body. Since the Maestro can live on for many, many years, things can only get worse. This leaves us vulnerable to exposure."

"The Maestro has a bad heart. Who knows how long he can live," voiced Pascal.

This information was of interest to the producer. "I wasn't aware of that. How bad is his condition?"

"It's very bad. He's been warned by his doctor not to do anything strenuous."

"Obviously, the Maestro wanted this kept a secret."

"Yes. I'm the only one who knows."

"I think we've arrived at a solution, Pascal."

"We'll have to put him away?"

"Precisely, Pascal. Look at this as an act of mercy. He'll be in a better place than staying in an apartment with you."

The producer and Pascal believed they were on the same page. In actuality, they were thinking of very different destinations to send the Maestro.

"I suppose it's for the best," conceded Pascal with a trace of sadness at the thought of confining his lover.

"Of course it is, my friend. If positions were reversed, the Maestro would be the first to propose this exact remedy to alleviate the worry."

"I understand, but what am I supposed to do for money with the Maestro away?" asked Pascal, again bringing up his personal needs.

"I'll take care of you. Don't worry about that," assured Baffi.

344

"You will?"

"I'll see to it that you get a good job."

The prospect of having to go to work wasn't exactly the help Pascal was looking for. "I have to go to work, Enzo? Why, I'm not sure I'd even be capable of working."

"If that's the case, I'll help see you through until we figure out a way for you to fly on your own, Pascal. But for now, we need to concentrate on taking care of our dear friend."

"Thank you, Enzo. That's a relief. How do you propose we start?"

"You don't have to worry about a thing, Pascal. Leave everything to me. You tell the Maestro that I'll be stopping by tomorrow evening. Tell him that I have a gift for him."

* * *

WHEN THE PRODUCER ARRIVED at the Maestro's digs, he heard violin music coming from within the apartment. Baffi shook his head in amusement at the tune being played. It was a peppy, modern number that was unusual for the Maestro.

Seconds after ringing the doorbell, Pascal came to the door to let Baffi in. The Maestro, lost in his music, continued playing his instrument vigorously. He had been oblivious to the sound of the doorbell.

"The Maestro is in a whimsical mood this evening, Enzo," whispered the jittery Pascal. "He rarely plays this kind of music."

The tune being played was a Tin Pan Alley classic. The Maestro's hair was sprouting in all directions as he gingerly worked his bow. He appeared to be the picture of a classic musical madman.

"Hello, Maestro," said the producer, interrupting the musician's playing.

"Oh, how are you . . . ahhh . . ." said the Maestro, forgetting Baffi's first name.

"Enzo," said Pascal, "it's Enzo."

"Of course," snapped the Maestro. "I know who it is," he barked nastily. "You do remember my friend the watch thief, don't you, Enzo?"

"Oh, come on now, Maestro," said Baffi. "Pascal would never steal your watch. You must have misplaced it."

"Hmm . . . hardly likely," said the Maestro sharply.

"I'm surprised to hear you playing that tune. Your usual preference is more along the lines of the Chaconne from Sonata No. 2 in D minor." Baffi was referring to one of the most famous of violin pieces.

"I'm not in the mood for something so serious," commented the musician. "What have you got in that big box?"

"I brought you a gift."

"What kind of gift?"

"It's an exercise bike."

"My doctor said all I should do is walk."

"Have you forgotten already, Maestro?" asked Baffi. "The doctor said intense exercise is the very best thing for you, my dear friend. Isn't that right, Pascal?"

"Uhh . . . I . . . think so," said Pascal, who was taken aback.

"Did he?" asked the Maestro before quickly adding, "Oh, that's right. I remember now."

Once the lightweight stationary bike was assembled, Enzo Baffi had Pascal tear up the box it came in and put it out with the trash. He then convinced the octogenarian to mount the bike. Once the old man was in position on the bike, Baffi had Pascal, upon his return, play a recording of lively music that the Maestro could pedal to.

"Go on, Maestro. Start peddling to the music," encouraged Baffi. "Faster now, FASTER, FASTER!" he urged. Baffi signaled Pascal to join him in his chant of "faster." Pascal couldn't bring himself to do it.

The producer continued to encourage faster pedaling. The octogenarian began huffing as he forced himself to maintain the ferocious pace. It wasn't long before the Maestro ceased pedaling altogether. Once the Maestro slumped forward, the producer instructed Pascal to shut off the music. Baffi checked the Maestro's pulse.

"He's gone," Baffi coldly announced.

Pascal took notice of the peculiar look on the producer's face. Rather than a grim expression of remorse, Baffi presented a look that seemed more in line with contentment. Pascal wasn't incorrect in his perception. The producer had gotten off during the process of killing the Maestro.

"Is he definitely gone?" asked Pascal.

"Yes, it's over for our dear friend," confirmed Baffi. "You disappointed me with your lack of enthusiasm, Pascal."

"I had no idea that this was the plan!" Pascal shouted defensively. "What do we do now?"

"Don't touch a thing. Just leave everything in the apartment as it is. You go take a shower as if nothing happened, then put on your pajamas, or whatever it is that you get into at night, and go to bed. In the morning, dial 911 and request an ambulance."

"How can I sleep? What do I say?"

"Your lack of sleep will come across as anguish, and that's a good thing. You tell the cops that you went to bed like usual. When you woke up, you found him this way."

"Are they going to believe that?"

"All you need to do is explain that our friend had gotten into the habit of riding his exercise bike after you went to sleep. Say that he did this at night to avoid having to hear you preach that he shouldn't be doing strenuous things. Can you remember that?"

"Yes, but what about you?"

"Me? I was never here. Don't forget that. You call me sometime tomorrow to notify me that our friend expired. Once I receive your call, I'll send someone to come by and help you with the arrangements."

"But the money . . ."

"I'll cover the cost."

On his way home the producer was thinking of how much of a liability Pascal posed. *I'll never be safe with him alive*, he thought. The idea of feeding Pascal to his incinerator excited the producer.

Once alone, Pascal came to realize that Enzo Baffi was a man without any semblance of a conscience. Having an association with someone as dark as the producer wasn't what Pascal wanted. However, he accepted that he had no choice but to go along until he found himself a soft landing with another Maestro.

* * *

PASCAL MANAGED TO COME through his end of the scheme with enough credibility to get by the authorities. As far as the world knew, the Maestro died of a heart attack as he exercised. While Pascal didn't disappoint the producer, the reverse was not the case.

Over breakfast the two men entered into a discussion as to the next step. Pascal was underwhelmed by Enzo Baffi's offer to employ him as the caretaker of his upstate home. The opportunity fell far short of what Pascal expected. Pascal, who didn't want to leave Manhattan, flatly rejected the proposition. Even the chance to live rent free failed to entice him.

"At least think it over, Pascal," suggested Baffi.

"I simply hate the woods, Enzo. I need to be around people, not squirrels," explained Pascal, who was used to being kept in an urban environment. "Why couldn't I work for you at your office in the city?"

"Doing what?"

"As your aide, perhaps?"

"Do you honestly think you could sustain yourself financially in the city on what I'd be paying you?" asked Baffi, forgetting his past assurances.

"What do you mean?"

"Since you can't afford the rent connected to the apartment you shared with the Maestro, you're forced to find more affordable accommodations, correct?"

"But you said that you would help me . . ."

"I'm trying to help you, but you must be appreciative of what I'm offering you. After all, you have no money. If you take the job I'm offering, you get to bank your money and live free in the log cabin. You'll be in a position to save a little money."

"I have a little money," voiced Pascal.

Outside of what was left to him by the Maestro, whatever money Pascal had came from pilfering what he could from the apartment before his lover's body was carted away. He stuffed his pockets with whatever watches, rings, and other jewelry that was there for the taking. He even slipped out of the apartment with the Maestro's most cherished violin.

"You'll run through that in short order," predicted Baffi. "You aren't a young man anymore, Pascal. Your days of being a catch are behind you. Do you relish returning to a Bowery flophouse? Do you miss the filthy wire cubicle that served as your abode?"

"Of course not . . ."

"Mark my words, Pascal: you'll be sitting alone in that chicken coop drinking cheap whiskey from the bottle to drown your troubles. Is that what you seek in your old age? At night, your lullaby will be the ranting of drunkards and the ravings of the mentally ill."

Pascal was shocked into the realization that his only chance of extricating himself from his dire situation rested in the generosity of Enzo Baffi. He asked Baffi to finance him enough money so that he could float a small studio apartment somewhere in Manhattan until he could find the appropriate roommate. He thought that since the producer was swimming in money, and considering their history, this was a reasonable request.

Baffi was noncommittal. All Pascal received for his trouble was the producer's reiteration of his original offer of taking him on as caretaker at his upstate home.

"But I'd go insane up there," voiced Pascal. "And how would I ever meet anyone who could take me out of this conundrum I'm in?"

"Eat your food, Pascal," stated Baffi, ignoring the question. "Aren't you hungry?"

"Why do you torment me, Enzo? All I need is to keep up appearances and some time to meet someone. Is that asking too much?"

The producer shrugged and continued to eat. His apparent lack of concern angered Pascal, who now played what he believed to be his trump card. "I'm warning you, Enzo . . . at this point I'm desperate. I'd rather live and die in jail than down on the Bowery, and I plan on having company if it comes to that."

Pascal's veiled threat wasn't lost on the producer. It sealed Pascal's fate.

"I believe you mean that, my friend. We've been through too much for this kind of talk. How about we just come to a compromise?

"I'm willing," agreed Pascal, feeling he finally had a say in things.

"You take the job I'm offering upstate. If, after a month, you still want to come back to Manhattan, I'll find suitable work for you and an affordable place to live. How does that sound?"

"Do you mean that, Enzo?"

"Oh, come, my friend. How could you doubt my sincerity? You and I have a special bond. We've shared experiences few can claim."

"If you feel that way, why not just set me up in Manhattan now?"

"Let me level with you. I need someone I could trust at the log cabin," replied Baffi. "I'm in the middle of a substantial land transaction that's going to require the upstate property be monitored for a month or so. Once the deal is consummated, you have my word that I'll satisfy your needs."

"So it'll definitely be a temporary thing?"

"Why, of course," answered the producer, continuing his falsehood. "I suspect that you're going to love the quaint log cabin. Trust me. The restful living will do you a world of good. When it's over, we'll get you something nice in the West Village."

Pascal accepted the terms without further discussion. The following day Enzo Baffi drove Pascal to his new residence. The Maestro's onetime lover spent his very first night upstate enjoying an eternal sleep inside Enzo Baffi's incinerator.

39

Making a Connection

WITH HIS CASES PUT TO rest and Fishnet Milligan no longer active, one would have thought that Markie was in a position to enjoy the holidays. Such was not the case for the sergeant. In years past, the holidays had always been something Markie looked forward to. However, since his divorce, the joy connected to the celebrated season waned.

At first, things had remained relatively cordial after the marriage was dissolved. Markie was still welcomed to stop by the house of his in-laws, where his wife and children resided in an apartment, on the holidays. Christmas gave him an excuse to visit his children and have a holiday drink with his father-in-law, someone he got along well with. Since Flo's father harbored hopes that the divorced couple would get back together, he usually insisted that Markie stay for dinner Christmas Day.

Things changed once Markie's electrician father-in-law passed away. With his death, the welcome mat was removed. This was primarily due to Flo's mother, who seemed more disgruntled over the divorce than her daughter did. The dynamics were further altered when the ex-Mrs. Markie entered into a committed relationship with her boss, a dentist. The combination of events found Markie shut out with no place to go.

Having no plans for Christmas, Markie was pleasantly surprised when his new girlfriend invited him to spend the day with her family. Karen's living situation was similar to Markie's ex-wife. She, her small children, younger sister, and widowed father all lived together in the patriarch's home. The family proved to be a welcoming lot.

Markie's alienation from his children and their mother provided Karen with the opportunity to solidify her own relationship with the sergeant. Christmas was the first of what Karen intended to be many invites to family doings.

Feeling bloated after a fine holiday dinner, Markie retired to the living room with Karen's father. The men chatted amicably in front of the television. The sergeant loosened his belt and glanced at the newspaper resting next to him on the couch. As Karen's father channel surfed, Markie began looking through the paper. In the entertainment section he happened upon a story about Enzo Baffi's plans for a new movie. Pictured with the story was an old photograph of the producer standing with several people connected to the arts. One of those identified in the photo by name was the Maestro, who was described as a prominent violinist.

Markie's seeing Enzo Baffi alongside the Maestro caused the sergeant to sit up straight. It was as if a great blur began to come into focus for the investigator. He remembered that Fishnet's girlfriend, during her interview, indicated that a violinist friend introduced Fishnet to Enzo Baffi. This caused Markie to start thinking that it might make sense to interview the Maestro.

When back at work, Markie had Von Hess conduct research on the virtuoso. He was disappointed to learn that the Maestro had recently passed on.

"What did he die of, Ollie?"

"It was a heart attack that killed him," answered Von Hess, who then went on to explain the circumstances surrounding the musician's death. "He supposedly had a bad heart and worked out against doctor's orders."

"Everybody is dropping dead," commented the sergeant. "What do you make of it, Ollie?"

"The Maestro was pretty old, Sarge."

"Yeah, but he croaked of a heart attack on an exercise bike he shouldn't have been on. That's as strange as Fishnet hanging himself.

"I don't know, Sarge."

"If you ask me, Ollie, there are interconnecting roads here," declared Markie. "And I'd like to know where they all lead."

"We have no proof of Dennis Bumper having anything to do with Fishnet, Sarge."

"Wait a second, Ollie. Let's break it all down. No Tax was the guy who told us about Father Billy, right?"

"Correct."

"We see this Father Billy with the crazy caddy Dennis Bumper and Fishnet in front of the rectory talking, right?"

"That's right."

"Fishnet then dies under, let's say, unusual circumstances. Fishnet's girl, Cheryl, puts him with that big- shot producer, Enzo Baffi. She said Fishnet met Baffi through an old musician. Correct?"

"Correct."

"Okay, we go on to find out that this Maestro guy was tight with Baffi. Now he turns up dead, also under unusual circumstances. You with me?"

"And . . ?"

"And my question is, was Fishnet hooked up with the Maestro? If yes, then how?"

"Are you saying that Fishnet and the Maestro may have both been murdered, Sarge? Ain't that kind of a stretch?"

"I don't know, Ollie—maybe it is," replied Markie, scratching his head. "But I'll tell you one thing, it's got me thinking. C'mon, let's go get something to eat."

The investigators decided to have lunch at a Chinese restaurant on Bayard Street in Manhattan's Chinatown. Over their meal, they continued their discussion.

"To be honest, Sarge, I still don't see it," said Von Hess. "Even if Fishnet knew the violinist and Enzo Baffi . . . I mean, what have we really got?"

"With Fishnet involved, we could have anything. I just can't see Fishnet hanging himself while packing a gun. You knew Fishnet as well as me. Did he strike you as the suicidal type?"

"Well, you have a point there, Sarge. Fishnet was the last guy you'd expect to kill himself."

"Exactly my point," said Markie triumphantly. "There has to be more to all this. And that old fiddle player croaking on an exercise bike—that's another crock to me."

"You really do suspect foul play, don't you, boss?'

"I don't know what to suspect, Ollie. This whole thing has me baffled."

"Well, there is nothing we can really do without evidence, Sarge. The only thing I can think of doing is to take a shot at grilling Dennis Bumper again. Maybe now the caddy would be willing to shed some light on all this."

"You know what I'd really like to do, Ollie?"

"What's that?"

"I'd like to poke around where the Maestro lived and get a line on him. You never know where that could take us."

"Sure, Sarge. Do you wanna start on that after we eat?"

"Yeah, let's do that. What are you ordering?"

"I'm having the pork-fried rice. You?"

"I gonna try the beef and broccoli."

After placing their order, Von Hess opened a fortune cookie. Removing the printed strip of paper, he read the fortune to himself.

"What does the fortune say, Ollie?"

"The answer to your question is closer than you think," stated Von Hess.

This resonated with the sergeant. "You know what? This fortune cookie is sending us a message."

"C'mon, Sarge. You can't really believe in that crap ."

AFTER EATING, THE DETECTIVES RESPONDED to where the Maestro had lived. They gathered through their inquiry that the Maestro had lived in his apartment with a man named Pascal. None of the people canvassed knew where Pascal currently lived. One neighbor indicated that Pascal was seen leaving the apartment with two large suitcases. The same neighbor advised that Pascal informed him that he was taking care of some business upstate for a month and would then be returning to Manhattan to live. A check with the post office revealed that Pascal had left no forwarding address.

The following day, the investigators consulted with the funeral parlor that tended to the Maestro. The funeral director advised that a man and a woman contracted the funeral home. When asked who paid the bill, they were told that the funeral was paid for by EBSMP, Inc. (Enzo Baffi Star Maker Productions).

"So where do we go from here, Sarge?" asked Von Hess after leaving the funeral parlor.

"I'll have to think it over. How about we go for a drink after work?"

"No, I have to get home, Sarge. Tonight is my turn to pick out the movie I watch with the old lady."

* * *

MARKIE ENTERED FITZIE'S with the intention of unwinding at his favorite watering hole. To the sergeant, this meant over-indulging in whiskey and beer.

Markie assumed his usual seat at the far end of the bar. As he regularly did when alone, he began looking at the framed pictures of celebrated people that Fitzie had hanging on the walls. He was stunned at the latest addition in the section dedicated to law enforcement. Hanging among notables of the past was a color photo of Fishnet Milligan.

"Where did that come from?" asked Markie after signaling Fitzie to join him.

"What?" asked the bar owner, who was working behind the bar.

"I'm talking about the picture of the guy between Johnny Broderick and Mario Biaggi."

"That's Fishnet Milligan. You know who he is . . ."

"Yeah, but what is he doing up there?"

"A detective from the local precinct came in a couple of weeks ago, saw the pictures on the wall, and came back a couple of days ago with a framed picture of Fishnet Milligan. So I hung it. Ain't he a hero?"

"Listen, Broderick was a legendary Broadway detective, and Biaggi was a lieutenant who ran for mayor. Joe Petrosino, over there next to Biaggi, was killed in Italy chasing the Black Hand. Barney Ruditsky and the rest up there . . ." Markie, who was worked up, stopped himself from continuing. "Do me a favor, Fitzie; just get me another shot and a beer."

Even in death, Fishnet Milligan continued to remain a stone in the sergeant's shoe. It took the consumption of several shots of Irish for Markie to get the bad taste out of his mouth. *I got time on my side,* he thought. *I'll get to the bottom of whatever this shit is about."*

As was usually the case, the magic of the intoxicants eventually activated Markie's libido. His carnal cravings caused him to telephone Karen, his girlfriend. Due to the short notice, Karen initially declined Markie's invitation to come and meet him. As was her way after coming home from work, she wanted to spend time with her kids. Markie, when drinking, was not one easily denied. Being manipulative, he pressured Karen by emphasizing his disappointment in her lack of commitment to him. With her guilt triggered, Karen told Markie that she'd try to make things work.

After ascertaining that her father and sister were both amenable to watching her children after the family ate dinner, Karen communicated to Markie that she'd be able to meet him. The sergeant couldn't have been more pleased.

While waiting for Karen, Markie continued drinking. Not having eaten all day, by the time Karen arrived the alcohol had gotten to the sergeant. Karen found Markie sound asleep while seated on a barstool, his head tilted toward his right shoulder as he napped. When she got close, a slight snore was audible.

Markie's drinking habits were known to Karen. For some reason, she was emotionally drawn to flawed men like the sergeant. When drunk, he presented a pathetic figure, a condition that made her feel needed.

"He's not in very good form right now, Karen," advised Fitzie. "I suppose something must have set him off."

"I can see that," answered Markie's lady friend. "What was it this time?"

"I don't really know, but he did mention something about rats slipping through the cracks. He wasn't more specific than that."

"Can we take him upstairs to your apartment?"

"I was about to suggest that," agreed Fitzie. "C'mon, let's put him to bed."

When being transported to the apartment above the bar, the sergeant began to come to. Propped up by Karen on one side and Fitzie on the other, Markie took notice of Karen. He expressed his happiness in seeing her by getting playfully affectionate. Although Karen feigned annoyance, she found his repeated attempts to kiss her reassuring.

"Easy bucko," said Fitzie from Markie's other side.

Once in the apartment the sergeant was placed on the bed. Seeing his role as being fulfilled, Fitzie left the couple to themselves. "If you need anything, I'll be downstairs," he advised before walking out the door.

The sergeant's words came out as gibberish, so Karen soothingly said, "Shhhh . . . lay down on the bed and close your eyes."

It only took Karen's rubbing of Markie's back for the sergeant to fall fast asleep. He didn't awaken until many hours later. When he finally woke up, he was unsure of where he was. Instinctively, he reached for the off-duty revolver he carried on his hip. He was relieved to find his gun was still there. After realizing his location, Markie went to the bathroom to wash his face. After pulling himself together, the sergeant returned downstairs to the bar.

"I was just coming up to see how you were doing," said the bar owner. "We're getting ready to close."

"Was Karen here?"

"She went home hours ago."

"Oh," said Markie, having a memory blackout. "Was she pissed off?"

"Don't worry. Karen's not going anyplace. She's the type who likes to suffer."

"Thanks, Fitz, I guess she found out I could be a handful."

"I'd say she already knew that," said the bar owner.

40

See No Evil

MARKIE AND HIS GIRLFRIEND were on their way to meet Von Hess and his wife for dinner at the Parkside Restaurant in Corona, Queens. The easy-going Karen sat in the car alongside the sergeant, enjoying the music of Johnny Cash on the radio. As Cash warbled "Folsom Prison Blues," Karen tapped her foot to the music. Her foot was coming down on the square piece of three-quarter-inch plywood that was used to cover the hole in the rotted floorboard.

"Be careful, Karen," cautioned the sergeant. "That wood isn't secured to anything. It's just there to cover the hole that rusted out."

"Isn't it time you got a new car?" she asked.

"I can't afford it," replied the sergeant, who had no intention of spending money on a new car.

"Why won't you get a new car? You could lease something like a Toyota. They're relatively inexpensive."

"Maybe next year," answered Markie.

Since they were ahead of schedule, Markie decided to make a detour. To Karen's surprise, Markie pulled into the entrance of the Cypress Hills Cemetery. Once she found herself surrounded by acres of tombstones, she questioned why they were driving through a graveyard.

"What are we doing here?" asked the puzzled Karen.

"I have to check out a couple of gravesites."

"Do we have time, Al?"

"This will only take a couple of minutes."

"Who is resting here?"

"A guy named No Tax. You wouldn't know him. While we're here, I want to take a look at the grave of Jackie Robinson too."

"The guy they named the parkway after?"

"That's right," commented Markie, not bothering to broaden her knowledge of the first African American to play baseball in the major leagues.

After his visit to the resting place of Robinson, Markie drove to where No Tax was buried. Locating No Tax was relatively easy because he rested just off the gate about forty yards from the cemetery entrance.

"Well, he got what he wanted," commented Markie, admiring the gravesite.

"What's with those panthers?" asked Karen.

"That's what he wanted."

"What was he to you?"

"Nothing, he was just a snitch who meant nothing to me."

"Then why are we here, Al?"

"I just wanted to make sure everything was the way he wanted it."

"Didn't he have a family to take care of that?"

"Nah, he had nobody," answered Markie. "No Tax was a live-for-today kind of guy. He was a degenerate gambler who died broke. I raised the money for his send-off."

"The police department does that?"

"Jeeze, you ask a lot of questions," said Markie, who was tired of explaining things. "Let's get to the restaurant before they run out of macaroni."

* * *

HAVING ARRIVED EARLY, VON HESS AND HIS WIFE were having cocktails while waiting for their dinner companions.

"I think I'm going to have the veal," announced Mrs. Von Hess after perusing the menu.

The wife of the detective was an attractive, dark-haired woman who appeared to be much younger than her years. She was free of facial lines and had a trim figure, making it hard to believe she was the mother of several children. The prim and proper sort, Mrs. Von Hess spoke intelligently, enunciating her words perfectly to a degree that she sounded more educated than she actually was.

"What are you having, honey?" she asked.

"I'm gonna wait and see what the waiter recommends," answered her husband.

As Mrs. Von Hess continued to study the menu, the detective scanned the restaurant. He noticed a priest at a nearby table having dinner with a party of six. Seeing the white collar awakened the demon that still haunted Von Hess.

The clergyman brought back unpleasant memories of Ross Holt, the Father Billy imposter. Von Hess still felt remorse over the assault he perpetrated. Making no efforts to justify his brutality, he lived with his guilt. Perhaps most disturbing to him was the hypocrisy connected to his enforcing the law while he himself was a lawbreaker. Being the survivor he was, Von Hess reconciled all this by reminding himself that if there was a price to pay, it would come after transitioning to the other side.

By the time Markie and Karen arrived at the restaurant, all the guilt within Von Hess disappeared. The foursome drank heartily, ate a fine meal, and chatted away amicably. When finished, the bill was split between the two couples. After donning their coats, Markie's girlfriend noticed a stain on the side pocket of the outer garment Von Hess wore.

"What's that on your pocket, Ollie?" asked Karen.

"Where?" asked Mrs. Von Hess, chiming in before the detective could reply. Her husband was totally unaware of the old blood stain.

"Look over here, by the pocket," pointed out Karen. "It looks like it might be ketchup or gravy."

"I swear, Ollie, you're so sloppy sometimes," criticized Mrs. Von Hess, who was a little embarrassed.

"I'll take it to the cleaners tomorrow," said Von Hess in an abrupt way.

"What will you wear then?" asked Mrs. Von Hess. "It's winter time."

"Will you stop all ready," barked Von Hess, looking to put an end to the conversation. "I said I'll take care of it."

Markie looked on without commenting. After exchanging glances with Von Hess, it was clear that both men were aware that the stain was blood. Von Hess never shared with Markie the origin of the blood. He didn't have to.

Markie now had a good idea where the beating of Ross Holt-Father Billy may have come from. The topic was one the sergeant had no intention of bringing up. He didn't need to hear something that he didn't want to know anything about.

* * *

BEFORE THE INVESIGATORS had a chance to do their homework on Pascal, they were given a new assignment by Lieutenant Wright. This one required that they look into the homicide of a retired police captain.

"Take Ollie and go to the Bronx," directed the lieutenant.

"What's in the Bronx, Loo?" asked Markie.

"They got a retired police captain found dead in the trunk of a car in the parking lot of the Split Rock Golf Course. The chief wants us on the case."

"Another golf caper?"

"Who the hell knows, Al. Go up there and see what it's all about. Then call me so I can post the old man."

"What's the name of the victim?"

"Masterson."

"I heard that name, Loo. I just don't remember from where."

"Go and see what's up, Al. The chief has an interest."

Markie rounded up Von Hess. After being filled in, the detective conveyed that he knew Captain Masterson.

"I remember him," said Von Hess. "Johnny Bronco worked in the Bronx.

"Now I remember where I heard of him," declared Markie. "He was a roughhouse guy."

"Everybody was back in the day, Sarge. Bronco Masterson was a bit of a character."

"How so?"

"His reputation was one of a womanizer and gambler, but he was well-liked."

"Nobody's perfect, I suppose. Let's saddle up, Ollie. We're off to the Bronx."

"It looks like we're putting this guy Pascal on hold."

"Yeah, for the time being, Ollie. We'll circle back to him down the road."

The duo of Markie and Von Hess wasted no time in embarking on their new adventure. This caper would eventually come to be known as "The Case of the Deadly Diary."

THE END